NATIONAL
SECURITY

NATIONAL SECURITY

MARC CAMERON

PINNACLE BOOKS
Kensington Publishing Corp.
www.kensingtonbooks.com

PINNACLE BOOKS are published by

Kensington Publishing Corp.
119 West 40th Street
New York, NY 10018

All Kensington titles, imprints, and distributed lines are available at special quantity discounts for bulk purchases for sales promotions, premiums, fund-raising, educational, or institutional use. Special book excerpts or customized printings can also be created to fit specific needs. For details, write or phone the office of the Kensington special sales manager: Kensington Publishing Corp., 119 West 40th Street, New York, NY 10018, attn: Special Sales Department; phone 1-800-221-2647.

ISBN-13: 978-0-7860-2494-0
ISBN-10: 0-7860-2494-1

First printing: November 2011

10 9 8 7 6 5 4 3 2 1

Printed in the United States of America

For Victoria: oh so smart and oh so pleasant.

Halibi had three, each half again as large—and the time had come to put them to use.

Contact with the night guard's blood made *Wudu*—ritual ablution—essential before an offer of prayer. And what was martyrdom but the ultimate form of prayer?

Halibi removed the lid to a new bottle of Aquafina. Beginning with his hands, he washed three times to his elbows, then moved cool water back and forth in his mouth, spitting away from his two cousins. He drew water into each nostril three times, touched his face, then moved to symbolically cleanse the remainder of his body, ending with his feet. His cousins repeated the same motions under the shadowed metal eaves of the Public Works garage. Devoted men of great piety, they were no doubt thinking as he was of the wondrous rewards that awaited them all in Paradise. All were freshly shaven, and now cleansed from the filth of the world. Halibi, the eldest, was not yet twenty-four.

"*Allahu akbar,*" Halibi whispered, as he grabbed a handrail and pulled himself up and into the first truck in line, squinting, curling his nose against the harsh odor of ammonia that shrouded the vehicles in an invisible cloud. Eighteen months of preparation had at last come to fruition.

Molly Roberson brushed a curl of sandy hair out of her eyes and took a long, critical look in the bathroom mirror. This mothering thing was turning out to be more than she'd bargained for. Twin eight-year-old boys took a lot out of a girl and she was beginning to show it. She patted the five pounds of extra fat that had remained on her once-flat stomach after the boys were born—Jared jokingly called it her peter belly and took full credit for causing it.

She ran a thumb across her eyebrows, in desperate need of a little wax and TLC. "I don't even have time to shave my legs," she whispered to no one in particular. "Guess my plans of becoming CEO of Microsoft will have to wait awhile. . . ."

She'd woken early to read the paper and see her husband off to work. The weatherman said it was going to be hot and Jared sometimes skipped wearing his bulletproof vest if she didn't get up with him and force the issue.

Now, resting both hands on the counter, she sighed, blowing at the curl that kept falling across her eyes. She needed a haircut and a long bath and a visit to the chiropractor. . . .

"Mom!" It was Sam, the older of the twins by fifty-eight minutes. She could picture him on the other side of the bathroom door, already dressed, blond hair moussed as only an eight-year-old could mousse it. "Trent says he's not coming with us, but I told him he had to because we're buying school clothes."

Molly smiled, taming the errant curl with a plastic clippie from her stash in a cup beside the toothpaste. She felt much too haggard for thirty-four. A stupid clippie in her hair and bags under her eyes—that's the way mothers of twin dynamos were expected to look, like they'd been on a ten-day drunk. She was lucky

Jared was the sort of husband who could overlook a little leg stubble.

She wriggled into a pair of clean but tattered black capris and a pink T-shirt before opening the door. "What's this about your brother, little dude?" She looked down at a freshly scrubbed Sam, his hair swept up in an earnest-looking pompadour.

"Playing Mario Kart on the Wii," Sam said, rolling his wide, blue eyes like an adult.

Molly looked at her watch. It was almost noon. They'd be lucky to find a place to park a mile from the mall. She leaned over the banister leading down to the basement. The smell of pizza and dirty socks rose up from the darkness to meet her. Jared called it the twins' man-cave—no place for a woman.

"Mister, you better march up here ready to go in three minutes!"

Trent, who was so slow it had taken him an hour longer than his brother just to wallow his way through the birthing process, plodded up the stairs dragging a blanket. He was slow, but he had a good-hearted glow about him that made it difficult to stay mad for long.

"I don't feel so good, Mama," he said, leaning his head against his mother's chest. She couldn't help herself and mussed his tangled bedhead of blond hair. "Seriously," he mumbled against her shirt, nuzzling her between the boobs in the naïve way he was sure to lose all too soon. "I know I've been playing games all morning, but I really feel sick to my stomach."

"The back-to-school sales are today, dude," Molly chided. "We've got to get your clothes and supplies."

She tilted his chin up with her finger so she could look him in the eye. "I was planning to go by Cold Stone for some ice cream. . . ." With Trent, ice cream was a tried-and-true tactic.

To her surprise he shook his head, puffing out his cheeks to show the thought made him nauseous. She put the back of her hand on his forehead. Maybe he was a little feverish.

"Sam's the same size as me. Can't you just get the same stuff for both of us?" he mumbled. "I'll barf all over everything if I have to go out."

Molly folded her arms and looked at both her sons. If Trent was sick, she couldn't make him go. That would be way too unmotherly of her. She pursed her lips in thought. He was only eight. Even eight-year-olds needed a little TLC when they were sick. . . . But there *were* the sales to consider and Trent was mature for his age. Maybe going out at all would be too un-motherly. . . . She was just not cut out for this.

Jared Roberson spit the frayed remains of a wooden toothpick out the window of his patrol car and tried to shrug off the unidentifiable nagging in his gut. A half mile below the rocky bluff where he sat overlooking the Denver suburb that was his domain, a parade of three garbage trucks rumbled single-file toward the Fashion Center Mall. Bits of cottonwood fluff floated up on the lazy summer air.

Roberson took a swig of Maalox, hoping the chalky stuff might drown whatever desert viper had slithered down his throat and coiled in his guts during his last tour in Afghanistan. It struck at him every other day or so, just to keep things interesting. Molly said he should see a therapist, but cops didn't visit shrinks—not if they wanted to keep their jobs.

The three trucks, blinding white under a noon sun, bore left on Spruce Avenue from the Interstate 25 access road. Something about the precise, almost choreographed way they moved reminded Roberson of a military convoy.

Glancing up, he caught a glimpse of his scar in the rearview mirror. Courtesy of a roadside bomb near some poppy fields outside Kabul, the grizzly war memento covered the left side of his face in tight, translucent flesh—and got a lot of second looks when he was writing tickets. It still ached—more than he confessed to Molly—and served as a constant reminder that he had survived when so many better soldiers had not. His twin boys seemed unbothered by the gruesome new look and reasoned that since their dad fought bad guys and had funny-looking skin, he must be a superhero. They called him Plastic Man.

On the streets below, the garbage trucks rolled to a stop at North Mall Drive, waiting for the light. They were perfectly spaced with a truck's length between them.

The serpent in Roberson's gut writhed impatiently. Plastic Man's instincts told him something was wrong.

Halibi's eyes flashed to the side mirror. Ismail was lagging behind. "Keep up, my cousin," he said, speaking into the prepaid cell phone. "We are very close. You do not want to waste our opportunity."

"Do you truly believe, Mahir? No doubts?" Ismail's voice quavered like a small child.

"I am here, am I not?" Halibi whispered as much to himself as his cousin. Beads of sweat ran down his forehead, stinging his already burning eyes. An infidel woman in a pair of short pants that revealed much of her jiggling buttocks crossed the street in front of his truck, licking an ice cream cone like a mindless cow. "The Americans call this the Sabbath, yet they spend their holy day shopping and stuffing gluttonous faces." He took his foot off the brake. "Follow me, my cousin. We have come too far to falter now. . . ."

Roberson hadn't checked out for lunch, but dispatch knew where he was. He came here every day. This was his spot. It was where he'd proposed to Molly, where she'd told him she was pregnant with the boys, and where he'd broken the news to her that he'd reenlisted with his old Ranger unit after September 11.

The muffled squeals and honks of traffic rose on waves of heat from acres of concrete and asphalt. The pungent smell of cedar mingled with the fragrance of freshly mown grass from the spacious Rocky Mountain estates that overlooked the city on the granite ridge behind him.

On the streets below, the light turned green and the trucks began to roll.

Fashion Center Mall was set up in a rough clover shape with its three anchor stores comprising the point of each leaf. Sun sparkled on an endless sea of windshields in the mall's three expansive parking lots. A steady stream of cars and SUVs poured in from I-25 like ants to a picnic. The big-box stores had advertised huge back-to-school blowouts for the weekend.

Molly would be there by now, buying the boys new jeans at the Sunday sales . . . the *Super Sunday Sales*. . . .

Roberson snatched up the radio mike from where it hung on the dashboard.

"Three-twenty."

The dispatcher answered immediately. "Go Three-twenty."

"Gina, I got three garbage trucks rolling up on Fashion Center. Any idea why the city would have trucks out today?" His stomach ached as if he'd gone three rounds with Rocky Balboa.

There was a long silence. "Uhhh . . . to pick up garbage?"

"On Sunday?" He slammed back another shot of Maalox.

"Ahhh." Now she got his point. "Public Works should be closed. I'll check with the fire department to see if they've heard—"

"Three-eighteen." The new voice on the radio was Brian Long, the officer working the northern sector. He was from Connecticut and his strong accent made it sound as if he was trying to eat the radio mike.

"Go ahead, Three-eighteen." Gina's voice bristled with this-better-be-good snippiness at having been interrupted.

"I'm out behind Public Works now. They're definitely closed, but somebody's gone and cut a big hole in the fence. You could drive a school bus through this thing. I got two empty box vans that don't look like they belong here and . . . holy shit!"

The radio went dead for what seemed like an eternity.

"Three-eighteen," Gina snapped. "Your status?"

Brian came back frazzled. "I . . . I got me a dead guy here. Looks like his throat's been cut. . . ."

"Ten-four, Three-eighteen," Gina came back, icy calm again. "I have two CSP units heading your way for backup."

Roberson watched as the garbage trucks picked up speed. The first two in line kept right at the entrance to the lower mall parking lot while the straggler hesitated, then veered left toward Sears.

"Three-twenty," Gina's voice broke squelch. "Three-fourteen and Three-twenty-two are leaving the station, heading your direction at this time. Looks like whoever took your garbage trucks is good for a homicide."

Roberson keyed his mike as the second truck peeled away, moving toward the packed lot in front of Nordstrom. "Ten-four," he whispered. Memories of Afghanistan and cordite and screaming pressed in around him. The viper in his belly struck with renewed vigor.

He dropped the mike in the passenger seat and jumped from his patrol car, punching his wife's speed dial on his cell phone with his thumb. His eyes locked on the mall.

"Molly!" he yelled as if he could shout his wife a warning from the ridge top. She was down there with the boys. Dread flooded his system like a debilitating drug, making it difficult to stand. Her cell rang twice before she answered

"Hey, Super Dude," she said. "What's up?"

Roberson kept his eyes glued to the scene below.

"Molly, where are you?" Bile seared the back of his throat. He knew it was foolish, but he searched the rows and rows of parked cars for her Impala. Of course he couldn't locate it from where he was. He wanted to run to her, but if he moved he'd lose sight of the trucks.

"Trent was sick so—"

"Thank the Lord," Roberson sighed. "So you're not at the mall?"

"Of course I'm at the mall. Trent stayed home. Sam and I are looking at boys' underwear in Sears," she said. "Why?"

"Moll—"

"It's incredible, Jared. You wouldn't believe the price—"

"Molly, shut up and listen to me!" he snapped. His wife could be stubborn and he needed her to be scared enough she'd do what he asked without question. "Take Sam and run toward the Home Depot—"

"Jared, that's on the other side of the parking lot—"

Roberson looked on in horror as the garbage truck bearing down on Sears jumped the curb. Throngs of shoppers fled as it crashed through the main doors and barreled into the mall, crushing anyone who couldn't get out of the way. He was too far away to hear their screams, but he knew they were there. It was like watching a tragic silent movie.

"Molly!" Roberson screamed into his phone. "Run. Now!" His voice caught hard in his chest. "Please . . ."

"Okay, Jared. All right, we're going," she said, still unconvinced. "I'll call you whe—"

The truck in front of Nordstrom broke through the red brick façade, sending a blinding orange fireball in all directions. It took a full second for the roaring boom to reach Roberson's ears. In an instant, four stories of steel, mortar, and glass vanished behind a mushroom of greasy black smoke. The initial blast tossed row after row of cars across the parking lot like so many pitiful toys. The screaming pulse and honk of car alarms followed the superheated wave of hurricane-force wind.

"Jared, tell me what's going on. . . ." Amazingly, Molly was still on the line, her voice hushed, fragile.

Roberson clutched the corner of his patrol car to keep his feet, leaning into the hot wind. "I love you, Molly—" he whispered as the two remaining trucks detonated.

Tornadoes of fire and flaming debris shot skyward. Curling dragons of black smoke completely obscured the mall. A searing pressure wave slammed into Roberson's chest, driving him to his knees and burning the scar on his face. Bits of shattered glass, shot skyward by the blasts, fell now to rattle off the hood of his patrol car in a constant rain. Three columns of inky smoke twisted upward from what had been Fashion Center Mall, blotting out the sun.

Roberson pressed the phone to his blistered ear, heard nothing but static, and began to weep.

Ash and debris were still falling like dirty snow when Nimble Rock Fire and Rescue screamed onto the scene eight and a half minutes after detonation.

Spot fires hissed among the twisted piles of steel and brick, looking more like war-torn Beirut than a

Colorado suburb. An entire section of escalator rested in the middle of one parking lot, perfectly intact, along with a charred baby stroller and assorted empty shoes strewn up and down the metal steps. The explosions that had reduced three huge department stores to smoking pits tore away half the center portion of the mall leaving all four levels crumbling, naked and open to the outside air.

Through the acrid smoke, arriving rescuers were treated to the grizzly sight of the mangled bodies of mall patrons thrown in pieces on top of counters and upturned clothing racks. Computers and cash registers dangled by sparking electrical cords. On the top floor, along what was left of the food court, a bewildered teenage girl, still wearing her bright red and yellow Corn-Dog-on-a-Stick uniform hat, staggered to the jagged edge of concrete and support steel in front of her store and collapsed, clutching a bleeding stub where her left arm should have been.

Children, blown from their clothing, stood blinking in wide-eyed shock, waiting for parents who had simply vanished. The pitiful screams and cries of the wounded and dying drowned out the wailing sirens of approaching rescue units from Denver. Panic-stricken mothers and fathers stumbled through the rubble and smoke on each sagging floor, their frantic searching exposed to the rest of the world as if they were inside a giant ant farm. Some, deafened by the explosions and unable to hear the shouts of arriving rescue personnel were driven by desperation in areas still on fire and jumped to their deaths on the jagged concrete three and four levels below.

Two of the first firefighters to arrive, both hardened professionals, well accustomed to sights of human misery and gory auto accidents, turned away to vomit.

FBI Deputy Director Paul Sanchez stood ankle-deep in a pool of greasy water and gray ash, wondering if he'd ever get the smell of cooked human flesh out of his head. Midnight had come and gone hours before, and his eyes felt as if he'd rubbed them with a handful of sand. The caffeine from five cups of coffee and the sea of strobing emergency lights combined in the pre-dawn darkness to drive a spike through his aching head.

More than fifteen hours after the three vehicle-borne improvised explosive devices—VBIEDs in the parlance of the Global War on Terror—had flattened a Colorado shopping mall larger than four city blocks, Sanchez still had no firm body count—at least not one firm enough to give to the President. Someone from FEMA had come up with the bright idea of counting the cars in the parking lots and doubling that number for an estimate. Mall shopping, they reasoned, was rarely a solitary pastime.

Sanchez looked at a tiny green cube of shatterproof glass smaller than a dime in the palm of his hand. It came from a literal ocean of the stuff, inches deep, in what had only a day before been a busy American parking lot. It would take days to sort through the twisted bits of plastic, metal, and broken glass to figure out the number of cars. It was like trying to guess the number of rocks it took to create the sand in a desert.

Initial estimates of the dead were coming in between twenty-three and twenty-seven hundred. Surveying the slabs of shattered concrete and steaming support steel under the harsh lights, Sanchez was sure those numbers were far too low.

Concussive shock waves from the three blasts had broken the windows in virtually every building within a one-mile radius around the mall. A frantic elderly woman who lived almost two miles away called 911 an hour after the explosions to report that her pet dachshund had found a human foot in the backyard and refused to give it up.

Colorado National Guardsmen had secured the perimeter of the bombing site with sandbagged roadblocks. The state of Colorado and the nation as a whole now teetered on the nervous edge of dismay and twitchy terror, ever concerned with the possibility of delayed or secondary attacks. The President, as well as the VP and key members of the Cabinet, had bunkered up in secure and "undisclosed" locations. Sixty miles to the south, the four thousand cadets at the United States Air Force Academy were buttoned up tight with F-15s from nearby Peterson Air Force Base providing overhead security patrols. A half dozen AH-64 Longbow helicopters from Fort Carson flew close air support, lights out to guard against possible assault from the ground. All aircraft was cleared hot, ready to fire on any enemy they found.

Sanchez had called in a hundred and sixty agents from as far away as New York and Miami to assist. By order of the attorney general, agents from the Bureau of Alcohol, Tobacco, and Firearms and the U.S. Marshals Service had also responded, along with FEMA and Public Health.

The Pit, as they were now calling the place, was a hive of activity. Three FBI HRT—Hostage Rescue Team—helicopters hovered overhead, spotlights cutting white beams through the night as they played back and forth around the gnarled, smoking mess. Emergency rescue crews crawled in and out of the rubble, working under the blinding glare of portable flood lamps, borrowed from a Denver road construction company.

Five Labrador retrievers, highly trained as cadaver dogs, scrambled up and down in areas their handlers considered safe enough to send them. Teams of forensic scientists used ground-penetrating radar to look for anomalies that might be human under tons of debris. They'd found a few survivors at first, huddling near the center of the mall, miraculously shielded by the twisted remnants of an escalator. All were badly burned and at least two had died later at the hospital.

Since 9 P.M. the Pit had yielded nothing living—or even intact.

Sanchez took a sip of his coffee, then spit it out, sickened by the thought of anything on his stomach. His nerves were frayed and he jumped at a sudden female voice to his right. The speaker was backlit by the glaring headlights of a waiting ambulance. He couldn't make out her face until she stepped closer, sloshing into his muddy pool to be heard above the pounding clatter of jackhammers and agonized whine of cable winches pulling up slabs of concrete.

"I think we might have an ID on one of the drivers,"

the woman said, almost screaming to be heard. She was Carol Victors, the Denver Anti-Terrorism Task Force supervisor. In the past ten hours, she'd become Sanchez's go-to agent in Colorado. No stereotypical Betty Bureau Blue Suit, Victors was tall, only an inch shorter than Sanchez at five eleven, and could hold her own in a battle of wit or muscle. Her dark hair was piled up under a navy-blue baseball cap with FBI emblazoned on the front in white letters.

"An ID?" Sanchez shook his head in disbelief. "No way. We don't even have a solid lead on the type of explosives yet. Somebody claiming credit for this?"

"We got lucky," Victors said, setting her otherwise full lips in a tight line. It was good news, but circumstances were too heavy for a smile. "There was a security camera at the Public Works garage. One of the drivers turned and looked directly at it after he killed the night watchman."

"So we got a face or an ID?"

"I ran the video stills through the facial recognition programs at State, Homeland Security, as well as ours at Quantico." She shrugged. "Again, we got lucky. State had a hit. Our driver was one Mahir Halibi, a Saudi student majoring in soil and crop sciences at Colorado State University in Fort Collins. He was using the name of Samir Mohammed and was here under a Jordanian passport."

"Soil and crops?" Sanchez reasoned. "If this turns out to be ammonium nitrate—which it probably will—that would make sense."

Agent Victors bounced from one foot to the other as if she had information that was to hot to hold inside.

"You've got more?"

"I do, boss," she said. "Halibi was already on our watch list. He's got ties to some serious people. . . ."

"How serious?"

Now Victors allowed herself the hint of a smile. "Does the name Farooq ring a bell?"

"Sheikh Husseini al Farooq?" Sanchez chewed on the swizzle stick from his coffee. "We're sure about this?"

"Our friends at the Agency say Halibi's father and Farooq attended the same madrassa in Damascus in the late seventies."

Sanchez pulled the BlackBerry from his pocket. "Like father like son, then," he said as he punched the speed dial. When the other party answered, he took a deep breath. "This is Paul. Connect me with the Director."

Four hours later
Saudi Arabia

Sheikh Husseini al Farooq leaned over the marble chessboard like a lion considering his kill. A slender hand poised over his knight, fingers tapping lightly. Islam's prohibitions against graven images of living things required the game piece to look like a squat painted mushroom instead of the more customary horse.

Farooq's opponent, a boy in his late teens, watched in rapt fascination. "Is it not glorious?" the boy said. "The Americans are broken, shattered as glass before a stone!"

A murmur of agreement rippled through the dozen men in the room. Each sat on a soft pillow watching the contest. With the setting sun, plates of food had been set after a day of fasting in observance of the holy month of Ramadan. The entire palace had been abuzz with congratulatory fervor as scenes of the Colorado mall bombing streamed on a plasma big screen tuned to Al Jazeera television.

"Do not underestimate the Americans," Farooq said, smiling as he maneuvered the knight in concert with his bishop, to put the boy in checkmate. "Underestimating one's opponent is the surest way to fail—"

"Forgive me, my sheikh." A man wearing a red Saudi *ghutra* on his head and a white, ankle-length robe burst into the room. Had it been anyone else but Dr. Suleiman, such an intrusion would have been met with quick and decisive violence.

Suleiman was in his mid thirties and clean shaven because of his need to wear protective masks during his experiments. His pink face beamed as if reflecting a great light.

"I suppose you have heard of the events in Colorado?" Farooq nodded toward the television in the corner.

"I . . . we have had a breakthrough in the lab." The doctor smiled, ignoring the others in the room. "I believe this will make the mere bombing of a shopping mall pale in comparison."

Farooq raised a brow. "Is that so?"

Suleiman stammered on. "Our Algerian friends have solved one piece of the puzzle. They are testing it as we speak. I believe I now know the answer to the problem that has always eluded us. . . . Of course . . . it will require another, more particular test. . . ."

Farooq clapped his hands. A brooding man with dark eyes and long, windswept hair rose from his seat in the corner, hand on a curved dagger at his belt. "Yes, my sheikh."

Holding up an open hand, palm out, Farooq turned back to Suleiman. His slender wrist protruded from the long sleeve of his white robe, identical to the doctor's. "You've actually done it then?" he said.

"I believe I have." Suleiman's eyes shifted uneasily back and forth from the sheikh to the brooding bodyguard.

A sneering grin spread across Farooq's angular face as he turned back to the man with the dagger. "We shall need a few more subjects on which to test the doctor's theories. Inform Ghazan at once."

CHAPTER 1

2 September, 2100 hours
Fallujah, Iraq

Jericho Quinn gunned the throttle, willing more power from the screaming motorcycle.

"Which one is Ghazan?" He threw the words over his shoulder, into the wind as he rode.

Blowing sand scoured his chapped face. He peered through the dusk, squinting, wishing he had a pair of goggles. Something pinched his nose in the gathering darkness—the telltale odor of wet wool seasoned with the sulfur that oozed up from the desert floor.

The smell of a sheep roasting in the flames of hell.

The scent of Iraq.

"There!" Quinn felt his passenger shudder behind him, his words ripped away by the wind.

"Which one?" Quinn scanned a knot of a half dozen FAMs—fighting-age men—loitering at the corner beneath the crumbling walls of a bombed mosque. In the three days following the horrific bombing of a Colorado shopping mall, any semblance of trust between cultures had evaporated from the streets of Iraq. Natives flinched and dropped their eyes when American patrols rolled past. Few in number from cyclical troop drawdown, U.S. forces stood on the edge of a full-blown assault at every encounter. Soldiers, sailors, marines, and airmen boiled with righteous anger that over three thousand Americans—most of them women and children—had lost their lives in the blasts.

The worst act of terrorism on American soil since 9/11, the media had dubbed it the Fifth Sunday Bombing—but it was impossible to put a title on something so horrible. Most just spoke in whispered reverence about *Colorado*. Hunting down those responsible was priority one for men like Jericho Quinn.

Ghazan al Ghazi was the HVT—the high-value target—of the moment. Quinn felt a familiar sensation in the back of his neck—the tingle that told him violence was close at hand—and wondered if he was enjoying this too much. He had no idea what he'd do if peace suddenly broke out in the world. Not much chance of that.

"Which one?" he asked again, leaning back to be certain Sadiq heard him.

"The large one . . . he wears aviator sunglasses. He is tall . . . there on the end with the neck of a bull." Sadiq groaned, hiding his head against Quinn's back as he spoke. "A blue shirt . . . open down the front. Please . . . you should drive on. . . ."

In the street, horns honked and beeped, churning up whirling clouds of yellow dust. Thick, angry voices rose into the dusk on ribbons of heat as the snarl of evening traffic came to a standstill. Stopped almost directly in front of their target, Sadiq began to twitch, so much so Quinn was sure it looked as though he was having some kind of fit.

"Hold on," Quinn yelled in colloquial Arabic as he tried to go around the jam. He nearly spilled avoiding the twisted hulk of a bombed Nissan pickup planted squarely in the road. Giving the bike enough throttle to keep it upright, he ducked down a side street away from the din of cars and military and NGO convoys. Slowing, he made a left turn on a quieter side street.

The motorcycle was a Kaweseki, a Chinese knock-off. Little more than a scooter, it had the look of a Japanese sport bike and the suspension of a skate-board. It was sure to rust or fall to pieces just when he needed it most, but it was what the locals rode. It was all they could afford. As an agent with Air Force Office of Special Investigations or OSI, Quinn had an impressive array of weapons and technology at his disposal. But for the moment he rode a piece-of-junk motorcycle and wore an ankle-length cotton *dishdasha,* called a man dress by American soldiers. His life, and more importantly his mission, depended on the ability to blend in with the locals.

He leaned over the handlebars, twisting the last ounce of horsepower from the protesting Chinese motor. The back tire shimmied, throwing up a shower of gravel as he ducked behind an abandoned café. Behind him, Sadiq clawed at his waist in an effort to hang on.

Despite the fact that he was surrounded by men who would be happy to saw off his head with a dull pocket-knife if they discovered who he was, Quinn found the orange-blue dusk oddly soothing. Above the rubble of bombed buildings and rusted vehicle hulks, a neat row of Medjool date palms lined the road, their straight trunks silhouetted against the evening sky. They were reminders of another Iraq, untouched by decades of war.

"Get off at the next corner." Quinn leaned back as he shouted to the lanky Sunni. The boy spoke passable English, but Quinn kept their conversations in Arabic to pacify any listening ears. "I must hurry and get back to Ghazan before he slips away."

"You will please pay me—*before* you go." The sallow university student's voice wobbled with a mixture of terror and the disorienting effects of the bumpy ride.

"Get off," Quinn snapped. "I don't have time to stop. I'll pay you later tonight." Sadiq was a good informant, but he liked to make things more difficult than they needed to be.

"I insist you pay me now."

Jericho let off the throttle, then gunned it suddenly to spite his rider.

"Must you Americans drive so fast?" Sadiq's voice was a curdled scream against the wind. "Ghazan is a dangerous man. He may kill you when you speak to him. Where would that leave me?"

One of the countless emaciated stray dogs that roamed the country darted in front of them, eyeing the men like a piece of meat. Quinn horsed the little bike to the right, fearing the flimsy handlebars might snap off in his hands. He took a quick moment to wish for his own motorcycle, a massive BMW 1200 GS Adventure. It was impossible to find a good motorcycle in the desert—at least one that allowed him to look like an Iraqi.

Sadiq yanked to the left to keep his seat, spewing an Arabic oath about Jericho's family history. Quinn popped the clutch, downshifting to coax just enough power to avoid a spill. The transmission squealed as if it was about to burst into flames.

They shuddered to a stop. Quinn shot a wary glance over his shoulder and ordered Sadiq off the bike in a voice that left no room for argument. He gunned the motor again. Unencumbered by a passenger, the little bike shot forward, back toward the men who would be all too happy to put a bullet in Quinn's head—or worse. Leaning forward, with the wind in his face, he considered his next move. His Arabic was flawless. Dark skin and a heavy beard helped him blend in with the population.

Very soon, none of that would matter. If all went according to plan, the Iraqi thug in the aviator sunglasses would find out more than he ever wanted to know about Jericho Quinn.

Ghazan split away from the others a half hour later, walking lazily in front of closed shops, their metal doors rolled to the ground and padlocked to discourage thieves. Quinn followed him a short way on the bike. He had smashed out the headlamp with a shard of brick from the side of the road. A broken headlight in a war-torn country wouldn't cause a second look and made him more difficult to spot cruising down dark side alleys.

Quinn watched from the shadows as the bull-necked man disappeared into a shabby, three-story concrete apartment building surrounded by heaps of garbage and rubble. He waited until a light on the second-level window flicked on, then took note of its position before stashing the Kaweseki across the street, behind a trash pile almost as high as his head. For a short moment, he considered calling in backup, but in the end settled back on what he'd known from the beginning— some jobs were better done without witnesses. It protected the innocent from having to report his behavior.

Men like Ghazan didn't worry much about heavy locks on their doors, relying instead on fearsome reputations to keep them safe. It would have been easy to assume the brute was alone, since the light had been off until he arrived. But Quinn knew relying on the probable had gotten a lot of men killed.

So, he would wait alone—and listen.

He crouched in the stifling heat of the concrete stairwell staring at the peeling white paint of Ghazan's door for what seemed like an eternity. The odor of urine and rotting lemons hung in the stuffy alcove. Feral dogs barked from distant shadows. A tiny hedgehog, no larger than an orange, shuffled by in the darkness. The wail of an ambulance siren cut the night. Here and there, the flat crack of an M4 rifle peppered the air. Quinn's knees began to ache. It was during just such moments, with sweat soaking the back of his *dishdasha*, staining the concrete wall behind him, that he took the time to wonder what he was doing. He had a little girl—a five-year-old—whom he hadn't seen for months. She was with his now ex-wife, back in the cool mountains of Alaska, so far from the grit and gore of this desert and the never-ending war. Missing her, he consoled himself with a quote from Thomas Paine. It was a favorite of his father's. "If there must be trouble, let it be in my day, that my child may have peace."

The telltale hiss of a running shower came through the flimsy wood door and drew Quinn back to reality. He tapped the Sig Sauer pistol beneath his robe taking a breath of solace in the fact it was there, then drew another item from the folds of his robe. This wasn't the time for pistol work. Quinn put a hand on the door, and took a deep breath, thinking one last time of his daughter before pressing her from his mind while he worked. He knew he should feel guilty about his absence, about the fact that he put his work even above those he loved the most—but he'd save the guilt for later. That's what made him so good.

Quinn surprised Ghazan with a snap kick to the groin as he stepped from the shower. Water dripped from the mat of black hair that thatched the Iraqi's body like a thick rug. The big man roared in alarm, attempting a kick of his own. The wet tile and newfound pain proved too much for his brain to handle and he hit the ground like a hairy sack of bricks.

Wasting no time, Quinn brought up the Taser X26, aiming the red laser dot at the center of Ghazan's chest. There was a static crackle as twin darts, barbed like straightened fish hooks, unspooled on hairlike wires to strike their target just below the right nipple and above the left knee. The Iraqi's body went taut and the muscles of his face pulled back in a grimace as fifty thousand volts of electricity arced between the two probes. He tried to cry out from the searing pain, but the best he could muster was a gurgle.

Traditional Tasers carried by law enforcement emitted a five-second burst of energy for each pull of the trigger. Quinn had taken the ride himself, along with his entire class of basic OSI agents. He found it to be like having a five-second full-body cramp, while completely engulfed in molten lava and stabbed in the back with an ice pick. It was something he hoped he'd never have to endure again.

The Taser he carried now had been modified to deliver four times that, completely immobilizing the target with pain and loss of neuromuscular control.

Ghazan's first twenty-second ride complete, Quinn pulled the trigger a second time. The muscles in the side of the Iraqi's neck tensed like thick cables, his glistening body arched up, bridging on shoulders and heels. Quinn took the opportunity to stick a small adhesive pad under each of Ghazan's ears. It was remarkably easy to find a vein and inject the contents of a plastic syringe, then secure his wrists and ankles with heavy plastic zip cuffs. The shock took the path of least resistance, which happened to be between the darts in the Iraqi's body, so Quinn felt nothing but a mild tingle as he completed his job.

Ghazan fell slack. He gave a pitiful groan and his head lolled to one side. Quinn slapped the man's cheeks, gaining his attention. He'd be no good if he passed out. The high-dosage scopolamine patches under his ears were already beginning to have the desired effect. His eyes fluttered, but he remained conscious.

"What . . . What do . . . you want?" The big man's words were a slurred mess, as if he had a mouth full of marbles. "You . . . you will suffer . . . greatly for this. . . ."

"The American soldiers you kidnapped," Quinn spat in Arabic as he hauled the slippery body upright, propping him against the rough tile wall.

Ghazan gave a rattling chuckle, blinked in an effort to clear his vision. The drugs and fatigue from the two bouts of electric-shock muscle cramping had exhausted him as surely as if he'd run a marathon. "You will die . . . for this insult. . . ." Ghazan swallowed. He smiled dopily. "I am thirsty, my friend. . . ."

Quinn grabbed a bit of the man's skin on the back of his upper arm, giving it a pinching twist.

Startled as if from another sudden shock, Ghazan yowled. "They will die tonight. . . ." he gasped.

"Where are they?" Quinn leaned forward.

The scopolamine began to combine with the drug Quinn had injected—a derivative of sodium pentathol developed by the Soviets called SP17. Together they induced a state of relaxed euphoria and, if all went well, would turn Ghazan into an Arab version of Chatty Cathy.

"What do you want with the American dogs? Fool! Farooq will kill you."

"Farooq?"

"You know of the sheikh, yes?" Ghazan stammered. "He is a powerful man . . . with many friends. Get me some water . . . and perhaps I will let you live. . . ."

Another pinch brought a scream and a renewed

sense of focus. Quinn kept his voice low, a menacing whisper, slipping seamlessly into English. "I need you to tell me about the Americans. They are my friends."

"Your friends . . ." Sick realization crept over the big Iraqi's face. "*You* are American?"

Quinn nodded slowly. "I am."

"Impossible," Ghazan sneered, momentarily coherent. "I don't know what you're talking about."

Quinn drew a long, slender blade from the back of his belt and held it before the Arab's face.

Ghazan blinked sagging eyes. He gave a tight chuckle, trying to convince himself. "Put that thing away. It does not frighten me. You Americans . . . you have told the world. You are disgusted by the mere idea of torture."

"We are disgusted by it," Quinn said, nodding slightly. "I am sickened by the act." He pressed the point of his blade up Ghazan's flared nostril until a trickle of blood flowed down his twitching lip. "And yet, I find myself needing the information inside your head." Quinn shrugged, drawing a fresh trickle of blood. "I am disgusted not for what it does to scum like you, but for what it does to the one inflicting the pain. Such violence does irreparable emotional harm to the torturer. . . ." The tip of his knife remained motionless, now more than an inch inside the big Iraqi's nose. "Some say it damages them beyond repair."

Quinn leaned in, almost touching the sweating man's face with his forehead, close enough to smell the odor of spiced chickpeas he'd eaten for supper. "The bad news for you," he whispered, "is that I'm already damaged. . . ."

* * *

Ghazan wept like a baby, but in the end, the drugs and the threat of a man even more cruel than himself loosened his mind and his tongue. He gave up an address in a bombed-over suburb outside Fallujah where American hostages were supposedly being kept. In his panic he offered information that some of the hostages were to be killed that very night as a show of insurgent solidarity.

The contents of a second syringe sent the Iraqi's head lolling against the wet concrete, snoring. Quinn stared at him for a long moment, thinking of the innocent people the terrorist was responsible for killing. He held the knife in his clenched fist and considered all the events that had brought him up to this point. He was not yet thirty-five, a government agent, Fulbright scholar, father, PTA volunteer . . . and an extremely talented killer. The world was a very strange place.

It seemed such a simple thing to slide the razor-sharp blade between Ghazan's hairy ribs and scramble his black heart like an egg. . . .

Instead, Quinn wiped the knife clean and reached inside the folds of his *dishdasha* for his secure radio, wondering just how damaged he was.

"This is Copper Three-Zero," he said. "I have high value target Juliet for immediate pickup. . . ."

Quinn dialed his encrypted cell phone on the way back to his stashed motorcycle.

Sadiq answered, "*Assalaamu alaikum*, Jericho. I am so pleased that you have remained alive to pay me."

Quinn returned the greeting and repeated the address Ghazan had provided.

"Mean anything to you?" he said.

"Nothing," Sadiq said. "But that neighborhood is a Sunni stronghold, very dangerous."

Quinn laughed to himself. All of Fallujah was a Sunni stronghold. "Ghazan mentioned a man named Farooq. Have you heard of him?"

The line was silent.

"Sadiq?"

"I know of this man. Most simply call him the sheikh." "It is said that this man was behind the bombing of your Colorado shopping mall. He has vowed to bring the Great Satan to her knees. Your Fifth Sunday Bombing, it is said, is just the beginning. He plans something far worse. . . ."

"In the United States?" Quinn held the phone against his ear with his shoulder as he pushed the motorcycle from the shadows behind the stinking pile of cans, rotting fruit, and pungent diapers.

"Most definitely in the United States," Sadiq said, preoccupied. "He wants to punish the Great Satan on American soil. . . . Jericho, these hostages, they are to be killed?"

"So says Ghazan al Ghazi."

"In that case," Sadiq said. "Be very careful you do not get killed yourself. Remember, I have yet to receive payment."

"Thanks for your concern." Quinn couldn't help but shake his head at his informant's abrupt manner. The kid was right though, lives ended in the blink of an eye in this part of the world. "I'll see that you are rewarded,

no matter what happens to me." He ended the call and sped into the darkness as fast at the rattling little Kaweseki would carry him.

Intelligence was a perishable substance and if he intended to save the American prisoners, he had to move fast. Worse, he'd have to enlist the help of a man he despised.

CHAPTER 2

3 September,
2035 hours
Paris
Charles de Gaulle Airport

Hamzah Abdul Haq ran—not for his life, but, Allah willing, to choose a less agonizing manner in which to die.

The hulking Algerian bolted down the long, arched hallway, heart pounding, lungs rasping for breath. Cheap, rubber-soled shoes squeaked on the cracked tile as he dodged startled pockets of tourists. A stinking vagrant—the airport was full of filthy people—sprawled across the floor directly in his path, but fear made Hamzah agile as well as fast and he darted around the derelict without losing any of his precious lead.

If the men chasing the Algerian had known what he had tucked in his huge fist they would have ignored the crowd and shot him on the spot.

Since 9/11 when people saw Hamzah with his sullen

eyes and wild, black goatee they naturally assumed he was a terrorist—a man on a sacred quest to destroy everything Western democracy represented. The American mall bombings had set nerves on edge. Commercial planes were only now beginning to be allowed back into U.S. airspace. Terrorists, they reasoned, lurked behind every shrub.

In Hamzah's particular case, these suspicions were correct.

Standing six feet four inches with the broad shoulders of a professional wrestler, the Algerian cut an imposing figure. The French girls with whom he spent his time called him *armoire à glace*—the mirrored wardrobe. His great bulk proved useful for bending others to his will or hurting them if the opportunity arose. At the moment, he would have traded size for more speed. This was his last run, but, Allah willing, it was the most important of his life.

Two officers of the French Police Nationale dogged his heals. Dark jumpsuits and shoulder patches identified them as Black Panthers—members of *Recherche Assistance Intervention Dissuasion* or RAID. As members of an elite antiterrorism unit they had their choice of weapons. These carried Glock semiautomatic pistols and the stubby, but deadly H&K MP5 submachine gun. RAID operators were said to shoot more than three hundred rounds each day and were all expert marksmen. The crowded terminal and their misguided desire to keep him alive for questioning were indeed the only things saving him from a bullet in the back of the head.

In desperation, Hamzah cut in front of a yellow

kiosk selling computerized foreign language courses. Unawares, a petite woman with blond braids pushed a baby stroller directly across his path. Her ribs crunched as he drove the point of his shoulder into her chest. The impact sent her crashing against a billboard with a sickening *whoof.* Hamzah yanked at the stroller as he bolted past, spilling a tangle of infant and blankets across the floor.

He held a feeble hope the officers would stop and check on the baby's safety, but a glance tossed over his shoulder confirmed what he already knew. RAID men were too professional for such a trick. They sailed over the dazed woman and her screaming child like Olympic hurdlers with automatic weapons.

A stately, graying gentleman dressed in the tweed sport coat of a university professor stepped from a bank of phones in an attempt to block the fleeing Algerian. He got a flat hand to the face for his trouble. His glasses shattered and he dropped to his knees.

Hamzah's heart sank as boots closed in behind him. Was it Allah's will that he should fail when he was now so close? Something had gone terribly wrong for RAID to be on him so fast. Someone must have informed.

Panting for breath, the Algerian rounded a bend at the great hall, near the main ticketing plaza. He felt a rush of wind as a RAID man swept at his neck.

Then, he saw his target, right where Rashid said he would be. Five more seconds, Allah willing, and nothing else would matter.

* * *

Ian Grant readjusted his tattered yellow backpack and took a look at his ticket. At nineteen he was already a seasoned world traveler, visiting places his friends back in Iowa had only seen in *National Geographic*. Charles de Gaulle Airport had fast become his least favorite spot on earth. Notoriously difficult to negotiate, even in September it was as muggy as a West African jungle and stunk like an overflowing toilet. Now it was packed with stranded travelers trying to get back to the States after a three-day flight embargo because of some stupid terrorists bombing a mall. He missed Africa already.

The flight from Abidjan, Côte d'Ivoire, the night before had been grueling. Before the cramped plane had lumbered down the tarmac, two haughty flight attendants had hustled down the center aisle, liberally applying the contents of two aerosol insecticide bombs into the already dank air over the passengers' heads. The smug women wore masks, but assured everyone else that the stuff was perfectly safe. Ian could plainly see a skull and crossbones on the orange cans. Twenty-four hours later, his T-shirt still reeked. It was a reminder of the many idiosyncrasies of the Dark Continent.

A year of sleeping on a reed mat and eating meals small enough to hold in the palm of his hand made civilization overwhelming. Small luxuries at the cheap hostel in Roissy the night before had been startling— light with the flick of a switch, a hot shower, and more food in one sitting than he'd been used to eating in a week. It gave him a melancholy pang at how he'd taken his entire life for granted.

Clarissa had warned him about that the night before

he left. She was twenty-five and freckled. A Protestant missionary, she was severely British and said whatever popped into her head.

Ian would never understand why a girl like Clarissa had taken up with someone like him. Six years her junior, he was all knees and elbows, with a perpetual bedhead of muddy brown hair. He was blind as an African fruit bat without his glasses, and his front teeth were on the big side.

With thoughts of Clarissa's herbal shampoo swirling in his head like a hot African wind, he didn't see the huge Arab until it was too late.

The tiny device in Hamzah's fist was called a cat's whisker. Roughly two inches long, it was nothing more than a hollow cellulose needle, sealed at both ends and housed inside a slightly larger cardboard tube with a plunger at the base. Once inserted into the body via the plunger, the inner needle would dissolve rapidly, releasing its contents into the bloodstream. It held little more liquid than a single drop of dew.

In this case, a drop was more than enough.

Ian's iced coffee spewed like a geyser as the massive Algerian ploughed into him from out of nowhere. Both men went down hard, the Algerian on top, driving the air from Ian's lungs.

The giant regained his feet in an instant, running again. Ian watched the soles of two black boots as a uniformed policeman leaped over him, only to slip in a puddle of spilled coffee. Another officer yanked his partner to his feet and the two tore down the hall cursing in French.

Ian shook his head as the trio disappeared around a corner beyond ticketing. He felt as if he'd been run over by a train. When he lifted the front of his coffee-soaked T-shirt he found the beginnings of an ugly bruise on his right side. He touched the spot with the tip of his finger. It was raw, like a bad carpet burn. The big guy must have led with his fist.

Ian grabbed a fistful of paper napkins from a nearby café stand and dabbed his shirt while he ordered another iced coffee. A veteran of West Africa, he'd endured far worse than a little bruise.

CHAPTER 3

The sounds of an American M4 assault rifle were distinctive—a friendly series of flat, supersonic whacks splitting the air—and hopefully the hearts and minds of more than a few Iraqi insurgents.

Sizzling arcs from falling Star Cluster flares illuminated the night sky to Jericho's left, past the motorcycle he'd stashed under a scraggly tamarisk tree. Male voices barked commands in English and guttural Iraqi Arabic. Moments before, a U.S. Army Cavalry "Peacekeeping Unit" had blazed through the streets in hot pursuit of two rusty Toyota Land Cruisers and an Opal sedan that supposedly carried several high-ranking insurgent leaders. The sounds of shouts and shooting moved four blocks away, then five, then six as American soldiers, many no older than twenty-one, ducked and dodged through dark, narrow streets and bombed-out buildings in this the City of Mosques.

So far, their quarry had eluded them.

Thirty feet above Quinn's head, a brisk desert wind caused the fronds of a lone date palm to hiss and rattle in the darkness as if shaken by an angry dog. There was no moon and as the Star Clusters burned away, the night closed back around him.

Dressed in the ankle-length *dishdasha* and a checked Arab head scarf known as a *shemagh*, Quinn lay prone. The rubble and broken pavement of the street gave up the heat gained from a long day, warming his belly. Though he wore his own M4 carbine and assorted other weapons, Quinn's robe made him look too much like an insurgent to take part in the present action without getting shot to pieces.

As a fluent Arabic speaker, Quinn was a rarity in the Air Force. With the copper skin of his Apache grandmother, he'd been able to blend in with the local populace, living "outside the wire" or beyond the protection of the base, for the past six days. A rash of kidnappings over recent weeks saw seven contractors, an Air Force TACP, and three soldiers from the U.S. Army Task Force out of Camp Fallujah go missing. Four of the civilian contractors and one soldier had shown up in various butchered body parts around the city. As other areas in Iraq appeared to be becoming more peaceful with the steady withdrawal of U.S. troops, minority Sunni insurgents in Fallujah had become even more violent. With the Colorado bombings, some now believed the Americans might just decide to stay for a while and were pulling all stops to make sure that didn't happen.

Though he ate everything he could get his hands on

when he was able to eat in the chow hall, Quinn had the gaunt look of a half-starved jackal that helped him fit in with the war-torn Iraqis. His Apache skin coloring, perpetual five o'clock shadow from his Irish father, and uncanny ability with the Arabic language allowed him to blend with the population outside the wire. His aggressive brand of fighting skill and elite fitness made him an obvious choice to spearhead the joint-service investigation tasked with finding the kidnapped personnel.

Since the Army had the most missing men, a lieutenant colonel named Fargo from Task Force 605 was put in charge of the operation. He was a blustering man with a red face and enough frustrated energy to start a grass fire if he stood in one spot too long. A logistics and supply officer by training, Fargo was rumored to have a relative in Congress who had helped move him into a more active role in the fighting before he rotated back to the States.

Quinn had been in Iraq for almost a year—double the term of deployment for an OSI agent. In that time, he'd developed a trusted stable of informants who had led him to Ghazan al Ghazi, an insurgent thug who was responsible for the deaths of hundreds of Iraqi civilians. Now, he'd finally developed a solid lead and the boneheaded Lt. Colonel Fargo had just blown right past with his men.

A nineteen-year-old Marine had been kidnapped the previous night during a protracted firefight in the far north end of the city. Since they had no personnel missing prior to that point, the Marine Corps had seen to its other duties and chosen not to take part in the task force.

For reasons known only to himself, Lt. Colonel Fargo had taken Quinn's intel and launched this rescue attempt without notifying the Marine Corps brass in Fallujah. Fargo was known as a "seagull colonel"—an officer who flew in, raised a riot with his infernal squawking, and then shit all over everything before he flapped off to annoy someone else.

At thirty-four, with the rank of Air Force captain, Quinn had no stomach for such leaders or the rancid politics they dragged around with them like a bad smell. If Fargo didn't see fit to call the Marines, that was his business. But the idiot ran right past Quinn and the target building, hot on the trail of a convoy of bad guys who were surely meant to do exactly what they were doing—drawing the Americans away.

Despite his best efforts, Fargo hadn't been able to keep the rescue a secret from the Marines for long. The radio net buzzed with activity as angry bulldog brass from Camp Baharia demanded to know what was going on. They were sending troops and advised all others on scene to "stay the hell out of their way."

Two minutes earlier, Quinn had seen a bright flash to the north and heard the shriek of an enemy RPG—rocket-propelled grenade—followed closely by the unmistakable groan and sickening thud of a chopper going down. Helicopters—likely Marine Super Cobras, dubbed "Snakes" by their crews—that had been on their way to save a missing hostage, now roared toward the crash scene to provide close air support with their mini-guns.

Quinn activated the high-intensity, infrared LEDs he kept in the pocket of the tactical khakis he wore under his *dishdasha*. Invisible to the naked eye, the tiny Firefly snapped to the end of a nine-volt battery could stay nestled in his pocket and still show up as an exploding fountain of light to patrolling aircraft. Quinn had witnessed firsthand the unholy mess American pilots and their magical weapons could make of unsuspecting insurgents. He didn't mind blending in on the ground, but he wanted the good guys in the sky to know he was a friendly.

Quinn raised his head just high enough to peer through a night vision scope at a clay building that slumped like a child's mud creation across the deserted street. Rusted oil drums, filled with sand and stacked two high, flanked the sides and much of the front of the rough two-story structure, giving it a bunkered, junkyard appearance. A hand-painted sign in Arabic swung from one broken hook above a dark, double-garage doorway. The faintest shaft of light peeked from the edges of shuttered windows on the second floor.

Quinn touched the tiny throat-mike that lead to the portable radio clipped beneath his *dishdasha*. "Tiger Four, Tiger Four, this is Copper Three-Zero. . . ."

Fargo's aide de camp, Major Tidwell, answered. Despite his tendency to brown nose, Tidwell was a decent and capable soldier. "Go for Tiger Four."

"Tiger Four, Copper Three-Zero," Quinn hissed. "You went past me. . . ." He consulted a wrist-mounted GPS and gave his coordinates. "My guy says the missing Marine and at least one other friendly are in the two-story building twenty meters west of my location. The sign out front says it's some kind of tire store."

Fargo came back, his voice crackling with energy. The pop of gunfire, likely his own whether he had anything to shoot at or not, caused the radio to cut in and out. "Stay put, Copper Three-Zero. Do not move. We're meeting resistance, but will work our way back to you." Fargo kept the button pressed on the radio while he shouted strained, nonsensical orders to his men. Quinn was forced to listen to an enormous amount of yelling and staccato gunfire before the officer finally came back to him. "I say again, do not take action! We'll rally at your location!"

Quinn tapped the Sig Sauer nine millimeter under his robe, to make certain it was where it was supposed to be. It was a habit he'd developed over his years of carrying a gun. He wore the pistol low on his thigh, in a tactical holster, so the ballistic vest he normally wore wouldn't interfere with his draw. The handgun was only for emergencies. The job of hunting men required something larger. Quinn's primary weapon was a Colt M4, the pug version of the venerable M16.

Rifle in hand, he rose up to peer at the shop but froze at a sudden hiss from his right.

"Copper Three-Zero? United States Marine Corps. I got your Firefly in my sights."

Quinn held his breath. "I'm a friendly."

"No shit," the voice chided. It was rock steady and rolled onto the night air on a heavy Southern drawl. "I'd have smoked your ass thirty seconds ago 'twere that not the case."

"How many men you got?" Quinn whispered at the dark shape, his brain already hard at work on a plan. It was a relief to have someone around besides Fargo.

"Two, but we're Marines so that's a dozen mortal men," the voice said. "We augered in hard on that Huey three blocks north. Damned hajji got us with an RPG. Crew chief and three of my men had to stay behind to move the pilots. Both of 'em got banged up on impact. Rat bastard Iraqis'll be swarming the place like maggots in no time flat. Me and Diaz broke away to come see about this missin' Marine y'all been squawkin' about on the radio."

Two forms scuttled up next to Quinn in the darkness under the lone palm tree.

"Gunnery Sergeant Jacques Thibodaux and Lance Corporal Diaz." Even in the inky black, Quinn could tell the gunny was built like a professional body builder. Biceps the size of grapefruit bulged from the rolled sleeves of his uniform blouse. Massive shoulders heaved with each deliberate breath. Corporal Diaz, who lay somewhere on the far side, was eclipsed by his giant sergeant.

Thibodaux gave Quinn a once-over, raising an eye at his Iraqi clothing. "You a civilian?"

"Air Force, OSI."

"Figured as much," Thibodaux grunted, his voice gumbo-thick with a Louisiana drawl. A square-jawed Marine Corps poster child, he put up with pilots from other service branches because they offered close air support when he needed it. Everyone else was a wing waxer . . . or worse. "So, Chair Force, where exactly is our Marine?"

Quinn rolled half on his side to look through his night vision scope at the shimmering green hulk of the Cajun. Thibodaux could have easily been an NFL lineman if he hadn't listened to the recruiter back in Baton Rouge.

"My information puts your Marine and at least one other American up there." Quinn nodded toward the dilapidated tire shop. "They're supposed to be executed tonight."

The muscles in the big Marine's jaw tensed at the news. "And your shitbird colonel wants you to wait 'til he gets here?"

"Those are his orders," Quinn said.

The men hugged the sand as an Opal sedan, covered in a layer of dust thick enough to obscure the color, sputtered up the road. Feeble headlights barely dented the night. The car ground to a creaking stop across the street, blocking the front door of the building from view.

A heavily bearded Iraqi got out and looked up and down the empty street, craning his neck as if stretching would help him see in the dark. When he was apparently satisfied that he hadn't been followed, he opened the trunk to retrieve a video camera and a large wad of clear plastic he stuffed under his arm. He gave the street another furtive look in either direction, then pulled an AK-47 from the back seat and disappeared into the building.

The giant Cajun took a knee. His voice was grim. "That dude just took in a camera and tarps. We all know what these rags like to get on video. . . ." The M4 looked like a toy in his shovel-sized hands.

Quinn slipped out of his *dishdasha* and tossed it under the palm tree. "We can't wait," he said. "That a problem for you?"

He could see from the look on the Cajun's face that it wasn't.

"You kiddin' me, Chair Force?" Thibodaux snorted. "I ain't responsible to orders some sand crab didn't even give me." He nudged Quinn in the side with his elbow. "Fact is, I was never gonna wait anyhow."

"Outstanding." Quinn pushed into a standing crouch. He tapped the CRKT Hissatsu fighting knife tucked in his belt before taking up the M4 from where it hung on the single-point sling around his neck. He paused to look at both Marines through the sullen darkness. To trust him, they had to hear this from his mouth: "No time for diplomacy here. We shoot anyone who isn't a hostage."

"Roger that," the Marines said in unison, stone-faced. That had always been their plan.

Quinn sensed the same torrent of white heat he felt before any life-threatening action—a fire, low in his belly.

Thibodaux turned and gave Quinn's shoulder a nudge as they began to move. "Time we got to know each other a bit, Chair Force. Let's me and you play a little game. Apart from the spending time in the company of a good woman—what are the top two things you wish you were doin' right now?"

Quinn broke into a fast trot, speaking as he went. His first wish was a no-brainer. "First, I'd be riding my BMW motorcycle up the Alaska Highway to see my little girl."

"Good choice," the Marine said, jogging beside him. "And if you couldn't do that?"

Quinn focused on the darkened building ahead, full of people who wanted nothing more than to see him and every other American dead.

"I'm doing it."

CHAPTER 4

Running alongside the two Marines dressed in their full battle rattle, Jericho Quinn felt naked in his mesh gear vest, OSI-issue dark blue polo shirt, and 5.11 Tactical khakis. The desert night was cold without his *dishdasha,* but the fact that he had no body armor sent the chill all the way to his bones.

"Take a look around back," Thibodaux whispered to Corporal Diaz as they drew even with the first row of oil drums at the left end of the building.

The plucky little Puerto Rican was dwarfed by the towering gunnery sergeant. He trotted off without a word with his bulky M240G machine gun. The Golf was heavier than an M4 but chambered for a 7.62 NATO round that packed a bigger wallop in return for the extra weight. He kept the weapon tucked in a high-ready position as he disappeared into the night.

Quinn and Thibodaux crouched alongside a grimy showroom window, adjacent to the main entry. When the shop had been up and running, the window would have revealed a small lobby full of tires and a few chairs for men to sit and drink strong Iraqi coffee while they waited. Now there was only a vacant concrete floor, some scattered rat droppings, and a darkened set of stairs in the far right corner leading to the second floor.

Diaz appeared from the opposite corner of the building in a tiptoeing sprint, having made a complete circle in just over a minute.

"There's a man-door up some rickety-ass stairs in back," he whispered, not even panting. "But it's sandbagged. Two sets of windows—one at the west end." He tipped his head toward the garage bay. "And another around back, ten feet west of the upstairs door. Windows are sandbagged too, but there's enough of a crack that I could make out two hajjis just inside the corner window."

"How about hostages?" Thibodaux asked.

"No sign of 'em, Gunny," Diaz said. "But I only had a half inch to peek through. The bastards already got on black masks. They're gettin' ready to make a video. . . ."

Quinn bit his bottom lip, understanding the urgency. "Any way to get a flash bang through one of the upstairs windows?"

"No way, sir." Diaz shook his head. "They got sandbags stacked up inside. I could blow the bags, but by the time we dug our way in, our guys'd be DRT."

DRT was dead right there—the worst kind of dead, absolutely, unrevivably dead.

The Puerto Rican jerked a thumb over his shoulder. "The only way in is up those inside stairs."

Quinn turned toward Thibodaux, caught up in the moment of the chase.

"Marines are big on charging the hill. . . ."

"Damn straight," Thibodaux said. "If I told you what I really want to do, it'd melt your little Chair Force ears."

"Roger that, Gunny." Diaz nodded in agreement.

Quinn shot another glance through the film of dust and grime on the showroom window. Suddenly struck with a plan, he took a step backward, looking up at the second story, then through the window again at the stairs.

"Gunny," he whispered. "You've been through this drill before, I'll bet. . . . Cleared building packed with insurgents."

"Chock-full of the rat bastards," Thibodaux said.

"They've learned from us to block all the entries but one—"

"Then fortify the hell out of the only way in," Thibodaux completed his thought. "I'll lay odds the hajjis Diaz saw got a fifty cal pointed straight at our only entry point."

"Okay, listen," Quinn said, thumb on the safety of his M4. "Fargo could be another half hour for all we know. If we wait for reinforcements—the guys upstairs are dead. If we charge the door and get ourselves killed—the guys upstairs are dead."

"Roger that." Thibodaux nodded, one eyebrow crawling under the front edge of his Kevlar helmet as he wrinkled his forehead in thought. "You look like a man with a plan."

"Here's the deal." Quinn hoped the idea didn't sound as crazy out loud as it did in his head. "We go in fast and quiet. Diaz will cut left to take a position in the back corner while you and I hustle up the stairs . . . keeping an eye out for trip wires." He added the last to show he'd cleared a building or two as well.

"The way those ceilings sag they're not much but plywood and rotten timber. Diaz, you give us a twenty-count, then spray the ceiling directly over that back corner with a good thirty-round burst. That's where they'll have their machine gun. After that, you better come running, because me and the gunny will be bootin' the door when we hear you shoot. If you don't get there quick, every bad guy in the place will be DRT before you get a chance to help."

"You're a scary man, Chair Force," Thibodaux grunted. "Death from below . . . remind me not to ever let you talk to my Delta-Whiskey."

"Your what?"

"Dependent wife . . . she's mean enough as it is. I don't want her to learn any of your sneaky-ass ways." The doorknob disappeared under Thibodaux's huge left hand. "It's open," he whispered. "We go in on three."

Safeties snicked off in the darkness. Thibodaux slid the door open an inch at a time, searching for wires and other telltale signs of alarms.

"What if the hostages are above the back corner?" Diaz said.

"Then they're dead anyway," Thibodaux winked, pushing open the door. "*Laissez les bon temps rouler.*"
Let the good times roll.

* * *

They made it up the stairs in three seconds without meeting any resistance.

"Since I got on my flak vest," the big Cajun whispered, "and you came to our little *fais do-do* unprepared, I'll take the lead."

"I'll let you," Quinn said.

Though the two men had known each other all of ten minutes, they were professional operators—and good tactics were good tactics. Each moved with a fluid surety that made the other man trust him as though they'd trained together for months. War, like no other catalyst, could forge an instantaneous and lasting friendship between men—if they survived.

Quinn held up his left hand, knifelike, pointing at the middle of the door. "Down the middle?"

The Marine gave a curt nod. He pulled the pin on a flash bang—to blind and deafen anyone in the room. "You take hajjis on the right, I'll take hajjis on the le—"

A clattering rattle broke loose below as Diaz tore up the floor with a barrage of 7.62.

Thibodaux reacted instantly, slamming a size-thirteen desert combat boot to the door. The flimsy, wooden jamb shattered with a loud crack. The door leapt from its hinges as if torn away by an explosion. A half second later, the Marine's stun grenade shook the building. Dust, smoke, and panicked Iraqi voices filled the air.

Quinn focused on threats in order of scale: guns first, blades second. He was aware of two bound men, kneeling in the center of the room. Both wore blindfolds, hands tied behind their backs. A dazed Iraqi stood behind each prisoner. Would-be executioners, they held short blades, no bigger than pocket knives— executions were supposed to bring agony as well as death.

The cameraman spun toward the door, his rifle dangling on a sling over his shoulder. He was less than three feet away, close enough Quinn could smell his sweat. Thibodaux moved fast, already behind the cameraman, busy with another target on his side of the room. It was too dangerous for Quinn to chance a shot with the M4.

Quinn's right hand stayed on his rifle while his left dropped to the Hissatsu killing blade in his belt. There were too many threats to devote inordinate time to any single one. Quinn strode forward, engaging the nine-inch blade point-first to shove the stunned cameraman out of his way. The razor-sharp weapon entered the soft flesh just above the V on the Iraqi's collarbone. The man's eyes slammed open in stark realization that the only beheading he would witness tonight would be his own.

Quinn was vaguely aware of warmth and moisture spraying his arm, and the sucking gurgle as the Hissatsu slipped though muscle and cartilage.

The knife slid back to its Kydex sheath with a positive click as Quinn advanced, a red palm print on his khakis where he'd wiped his left hand. The M4 back at eye level, he scanned the room for his next target.

The cameraman twitched on the floor behind him, no longer a threat.

Five feet away, a masked Iraqi who'd been in the

process of reading a statement for the camera staggered backward in surprise. He tripped over a startled hostage to fall toward the left side of the room.

"*Allahu akbar!*" he shouted, before two rounds from Thibodaux's M4 tore his throat away.

Quinn's rifle spat and a tall Iraqi behind the two kneeling hostages stumbled forward, dropping his AK-47. The teenager who'd been posted with the 50-caliber machine gun, badly wounded by Diaz's withering fire from below, poked his head over a row of sandbags in the far corner. He made a feeble attempt to fire a pistol.

Thibodaux bounced a grenade off the back wall into the makeshift bunker and turned the kid to jelly. The sandbags directed the blast upward, away from everyone else, but the noise was deafening.

Flanking each blade-wielding executioner, two more insurgents brought long guns to bear as they shook off the effects of the concussion.

Quinn breathed in the smell of cordite and blood, swinging his rifle methodically, resting the glowing red circle on the M4's EOTech holographic sight on the chest of one target, squeezing the trigger twice, then moving to the next a half a heartbeat later. He had no doubt Thibodaux was doing the same. If Marines were anything, they were expert riflemen.

All the gun-wielding insurgents in his area of responsibility DRT, Quinn rushed forward to get a better angle on the one with the blade, who'd now grabbed the nearest hostage by the collar and used him as a shield.

The young prisoner was difficult to identify through

the filth that caked his face and grimy brown T-shirt, but his high-and-tight haircut above the duct tape blindfold made Quinn guess he was the missing Marine.

He fought like a Marine.

The hostage gave a muffled yell beneath his gag and pushed himself backward, rolling over the top of his assailant. Spinning as he rolled, he kicked out with bare feet, connecting with a satisfying thud to the masked Iraqi's ribs. Enraged and still screaming under his duct tape, the young Marine lashed out blindly, legs pumping as if he were riding a bicycle. The Iraqi shifted away to avoid another blow, giving Jericho enough room to put two rounds below his left ear.

"Clear!" Thibodaux shouted through gray curls of gun smoke and settling dust. His weapon still pressed close to his shoulder, tree-trunk arms tucked tight as he scanned the room.

Jericho did the same.

"I'm a friendly!" Corporal Diaz warned as he came through the door behind them. He blinked in dismay at the nine dead Iraqi's that littered the room. "Holy shit, Gunny! You guys done already?"

"Roger that," Thibodaux said. He'd let the M4 fall against the sling on his chest and now knelt above the bound Marine. He cut the young man free and offered him a badly needed sip of water from the CamelBak attached to his ballistic vest. "What's your name, son?"

The young Marine stretched his jaw muscles, unaccustomed to being free of the duct tape. "Corporal Lark, Gunnery Sergeant. I got separated from my platoon two days ago. My buddy got shot and I woke up half beat to death with my hands tied." His entire body shook from relief and adrenaline.

Quinn tugged the tape away from the other hostage's mouth and eyes. This one was older than the Marine by at least fifteen years, with thinning blond hair and a scraggly goatee—one of the missing contractors.

"I thought I'd never see Americans again," the man said, his voice shaking. He blinked in dismay as his tearful eyes adjusted to the light. "You killed them all." He swallowed hard when, for the first time, he looked to the floor and saw the tiny knife that had been meant to cut his head off.

The contractor hung his head between his knees and vomited.

Diaz looked impatiently at his watch and tapped the toe of his boot against the wooden floor, which was now awash with pools of blood and bits of Iraqi insurgent.

"We should haul ass, Gunny," he said. "Been here too long alre—"

As if to punctuate the urgency of the corporal's plea, a mortar round screamed in from the darkness smashing into the side of the building. The sandbag bunker in the corner exploded in a flash of light and yellow smoke. Wood and sand flew through the room as if sprayed from a hose. A shard of metal from the demolished fifty cal whirred into Diaz like an airborne saw blade. He dropped to his knees, screaming in pain.

"*Cochons!*" The big Cajun's head jerked up from tending a blood-caked Lark. His eyes bored holes through Quinn. "Rat bastards are givin' me the red ass!

Chair Force, get on the horn and call us some close air support, pronto!"

The gunny rushed to Diaz's side. The huge piece of shrapnel had hit him below his calf, severing the Achilles tendon and both bones in the lower leg. His foot was attached by only a thin strip of skin.

Thibodaux applied a tourniquet from a pouch on his vest. He shot a worried look at Quinn. "How about that air, beb?"

Another mortar exploded outside. Twisted oilcans flew by the gaping hole in the wall. Like dogs to a dinner bell, insurgents were drawn to the sound of American presence.

As soon as Quinn tried the radio, Lt. Colonel Fargo launched into a fulminating volcanic eruption, screaming as if Quinn had single-handedly started the whole Iraqi war. Quinn ignored him. If Fargo wasn't going to help when they were under direct fire, it was hardly worth the trouble to mount a defense over the radio.

After two calls for help on the open radio net, a patrolling pilot answered. "Copper Three-Zero, this is Psycho bringing my Warthog in from the north. Is that you, G-Man?"

A third mortar whoomped in front of the tire shop, destroying the dead Iraqi cameraman's rusty Opal. Whirring metal reduced the palm tree across the street to a three-foot stump.

Thibodaux arched massive shoulders over Diaz, shielding him from falling debris. "The sons of bitches got us dialed in for sure now. Tell your flyboys to light a shuck!"

Quinn gave him a grim nod, then turned back to the radio. Psycho was Major Troy Bates, an Academy classmate who'd gone on to fly A-10 Warthogs. "Psycho, this is Copper. That's affirmative. It's me all right." Jericho was careful not to give out much information. Too many bad guys had stolen U.S. communications gear. He already had a price on his head—no point in jacking up the pot.

A hidden fifty-caliber machine gun opened fire from the dark tumble of clay buildings less than half a block away and began to chew up the tire shop.

"Psycho . . ." Quinn keyed his radio, his voice a taut wire. "We could use that support sooner rather than later. Lt. Colonel Fargo has Echo Company coming back from the northeast and we're taking fire from our west." He checked the GPS on his wrist and gave his coordinates.

"I'm cleared hot and I got good eyes on your bad guys," Psycho said, a half moment later. "Hold your ears, G-Man."

The Warthog's GE turbofan engines roared overhead a moment before the GAU 8 nose gun burped with a throaty growl, like a smoker's cough on steroids. Seventy rounds per second, each roughly the size of a fat carrot, shredded the rooftop insurgents like coleslaw.

Quinn sighed, relaxing for the first time in a week. With an A-10 spitting death from the sky, other bad actors would lay low for a time. "I owe you, Psycho."

"Yes, you do," the Warthog pilot came back. "But

it'll have to wait. I'm getting another call. The bad guys must be smokin' crack tonight. . . ."

A Marine Corps Huey landed two minutes later to medevac the wounded. The pilot offered to take the American contractor as well, but Lt. Colonel Fargo would not permit it. He had to have something to show for his efforts. He treated the contractor little better than a prisoner, forcing him to ride in the command Humvee instead of taking the relatively quick chopper ride back to a hospital and hot food.

Insurgents or no insurgents, before Fargo left the scene, he wanted a piece of Quinn. Spittle flew in all directions as he ranted and fumed. A desert camo helmet perched on an ostrichlike neck; veins throbbed and tendons tensed. His words were little more than seething, apoplectic grunts, but his meaning was clear. He had "important" connections—all the way to Congress—and he intended to see that Quinn was drummed out of the service for his disobedience.

Through the dust at the landing zone beyond the splintered palm tree, Quinn caught sight of Thibodaux loading his brother Marines into the Huey amid flashing lights and rotor wash. Two Apache gunships circled overhead, patrolling for any bad guys who might want to crash the evacuation party. Thankfully, their engine noise drowned out most of Fargo's tirade.

As two Navy corpsmen took custody of Diaz's stretcher, the corporal pushed himself up on one elbow. Quinn watched as he tugged on Thibodaux's arm, then pointed back across the street, directly at him.

". . . putting you on report, mister!" Fargo's threats jerked Quinn's attention back. "Captain, are you hearing me?"

Quinn decided he'd had a gut full. "I am, sir, loud and clear. Your wife's sister is the President's dishwasher's nephew's nanny, and you plan to use these connections to get me kicked out of the Air Force."

Fargo snorted. "Laugh it up now, bucko. You think you're some kind of hero, but that kid got his foot blown off because of your stupidity. The Marines will want your hide—*if*, and that's a big *if*, bucko—there's anything left after I'm through with you. I had tactical command on this operation and you disobeyed my direct order. You are done!" Fargo started to poke him in the chest with a finger, but luckily for both of them, had enough brains to decide against it at the last moment.

Quinn turned away, shrugging off the encounter before he did something that would really get him in trouble. It was impossible to take seriously anyone who used *bucko* twice in the same breath.

As Fargo stomped off, Gunny Thibodaux rattled Quinn's fillings with a smack between the shoulder blades. The two men stood together, shielding their faces from flying sand as the Huey spooled up and leapt into the black night. It disappeared quickly, flying lights-out to confuse RPG shooters among the rooftops and mosques.

"Chin up, Captain." Thibodaux grinned. It was no small thing that he'd elected not to call Quinn "Chair Force." "Forget about that sand-crab son of a bitch. We saved two American lives today. That's gotta count for somethin'. How you gettin' back to your base?"

Quinn nodded toward the wispy boughs of a haggard tamarisk bush across the street. "My bike's stashed over there where you snuck up on me. It's a piece of crap, but I'll ride it back. I think more clearly when I'm in the wind." He glanced up at the giant Marine. "How's Diaz?"

"He'll make it."

"And his foot?"

"The foot's DRT, beb." Thibodaux gave a somber grin. "That dumb-ass Puerto Rican, he's worried 'bout you. He asked me to pass you a message."

"Yeah?"

"Hell yes, he did." Thibodaux shook his head in disbelief. "'Gunny,' he says to me, 'you tell Chair Force not to worry none. I'd give my left nut to save another Marine. A foot—well, that ain't nothin'.'"

CHAPTER 5

Paris

By the time Ian Grant cleared security and reached his gate an hour later, his neck was incredibly stiff. He shrugged off the pain as a side effect to the collision with the big Algerian and made a mental note to go see a chiropractor once he made it home to Iowa City.

Northwest Flight 2 began to board forty-five minutes later, just before 10:00 P.M.

Ian's seat was 61E, near the back, so he was called early in the process. His passport was checked for the sixth time by a sneering gate attendant who seemed eager to add one last layer of bureaucracy before his victims got out of France.

Finally on board, Ian found the loud behavior of the American crew disconcerting after so many months among the quieter people of West Africa. A smiling flight attendant with blond hair piled high and a gold tag that said her name was Samantha, helped him find his seat—which happened to be crammed between two gray-haired women from New Jersey.

"Are you all right, young man?" the woman on the aisle said, as she gathered up her knitting to let Ian slip into his seat. "You look green at the gills." The lines on her smiling face said sixty was a distant memory.

"I'm fine," Ian lied through a halfhearted smile. He kept his neck locked in place as he lowered himself into his seat.

The old woman reminded him of his Aunt Ellen back in Iowa City. If the resemblance went any further than physical this was going to be a long eight hours to New York.

Aunt Ellen leaned forward to talk to her traveling companion, who turned out to be her sister, Theresa. "He look a little peaked to you?"

Theresa lowered her paperback bodice-ripper and put the back of a veiny hand on Ian's forehead. "Feverish, indeed." She peered across gold-rimmed granny glasses that were chained to her neck. "I trust you're not contagious." She looked and sounded very much like Ian's seventh-grade English teacher. A more humorless woman, he'd never met.

He tried to shake his head, but had to make do with shifting his eyes. He was beginning to worry that he'd broken something. "Touch of malaria." He swallowed. Razor blades suddenly appeared in the back of his throat.

"Malaria's not catchy," Aunt Ellen said, settling back in with her knitting for a moment, and then suddenly leaned to look across Ian. "It's not, is it, Theresa?"

"Not unless we happen to share mosquitoes," Theresa mumbled, engrossed again in her pulp romance. "But he'll likely get sweat all over us."

Roughly three hours after Ian's collision with the Algerian, Samantha and a flight attendant named Liz brought the beverage cart to a rattling stop beside row sixty-one.

Samantha leaned across Aunt Ellen to give Ian a napkin. "Can I offer you a turkey sandwich and something to drink?" She put a wrist to his forehead. "Are you okay? You look feverish."

"Malaria." Aunt Ellen looked up, a twist of sky-blue yarn wrapped around her boney index finger. "It's not catchy."

"Just water," Ian croaked, surprised at how raspy his voice had become.

He sucked a piece of ice, hoping it would soothe his throat, but it only made the pain worse. He spit the cube back in his glass and sank against his seat, exhausted. His entire body was on fire.

Aunt Ellen raised an eyebrow and clucked like a mother hen. "You poor thing." She dabbed at Ian's forehead with her napkin, between bites of her turkey sandwich.

The boy in row sixty popped up and down like a redheaded Whac-A-Mole target, gawking at Ian and his two elderly seatmates. His name was Drew and he found it extremely entertaining to throw his pretzels one at a time, backward over the seat while his mother was in the restroom.

Theresa scolded the boy, going so far as to smack him over the head with her paperback. Drew retaliated by tossing more pretzels, one of which landed in Ian's water. Theresa fished it out with a wink and threw it back at the boy. The boy poked his freckled face above the headrest with the soggy pretzel between his teeth. He swallowed it with a devilish giggle just as his mother returned to her seat.

Fifteen minutes later, Theresa and Drew began to cough.

Two hours into the flight Ian awoke with his stomach on the verge of eruption. He had just enough time to grab an airsick bag from the seat pocket.

Theresa rolled her eyes behind her book. Aunt Ellen rubbed her belly. "I've always been a sympathetic vomiter." She dropped her knitting on the floor and waddled up the aisle toward the restrooms.

Samantha Rogers heard the boy in 61E retch as if he was about to lose his entire stomach. Airline policy dictated she put on latex gloves immediately, but she usually just carried them until she checked out the situation. People upchucked all the time on these long flights, but they usually made it to the airsick bag or the restroom. She'd gotten a new manicure at the Hotel Meurice during her layover and wasn't about to wreck her nails if she didn't have to.

The kid's upper lip was beaded with perspiration. His T-shirt was soaked. Though slender, his belly was bloated as if ready to burst. A ring of what looked to be chocolate cookie crumbs encircled grimacing lips.

No need for gloves here—just an overindulgent sweet tooth. Thankfully, he'd used the airsick bag. Samantha held out a plastic sack to take the smaller bag. She gave him an empty one in return.

"Too many Oreos for you, mister," she scolded, touching the corners of his mouth with a moist towel she kept in the pocket of her apron.

"He hasn't been eating cookies." Theresa leaned across to scowl at the flight attendant.

"Then what . . . ?"

Samantha's face went pale as the boy's eyes flicked open. Tears of blood trickled from a web of swollen vessels. A muffled croak escaped cracked lips. To her horror, she realized the flecks of what she'd thought were dried bits of cookie was dead flesh sloughed from the boy's raw tongue.

A moment later, Liz ran up the aisle. Her mousy brown hair had escaped its bun and hung beside a flushed cheek as if she'd just been in a scuffle.

"She's dead!" Liz gasped in Samantha's ear. Her voice shook with abject terror. "I went in to check on her and she's dead—"

Samantha grabbed her by both arms. "Who?"

"She was sitting right here." Liz's eyes were wild. Her voice quavered as she pointed to the empty seat beside Ian Grant. "I heard an awful groan in the bathroom, and when I checked on her . . . she was slumped over the toilet. . . ." Liz dropped her voice to a grating whisper. "Sammie, she was bleeding out of her mouth. . . ."

On the other side of Ian, Theresa stared mutely as a single drop of blood fell from her nose to land on the pages of her novel with a sickening plop.

Samantha took a step toward the restroom, seized by a sudden wave of nausea. "Get it together," she told herself through clenched teeth.

From behind her, came the unmistakable sound of a child vomiting.

"Drew!" The terror in a mother's voice was unmistakable.

Samantha swallowed, trying to regain some semblance of composure. Her throat was on fire.

CHAPTER 6

"Are you hearing this, Karen?" Northwest Captain Steve Holiday stared in dismay at his first officer as they listened to the flight attendants over the intercom. One passenger dead and four more were unconscious.

"Food poisoning?" Karen Banning said as she unfastened her seat belt. If it had been a terrorist incident, both pilots would have barricaded themselves behind the armored door of the flight deck. In a medical scare, it went without saying that she would check things out.

Captain Holiday reached behind his head and grabbed the oxygen mask. When alone at the controls, he was supposed to wear supplemental oxygen. His voice took on a detached, Darth Vader quality as he spoke through the mask.

"Be careful out there. Scoot back here to let me in on what's going on. Follow protocol." If Steve Holiday believed in anything, it was protocol. It drove his wife crazy.

The 747 was a spacious aircraft. It took the first officer three minutes to make her way through the upper-deck business class, negotiate the stairwell down to the main passenger compartment, size up the situation, and call back up to flight deck. To Holiday, each minute was an eternity.

Normally almost giddy, Karen's voice was deadly somber as it crackled across the intercom. "You're not going to like this, Steve. . . ."

Her vivid description of the pandemonium in the rear of the aircraft hit Holiday like a straight jab to the nose. He ordered her back to the cockpit, where hours of training and well-established emergency procedures kicked into gear.

Holiday noted their position on the GPS—still five and a half hours from JFK—and called in a medical emergency via the satellite phone. He was told to stand by while a doctor was summoned.

When the doctor came on the line ten minutes later, Karen described what she'd seen like a child recounting a nightmare—coughing, fever, vomiting, bleeding from the nose and eyes. She looked across at Holiday, slight shoulders trembling as she spoke.

"It's not isolated among a particular group of passengers?" the doctor mused, almost to himself.

"It is not," Holiday snapped. He hated it when people talked to themselves when they should be talking to him. "This thing's moving through my airplane like the plague. We haven't been in the air four hours and already have five dead and . . ." Karen mouthed a number that surprised even him. ". . . and at least forty-two showing advanced symptoms."

The doctor advised the pilots to use continued oxygen and have no more interaction with the passengers. With hardly a good-bye, he promised to make contact again in fifteen minutes and cut the connection.

Holiday gave a tight grin to his copilot. Blond, pert and almost elfin in appearance, Karen had always reminded him of his daughter. The sight of her trembling beside him broke his heart. She had to know she could still depend on him. "Chin up, kiddo. They're probably trying to figure out what leper colony to divert us to."

CHAPTER 7

Thirty-four minutes after Captain Steve Holiday placed his initial call to FAA Flight Following, Dr. Megan Mahoney of the Centers for Disease Control found herself pulled from the a plush corner booth at The Dining Room in Buckhead, on the outskirts of downtown Atlanta, and escorted to an armored limousine that smelled faintly of cigar smoke. She had been on her first date in months, with a cardiologist from Emory University Hospital. He was a handsome enough man, but loved to hear himself talk. Megan had to admit she wasn't disappointed at the interruption.

"I have to go," she'd said as the two young, athletic-looking men wearing dark suits and dour expressions invited her to "please come along" with them. She'd shrugged and dropped her napkin on top of her lamb shank osso buco, which she was much sorrier to leave behind than the gabby cardiologist. "Duty calls."

"They send secret agents to fetch you from dinner?" Her date had smirked. "Who are you, Batgirl?"

"Batgirl . . ." Megan had nodded at that, thinking of

the hundred of bats she'd dissected under lantern light in dank forests around the world. "I suppose I am. . . ."

Mahoney was a compact woman, barely five-three, but when she wasn't peering through a microscope at deadly pathogens, she was at the gym or in the pool. She demanded the two agents show her their credentials—though they both gave the impression she would get in the tinted limo one way or another.

Inside, Megan found herself alone. A built-in webcam in a plasma screen on the teak table broadcast her image to representatives from Homeland Security, NORAD, and the White House. James Willis, the director of the CDC leaned across his deceptively uncluttered desk, making eye contact with her over the computer screen. He'd spent the last four days and nights working nonstop in Colorado. His face was drawn with fatigue and worry.

Megan straightened her shoulder-length hair—her father called the color *claybank*—in an effort to look more professional and tried to settle into the overly soft leather seat.

Each of the conference participants got their own portion of the split screen so all were visible to one another, even when they weren't speaking. She recognized several of the Joint Chiefs and other high-level bureaucrats from too much time watching C-SPAN.

"She's four hours and twenty-one minutes off the Eastern seaboard at her present speed and course," General Brian Randall, United States Air Force, advised the group, as if Northwest Flight 2 was an enemy missile. LEDs blinked and flashed on a wall map behind him in USNORTHCOM's version of a Larry King backdrop.

"Is that enough time to put a plan in order?" a frumpy woman from Homeland Security asked. "I'm not sure that's enough time. . . ." She wrung her hands on the oak table in front of her, as if squeezing out a washcloth.

"Depends on the plan," said Army Lt. General Adam Norton. "French sources tell us their antiterrorist units took down a lab a little over an hour ago near Roissy, an area adjacent to the Paris airport. They discovered the makings of what looks like an attempt at some kind of biological weapon."

In the back seat of the limousine, Dr. Mahoney ran a hand down the front of her black cocktail dress and took in the information. Of course the government had plans in place for the quarantine of incoming aircraft, but every incident was different and required a slightly different protocol. She'd scanned the contents of a powder-blue folder from the seat beside her. As she spoke, she leaned into the microphone beside the plasma screen.

"Megan Mahoney with the Centers for Disease Control and Prevention." She possessed the well-coifed classiness of a CNN news anchor and, having grown up in Fulton County, the magnolia-soft drawl of a bona fide southern belle. "Forgive me, but I'm assuming you've put the DEOC on alert?" The CDC director's Emergency Operations Center stood fully staffed and ready 24-7 to help support national health emergencies.

"For the time being, *you* are the DEOC." Willis shook his head. "The White House wants this close hold—the fewer people made aware of it, the better. With everyone spooled up over the Colorado bombings, nerves are on edge, as you can imagine. Something like this could shut down the country."

"Very well," Mahoney sighed, knowing better than to argue with all the egos at the meeting. "The symptoms the pilot describes indicate a hemorrhagic virus—something like Marburg or Ebola—but we've never come across anything that acts this fast. Has anyone looked at the passenger manifest? This would make a lot more sense if a large group traveling together began to develop symptoms at the same—"

General Randall held up a sheaf of computer paper. "We've been over the passenger list, Dr. Mahoney. No large groups. According to the pilot in command, it looks like an American kid named Ian Grant seated at the back of the airplane was the first to get sick. We've run this kid's passport history. He was on a flight to Paris from the Ivory Coast day before yesterday."

Megan made some notes in a small notepad she carried with her everywhere. "And he isn't traveling with anyone?"

"No, ma'am." Randall shook his head. "But he and the old ladies who were sitting next to him are dead."

"And farther forward?" Megan felt her chest go tight as she thought through the possible ramifications of a hemorrhagic virus trapped in the tight confines of a commercial airliner.

General Norton leaned back in his chair and stared

at the ceiling. "The pilot says there are five dead and over forty showing symptoms."

Megan nodded. It was exactly what she'd feared. "If an agent this fast is also airborne . . . that entire airplane is doomed—"

General Randall harrumphed, rolling his eyes. "Doomed is a strong word."

Megan Mahoney chewed softly on her bottom lip. She was all too used to dealing with know-it-all managers who, in truth, knew less than the guys who vacuumed their spacious offices. She leaned against the teak table, both hands clasped at her chest. A string of Mikimoto pearls was draped across her fingers.

"You are right. We do have plans in place for this sort of thing, General. Northwest 2 should proceed to the quarantine isolation gate at JFK. If those passengers aren't quarantined the moment they step off that airplane, this illness would almost certainly infect any unprotected people who get within breathing distance. I suppose I don't have to point out that Marburg kills one in four of those it infects. . . ."

"Maybe it's not Marburg," Randall said.

"You're right. It could be worse," Mahoney said. "Ebola Zaire kills nine out of ten. Once those passengers get cell coverage they'll be on the phone with their families. If they describe even the smallest fraction of what they're going through, mass panic will ensue on the . . ." Her voice trailed off as she scribbled some figures on a legal pad in front of her.

"What?" Randall asked, appointing himself as CDC's unofficial interrogator. "You're the disease expert. What are you thinking?"

"The air onboard a commercial jet is recirculated throughout the plane. . . ." Megan blew a strand of copper gold hair out of her face as she tapped her pencil on the pad. "A 747 carries roughly four hundred passengers. So far, they've eaten up fifty percent of their flight time and a little over ten percent of the passengers are infected. If this is anything like the hemorrhagic fevers we've seen, as soon as they show symptoms, each of those passengers will become a fountain of leaking virus and, from the look of things, be spewing it into the air with each breath." She threw her pencil on the table. "I'm tellin' y'all, Ebola does things to the human body you don't want to see in the guy scrunched up next to you in coach."

Director Willis leaned forward. "Dr. Mahoney," he said, giving her a knowing nod. "Why don't you explain to the rest of the group what a hemorrhagic virus does?"

"If it hasn't happened already, very soon, the inside of that airplane will be awash in every bodily fluid imaginable. Connective tissue breaks down so skin looks like it's falling off the bone. Cells rupture, men's testicles swell, then die and turn black. Skin becomes hypersensitive to touch, making even the brush of clothing unbearable. There'll be lots of bleeding—even from the pores—loss of bladder and bowel control . . ."

Mahoney saw all eyes on the plasma screen were focused heavily on her. "Look, I apologize for being so blunt, but it's important y'all understand just how dangerous this is. Ebola . . . *digests* you, for lack of a better description, from the inside out. By the time it's finished, it's replicated itself in exponential proportions.

Each drop of blood in an infected body can contain over one hundred million viruses . . . and every single one of those little guys wants to find a way out, because you're dead, and he's gonna need another host. . . ."

"Thank you, Doctor." A towering man in a crisp blue uniform and a full head of gray hair rubbed tired eyes. "Admiral Tobias Scott," he said, though the chairman of the Joint Chiefs needed no introduction. "Whatever our decision, we owe it to Captain Holiday to get back to him quickly. He's got be awfully lonely."

"I have two F-15s on alert at Lajes Field. With your permission—"

"I appreciate that, General Randall, but our 747 is well beyond the Azores by now." The admiral leaned sideways and spoke for a moment to an aide before turning back to the group. "Ladies and gentlemen, it looks as though the U.S. carrier Theodore Roosevelt is almost directly under Northwest 2's present position. I'll have her skipper send an F-18 Hornet up as an escort. He can jam the radio and satellite phone traffic so Captain Holiday or anyone else on board will be unable to get a signal out without coming through us. That should solve our mass-panic problem for the time being." Scott looked directly into the camera. "Forrester?" he said, almost barking.

Guy Forrester, a balding civil servant who'd risen inexplicably through the ranks of government to land high in the newly formed Department of Homeland Security, had jowls that were puffed and green, as though he might be sick. "Yes, Admiral Scott?"

"Have someone pick up that FAA controller and the doctor who spoke to Captain Holiday. We're going to have to bring them in to . . . protective custody, shall we say."

Forrester blinked bleary eyes and took a deep, shuddering breath. He did not move.

"Right away, man," Scott barked. "I can not emphasize containment enough here. You're dismissed to go make your calls."

The admiral leaned back and steepled his fingers in front of closed eyes. "I need to brief the President in five minutes. Let's hear some options, people."

CHAPTER 8

4 September

Captain Steve Holiday drew a breath from his oxygen mask through clenched teeth. Samantha, the lead flight attendant, was dead. Perky Liz, who'd just been showing off photos of her little boy's first birthday, was dead. Four of the remaining nine crew members were having trouble standing, and from all accounts, two of those would be gone in a matter of minutes. He'd deployed emergency oxygen masks for the passengers but lied when he announced that doctors had advised this would help staunch any further spread of the mysterious illness. No one was telling him a damn thing.

Beside him, slouched in the right seat, Karen Banning had figured out she was dying. A pile of tissues at her feet was stained with the steady flow of blood that dripped from her nose and came up with every raw, spasmodic cough. He'd tried to comfort her with a pat on the shoulder, but she jerked away, shrieking in pain at his touch. Any pressure against her skin threw her into agony.

Once-smooth skin hung loose and lifeless off her cheekbones. Dull eyes bounced oddly in all directions as if hung on the end of cartoon springs. It was the stuff bad dreams were made of.

The few unaffected passengers had barricaded themselves in the upper deck, outside the cockpit, and threatened to roll a beverage cart down the stairs at anyone who tried to come up the stairs from below. A look at the video monitor that viewed the back galley showed a surreal scene of dangling yellow oxygen masks, slumped bodies, and exhausted passengers shuffling zombielike to and from overflowing rest-rooms.

Holiday switched off the monitor, surprised by a sudden squawk on the radio.

"Northwest Flight 2, this is United States Marine Corps F-18, Nickel Five-Five hailing on one three one point one"

Holiday bounced a fist off his knee and nearly howled in delight. "Hot damn, Nickel Five-Five, it is good to hear a friendly voice."

"Northwest 2 switch to Tango Niner-Niner."

Holiday complied. It was an encrypted frequency, used during hijackings.

"You there, Nickel Five-Five?"

"Roger that, Northwest 2."

"Outstanding," Holiday said. "I've got an airplane full of dying people, and to top that off, we're having radio trouble. Think you could relay for me?"

"Happy to, sir," the F-18 pilot answered back. "I'm a half mile off your starboard wing."

Holiday passed on details about the crew's medical

condition, the rapid spread of the illness, and the latest update on the number of dead.

"I'm switching to a military frequency," the fighter said after he'd repeated the information coolly. "Be right back, sir."

"You know where to find us," Holiday chuckled.

He shook his head at the luck of it all—running into an F-18 pilot at thirty-four thousand feet over the Atlantic. But as the quiet thrum and muted green glow of the cockpit closed in around him, he thought of his friend and first officer sitting only inches away with her eyes wobbling around in their sockets like loose marbles. Holiday realized luck was pretty damned scarce.

The Marine fighter pilot from the *Roosevelt* gave the group a curt radio briefing on what he'd learned from Captain Holiday. Megan had worked with the military many times and was used to their deadpan delivery. She supposed it was trained into them, but they always sounded bored when talking to civilians.

The news was grim. Everyone on the video link sat in stunned silence as the F-18 pilot recounted the way the virus had burned through half the passengers in the last hour.

With nothing more to tell, the fighter pilot signed off to resume contact with Northwest 2.

Lt. General Norton leaned forward, clutching what was left of his thinning gray forelock. He looked like a young boy stumped by an unanswerable test question. "We thought 9/11 was bad. . . ."

"General," Megan said. "Don't misunderstand what I'm—"

Randall cut her off. "We talked about a worst-case scenario like this well before 9/11. There is only one alternative here." The general slapped the flat of his hand on the table for effect. "And we all know what it is."

Mahoney took a deliberate breath, mentally kicking herself. In her haste to point out how bad a hemorrhagic virus could be, she'd made this sound like the end of the world. "Gentleman, plea—"

"I have to agree with General Randall." It was Norton's turn to cut her off. His voice was hollow and he spoke without looking up.

Admiral Scott nodded slowly, as if passing judgment. Everyone on the video con went quiet. At length, he turned to his aide.

"Get our F-18 pilot on the horn again, please." That order given, he turned to face the monitor again. "Dr. Mahoney, you were saying?" Even on the plasma screen, the man's blue eyes locked on to her, missing nothing.

"It's vital that we all understand something, Admiral." She cleared her throat. "Though this incident is bad, it is not the *worst* possible scenario."

Scott's aide turned to call the F-18 pilot, but the admiral flicked his hand, motioning for him to hold.

"And exactly what would the worst be?" the admiral asked.

All eyes on her again, Megan smoothed a hand down the front of her dress, nodding. As a scientist she'd always been more comfortable surrounded by deadly germs than politicians and bureaucrats; she found them more predictable. Her Georgia accent came on thicker when she was nervous and it was honey sweet at the moment. "For one thing, hemorrhagic fevers—like Ebola—tend to burn themselves out, in many cases killing their victims before they have a chance to spread to anyone else. Faster is not necessarily better for a virus's longevity. If the illness aboard Northwest 2 was implemented by a terrorist cell, then they succeeded in something remarkable only by making it airborne."

"Still pretty damned terrifying," Randall said.

"There's no doubt," Megan continued. "This scares the hell out of me . . . and it would cause a tremendous amount of panic. But we could more than likely isolate something like this almost as quickly as it began—especially now that we know what to look for."

"So?" Randall threw up his hands. "That's supposed to make us feel better—that we are 'likely' to be able to contain it?"

Megan clenched both fists beneath the table, out of the camera's view. Randall was getting under her skin, so she focused on Admiral Scott. "First, viral pandemics aren't something to screw around with. In the early nineteen hundreds Spanish flu killed more Americans than Vietnam, Korea, and both World Wars combined." Megan spoke slowly so imbeciles like Randall could understand. "AIDS is able to infect so many because it is insidious. It kills slowly. In fact, a carrier can infect hundreds of others without showing any signs they are contagious. If an airborne virus such as the one on Northwest 2 were to shift, or be caused to shift into something that killed a little more slowly . . . it wouldn't even show up on our radar until it's gone too far to stop. In the deadly disease business we even have the name for such a bug—Pandora." She paused to let her words sink in. "Once she's out of the box . . . there would be no stopping her. *That* is the worst case."

Admiral Scott sat motionless for a long moment. "Thank you for your assistance, Dr. Mahoney. Dr. Willis, I know you're busy with your duties in Colorado. I'd like Dr. Mahoney to get herself to Washington on the next available flight. We should discuss this face-to-face. Now, if you all will excuse me, I need to have some words with our F-18 pilot."

The plasma screen in front of Megan switched off and the limousine went dark.

CHAPTER 9

"You out there, Nickel Five-Five?" The 747 pilot's voice crackled over the Super Hornet's radio.

"Go ahead, sir." The young Marine turned his head to the left and watched the heavy airliner glide against the lumpy backdrop of white clouds. They traveled at the same speed and the big bird appeared to hang motionless in the air.

He'd allowed his fighter to inch closer and was now less than two hundred yards off the 747's wing, flying behind and slightly above. It was a position he called *owning*—though in a weapons platform as sophisticated as the F-18 Super Hornet, he *owned* all he could see and then some.

"Call sign *Nickel* . . . one twenty-second Crusaders, right?"

"Aye, sir," the fighter pilot said, snorting. He was genuinely impressed. "If you don't mind me asking, are you a Marine?"

"Negative, son," the 747 pilot came back. "United States Navy."

"I'm sorry, sir," the fighter jock chuckled. "Didn't mean to bring up a sore subject." He wished the brass would come back and tell him what was going on. This chatting with a bus driver was going to get old fast.

"Good one, Marine. I'll let that slide since you happen to outgun me. Not to mention the fact that I'm partial to the airframe you're flying."

"Got a little time in an F-18, sir?"

"A little," the 747 pilot said. There was something faraway in his voice. "Mind if I ask your name, son?"

He really hated when these old geezers called him son. "Stoner, sir, Captain Brad Stoner."

"They got the Crusaders flying off *Rough Rider* now?"

Stoner snorted again. This guy knew a lot more than an ordinary bus driver. *Rough Rider* wasn't the ship's real name—the President had co-opted that one—but the folks lucky enough to serve aboard the *Roosevelt* still called her that from time to time. "Aye, sir, we're on our way home from the Persian Gulf. You spend time aboard the TR?"

"Fair amount."

Man, this dude was cagey. "May I ask your name, sir?"

"Holiday," the 747 pilot replied. "Steve Holiday. I was likely retired before you graduated high school."

Why did that name ring a bell?

"What squadron were you with before you retired, sir?"

"Flight Demonstration," Holiday said.

"Captain Steven Holiday of the Blue Angels? That's you, sir?"

"My friends call me Doc," Holiday said.

"It's an honor to fly the same patch of sky with you, Captain Holiday," Stoner gushed in unabashed hero worship. "I had a model of your F-18 hanging from my ceiling when I was a kid. I still got a poster you signed at the Oshkosh air show. Wait until I tell the guys in my squadron."

Stoner had dreamed of being a Blue Angel from the time he was in the seventh grade. He wanted to say more, but the radio squawked.

"I'll be right back, sir. I've got HQ on the other freq."

"Roger that, son," Holiday's voice crackled. It was breathless, as if he'd just finished a long run. "Glad you're here, Marine."

The USS Theodore Roosevelt relayed an encrypted patch from the Pentagon to the F-18 Hornet. Only five people were privy to the ninety-second conversation. By the time it was over, Brad Stoner thought he might cry.

"You . . . hangin' in there, Captain Holiday?" Stoner's throat convulsed.

"Roger that."

"Listen . . ." Stoner shook his head, trying to focus on the instruments in front of him. "Sir . . ."

Holiday, ever the warrior-gentleman, saved the distraught younger pilot from having to explain himself. "Say, Brad . . . I did some thinking while you were gone. . . ." His voice flickered like a failing light. "You might want to know that my good friend and first officer just passed away. . . ." He coughed. "The way she went wasn't pretty."

"Captain—"

Holiday cut in. "They still strap a Slammer on those birds?" A Slammer was the AIM 120—the big sister to the Sidewinder Air Interceptor Missiles the Super Hornet carried at the end of each wing.

"They do indeed," Stoner said in a reverent whisper.

Holiday gave a ragged cough. "I gotta tell you, Brad, I never considered myself a coward, but I don't relish the thought of dying like my friend just did. . . . You hear what I'm saying?"

"Aye, sir."

"Outstanding—"

"Captain Holiday, would you do me the courtesy of looking out your starboard window?"

Stoner maneuvered his F-18 twenty yards off the jumbo jet's right wing. He turned on the cockpit light, flipped up his helmet visor, and snapped a crisp salute. He held it for a long moment as tears welled in his eyes.

Across the dark void of sky between the two men, in the cockpit bubble of the 747, Navy Captain Steven "Doc" Holiday returned the gesture.

"A small favor, Brad?"

"Name it, sir."

"This is gonna be awful hard on my wife. . . ." His cough was more ragged now. "If you ever get a chance . . . her name's Carol. Tell her you met me once—and that all I ever talked about was her."

"Aye . . ." Stoner couldn't finish.

"Tallyho, Marine—" Holiday broke into a coughing fit and cut radio contact.

Stoner pulled back on the stick, gaining the altitude and distance he'd need to carry out the admiral's order. On his console, a small light reading A/A—air to air— blinked red.

He'd never be able to tell anyone what he was about to do—nor would he want to.

CHAPTER 10

7 September, 1100 hours
Al-Hofuf, Kingdom of Saudi Arabia

Sheikh Husseini al Farooq never traveled unless accompanied by at least two of his three most trusted men—and Zafir knew he was favored above all. Ratib and Jabolah had grown up with the sheik, and indeed these two men were considered family. But Zafir had *proved* his loyalty when he lost three fingers of his left hand saving the sheikh from an assassin's sword. For the lowly Bedouin, Farooq reserved a trust beyond that given even to his closest brother.

At forty-one, Zafir was ten years the sheikh's junior. Where the master was short and neat with finely chiseled, almost feminine features, the Bedouin was tall and unkempt. His black hair swept from a high forehead in a wild mane, revealing dark eyes that pinched into a permanent scowl. He looked as if he'd just ridden a fine horse to death only to walk the remainder of a long journey—every step in service of his master.

Today, he was dressed, as were Farooq and the other

seven men at the meeting, in the dazzling white cotton *dishdasha* of a Saudi businessman. Unlike the others, Zafir's face twitched and his body ached for the rougher robes of the Bedouin. He took a sip of strong coffee, letting the bitterness and familiar bite of cardamom soothe his nerves. As always, he kept a wary eye on all those near the sheikh.

Dictated by long tradition, Farooq, as the host, had ground the beans in front of his guest and served the coffee himself.

"The Americans are reeling," the sheikh said as he served a tiny cup to Malik, a fat man from Baghdad. "They are full of self-righteous indignation over our little bombing at their shopping mall. But they believe bombing is all we know how to do. They believe us to be weak and ignorant."

The men sat on quilted cushions around a low mahogany table piled high with fruit, flat bread, and al-kabsa—a dish of rice and spiced lamb. Malik had hogged nearly all the dates, though no one but Zafir appeared to notice.

"They think us inferior because we choose to live in a desert and keep control of our women where they cannot."

Each man at the table nodded in somber agreement. Nassif, the dapper first deputy to the Saudi foreign minister sipped his coffee, but all there knew he agreed. A man of his standing would have never met with the sheikh unless they had already come to some accord. The fat Iraqi snorted over the last two dates he'd shoved in his mouth, highly offended that anyone would think him inferior.

Farooq continued, "The Americans are bad players of chess. They have failed to see the mall bombing for what it was, the push of a pawn. They believe their ultimate win is inevitable merely because they have the greater number of pieces on the board. And that is exactly what I want them to think. For now, we will play their game—"

"I have heard," Malik, the Iraqi, interrupted, wiping thick hands on a linen napkin as his spoke, "that the Prophet—may Allah be pleased with him—forbade the playing of chess."

Several of the men at the table, all adherents to the strict Wahabi sect of Islam, nodded in agreement. Nassif, the deputy minister, kept his thoughts, if he had any, to himself.

Haziz al Duri, a wealthy hotel owner from Riyadh, put a hand to his goatee. "Indeed Ali—may Allah be pleased with him—said chess was gambling—worse even than backgammon."

"Oh, I beg to differ," the Iraqi shook his jowly face. "It was Ibn Umar—may Allah be pleased with him— who said it was worse than backgammon."

"Gentlemen, please." Farooq raised his hand and smiled meekly. Only Zafir saw the twitch in his left eye that revealed his true displeasure with the Iraqi. "Though I am certain chess has value to the mind and is indeed halal if it does not cause us to miss prayers or gamble, I speak here only of a figurative game. Perhaps we might save our discussion of such merits for a later time."

"I have pledged my assets to the effort," Malik said.

"I wish to see the Americans crumble as much as anyone."

"And your generosity is appreciated," Farooq said. "Our latest operation in France was only a test, but it was far more successful than we'd imagined it would be."

"But we have heard nothing of consequence in the news," the merchant from Riyadh said. "Only that an American airliner crashed into the ocean. I fail to see how that is a success."

Farooq took a deep breath, then held it for a moment before exhaling through thin nostrils. "Again, if I might compare our work to the strategy of chess without beginning a debate. The American news reports the plane crashed, but I believe the Americans shot it from the sky. The U.S. is frightened because they believe they know what we are up to. At the same time, they believe they have won, because the French killed our Algerian brothers and took the contents of their lab. They are certain to think us incapable of anything more intelligent than infecting an airliner.

"Of course there will be those among the Americans who suspect more, but they will be disbelieved. It is their defense mechanism. And even if some do choose to believe, while they stand mesmerized by one battle raging on the board, we will strike from a completely different angle, ending the game while the haughty devils still believe they have beaten us."

"Would you care to enlighten us with the remainder of your plan?" The fat Iraqi scooped a pile of al-kabsa onto his saucer with a piece of flatbread.

A smile blossomed on Farooq's face, turning his lips into a pale gash beneath a sparse goatee. "My friend, I would be delighted to do just that. If you would all be so gracious . . ." The sheikh raised a hand. Ratib slid back the woolen curtain that covered a heavy glass partition separating them from a dimly lit room.

The men around the table grew pale. The hotel owner's hand shot to his mouth and he turned away in horror. Nassif, the government man, tried to take another sip of coffee, but his hand shook too badly to get the cup to his lips.

Sheikh Husseini al Farooq reclined against his cushion and yawned. He considered the back of his manicured hand as he spoke. "We are fortunate, I think, to have the laboratories and veterinary scientists so near at King Faisal University. Of course, to do this to animals would be strictly haram. I would take no part in such a thing. Americans are worse than devils to be sure, and Allah, may it please him, will surely sanction our plan. What you see, Allah willing, is but a small taste of what the infidels have in store."

Zafir stared at the glass, transfixed at the scene on the other side. Tonight was the night he would ask of his master the greatest of all favors—to play a more central part in the game. That's what the sheikh called it—*the Game*. And with a man as supremely wise as Farooq pushing the pieces on the board, it was a game they were certain to win.

A rumbling gurgle drew the Bedouin's attention away from the window. Malik, the fat Iraqi, had vomited in his plate.

CHAPTER 11

Jericho Quinn's BMW GS Adventure mirrored his personality. It was a powerful bike—tall, gunmetal gray, fast, and intensely aggressive. As a boy, he'd tacked Molly Hatchet's debut album to the wall above his bed. The cover art was a Frank Frazetta painting of a horn-helmeted fantasy warlord, clothed in dark robes atop a muscular black warhorse—*The Death Dealer*. Sullen red eyes glowed under the knight's helmet. Blood dripped from a battle axe in a brandished fist. Vultures circled overhead and steam blew from the beast's nose. Jericho's mother hated the painting, complaining that such a dark image was bound to inspire her son toward horrible things. His father, on the other hand, had only smiled and told his mother to be glad that was the only Frank Frazetta art Jericho had decided to hang on his wall.

The album cover did turn out to be an inspiration. Quinn had ridden motorcycles virtually all his life, from the first Honda 125 he used to scoot up and down the beach on while the family dug for razor clams, to the broken-down Harley Panhead he'd bought to tinker with during high school—and a dozen other bikes since. He loved them all for differing reasons. Some were fast, others were nimble, still others were hell on wheels off road. But he was never able to choose a single favorite bike—until he saw his first 1150 GS shortly after he'd graduated from the Air Force Academy. The first time he set eyes on one of the big black BMWs stopped at a light in downtown Anchorage on a drizzly gray afternoon, his mind had immediately flashed to the Death Dealer's muscular warhorse. He'd sold his Firebird, a Honda CBR sport bike, and a Harley Davidson Road King to buy his first one. Though he'd eventually moved up to the 1200cc model, he hadn't once been disappointed.

GS stood for *Gelande Strasse*, German for *trail* and *street*. Though the Beemer handled tamely enough on the manicured, vegetarian pavement of Andrews Air Force Base, the 1,200cc was a predator. A two-wheeled raptor, a hundred and five warhorses of beaked meat-eater, built to chew up rougher terrain.

The crossed war axes on his metallic gray visored Arai motocross helmet, complete with blood dripping from the blades, were a custom-painted tribute to the Frazetta painting of his youth.

Helmet in hand, Quinn stood beside the bike in the sunny parking lot outside AFOSI Detachment 331 Headquarters. A cell phone was pressed against his ear.

A black leather Vanson motorcycle jacket covered his light blue uniform shirt. His darker dress tunic was folded neatly in the Touratech aluminum-top case on the back of the bike. The air was heavy with humidity and the scent of newly mown grass.

As an OSI agent, he normally worked in civilian clothes. It made interviewing people who outranked him much easier when he identified himself as special agent rather than a lowly captain. A Court of Inquiry, however, required service dress blues. He didn't know if it was the gravity of his present situation or his starched collar, but Quinn felt as if someone were sawing off his head. He found it oddly entertaining that he considered himself in more danger now than he ever had in Iraq.

His ex-wife's attitude didn't help.

"So . . ." Her voice was distant, both in tone and geography. "How did it turn out?"

"What?" He put a finger to his free ear to block the roar of a passing lawnmower.

"That little court thingie."

It was mind-numbing that Kim would minimize a proceeding that might very well cost him his military career by calling it a "little court thingie." She did it with anything that frightened her. It was her way of coping, her way of not going crazy in an insane situation. She didn't mean anything by it.

"Hasn't started yet," he said, rubbing his eyes with a thumb and forefinger. He almost told her how the worry was eating a hole in his guts. Luckily, she cut him off.

"We had a cow moose eating my apples along the

driveway this morning," she said. "Mattie couldn't get to the bus stop so I had to drive her to school."

It was better this way. Keep things light. "Was she scared?" As if Mattie Quinn was scared of anything. Jericho knew his little girl took after him in the bravado department. He wondered if that fact would serve or damn her.

"She's fine," Kim said. "This morning she asked when you were coming home." She had to slip that in. "You think you'll get leave anytime soon? I mean, they did keep you over there nearly a whole year."

"I may get more time off than I want if they boot me out of the Air Force." He couldn't help himself. His stomach was in knots and he needed someone to talk to. It turned out to be a mistake.

"Would that really be so bad, Jericho?" You could come back home and spend some time with Mattie—"

"What about Mattie's mom?"

"You know how I feel about you," Kim said. She could be very guarded in her words now. He supposed he deserved it with the kind of life he'd put her through.

"And what if I did quit?" Quinn heard himself say. "I could get out and come back to Alaska. How would you feel about me then?"

There was a long silence on the phone. He could hear Kim breathing, as he'd heard her so many times as they lay beside each other in bed, touching but incredibly far apart, not saying the things that should have been said.

"Don't do this to me, Jericho."

"So it wouldn't matter?"

"Of course it would matter," she said. "Mattie needs you here."

"And you?"

"You know I do."

"All right, then," Quinn said, feeling dizzy even as he said the words. "If they don't kick me out, I'll give them my resig—"

"What would you do?" Kim said, suddenly bent on playing devil's advocate. "If there's one thing I know about you, it's that you're not cut out for normal life."

Quinn shrugged, gritting his teeth. She had to make things so hard. "I don't know. . . . I'd get a job with the Troopers or Anchorage PD."

"You're serious?" Kim said, her voice a breathless whisper.

"Dead," Quinn said.

"Listen," Kim said. "It's nearly noon here. This is a lot for me to process. I've got to run to the store before Mattie comes home. Call me later."

"Okay," he said. "I love you."

"I know you do," she said.

Kimberly Quinn wasn't much for good-byes. He'd left her so many times during their three-year courtship and eight-year marriage; he supposed she'd had enough of them.

Quinn flipped the phone closed and traded his leather riding jacket for the uniform tunic in the aluminum case. He took a moment to look around the manicured lawns and shrub-lined sidewalks of the base. He'd just told his ex-wife he would quit the very thing he was best at doing—for her and their daughter. Wasn't that what good husbands and fathers were supposed to do? He was tempted to climb back on his motorcycle and ride as far as a tank of gas would carry him. Instead, he straightened his tie and walked through the yawning double doors of the red brick building—as a resigned man might walk to his own execution.

Lt. Colonel Fargo had gone in first. He still had the pulsing tendons in his jaw and fiery look of retribution in his otherwise vaporous eyes, but his intensity was muted by the post-sunburn peeling of his nose courtesy of his time in the desert—and the way he thought himself impervious to the rules of nature.

After the adrenaline of the rescue had faded and Quinn took the time to consider, he'd not expected things would go this far. His commanding officer appeared to like him—and they *had* saved two American lives. But, as Fargo was quick to point out, Lance Corporal Diaz had lost his foot, and right now the Monday-morning quarterbacks were using that foot to give Quinn the boot.

As it turned out, Fargo had enough political juice to reach across service lines and seriously screw with Quinn's career—at least enough to get his boss to convene an official Court of Inquiry.

Waiting, Quinn did what he always did when the going got dicey. He took a dog-eared photograph of his five-year-old daughter from his wallet and stared at her big blue eyes. Poor kid, he treated her like some kind of worry stone. He supposed it was lucky he didn't get to see her too often or she'd grow up realizing her dad was the biggest whack job in the Air Force. . . . He wondered how much their relationship would change if he returned to Alaska and went to work for the Troopers. It suddenly occurred to him that if he was discharged he wouldn't likely find a job anywhere in civilian law enforcement either.

Quinn looked up at the echoing snap of dress shoes on the polished tile floor.

"If it ain't my ol' buddy Chair Force." A friendly Louisiana drawl yanked Quinn out of his self-pity. "That your bike out front?"

Quinn shook off his thoughts and reached to shake Thibodaux's hand. "Yep."

The Marine's kettledrum chest came in handy as a billboard to hold the palm-size placard of service ribbons hanging from his green tunic. A red and blue ribbon signified he'd received the Bronze Star for Valor.

"A Beemer . . ." Thibodaux gave a low whistle. "Us lowly enlisted boys can't afford the German stuff. My KLR is a good enough motorcycle, but I wouldn't mind keepin' your BMW exercised, so to speak, while you're in the brig. It's what friends are for."

Quinn sighed. "Good to see someone has faith in me."

"Corporal Diaz says to tell you hey. He's pushin' the envelope to stay in the Marine Corps when he gets his new bionic foot."

Quinn shook his head, thinking of all the bureaucracy the poor kid would have to wade through on one leg. "Yeah, good luck with that."

"Well, beb." Thibodaux took a seat on the polished wooden bench next to Quinn. "I sure enough owe your ass. Only two months into my umpteenth tour in the desert—but thanks to you, I get orders to come back to the good ol' U S of A and testify at your hearing. I got to stop off for a visit with my wife and play with the box the kids came in."

Quinn chuckled. "How many kids?"

"Well, considerin' how much I'm deployed, we got us a mess of 'em."

"How many in a mess, exactly?"

Thibodaux winked. "Six . . . so far."

Quinn pictured his little girl again, his dark hair, her mom's blue eyes. . . . If that's what she needed, he would quit. He'd actually do it. . . .

The heavy wooden door beside them creaked open and saved him from his thoughts. The most influential member of the general's staff, a short, female Air Force major named Babcock peered over a pair of heavy, black-framed glasses—the kind they'd called birth control goggles or BCGs in the Academy. Most reverted back to their more comfortable—and vastly more flattering—styles of eyewear after training ended, but not Major Babcock.

"Captain Quinn," she said, her face showing as much emotion as a bran muffin. "You're up." She gave Thibodaux a quick up-and-down from behind her BCGs. "You, too."

"Both of us?" Quinn had assumed the general would want to question them separately.

Major Babcock's heels clicked as she turned, apparently unwilling to use more energy than necessary to explain things. "Both."

"She's hot," Thibodaux whispered.

Quinn looked at the big Cajun as if he'd lost his mind. "Well, you're certainly not a credible witness."

Base Commander Lt. General Ted Powers was a straight shooter, and it was common knowledge you didn't want to be in his sights, especially when he was pissed—which, at the moment, he was.

The balding general slumped behind a raised wooden table scowling under a forehead furrowed with wrinkles. Lt. Colonel Fargo gloated at the table set aside for what would have been the prosecution had it been an actual trial court.

The general gave a cursory nod as Major Babcock led in her two charges. The clack of her stark, black shoes echoed off the tile in the cavernous room. Her perfectly creased blue uniform slacks swished as if she'd starched the polyester.

Quinn snapped to attention as he approached the commanding officer. He'd expected a colonel or even a one-star. Fargo must truly have had some juice to manipulate the system and get a three-star general to hear a complaint like this one.

Four men in dark suits whom Quinn didn't recognize sat at the back of the room in a double row of wooden chairs.

"Thank you for attending these proceedings, Gunnery Sergeant Thibodaux." Powers shuffled some papers and put on a pair of skinny reading glasses. He glanced up at Quinn and motioned at the table opposite Fargo. He spoke crisply as if the words tasted bitter in his mouth. "Be seated, Captain. This won't take long."

Fargo's gloat grew bolder with that. Thibodaux sat, ramrod-straight in a wooden chair along the far wall, broad shoulders silhouetted by a row of windows that ran from floor to ceiling.

"Captain Quinn," General Powers began, "I've been reviewing your record. . . ." He scanned the documents in front of him as if he was searching for something in particular.

Fargo shot a smirk across the aisle. Quinn tried to ignore him, since anything less than choking out the miserable excuse for an officer would give him little satisfaction.

The general shut the folder with such obvious finality it was easy to see he'd come to a decision. "You have a stellar background, Captain Quinn. There's no disputing that. There is, however, this issue regarding following the orders of a senior officer. Do you dispute that Colonel Fargo had tactical command of the operation that led to the charges he's levied against you?"

"No, sir, I do not."

"Do you dispute the fact that Lieutenant Colonel Fargo ordered you to wait to mount your rescue until he was able to return to your location?"

"No, sir," Quinn said, his meager hopes falling fast. The general was merely going through the pre-court martial formalities. Quinn had already made his case for disobeying what he considered to be a foolish order. It was all in his report. He saw no reason to waste effort defending himself now. Fargo would enjoy that too much.

General Powers peeled off his reading glasses and pushed away from his desk.

"Captain Quinn," he said. "I want to be clear about this—for the record. Have you and I ever met?"

Quinn took a deep breath wondering where this was heading. "I have not had the pleasure, sir."

"Well, if we had met," the general went on, "there would be zero doubt in your mind that I am a stickler for obedience."

"Yes, General," Quinn said, trying not to slump in defeat.

The general shifted his gaze to Lt. Colonel Fargo. "You would agree, would you not, that obedience to a superior officer is imperative?"

Fargo gave a smug nod. "I would indeed, General Powers."

"Outstanding. We are all in agreement." Powers leaned in to the desk microphone, close enough that his voice reverberated around the room. "My orders to you, Lieutenant Colonel Fargo—and I assure you that no matter the military branch in which you serve, the orders of a general officer bearing three stars will hold some sway—my orders to you, are to stand down with these ridiculous charges."

Fargo blinked as if he was staring into a fan, dumbstruck by the sudden turn of events. "Sir, I must—"

"You *must* obey my orders," the general snapped. "I have nineteen letters—not e-mails, mind you, but genuine handwritten letters—including one from a Marine Corps general, and one from your commanding officer in the United States Army—all lauding the efforts and accomplishments of Captain Quinn and Marines Thibodaux and Diaz."

Powers put on his reading glasses again. "Here's one

that struck me in particular. And I quote: 'I have no doubt that the Iraqis who held us captive were only seconds away from taking our heads. Were it not for the heroic actions of . . .' "

The general peered across the desk. "Do I need to keep going?"

The sand crab shook his head and snapped to attention, begging to be dismissed. Major Babcock escorted him out and General Powers adjourned the proceeding.

"Quinn," the general said, almost as an afterthought. He popped a peppermint candy in his mouth and rose from his chair. "Step up—and bring your Marine friend with you."

Powers put his hand over the microphone as the two men approached. "Just so we're all clear, if you'd disobeyed one of my orders I'd have kicked your ass from Baghdad to Washington and back. Do you read me?"

"Yes, General," Quinn said, stifling a grin. "But with all due respect, I don't believe you'd have given such an order."

"Damn straight," Powers said. "But don't be thanking me yet for the rosy way your day's turning out." He gave a somber nod over his shoulder toward a large oak door along the wall behind him. "There's a man in that office who wants to speak with both of you. He's wearing a very expensive suit and it's been my experience that men in uniform should be extremely wary of men in suits."

CHAPTER 12

1550 hours
Centers for Disease Control
Atlanta, Georgia

The black telephone on Megan Mahoney's desk rang for the fifth time, then fell silent. Like a soldier in a garrison, Mahoney found the pressed uniforms, seedy politics, and confines of public health stifling. If she had wanted an office, she'd have been a surgeon or some other kind of specialist.

Even the walls of her posh apartment outside Atlanta threatened to crush her if she stayed inside too long. She belonged in the field.

The phone rang again, more urgently this time, if such a thing was possible. Mahoney picked it up.

"Dr. Mahoney. How may I help you?" She was put off by the interruption but saw no reason to let her Southern manners slip.

"Hallo, Dr. Mahoney. Dr. Alain Leclair here . . . National Institute of Health." It was a male voice, slightly nasal and thickly French. He pronounced her name

"Mayho-knee" with a heavy accent on the last syllable. "I must to speak with you regarding the shipment of certain culture specimens. . . ."

Mahoney got a half dozen such calls a month, usually from third world countries with no labs of their own.

"The instructions for mailing bio samples are all online." She started to give him the Web address.

"I am familiar with the CDC website," Leclair said. "In truth, I'm not certain why I was given your name. I have not looked at the samples, myself. My counterparts in the Ministry of Interior had sealed them before they came into my possession."

Leclair blew his nose, loud enough that Mahoney had to hold the receiver away from her ear. Sniffing, he continued. "These are blood and tissue samples—collected in Roissy."

Mahoney sat upright, pushing herself away from the computer. She bit her bottom lip.

"Did you say Roissy?"

"*Oui*. A small community near the Paris airpor—"

"Tell me, Doctor, exactly how are the samples packaged?" Mahoney felt as if someone heavy was sitting on her chest. "You are positive you didn't try to examine them yourself—touch them in any way?"

"*Oui*, I did not." Leclair said. "They were packaged when I rec—"

"Okay." Mahoney felt herself begin to breathe again. "Listen to me very carefully, Dr. Leclair. You must place the Roissy samples in a biosafety level-four containment lab immediately."

Neither Leclair, nor anyone in the French government, would have been told the whole truth regarding the incident with Northwest 2. They knew only of an Algerian lab with some sort of bioterrorism connections. Mahoney had been told the place was firebombed to ashes or she'd have been on the first flight across the Atlantic. She fumed that no one had seen fit to inform her of any surviving cultures.

The French had no way of knowing that the virus from Roissy was, in all likelihood, responsible for the death of over four hundred people.

"I can assure you, the samples are quite well packaged, Dr. Mahoney," Leclair protested. "We are professionals here in France. The CDC protocols were followed to the letter. You have no need to—"

Mahoney's Southern sweetness had its limits.

"Damn it, Leclair," she snapped. "Hang up the telephone right now and take the specimens to the nearest BSL-four containment—someplace you'd take the deadliest stuff you'd ever even thought about."

"Impossible," Leclair huffed.

Mahoney threw up her hands. "And just why is that?"

"Quite simple," Leclair sniffled. "I do not have them. The FedEx messenger picked them up from my office five hours ago. They are already en route to you."

CHAPTER 13

The two men with the suits were operators, there was no mistaking that—Secret Service or some other steely-eyed protective agency who knew their stuff and hired their beef by the pound. Both wore pressed but not overly expensive suits, cut full to allow for athletic shoulders as well as an assortment of hidden weapons underneath. Quinn had several identical suits stashed in his own closet, complete with gun patches to keep his sidearm from wearing out the lining. Earpieces with flesh-tone wires hung from each man's left ear. Their eyes locked on the newcomers like targeting radar as they flanked their boss, who was finishing a conversation on the phone.

Quinn couldn't place the suit's face. He was a tall man, with close-cropped charcoal-gray hair and a ruddy, smiling face. He looked familiar, even fatherly, like a television news anchor you might let into your living room every night, but not quite recognize on the street.

"Winfield Palmer," the suit said, extending a strong hand. "Director of National Intelligence. My friends call me Win."

Of course, Quinn thought. That's why he recognized the man. Winfield Palmer was arguably one of the most powerful men in Washington. As DNI he was said to have the President's ear—and support—on anything and everything of consequence regarding the Global War on Terror—and no matter what they called it in public, to those fighting it, a global war was exactly what it was.

Quinn shook his hand, as did Thibodaux.

Palmer dismissed the two bodyguards with a nod. They left without making eye contact.

"Gentlemen, I know you've both had an extremely long day. I appreciate your taking the time to see me." He glanced at the stainless TAG Heuer Aquaracer next to the platinum cufflink on his French shirt, giving a nod of approval to the identical dive watch on Quinn's left wrist.

"Please, have a seat." Palmer pointed at two leather chairs beside a long mahogany coffee table. He came around to sit on the edge of the general's highly polished wooden desk.

"Let's cut to the chase. I've been around enough to know men like you two don't trust guys like me from the get-go. Lark—the young Marine you saved in Fallujah—happens to be my grandson. What you men did was incredibly brave—"

Thibodaux cut in. "With all due respect, sir, we were only doing—"

Palmer held up an open hand and wagged his head

with a smile. "I get that, Gunny. Certainly, there are thousands of men and women in the desert doing brave and dangerous things for our country every day. You are right. Neither one of you have a corner on the bravery market. The fact is you two fell under my radar so I took the liberty of looking over your files." The DNI turned slightly and retrieved a thick, red-striped folder from the desk behind him. "I have to say I'm impressed, Gunnery Sergeant Thibodaux. Starting shortstop for LSU, where you graduated summa cum laude. . . ." He glanced up with the chuckle of someone holding a winning hand. "I'd ask why you aren't an officer, but I don't want to hear your BS about wanting to work for a living. . . ." Palmer's eyes fell again to the file. "Let's see . . . an only child, your parents own a restaurant in the French Quarter . . . champion Greco Roman wrestler, ranked mixed martial artist where you fight under the name 'Dauxboy'. . . . You're fluent in French, and surprisingly enough, Italian—"

"My wife's Italian." Thibodaux gave a modest grin, dipping his nearly shaven head. "It comes in handy so I know when to duck if she goes on one of her tirades."

Palmer ignored the comment. "Your file goes on to say that you're an expert marksman, defensive tactics instructor at Quantico, and somehow, in between four deployments to the desert, you've managed to sire six sons, all of whom are under the age of eleven."

Quinn started at this, stifling a grin. Six sons. There was definitely more to Jacques Thibodaux than met the eye.

"And every one of 'em a bouncing baby stud," Thibodaux beamed. "Does my file mention I play a mean mandolin?"

"As a matter a fact it does." Palmer dropped the folder on the desk. "It also notes that you are a smart-ass. A valuable and talented smart-ass, but a smart-ass nonetheless." He clasped his hands in front of him. "So, do you recall the protective operation you worked a year ago when the commandant of the Marine Corps visited Mosul?"

"I do, sir."

"DOD did an investigation for a top-secret clearance on all personnel involved with that op. That certainly makes things handy for me. . . ."

Palmer chuckled, turning to Quinn, who couldn't help but wonder how much of his file this man had in front of him. As the Director of National Intelligence and as such the top dog of both the National Security Agency and the CIA, Quinn supposed he'd have access to the whole of it.

Palmer skimmed the three-inch ream of dog-eared papers, nodding here and there, muttering quietly at various points of interest along the way. Finally, he began to speak without looking up.

"Captain Quinn, as an agent in the Air Force Office of Special Investigations you already hold a TS clearance. I see here you swam varsity for your high school in Alaska—did quite well in swimming and track. Looks like you hold some kind of state record in the eight-hundred-meter run."

"It's a sparsely populated state, sir," Quinn said.

Palmer peered over the top of his folder, apparently

unimpressed by the show of modesty. "I see. So, your father is a commercial fisherman and your mother teaches eighth-grade history—both dangerous jobs." Quinn smiled. Palmer went on playing *This Is Your Life.* "You have one brother . . . but we'll get to him in a minute. After high school you received an appointment to the Air Force Academy, where you participated in Army Jump programs and the Navy's Mini-BUDS course. I happen to be an old West Point man. What I can't figure out is why in the world you'd pick the Air Force if you weren't going to fly?"

Quinn made it a point not to answer rhetorical questions.

Palmer studied him a moment with flint-hard eyes before returning to the file. "Your record says you speak Japanese, Mandarin Chinese . . . and Arabic. That's amazing. Are you fluent in all three?"

"Chinese and Arabic," Quinn said. "More what you'd call conversant in Japanese."

"We'll see," Palmer said before changing the subject. "You won the Wing Open boxing tournament your junior year—that makes you quick with your brain and your fists. . . . Sandhurst Military Competition each year, team captain while you were a firstie . . . though you spent the first half of that year in Morocco taking part in a study-abroad program. Did a Fulbright Fellowship there as well after graduation. . . . No offense meant here, son, but you have a dark and swarthy look about you. I'm thinking you could pass for an Arab without too much trouble."

Quinn nodded. "My great-grandmother was a Chiracahua Apache. I got her coloring."

"Among other things," Palmer said, perusing something else in the file. "Tell me about your graduation."

Quinn took a deep breath. The man had the file. He hated telling the story, but was quizzed heavily about it by his commanding officer every time he moved to a new assignment. It had become the stuff of Air Force Academy legend and it was better he did the telling than let it grow out of proportion.

"I very nearly didn't graduate, sir," Quinn said.

Palmer nodded. "Report says your younger brother—what was his name . . . Boaz—started some sort of brouhaha during the graduation parade the day before commencement."

"I believe he'd say the drunks waving a Russian flag during our national anthem started it," Quinn said. There was no use in holding anything back. "Bo happened to be standing next to some Russian men visiting the Academy. They started talking smack about the United States and, for all his faults, that's one thing Bo won't stand for. Just as my squadron marched by, I saw two of them jump him from behind while the other three squared off in front of him. . . ."

"So let me get this straight. You, as a flight commander, broke ranks from your squadron during pass in review, and jumped into the scrap to help your brother." Palmer grinned. "In front of ten thousand people and the superintendent of the United States Air Force Academy. Four years of putting up with the grind of cadet life and you were willing to toss it to the wind one day away from graduation?"

Quinn looked ahead, his eyes locked on Palmer. "Some things you just do without thinking, sir."

"Like saving your little brother from an ass kicking?"

"Exactly like that."

Palmer nodded. "You and your brother put three Russian nationals in the hospital before security forces broke up the fight. Two of them had to have their jaws wired shut. As much as I admire your courage, I find myself forced to ask you a question. Do you have a temper problem, Captain Quinn?"

"No, sir," Jericho said. "I believe I have an excellent command of my emotions."

"Where do you stand on Arabs?"

"I beg your pardon, sir?" This was definitely not what he'd expected.

"Arabs. Muslims," Palmer said, locking eyes in a sort of visual jousting match. "Your record shows you've had a hand in sending more than a few to meet their maker."

Quinn nodded slowly, taking time to choose his words. "I don't have a problem with any particular group or religion. My problem is with thugs—of any kind. If the U.S. was being attacked by the militant Irish terrorists, I'd respond the same way I always do. And my father is Irish. If you'll note my file, you'll see the time I spent in Morocco was more of a humanitarian mission—no guns, just hammers and nails, building houses for the poor." It wasn't like Quinn to try and defend himself, but for some reason, he felt a compelling need to have this man understand him—as much as that was even possible.

At length the DNI peered up over the open folder. "Well, I guess the Academy thought it would be imprudent to hold up the graduation of their top athletic cadet and distinguished graduate just for protecting his kid brother."

"The district attorney in Colorado Springs declined to file charges," Quinn said.

"So, let's see here," Palmer said, as if eager to change the subject. "Turns out you're quite a motorcycle enthusiast. Your file says you raced the Dakar Rally in 2004 along with that same kid brother."

Quinn smiled. There had been another fight just after he and Bo had crossed the border into Senegal—one that made the graduation-parade scrap look like a church dance—but he didn't think that one had made it into the file, so he said nothing.

Palmer continued, "You entered the pipeline for Air Force Special Operations right after the Fulbright Fellowship. That's pretty tough duty—a year and a half training in firearms, scuba, running, swimming, HALO, more running, advanced trauma medical, more swimming, escape and evasion. . . . Did I mention running and swimming?" Palmer smiled. "Graduated top of your squadron to become a combat rescue officer. So, what made you leave the CROs after just two years?"

Thibodaux looked on from the sidelines with renewed interest. CROs weren't Marines, but they weren't wing waxers either.

Quinn took a slow breath. For the first time since he'd met Win Palmer, his mind fell to the last conversation he'd had with Kim. "My wife worried about me being in harm's way quite so much."

"So you chose to switch to OSI thinking that would calm her sentiments?"

"I did," Quinn said matter-of-factly. "Then when the Gulf heated up, so did OSI."

"And you divorced."

"We did."

"One daughter."

"Correct."

Thankfully, Palmer changed gears, allowing Jericho to think of something else besides the cell phone call with his ex-wife, for the time being. "All right, men, enough of this getting to know each other. Let me, as they say in the Kashmir, get to the yolk of the egg. Your reports from Fallujah mention a man named Farooq."

Quinn was happy to be out from under the microscope. "My informant didn't have all the details, but there's word this guy is one of the ones behind Colorado. He's got something to do with all the kidnappings going on in Iraq as well—at least where American personnel are involved."

"You know," the DNI said, folding his arms, "everybody's been so damned knotted up over Osama bin Laden. But I'm worried about the next one. We start to think everything bad comes from one man and we miss something important, like a Colorado shopping mall."

"And we think Farooq is the next bin Laden?" Thibodaux asked, letting his big head loll to one side as if he was trying to let water drain out of his ear.

"We had indications Osama was going to hit us. Hell, Ollie North warned us about him years ago. I'm not anxious to keep repeating the same mistake."

"So you want us to kill this guy Farooq?" Thibodaux voiced Quinn's thoughts. It was odd enough they'd even have a meeting with the Director of National Intelligence, but for him to give the two of them such a high-level briefing brought to mind so many questions his head hurt.

"*Ruguo ni zhiyou yiba chui, mei yige wenti jiu kanqilai dingzi,*" Palmer rattled as if he was native Chinese. "Did I get that right, Captain Quinn?"

Jericho nodded, impressed at the Director's flawless Mandarin. "*If you only have a hammer, every problem looks like nails.* You have a good ear, sir. You must have spent some time in China."

Palmer gave a wry smile, as if remembering better days. "As a matter of fact I have. But, since my Senate confirmation seven months ago, I have come to see that we have exactly the opposite problem of that particular proverb. I have at my disposal a myriad of sophisticated tools: vast communications systems, crack military units, spy satellites, billion-dollar warplanes and ships . . . the list goes on and on. But there are times when a fancy, more specialized tool just won't work. What I really need is a bona fide pipe-hitter that's unencumbered by the cords and fancy systems of red tape."

Jericho knew from the look the DNI gave him, the next conversation he would have with Kim was not going to be a good one.

Palmer nodded slowly, as if passing judgment.

"I need a hammer."

CHAPTER 14

Al-Hofuf

Sheikh Husseini al Farooq gazed serenely through the one-way glass. Small, feminine fingers toyed with the ruby ring on his right pinkie. His long white robe just brushed the marble floor.

"How long?" Zafir, who stood to the sheikh's immediate right, asked. He kept his head slightly bowed but could still make out the reflection of his master's waspish face in the tinted glass.

"Mm?" Farooq looked up, startled from a thought.

"How long until they die?"

"Soon," Farooq said. "If not from the disease, then from dehydration."

On the other side of the thick partition, a scene from an American horror movie stared back at them. Even Zafir, who'd spilled his share of blood and misery, was repulsed by the sight. Farooq appeared to marvel at it. Five of his test subjects lay in a row of mean cots. The sheets, once white, were filthy, stained in unclotted blood and human filth. The room was now so contaminated, no one, not even Dr. Suleiman, the veterinary scientist Farooq had paid to conduct the experiments, would enter to feed or tend the dying souls.

Zafir mused at the dying people, consoling himself as to what they represented. Three were men—two American hostages and a Shiite pig who deserved the flesh-eating death that now ravaged their bodies. The fourth was a woman, a prostitute from Riyadh. Even the sight of her bleeding from the nose and dull, sightless eyes failed to arouse any sense of pity. The woman's daughter, a child of seven lay in the bed next to her. Younger than the rest, she'd been stronger, her slight body more adept at fighting the virus. But in the end, it had claimed even her.

There was a microphone inside the lab so Farooq could listen to the moans of the patients. He had it turned off for now, but Zafir could tell by the way the little girl's shoulders heaved that she was crying. So much the better—a child of corruption deserved no happiness in this world or the world to come.

"What of Malik?" Farooq said, still gazing into the glass. An ever-present grin perked the corners of his mouth.

Zafir nodded in thought. It was his habit to pause for a few moments before answering the sheikh. The fat Iraqi had been talking far too much, this was true. With the recent success of the experiments, they would have no more need of his prisoners. . . . It all seemed simple enough.

"You rewarded Malik well, but you cannot buy the allegiance of such a man. You may only rent it. He has reached the end of his usefulness," Zafir said.

"We think alike, my brother." Farooq's voice buzzed slightly against the glass.

"Shall I bring him here?" Zafir asked. "For the experiments?"

Farooq smirked, shaking his head. "No, I think not. The flood that would come from that fat body would be uncontainable. Kill him and be done with it."

"I'll see to it right away," Zafir said. "Personally."

Farooq suddenly turned to face him, cocking his head. "Have I not treated you well?"

Zafir knew where this was going. "Much better than this humble Bedouin deserves," he whispered.

"Then why do you wish to leave us?"

Zafir had prepared himself for this question. He grit his teeth, paused another moment, then answered slowly. "I do not want to *leave*. But, Allah willing, I wish to play a larger part."

"If you do this," Farooq whispered, "your death is a certainty. It is a divine thing to be a martyr in our holy struggle, my friend, but you are needed here." He wagged a slender finger. "I am informed you have news of the woman in Texas."

Zafir sighed, deep within himself. There was little Farooq did not know.

The sheikh pressed the issue. "Is it because of the American you wish to play such a role in the game?"

Zafir shook his head, slowly. "No." It was the first time he'd lied to his master. The very thought of what the woman had done boiled in his stomach.

Of course it was because of her.

Farooq's thin lips parted, but he waved the idea away as if it was a bothersome fly and started again. "I have no quarrel with you going to America—and I certainly find no fault in seeking your pound of flesh from the infidel woman. But, when you are finished, return to me, where you are needed. . . . I see no point in your playing the role of the pawn when you could stand here, beside me."

Zafir bowed his head. "I will do as you wish . . . as I have for these many years. But you now know my heart. I am weary of watching others punish the Americans for their insolence. Allah willing, I might be of a greater service in my master's game."

The sheikh nodded slowly, pondering. He put an index finger to the glass, pointing to the Riyadh prostitute. She was no more than twenty-five but looked twice that. "See how the woman bears her agony in silence. She is the bravest of them all."

"Perhaps she has lost her mind," Zafir said. "If she could see how her child suffers she would not be so brave."

"Perhaps," Farooq said. "Yes, perhaps that is it." He looked up. "Let us consider your request after *Salat ul Isha*. I will think better after prayers."

"I leave for Iraq tonight then." Zafir withdrew a half step, waiting as always for the sheikh to dismiss him.

"I understand our Iraqi friend is close to a certain university student in Fallujah," Farooq said, smoothing his thin goatee with boney fingertips. "We are, as they say in chess, at the endgame, Allah willing. The Americans must not learn too much until the time is right. Pay the boy a visit as well. Find out what he knows."

"As you wish," Zafir said. He looked forward to the task. The methods he used to obtain information would be a pleasant diversion from thoughts of the infidel whore—until he could go to Texas and settle things with her as they should have been settled long ago.

CHAPTER 15

Harris Methodist Hospital
Outpatient Psychiatric Clinic
Fort Worth, Texas

Carrie Navarro exhaled through pursed lips, sank back against the chilly cushions of a leather couch, and tried to focus on the most horrible moments of her thirty-two-year life. Dr. Soto had agreed to meet her for an evening appointment, after a long day at work, so she was already exhausted. Her eyes were closed, her hands lay flat and loose on top of her thighs. She was pretty, in a world-wise sort of way, with dark features and full red lips. Her eyelids and fingers seemed in constant motion, quaking slightly like leaves in a gentle breeze.

"Let the memories flow back slowly . . . water filling a cup," Dr. Soto said in her cool-cloth-to-the-forehead voice. She was a professional, dressed in fashionable red slacks and a white silk blouse, the kind of mature woman Carrie found it easy to trust. "You are completely safe, watching events unfold as an objective by-stander, not a participant. . . ."

Throughout three years of therapy, Carrie had learned to trust the mild-mannered doctor as much as she trusted anyone in the world. Andrea Soto knew more about Carrie than her own mother—the intimate details, private things you didn't tell your closest friends. Even friends made judgments. Everyone made judgments about certain things—everyone except Dr. Soto.

Soto's voice was firm and matter of fact. It had surprised Carrie at first that the doctor hadn't whispered when she put her under. "Okay," she said. "How do you feel?"

"I feel fine," Carrie said, watching the movie of her earlier, unspeakable life unfold before her eyes.

"Are you comfortable?"

Carrie's long eyelashes fluttered but didn't open. "Yes," she said, feeling thick and sleepy.

"Good," Soto said, and Carrie heard the sound of her pencil zipping across her notepad. "Let's begin."

"What is the date?"

"Today or then?" Even under hypnosis, Carrie couldn't help but be argumentative. It was her nature, and in the end, it was what had gotten her into such trouble.

"Then," Soto said, ever patient.

"June 8 . . . al-Zarqawi has just been killed by a U.S. air strike."

"Where are you?"

"Baquba," Carrie said, holding her breath. Her moist

lips were set in a hard, grimacing line. "Do I really have to come back here?"

"No, honey," Soto said gently. "You don't have to. But I think it will help you heal if you do."

Carrie sat for a moment, saying nothing. Long purple nails with snow-white tips dug at her jeans. The trembling grew more pronounced.

"All right," she sighed. "I'm here, in Baquba."

"What do you smell?"

"Earth . . . orange groves . . . trash," Carrie said. "And gunpowder."

"Good. Now, when you're ready, tell me what you see."

Carrie Navarro suddenly grinned. "Damn, Doc!" she said. "I'm lookin' hot in my sexy reporter outfit!"

Baquba, Iraq

Carrie Navarro got up early, stepped into her purple Crocs and shrugged on a heavy flak jacket. They didn't call the place *Baquboom* for nothing. It was not uncommon for a half dozen mortar rounds to pound the camp each day. It was a short slog from her bunkered CHU—containerized housing unit—through mud and pelting rain to the concrete shower stalls so she decided to carry her towel and toiletries inside her folded poncho. Wind whipped shoulder-length black hair against her sleepy face. Soaked to the skin in her T-shirt, perky little gym shorts, and incongruous flak jacket, Navarro got more than a few raised eyebrows from passing soldiers. She *was* on her way to the shower. Why shy away from a little water beforehand? Besides, if the solders at Camp Warhorse weren't used to her behavior by now, they would never be.

For some female reporters, being embedded with a crew like the Alaska-based 172nd Stryker Brigade would be seen as tough duty. Navarro considered it a plum. She ran with them, drank with them, and matched their dirty jokes punch line for punch line. If she fluttered her long, curly eyelashes and pouted her lips at just the right moment, she could even shoot with them once in a while. They were good boys, treating her more like a baby sister than a would-be girlfriend. She supposed the suicide bombings and daily mortar attacks had a lot to do with their desire to lord over and protect her. Most times their efforts were appreciated, but today she had a meeting and it just wouldn't do to have an armed convoy of overprotective Stryker vehicles dogging her every move.

Almost giddy at the prospect of her interview, she toweled off quickly after the tepid shower, stepping into a relatively clean pair of khaki cargo pants and her favorite sky-blue button-down. Stuffing the pockets of her desert camo photographer's vest with pens, paper, and a small digital camera, she threw on a rain jacket, then looked at her watch. 0730. She'd still have time to run by the Green Bean and grab a cup of coffee before her ride made it to the front gate.

The stubby black Mercedes box truck slowed to a creaky stop in front of the water station tent. The driver, a nervous-looking Jordanian man named Hamal reached across the seat to fling open the passenger door. He smiled a forced, half smile.

"Please to embark to my truck," he said in halting, book-taught British English. "No delay . . ."

Carrie tossed her small day pack full of PowerBars and water bottles into the front seat and climbed in.

The overwhelming smell of cardamom and human sweat hit her like a punch in the face. Hamal was evidently chilled by the rains and had the heat turned to full blast. He smiled at her again, patting the chest strap of his seat belt.

"Please to fasten safety belt," he said, fluttering dark eyelashes. "American soldiers wish all be . . . safety."

Carrie snapped the belt at her waist and cracked the window a hair to keep from suffocating.

"So," she said. "This Dawud has finally agreed to meet me?" Dawud was a tribal leader in the village of Chibernat, on the outskirts of Baquba proper. According to Hamal, the man was willing to give an interview about how the American presence in this Sunni stronghold was affecting local lives. If it panned out, it would be a tremendous coup and very likely get her promoted to editor.

Getting out of Camp Warhorse proved a lot easier than getting in. Hamal was a regular as was his Mercedes delivery truck. Though the sentries at the front gate gave her some funny looks at leaving the compound alone with an Arab, no one stopped them. One, a freckle-faced, blond specialist named Brennan, tossed her an infatuated wave from his post at the fifty-caliber machine gun.

"Please to cover head, young miss," Hamal said as the Mercedes sloshed away from the bunkered gates of Camp Warhorse and into the mean and muddy streets of Baquba.

Carrie pulled a navy-blue scarf from her daypack and wrapped it around her head and face. They passed a patrol of "her boys" from the 172nd Strykers. She waved, but didn't realize until they'd passed that there was no way they could have recognized her behind the scarf.

Ten minutes out of the camp, Hamal began to tap a weathered hand on the steering wheel. Carrie tried to make small talk but got little more than grunts and single-word answers. The Jordanian had always been the quiet type, but this was way outside the norm. A tiny nagging began to push its way to the surface of Carrie's gut as Hamal turned west toward the winding Diyala River.

She decided to bring up the only thing the quiet Jordanian had ever been happy to talk about.

"I spoke to my editor about your reward," she said, watching the man for a reaction. The corner of his mouth twitched, but he said nothing. He didn't even look in her direction. Her belly tightened.

"If this interview with Dawud turns out like I think it will," she baited, "I've been authorized to pay you two times our agreed sum."

Hamal nodded slightly. "Very well," he all but grunted. This from a man who literally had to lick the drool from his lips when money was mentioned. Something was wrong.

He slowed the truck to make a sharp right onto a deserted stretch of muddy road that reminded Carrie of the scrubby patch of land her grandfather had owned in West Texas. Through the road grime and pelting rain, she could just make out a rough tumble of earth-toned buildings in the distance, half hidden by a lone copse of orange trees. It looked like some sort of dilapidated power plant.

"I thought we were meeting Dawud at a coffee shop in Chibernat," she said, trying to keep her voice from sounding as shrill as she felt.

"We indeed meet Dawud, young miss," Hamal said, eyes still glued to the road. "Please to refrain from speak now."

"Hamal," Carrie nearly screamed. "I am paying you well. You need to follow our plans or tell me before we leave."

Now the Jordanian turned to face her. His lips drew back into a cruel sneer. "Plans?" He shrugged bony shoulders under his white *dishdasha*. "Plans change, young miss. Now, no more speak to me." His right hand let go of the wheel long enough to punch her squarely in the jaw. A cascade of lights popped in her brain, first blinding, then falling like spent fireworks into nothing but blackness.

Navarro's manicured nails dug into her jeans again. "That son of a bitch hit me in the face," she said, eyelids closed but fluttering. "Why can't I see anything, Doc?"

"You were unconscious. It's a time for which you have no memory." Dr. Soto cleared her throat, as if she'd been crying. "Let's move forward now. Walk me through what happened when you woke up. Remember, none of what happened was your fault, Carrie. It's important to know you won."

"Won?" Navarro scoffed. "Is that what you'd call being tortured by a sadistic bastard for month after never-ending month?" Her shoulders shook uncontrollably. "I . . . I don't think I can face this today, Doc. I've got to stop."

"Very well," Soto said, in her ever-soothing voice. "We'll continue in a few days . . . if you're ready. I'm going to count backwards from five, then snap my fingers. You'll remember everything we talked about, but all your anxiety will disappear. . . ."

Five seconds later Carrie opened tearful eyes. Her entire body shuddered with pent-up sobs. "I know you're doing your best, Dr. Soto." She took a tissue from the coffee table and blew her nose. "But after what that son of a bitch did to me . . . no amount of backwards counting or finger snapping is gonna take away the anxiety I got."

CHAPTER 16

Mahoney looked skyward, shielding her eyes from the drizzling rain as she watched the flashing strobe lights on the white FedEx 747. It lumbered in from the east and overflew the airport to make a slow, rolling turn over the Everglades and land from the west. Since reporting her conversation with the French Ministry of Health to Admiral Scott, she'd half expected the FedEx plane would be blown out of the sky before it ever made it to land.

Fourteen heavily armed deputy U.S. marshals, each dressed in orange full-body biosafety suits, stood along the dark ramp. Blue lights glowed in the steamy mist along the hot tarmac. Self-contained breathing units hummed in the drizzle. Mahoney was similarly dressed, albeit without the submachine gun, as was her lab assistant Justin, a twenty-four-year-old doctoral student who made no secret of the fact that he was clearly infatuated with her.

Justin looked over his shoulder, wiping rain off the front of his clear bubble face shield. He patted his rear with a gloved hand. "What do you think, Megan? Does this suit make my butt look big?"

He was a cute kid, with mischievous, brown eyes, muddy-river hair, and the muscular shoulders of a baseball player. He was also young enough to cause a scandal of Fox News proportions if she yielded to his relentless advances.

"Justin," Mahoney sighed into the tiny microphone inside her rubberized helmet, fighting the urge to flirt back with such a good-looking hunk of man. "Knock it off. The stuff on that airplane is nothing to screw around with. Besides, I'm old enough to be your—"

"Sorry," he cut her off. "I'll stop."

"Thank you." Mahoney walked past him. The battery pack that powered the breathing unit at her waist whirred as she made her way toward the approaching aircraft. Ensconced in the cumbersome suit, she couldn't hear Justin sniffing along behind her, but she was sure he was there. Maybe she was giving off the wrong vibes. Maybe she was leading him on subconsciously. She certainly didn't intend to appear needy—no matter how available she was. In point of fact, her social calendar was incredibly lacking. She told herself it was because she was too busy with work, but wondered in her heart of hearts if she just wasn't overly picky.

When Megan was a little girl her father, the Fulton County sheriff, had described her hair as claybank, comparing it to the coat of his favorite dun mare—not blond, not red, and not brown but somewhere in between all three, depending on how the light hit it. As she'd grown up he compared her in other ways to his beloved horse. When she'd placed third in the state high school swim meet, he'd put a hand on her shoulder and said: "You know, you and your mama are more like quarter horses than thoroughbreds—built for comfort over speed." She'd looked around the pool and, for the first time, noticed that all the other young female swimmers standing around with their families towered over her by at least four inches.

"Third in state is nothing to be ashamed of," her mother had said, draping a towel over Megan's shoulders.

"I ain't sayin' she should be ashamed," her father tried to defend his reasoning. "I'm just pointing out she's been blessed with a little more hip and a little less length than these bags of bones that are taking first and second."

The quarter-horse comparisons not withstanding, Megan knew she was attractive enough. The men who did ask her out all looked like Ken dolls. Roger, the cardiologist she'd been having dinner with in Buckhead when she'd been summoned away to the limousine conference, was exactly the sort of man she seemed to attract, and exactly the sort she couldn't stand—rich, well-groomed, highly educated, and incredibly boring. She wondered if working surrounded by life-threatening germs day in and day out had somehow dulled her senses, made her crave more excitement from a man than any human being was capable of giving. Justin was certainly willing to show her some excitement, albeit of the fumbling kind. She could see it in his hungry, young eyes every time he looked at her. Somehow, she'd have to figure out a way to hit him in the head with a figurative two-by-four to let him know she wasn't, and never would be, something on his menu.

The jet made a slow turn off the taxiway and lumbered toward them amid pulsing lights, turning Mahoney's thoughts back to the deadly task at hand.

Luckily, FedEx traveled with a flight crew of only two and no attendants, making it far less likely that anyone would have come into contact with the package containing the virus.

"I know what you were going to say, Megan," Justin said from behind her, his voice dripping with impish enthusiasm. She'd started their relationship off badly by insisting he call her Megan instead of Dr. Mahoney. She made a mental note to remain more aloof with her next intern.

"You were going to say that you're old enough to be my sister."

Mahoney spun on her heels. Every breath threw a tiny puff of fog on her clear plastic face shield. It was uncomfortable enough to begin with stuck in the clammy suit. She wasn't about to put up with this for one minute longer.

"Justin, I'm serious." She jabbed him in the chest with her glove-encased finger. "If you want to work with me, you gotta rein in that horn-dog libido. If I was a twenty-year-old cheerleader at Georgia Tech, maybe you and I could have a hot roll in the hay. We could catch us a nice case of campus clap—then set up a romantic date to get treated together at the health unit. But I'm old—"

"Thirty-something isn't old." Justin amped up his perfect grin. "*Cosmo* says you're in your sexual prime."

"I've seen too many deadly bugs to screw around with you, or anybody else who hasn't been living inside a plastic bubble all his life." That was a lie, but it sounded good. Mahoney hooked a gloved thumb over her shoulder toward the FedEx jet as it powered down behind her, lights pulsing in the dark rain. "It's time to get serious. You hear what I'm saying? There is no vaccine for what's in there, no cure."

The intern slumped. "I understand. Won't happen again."

"Good," Mahoney said, knowing that it would most certainly happen again . . . and again. They had a similar talk about every other day. Talking about a roll in the hay with the beefy youngster had caused her hood to fog up even more.

When this is over, she thought, *I've gotta find a full-grown man who can really fog my face mask.*

Seven yellow airport fire trucks moved in to form a loose perimeter outside the ring of deputy marshals who now surrounded the aircraft. Tentatively, the co-pilot opened the door and stepped out onto the rolling metal stairway. He waved sheepishly, looking relieved to be on the ground. The lead marshal pointed back in the plane, shaking his head.

"Please stay aboard, sir," he shouted. "No one out until we give the order."

"I'll be the only one to go aboard," Mahoney said

over the radio so the marshals could hear her. "My team and security contingent will take the package. The rest of you can secure the aircraft and crew for decontamination." She turned to her pouting assistant. "Justin, grab the bubble stretcher and wheel it up to the base of the steps."

The bubble stretcher was a Plexiglas box, long enough to hold a human body, fitted with an electric air pump and HEPA filter. Any virus or bacteria was kept inside by the constant negative air pressure provided by the pump.

"On it, Doctor," Justin said, professional, for the moment.

Mahoney stopped and took a deep breath at the base of the Jetway. Through unthinkable errors of miscommunication between governments, FedEx had just accomplished the very act terrorists had failed to complete on Northwest 2. They had landed a weaponized version of the deadliest virus known to man on American soil.

She glanced at her watch to confirm what she already knew.

It was September 11.

CHAPTER 17

11 September
Mount Vernon, Virginia

In the back of a dark blue armored limousine, where the Director of National Intelligence conducted the lion's share of his work, Win Palmer briefed his new agents on the events surrounding Northwest Flight 2 and what he believed to be the inevitability of a bioterrorism attack with weaponized Ebola.

Quinn let out a deep sigh. The conversation with Kim had gone as expected. There was no ranting, no screaming, just a long, resigned sigh and a sullen "I knew better than to hope." Quinn was sure that wasn't the end of it. Rather than dwell on his own sorry problems, Quinn turned his thoughts to the tragedy of the Northwest flight. He'd heard of Steve Holiday, one of the most beloved squadron leaders ever to command the Blue Angels. He thought back to what Sadiq had told him outside the mosque that night in Fallujah.

"My informant says this guy Farooq is determined

to do something worse than the mall bombings—to bring America to her knees."

"And then shoot us in the head." Palmer gave a somber nod. "Unfortunately, everything we have on Sheikh Husseini al Farooq—or his organization— wouldn't fill a double-spaced page. We could kill him—if we could find him—but for all we know he has a second-in-command that's even worse. Are you still in contact with your informant?"

Quinn nodded. "He's got my secure cell phone number and I gave him a stack of phone cards before I left Iraq. He's too greedy not to call me when he gets anything.

Thibodaux scratched his buzz cut, staring at his reflection in the tinted window. "I got a question or two if I might be so bold."

"By all means," Palmer said, smiling like a friendly uncle. He nursed a bottle of water across a low teak table from Quinn and the Cajun. Both still wore their uniforms, though they'd taken off the tunics and, thankfully, the ties—to Quinn, wearing a tie was like being choked by a very weak man. It was late, after eleven, and the heavy armored limousine thumped slowly down deserted residential streets. Compared to his BMW, the limo was a cage. Palmer had assured him the motorcycle would be transported to meet him, but the thought of someone else riding, or even trailering, his baby ate a hole in Quinn's gut.

"Well, first off," Thibodaux said, "do I still report to my same command structure? I ain't no mercenary, but the wife will want to know about little things like where my pay will come from. I got a few mouths to feed."

"Fair enough question," Palmer said. "The paperwork has already been processed to put you on loan to OSI—"

"Hang on a damn minute there, sir," Thibodaux said. "I'm a Marine. No offense, Quinn, but I didn't sign on to be a wing waxer."

"You're still a Marine, Jacques," Palmer chuckled. "You're just on loan to the Air Force. We have an arrangement with OSI that makes it easier this way. You are now both what we in the business call OGAs— Other Governmental Agents. I've found it's much easier to hide my OGAs in plain sight rather than trying to set up some clandestine agency. It's not at all uncommon for agents of the federal government to go on various assignments they don't talk about. As you would assume, most of those assignments are yawners—dignitary protection, diplomatic missions, things like that. Even James Bond could get lost in a bureaucracy as big and complex as ours. Take it from me; it's much easier this way than putting you on the CIA or NSA payroll. You both have clearances and I can read you in above TS. Your pay and benefits mechanisms are already in place. You'll start to receive oh-six pay as of last week."

"A colonel's salary?" Thibodaux whistled. "The child bride's gonna wonder what kind of deal I've made with the devil for that one. I'm still not sure what our duties will be on this 'Hammer Team' of yours."

"Your duties"—the DNI grinned—"are whatever I

find necessary. Apart from the fact that you saved my grandson, I chose you two because of your particular skill sets and above all, your personalities. Your records demonstrate you don't kill just because you have the opportunity . . . but when it's the correct thing to do, you don't hesitate. Thankfully, the President has removed the chains of red tape from me. We can act when we need to act—without waiting for fifteen others to sign off on our actions."

"Are there more of us?" Thibodaux asked. Quinn had the same questions but was happy enough to let the big Marine do the talking.

The limo turned into a tree-lined circular drive off a shadowed side street a stone's throw from George Washington Parkway.

"There are a few, but I doubt you'll ever meet. Terrorists learn from us . . . and we learn from them. Small, independent cells can act on their own and, better still, they can act with speed. It gives the President deniability."

"Deniability . . ." Quinn mused, mouthing the distasteful word.

"Correct," Palmer said. "You report only to me and I report to the President. No matter the politics, the person sitting in the Oval Office feels the harsh weight of reality settle on them pretty fast. Torture, enhanced interrogation—call it what you want, but every great once in a while such a thing becomes a necessity. Some play the game in the open, some more discreetly. The events in Colorado have purchased a new sense of realism from the citizens of the United States. For a time at least, they see the need to fight back."

Thibodaux crunched his brow like his head hurt. "But if the President knows, he doesn't have deniability."

Palmer smiled. It was the sort of smile the general had warned them about when he mentioned men in suits. "He knows what I say he does."

"So you'd lie?" Thibodaux released a deep breath.

"In a heartbeat," Palmer said simply, "for a greater cause."

"What about Congressional oversight? Isn't it illegal to do this sort of thing without legislative approval?" Quinn studied the man's cool eyes under the dim yellow dome light.

"We have our supporters," he said, shrugging. "Call it a *Select Committee* of the Senate Select Committee on Intelligence—I call them the Gang of Five. The SSCI has fifteen members, the majority party having one more seat at the table. Our Gang of Five keeps that same ratio—but again, they only know what I tell them—and generally they don't do too much asking. I think they prefer to bust my chops after the fact than to know the whole truth up front. No matter what anyone weeps about in front of the television cameras, we have the backing we need—sometimes even from the same people who bash us on CNN. The Gang of Five likes to have their deniability, too."

"So you'd lie to the Senate, but you won't ever lie to us?" Thibodaux said.

"Never."

"Is that a lie?" The Cajun grinned.

Palmer leaned back to study the limo's carpeted ceiling a moment, and then put both hands flat on his knees. "I'll make you this promise, gentlemen. I may not *always* tell you everything, but I'll never send you to get killed without giving you the whole of it. That kind of mission should be voluntary and fully disclosed."

"Sounds like it'd be pretty easy to drop us in the grease," Thibodaux said, stone faced.

Win Palmer sighed, closing his eyes. When he opened them he looked directly at each man in turn. "Neither one of you would have stayed alive as long as you have if not for the ability to read people. You saved my grandson's life and that's something I don't take lightly—but more than that, you have talents that can save countless other lives. I love my country, gentlemen, and from your records I can tell you do as well. I don't believe I'll ever have to 'drop you in the grease'— I think you'd jump in on your own."

Quinn kept quiet.

"Get some rest." Palmer nodded toward a sprawling brick home behind an alternating row of sycamores and oaks that had already been big trees when George Washington was still receiving guests at Mount Vernon. "Miyagi will settle you in and see to your equipment issues in the morning."

"Are you shittin' me?" Thibodaux grinned. "Mr. Miyagi works for you?"

"*Mrs*. Miyagi," Palmer corrected. "And no 'wax on, wax off' jokes. This woman might not look like it, but she could seriously kick your ass."

Quinn's cell phone began to buzz in his pocket.

"Go ahead and take that," Palmer said, pushing open the door. "But don't loiter out here too long. Mrs.

Miyagi is expecting you—and she's not someone you'd want to have mad at you."

Red oak and yellow sycamore leaves, the beginnings of an early fall, swirled under the tires in the feeble glow of the taillights as the limo crunched down the deserted street to leave the two men alone.

Quinn pressed the button on his cell. "Hello."

Thibodaux leaned against the ghostly white bark of a sycamore tree and stared into the night.

"Daddy?"

Quinn put aside thoughts of grimy politics and let himself go soft inside. His five-year-old daughter was the one person in the world who never disappointed him.

"Well, hello, Mattie. What are you doing up so late?"

She gave her trademark giggle. "Daddy, it's always late where you are. It's only eight in Alaska."

Quinn looked at the Aquaracer on his wrist. Midnight. She was so far away.

"Daddy?"

"Yes?"

"Are you killing surgeons?"

"Where did you get that idea?"

"On CNN they said that Americans are killing surgeons in Iraq. You're an American."

"I think you should stop watching CNN."

Thibodaux chucked softly in the darkness. "Tell her to watch Fox," he whispered. "I don't let my boys watch nuthin' but Fox."

Quinn waved him off.

"I saw a girl moose today in our yard," Mattie said.

"Wow." Quinn didn't care what they talked about.

Just hearing the kid's voice soothed his soul. "Mom told me she had to drive you to school."

"I heard Mom tell Grandma she's worried about you."

"Is that right?" Quinn couldn't help but smile that Kim would talk about him at all. Still, he didn't like the idea of her worrying Mattie. "Can I talk to Mommy a minute?"

"She said to tell you she's sleeping."

Quinn nodded, loving his daughter's naïve honesty.

"I have to go, Daddy. Don't let the surgeons get you. You're my bestie."

"You're my bestie too, sweetheart. Love you . . ." Quinn returned the phone to his pocket, fighting back a tear.

Thibodaux hung his big head. "I thought I'd be home spoonin' the delta whiskey tonight. Hell, I don't even have a toothbrush. I hope Mrs. Miyagi has an extra."

Quinn stared down the empty road, toward the orange glow of D.C. He thought of what Win Palmer had said. *Deniability*—it gave any professional soldier pause. It was another word for throwing someone under the proverbial bus.

Dry leaves skittered across the pavement on the cool breeze, sending a chill crawling up Quinn's neck.

He threw on the Vanson jacket and glanced up at the forlorn Thibodaux. The mountainous Cajun studied him, cocking his head.

"Somethin's eatin' at you, ain't it, Chair Force?"

"I was just thinking." Quinn shrugged. "You know I grew up in Alaska, right?"

"Always wanted to see the place . . . in the summer, mind you."

"The year before I left for the Academy," Quinn said, "I went on this big deer hunt with my brother and dad on Kodiak."

Thibodaux raised an eyebrow. "There's some mighty big bears on that island, beb."

Quinn put his hands in his pockets against the chill. "It was dark and cool . . . just like tonight. We took three Sitka blacktail deer about dusk and were covered with blood by the time we headed back to camp with the meat in our packs."

Thibodaux gave a low whistle. "Not a good way to be in bear country."

"You're telling me," Quinn said, remembering the event as if it had just happened. "On the way back, we came around a corner in the alder brush next to a little mountain stream and there was this live salmon lying in the middle of the trail. Its skin had been peeled off right before we happened along and it was still flopping around in the mud. It had some pretty serious teeth marks in its tail. The bear was still nearby and pissed, thrashing around in the alders, close enough we could smell him. No doubt, he wanted to get back to his meal of freshly skinned salmon."

"You feel that way now?" Thibodaux asked. "Like a hunter covered with blood in the middle of bear country?"

"Nope." Quinn sighed, walking toward the darkened brick house. "I feel like the fish."

CHAPTER 18

0700 hours
Fort Detrick, Maryland
U.S. Army Medical Research Institute for
Infectious Diseases (Usamriid)

A half dozen blue Chemturion suits hung on pegs along the cold tile wall, looking like the flayed skins of gargantuan Smurfs.

Dressed in a fresh pair of green hospital scrubs complete with paper slippers, Mahoney stepped into her rubberized suit just as the heavy bass beat of "Short Skirt and Long Jacket" began to thump in her earpiece. Cake was Justin's favorite band and playing the song on the intercom was just another one of his ways of paying homage to her. He clipped the iPod onto the drawstring of his scrubs and stepped into his own anti-exposure suit—a larger version of Mahoney's.

She checked the gaskets at her wrists, stretching fingers inside the heavy-duty rubber gloves. They were the first line of defense in a series of three layers, the next being cut-resistant Kevlar, followed by purple nitrile gloves. Nitrile ripped easier than latex when it was punctured, but in the deadly stuff they worked with, that was a plus. A glove with an unnoticed hole, even a tiny one, could spell a slow and agonizing death. Better the thing just fell to pieces once it was compromised.

Turning slowly, one at a time, each checked the other's gear, looking for correct closure on all the zippers and latches on the bulky full-body suits.

Justin did an ungainly pirouette but, thankfully, kept his mouth shut.

Mahoney punched her code into the pad beside the first airlock. The heavy steel door slid open with a sucking whoosh. She had to pass through four doors to get to the Biosafety level-four containment lab, the place where scientists worked on the nastiest bugs—*animalcules*, the pioneers had called them. Past the second door, down a long hall to the left, was the airlock to the infamous Slammer, the quarantined medical unit where researchers were sentenced if they suffered exposure, or even possible exposure, to one of the booger bugs in BSL-4—highly contagious and with no known cure. The place got its name from the sound the heavy door made when they sealed you inside for observation—maybe to never again come out and breathe fresh air.

A visit to the Slammer wasn't exactly a death sentence, but the only two people she'd seen go in had cracked under the isolation, emerging three weeks after their initial interment with no symptoms of the threatened disease but a multitude of facial twitches and body tics they hadn't had when they went in. Mahoney had been inside once, on a tour, and found it to be like the inside of a sterile submarine with grommeted armholes for unseen medical staff to work on isolated patients. One of the Slammer veterans had described it as living for three weeks inside an empty bleach bottle. Even the outer door gave Mahoney the creeps and she shuffled past as quickly as her blue suit would let her.

"All right," she said, moving through the third lock. "Time to get to work. Two monkeys dead, two still alive?"

"That's what the instruments read," Justin said.

"Curiouser and curiouser . . ." Mahoney mused as she moved toward the last door. "I thought they'd all have crashed by now."

With roughly five minutes of air in her sealed suit, Mahoney's first order of business was to attach one of the red air hoses that hung coiled from the ceiling every twelve feet. The hose provided her suit with a positive air flow and kept her face shield clear from fog. More importantly it gave her clean air to breathe.

Those who worked the Special Pathogens Branch followed safety precautions to the letter, but deadly viruses had to be kept alive in order to be studied. Working in a BSL-4 was like swimming in a feeding frenzy with billions of invisible, microscopic sharks—except it was far more dangerous.

Mahoney's suit filled with a constant stream of air, turning her into a hissing blue version of the Michelin Man.

The French had done a remarkable job of packaging

the samples. There were two, each in a separate, unbreakable tube, sealed in foam tape and stored with a chemical gel coolant that would keep anything, virus or otherwise, viable. One of the samples was easily identifiable as blood. Primary tests revealed it was human, but a mix containing the DNA and blood types of at least four individuals.

The second sample, also taken from the Roissy lab according to the French, was not so easy to identify. It was clear and viscous, the consistency of syrup, with microscopic flecks of black and red Mahoney had supposed was occult blood. It turned out to be vitreous gel, the fluid from inside a human eye, again from multiple donors.

Inside the BSL-4, the stainless steel surfaces and shatterproof glass equipment were dazzling in their sterility.

Mahoney, followed by a very serene Justin, made her way across the spotless tile floor—it was severely uncluttered, devoid of anything that might pose a trip or cut hazard. Two Pyrex vials sat in separate airtight glass containment boxes on her workbench, right where she'd left them.

It took hours to ready samples for study. They'd started the process as soon as they'd arrived from Miami. Now, Mahoney put Justin in charge of slicing dried droplets of amber resin containing cultures from each of the two specimens and studying them under an electron microscope.

She would deal with the macaques.

A long row of eighteen enclosures, connected by a

series of metal and PVC piping ran along the walls of yet another sealed room inside the BSL-4. Only ten of the enclosures contained macaques.

Mahoney had never been able to bear naming the animals involved in her research and called them by the control number tattooed on their chest. The primates were the worst, with their intelligent eyes and human expressions—it was far too easy to become attached to them. She'd spent months in the jungles of Africa and South America staring the world's deadliest diseases square in the face, watched people in the worst forms of pain and human agony, and still it was the monkeys that haunted her dreams.

She told herself the work she did was so important. The deaths of a few had the potential to save millions of lives. Mahoney listened to the muffled thump as the doors leading to the monkey unit slid shut behind her and wondered if the man who gave the order to shoot down Northwest 2 had used the same line of reasoning.

All eight of the surviving monkeys broke into a chorus of "Krraa! Krraaa!" as soon as Mahoney walked in and attached her breathing hose. Though slightly muffled by their airtight pens, the monkeys' screaming cries filled the room. She always tried to be gentle, but brought the creatures little but pain. She knew it and they knew it. Though each monkey could see the animals in the enclosures on either side of it, the air going in and out of the cage only mixed with that of the adjacent animals if Mahoney wanted it to.

In the far corner of the room the enclosures for C-08 and C-11 were quiet.

Five hours before, Mahoney had injected C-08 with

a serum made from the Roissy blood mixture, then connected the air ducts from that cage to the cage of C-11. No other contact was allowed. Megan groaned when she looked in the metal enclosures and found each animal slumped dead with uncoagulated blood still dripping from their old-man faces. C-11 had had no direct contact with the Roissy virus, but seven hours after beginning to breathe common air, he had crashed and bled out, just as surely as C-08.

She'd have to do a necropsy, take some blood and liver samples for further study, but first she needed to check on her two other test subjects.

Mahoney had given C-45 two cc's of a serum made from a sample of the vitreous eye gel found along with the blood in the terrorist lab in Roissy. C-45 was a robust, bearded male tipping the scale at thirty-one pounds—much of it teeth and claw. It had taken a double dose of ketamine to sedate the animal long enough to give him the test serum. It was one thing to get poked with a needle containing an anesthetic, quite another to get even a nick from a syringe containing a deadly agent like Ebola.

Though heavily sedated with a drug that should have had amnesiac effects, C-45 had stared up at Mahoney during the short procedure with pure, unblinking hatred right up to the time Justin had returned him to the enclosure.

Now the big macaque paced his tiny metal prison, still very much alive. C-6, whose enclosure shared the same air system as C-45, screamed and scolded Mahoney as she approached for a better look. C-45's huge brown eyes still burned with hatred, but he was unsteady, apparently under residual effects of the keta-mine. She wondered vaguely if he was having a bad trip. Ketamine, known as Special K on the street, could send humans into wild hallucinations.

Mahoney made a note in the chart hanging below the enclosures while she worked to connect the dots in her mind. Maybe the eye gel was just some byproduct at the lab. Vitreous gel was mostly water with a few proteins; maybe it had been used as a culture medium. The thought of where anyone had gotten such a thing turned her stomach. If the stuff had contained the same variant as the blood, C-45 and C-06 would be goners by now. Maybe it was something else altogether. Inside the cumbersome blue plastic suit, Mahoney shook her head. Hers was not a job where you could afford to miss things. . . .

"Boss . . ." Justin's voice crackled across her ear-piece. "You're gonna want to see this."

It was his favorite trick—to lure her to the micro-scope with the promise of something interesting and use the opportunity to slide his arm around her while they stood cheek to cheek, or at least bubble to bubble.

"I'm really busy in here, Justin," she said. "What have you got?"

"Okay, but I'm telling you—"

"Just tell me what you see."

"Okay," Justin groaned, sounding slightly bored. To him, this was just another of many brushes with killer animalcules. He could never know the particulars of Northwest Flight 2. "The Roissy blood contains large amounts of filovirus. . . . Looks a lot like Ebola Zaire—shepherds' crooks and spaghetti worms everywhere."

Mahoney leaned against a metal table, stretching her back. "That's what I suspected. And the vitreous gel . . . nothing, right?"

C-45 suddenly went berserk, banging his head against the front of his enclosure.

"Kraaa! Kraaa!" The enraged macaque bared long yellow fangs, focusing all his anger on Mahoney.

Justin paused from his rundown. "You all right in there?"

"We're fine." Mahoney turned away from the cage, hoping that might calm the enraged beast. "You were telling me about the second sample."

"That's what you'll want to see, Meg." He had to throw in her name. "The vitreous gel is teaming with virus, more even than the blood. The thing is, each strand in the gel appears to be encased in some sort of heavy sheath . . . maybe a protein. . . . I'm guessing that's why C-45 and C-6 aren't showing any symptoms. Maybe it affects them same way Ebola Reston hits humans—communicable but not deadly. I'm thinking what we have here is one of the bad guys' failures in the bioweapon department."

"Good." Mahoney nodded, tapping the clipboard with her pen. "Failure is a good thing when it's them doing it. Of course, we don't know how the stuff will affect a human. . . ." She looked up to see Justin on the other side of the window, his young face drawn tight in abject terror.

"What?"

"Dr. Mahoney, you need to get out of there now!"

"Justin," Mahoney said, glancing up to make certain

she was still attached to an air hose. "What the hell are you talking about? Is my su—"

The metal clang of a cage door behind her answered her question. She turned slowly, to find C-45—all 31 pounds of him—hunched on the spotless tile floor. In his fist, he held his wooden gnawing stick like a club.

"Justin, honey," Mahoney said, voice sticky as a Georgia peach. "Did you remember to fasten the door after you put C-45 back in his cage?"

"I . . . I . . . thought I did," the boy stammered. "I'm sorry, Doctor. I'll come in and help you get him caught."

"Stay put!" Mahoney barked. Justin underfoot was the last thing she needed. The horny idiot would flirt on his way to the guillotine.

Mahoney clutched the clipboard in front of her chest. The tiny square of Formica would work about as well against a running chainsaw when C-45 attacked, but it was all she had.

The big macaque heaved as it squatted on the floor not ten feet away. She'd been the one to give him the needle full of virus-laden juice. The scowling face said he held a grudge. Blue lips pulled tight. Fangs dripped ribbons of thick saliva down the green numbers tattooed across his pink chest—saliva that was surely hot with an unknown strain of hemorrhagic fever.

Mahoney reached slowly to unhook her breathing hose, then began to ease—inch by inch—toward the door. She didn't think about the pain of teeth ripping into the flesh under the flimsy layer of her rubberized suit. The agony and almost certain death from exposure to the virus didn't even cross her mind. One sound dominated her thoughts, a sound that pressed at her chest and made it impossible to catch a full breath. The whooshing thud of a three-hundred-pound metal door echoed in her imagination like a recurring nightmare—the Slammer.

The angry macaque didn't even have to break her skin. A simple tear of her suit—one breath of ambient air—and her next stop would be the stuff of nightmares. She could already hear the door crashing shut behind her, trapping her in the empty bleach bottle that would be her prison—possibly for the remainder of a very short and agonizing life.

CHAPTER 19

"I don't think she likes me very much." Thibodaux grunted, tossing back a liter bottle containing a mixture of water, chocolate protein powder, and a cup of raw oatmeal he'd let soak long enough he could chew it.

Across the breakfast table, Quinn made do with granola and soy milk. "Why do you say that?"

"I dunno . . ." The Marine wiped his mouth with the back of his forearm. "Because I can't do a handstand on my nose or some shit like that."

Mrs. Miyagi had woken them before five with an entire new wardrobe, including T-shirts, running shorts, and shoes. They'd arrived with literally nothing more than what they had on their backs and had given their sizes to Palmer the day before, but neither expected to have the promised clothes by the next morning.

Each man was accustomed to a strict regimen of exercise and they put the new gear to use without being told. Thibodaux didn't look like a runner, but as big as he was, he stayed shoulder to shoulder with Quinn for six miles through the neighborhoods around Mt. Vernon at a blazing seven-minute-mile pace. When they sprinted up Mrs. Miyagi's tree-lined driveway, they found her in the backyard, resting serenely in a sort of handstand on her forearms; her back arched slightly, legs straight up in the air. It was, she explained, a yoga move called *Pincha Mayurasana* and the sooner they mastered it the better for everyone involved.

It was impossible to tell the mysterious woman's age. She was compactly built, just a breath over five feet tall. Her black leotard revealed the muscular upper body of an Olympic gymnast, the defined hips and thighs of a sprinter. She moved like an athlete with a sort of fluid, feline confidence that took immediate control when she was present. Her coal-black hair was pulled back in a short ponytail. She wore no nail polish or any apparent makeup; her only adornment was the fleeting, crimson edge of an unidentifiable tattoo, barely visible at the scoop neck of the leotard over the swell of her left breast.

Her workout over, she dressed in faded jeans snug enough to accentuate the curves of her figure, and a white oxford polo that left the tattoo a hidden mystery. Under some lights, her flawless skin and ever serene demeanor made Quinn guess she was still in her thirties, but in momentary flashes, particularly when she spoke, the deep, ageless wisdom in her eyes said she was much older.

Miyagi joined the two men in the dining room just

as Thibodaux finished his protein and raw oats. She carried an aluminum Zero Halliburton briefcase in each hand.

"The DNI tells me I am to issue your equipment immediately," she said.

"*Arigato gozaimasu.*" Quinn accepted his case with both hands and a slight bow. It was large, at least five inches deep, and it had some heft to it.

"You are welcome." Mrs. Miyagi's lips perked into just the hint of a smile, the first Quinn had seen of such sentiment in the mysterious woman. "Palmer San said I should watch what I say around you." There wasn't the slightest trace of a Japanese accent in her words. Her teeth and her emotions vanished as quickly as they had appeared. "Now, if you gentleman will please open your cases, I will explain your new weapons.

"New weapons?" Thibodaux rubbed his big hands together. "I like the sound of that."

Quinn snapped the latches and raised the lid on the brushed aluminum case to find a pair of Kimber Tactical Ultra II pistols chambered in ten millimeter. The Kimber was built on the venerable 1911 design some operators felt had to have been revealed by the Almighty to John Browning.

Nestled between the matched handguns was a custom Glock in .22 caliber with a threaded barrel, Gemtech silencer, and a box of subsonic ammunition. There were extra magazines and a variety of concealment holsters for each weapon.

Miyagi waved an open hand over the contents of both cases. "The Director leaves the choice of sidearm up to each of you, since that is a personal issue. He makes you the gift of these pistols and reminds you that you are no longer constrained by the need to carry NATO-approved ammunition. The ten millimeters are for times when immediate stopping power is required."

"I can't think of a time when it's not." Thibodaux smiled. He peered down the sights of one of the Kimbers with the broad grin of a boy on Christmas morning. As a special agent with OSI, Quinn was accustomed to carrying a pistol wherever he went, both in and out of the United States. Thibodaux only carried a weapon when he was overseas or in training, and in the Marine Corps that was customarily a rifle.

"When silence is paramount"—Mrs. Miyagi smiled serenely as if she'd done her share of specialized pistol work—"the .22 caliber Glock fitted with the Gemtech should serve you very well. From my experience with the Director, it is my belief that you will employ this system far more often than you will the Kimber." She turned to Quinn, studying him for a long moment. "I understand you often use a blade in such circumstances."

"I have on occasion." Quinn nodded, wondering how much this woman knew about him.

With his particular skills and the broad range of opportunities to put them to use in Iraq, Jericho had learned to utilize the weapon that got the job done. In the beginning, he'd never set out to kill a man with a knife, but it had happened more than once. Quinn had discovered the method to be supremely effective and silent. The aftermath of blade work had the added benefit of throwing a psychological headlock on others among the enemy camp who came upon the bloody scene. It also gave him a reputation that made other OSI agents steer clear of him at parties but jump at the chance to work with him in the field.

Mrs. Miyagi bowed slightly, folding both hands in front of her waist. "Would you permit me to see your blade?"

Quinn drew the CRKT Hissatsu killing tool from his waistband. Modeled in the style of an ancient Japanese dirk, it was one of the few knives on the market that wasn't meant for double duty as a letter opener, or camp tool. The long, slender blade had no other job than the quick penetration of vital organs where it could inflict the most lethal damage.

"A knife?" Thibodaux tilted his big head, unconvinced.

"Why not?" The enigmatic woman peered through narrowed eyes. "Sicarii Zealots in first-century Palestine killed in broad daylight with a short sword known as a *sica*. The Fidaiin, most feared of the ancient assassins, always used a dagger to work their acts of terror. Even Spartans, whom you Marines revere so much, were renowned for their use of a short sword."

"Short being the operative weakness," Thibodaux said.

"Ah," Miyagi said, scolding the Cajun. "When a Spartan youth once complained to his mother that his sword was too short, the warrior mother told her boy the weapon would be long enough if he would only step forward."

Thibodaux sighed. "Touché," he said, giving Quinn an I-told-you-so look.

Her history lesson over for the moment, Mrs. Miyagi turned her attention back to Quinn, who was grinning ear to ear at Thibodaux's mental thrashing. "Very nice," she said, drawing the twelve-inch blade from its Kydex scabbard. "I'm sure it has served you well."

Quinn tipped his head, agreeing but saying nothing.

Mrs. Miyagi examined the Hissatsu under the natural light streaming in from her dining-room window. "Do you know of the ancient swordsmith Masamune?"

"I do indeed," Quinn said. "Some feel Masamune was the greatest of all Japanese sword makers during the late thirteenth century. Leaves floating down a river toward his blade were said to have sensed the sharpness and veered away in the current. While other weapons were sharp, Masamune swords held a certain mystical power—discerning about what they cut."

"You know your history." Mrs. Miyagi gave an approving smile. She held the Hissatsu flat, across both hands. "Many years ago I was given a Masamune dagger—much like your blade. It is called *Yawaraka-Te . . .*"

"Gentle Hand, like the legend of the river and the leaves," Quinn mused. It was so typical for the Japanese to give an instrument of death such a serene name.

"Yawaraka-Te now rests in your Halliburton case, under the guns," Mrs. Miyagi said. "I make it a gift to you."

Quinn caught his breath. A pair of pistols was one thing, but a centuries-old blade forged by a Japanese master was a heavy burden. He may have saved the Director's grandson, but this woman didn't know him at all. For her to give him a sword that for all practical purposes was a Japanese national treasure was unthinkable. Still, he could see from the set in Mrs. Miyagi's jaw to refuse it would be unthinkable.

"Do I get a cool knife?" Thibodaux peeked under the corner of the foam insert inside his aluminum case.

A mischievous sparkle formed in Mrs. Miyagi's bottomless brown eyes, flashing at Quinn. He nodded, understanding her meaning without words passing between them.

She pushed the Hissatsu toward the Cajun. "Blades are far more powerful when they come to us as a gift. Quinn San wants you to have this one." Offering him Jericho's knife with both hands, she changed the subject. "Now, there is much to do. Please put that away and follow me."

Thibodaux slumped, shoving the present in his aluminum case. "I told you she didn't like me," he whispered. "But hey, thanks anyway for the pigsticker, beb."

Quinn was severely tempted to look under the pistols in his case. He longed to touch the eight-hundred-year-old blade. That would be rude though, so he let it wait.

Mrs. Miyagi stepped out to her front porch and motioned toward the circular driveway. "The Director authorized a second BMW Adventure, identical to yours, Quinn San, but for the color."

Thibodaux all but vaulted onto the red and black GS. Except for the color it was the twin to Jericho's gunmetal bike, complete with Touratech aluminum cases.

Mrs. Miyagi ran her hand over the huge gas tank on

Quinn's motorcycle. "The Shop made a few adjustments while you slept. A little more travel in the front suspension . . . tuned the engine to coax out an additional ten horsepower to your original one oh five . . . and added run-flat tires."

Sitting astride his new bike, Thibodaux tipped back and forth on the center stand. He looked like a giant kid on an electric pony. "I'll bet they shoot rockets or some—"

"Don't touch that!" Mrs. Miyagi snapped. She stepped closer, pointing at a gray button on the handlebars.

"Really?" The Marine jerked his hand away as if he'd been bitten.

"No, Thibodaux San," Mrs. Miyagi laughed. "That controls your heated hand grips. Motorcycles do not make a good platform for rockets." Her smile vanished as quickly as it had appeared. "However, these particular motorcycles will carry you from point A to point B very fast, in places where a conventional vehicle can not always go. As riders you won't stand out when wearing armored clothing. We have full custom suits based on the measurements you provided. They are fashioned from Aerostich Transit Leather—both the pants and the jackets. Breathable and waterproof, but engineers at the Shop have installed a small cooling system for more pleasant summer wear. Ballistic shielding has been added to the crash armor already in place."

"I'd like to visit this Shop," Quinn said, giving his bike a quick once-over to make sure everything was in the proper place. He called it his pre-flight.

"Ah." Miyagi smiled. "Perhaps someday I can arrange

this. The Shop is a small, subunit of DARPA specializing in equipment for teams such as yours." DARPA—the Defense Advanced Research Project Agency—was a component of the Department of Defense comprised of government and contracted research specialists in everything from nano-bots to guided missile lasers.

Miyagi continued with her gear issue. "Our engineers have added a heads-up display to the visor of your helmet, using the same technology employed by fighter pilots. You will be able to keep your eyes on the road but still access night vision, GPS, and even a video link if that should become necessary—though I don't recommend it while riding, for safety's sake. Your helmets have also been wired with a voice encrypted, wireless STU." The STU was a secure telephone unit usually operated with an encryption key.

"Once they are imprinted, you'll be able to speak securely to the Director's office as well as to each other and, when needed, more conventional telephones."

Thibodaux rolled the black, visored helmet in his beefy hands. "I'll bet I could check my Facebook on this thing."

Quinn's head snapped up. "You're on Facebook?"

"Sure 'nuff." Thibodaux grinned. "You're not?"

"Indeed, you could use the equipment to check such things. . . ." Mrs. Miyagi pursed her lips as if she was about to say something else but turned her attention to Quinn instead. She rested a bronze hand on the handlebar of his motorcycle. "There are quite a lot of improvements, too many to comprehend in a short briefing. They were designed to be intuitive so nothing should surprise you. I believe you will be pleased as you learn of them. Some may even save your life."

"So," Jericho said, already feeling the calm waves of normalcy his bike provided, "we train with you?"

"That is correct," Miyagi said. "I am aware of your previous curriculum. I will provide a more spiritual . . . esoteric sort of guidance to prepare you for what the Director has in mind."

"And we are to stay here?"

Miyagi remained stone-faced. "For a time . . ."

The buzz of Quinn's cell phone interrupted Mrs. Miyagi's answer. She stepped back, motioning for him to take the call with a wave of her open hand.

"Hello?"

"*Assalaamu alaikum*, Jericho." The Arabic voice was unmistakable. It was Sadiq. "I hope you have much money, for I have much news for you."

In his typical fashion, Sadiq meandered on about the weather, his ailing grandmother, and his fat uncle, all in windy, unending detail, refusing to get to the meat of the matter. After two minutes, Quinn had had enough.

"Well, well, my friend . . ." He risked butting in, hoping the thin-skinned boy's lust for money would win over his ego. "You said you have important news . . . ?"

The line went quiet. "I do," Sadiq said at length, the irritation at having been interrupted clear in the staccato clip that had fallen on his speech. "News the Great Satan will, no doubt, find extremely vital."

"I am authorized to pay you well."

"This is much more than I've ever given you. . . ."

"How much more?"

"Come now, my friend. Can one put a price on human life?"

Jericho nodded at that. "Tell me what you have in mind."

"Four hundred American dollars bought the lives of two American hostages. What would the Great Satan pay to save millions?"

CHAPTER 20

Quinn directed Sadiq to call him back on a landline inside Mrs. Miyagi's house. Unless fitted with sophisticated adapters, cell phones were about as secure as shouting from the rooftops, and though Quinn's was secure, he'd only issued such a device to Sadiq when they were actually on a mission.

Once connected on the hard line, they exchanged code words. Jericho quizzed the boy for a short time about a few of their past experiences to be sure he hadn't been compromised. In the meantime, Thibodaux called Win Palmer and briefed him on the situation. The Marine listened intently, then scribbled something on a notepad and handed it to Quinn.

"Two million U.S. dollars," Quinn read aloud, raising his eyebrows. "*If* the information is as you say."

"*Raa'irh*," Sadiq gasped. *Splendid*. "But, I cannot spend even one penny if I am a dead man."

"We'll get you out of the country, give you a new name."

"That is better," Sadiq said in passable English. "I have always wanted to attend Harvard. You think I could go to Harvard? Maybe become a learned man in the law?"

Quinn thought of the quick two million the kid had just negotiated by spying on his friends and relatives. "I think you'll make a fine lawyer," he said.

"Very well," Sadiq said. "Since we are in agreement I will tell you what I know. My uncle has an acquaintance, a very fat man from the south of the city—his name is Malik. I am told he supplies American prisoners to this man, Farooq, just as Ghazan al Ghazi did. Lately, Malik has spoken of unspeakable experiments in Saudi Arabia, a laboratory where the prisoners he has supplied are used to test a special weapon that will certainly kill millions of infidels."

"The Saudi Kingdom is a big place," Quinn mused. "You'll have to do better than that to get your law degree."

"Of course, of course, my friend." Sadiq chuckled with a little more abandon that he should have, considering what his life was worth at the moment. "I know this laboratory is at a university that trains . . . how do you say . . . medical doctors for animals. . . ."

"Veterinarians?"

"*Ajal*," Sadiq said. *Precisely*. "That is the word. There is a campus of King Faisal University there for agriculture and veterinarians. Women may also study at this university. I understand you allow women to study at Harvard. Do you think this is wise?"

Jericho rolled his eyes. "Stay focused, my friend. We are talking about the lab"

"Yes, the lab . . . Farooq is said to have a small residence near the oasis of Al-Hofuf, adjacent to the stud farms belonging to the university. That is all I know." Sadiq's voice fell to a whisper. "But I think it is enough. Is it not?"

"Farooq is in Al-Hofuf now?"

"According to the information I have. This is timely, is it not?"

"It is enough," Quinn said. "Tell no one that we've spoken. Stay where you are. I'll send someone to pick you up."

Quinn hung up Miyagi's phone as Thibodaux handed him the cell with Win Palmer on the line.

"Looks like someone needs to go to Al-Hofuf," Quinn said, knowing as he spoke who that someone would be.

"I've got the Shop working your background even as we speak," the Director said. "The Bombardier will be waiting at Langley inside the hour. I'll meet you there for a better briefing."

"And Jacques?" Quinn asked, reading the concern on Thibodaux's face. "What's his role in this?"

"He'll be backing you up in spirit from a remote location. Unless you can teach him Arabic in the next few hours, you'll have to go this one alone."

"I have to ask, sir. . . ." Quinn paused, not wanting to overstep his bounds with a member of the President's Cabinet. "The Saudis are our allies. We're not going to try any diplomatic channels here?"

"This is one of those times I mentioned when we first met. We can't use you *and* the diplomats. If our experts at CDC are correct about the stuff these guys are making in their lab . . . we don't have the luxury of waiting for the glacial pace of diplomacy. Besides—" Palmer chuckled. "Diplomats aren't very good with hammers." Then he cut the connection.

"You trust this kid Sadiq?" Thibodaux asked fifteen minutes later as they packed new gear in the Touratech aluminum cases on their respective motorcycles. "I mean, he could be setting you up."

Quinn shook his head. "I don't trust anyone over there. But there were a lot of times he could have gotten me killed if he'd wanted to."

"My experience," Thibodaux said, stepping in to his black Aerostich Transit leather pants and shrugging on the jacket. In the tight, armored leather he looked like a superhero without a cape. "Snitches just love to hear themselves blab. Wonder how many folks he's told about Al-Hofuf besides little ol' you."

"There is that." Quinn swung a leg over his BMW, happy to be back aboard his beloved bike. "But it can't be helped."

He'd been itching to see what the bike could do ever since Mrs. Miyagi told him "the Shop" had tweaked it. The engine popped to life with the same purring roar he was accustomed to. He toed the shifter into first and held the clutch, letting her roll forward a few feet before gassing to a wheelie. After a short fifty feet, he let the front wheel settle back to the pavement and made a tight circle next to a waiting Thibodaux. He waved a good-bye salute to Mrs. Miyagi, nodding slightly to let her know he was pleased with the modifications.

"Well, here we go, Chair Force," Thibodaux said, gunning the throttle. "No matter how this turns out, at least you'll get to take care of some 'surgents."

CHAPTER 21

Fallujah

From his years of service to the sheikh, Zafir had learned that black trousers were less likely to show blood. He would have worn a black shirt as well, but decided that would look too conspicuous if he was forced to make a quick escape. He slipped a pair of vise grips and a small roll of duct tape wound around a Popsicle stick into the pocket of his slacks and bounded up the concrete stairs to Sadiq's tiny apartment. He'd dressed the part of a simple Iraqi shopkeeper and taken an overly contrite mood at every American checkpoint. Since he carried nothing they recognized as a weapon, none of the U.S. military personnel who detained him had paid him a second notice after the initial humiliation of being stopped in the first place.

They had no idea what he had planned for the vise grips and duct tape.

At the top of the fourth flight of stairs a dusty tangle

of dead spiders and a stack of old newspapers lay piled on the concrete at either side of a gray metal door. Zafir smiled to himself. He went through the motions of knocking in the event anyone was watching. It seemed American informants were behind every tree and bush. If he killed ten random people, nine would be *kafir*—apostates of Islam, in bed with the Americans in one way or another.

A muffled voice came from inside, followed by the shuffling hiss of slippers against a tile floor.

"Who's there?"

Habit caused the Bedouin to stand to one side of the entry—out of the line of fire. Even meek little lambs sometimes carried weapons, and the more frightened they became, the more likely they were to shoot through a closed door at an unseen threat.

"I am a messenger from the U.S. embassy," Zafir mumbled in English. He didn't particularly care if the boy understood him or not. "I have good news."

"Do you know the code word?"

To his surprise, the door creaked open a fraction, waiting for the code. When the boy saw his caller was not an American, he threw his body against it, trying to shove it closed, but it was too late. Zafir slammed his fist against the startled boy's nose as he shouldered his way in.

Zafir shut the door behind him so no neighbors would interfere with his methods. Sadiq cowered on the floor, blood pouring from his shattered nose in pools on the chipped tile.

"If you are from the embassy why do you do this to me?" he groaned, hand splayed across his bloody face.

"I am not from the embassy, you idiot," Zafir laughed. Methodically, he began to unbutton his shirt. "I am a messenger—from Allah. And you have been talking to the Americans."

"Everyone here talks to the Americans. . . ." Sadiq's voice quavered. "What are you doing? I'm a student . . . waiting to return to Baghdad and the university when it is safe. . . . Why are you taking off your clothes?"

Zafir draped the shirt in the seat of a padded chair beside a cluttered table that occupied a quarter of the cramped apartment. "I wish to keep it free of blood— your blood—while I work." He took the roll of tape from the pocket of his slacks and bound the boy's wrists behind his back. As Zafir expected, Sadiq held out a pitiful hope that if he complied, he wouldn't get hurt. Foolish boy. Zafir threw him on the shabby couch under a poster of an American actress wearing a swimsuit. The Bedouin spoke slowly, lips pulled back in disgust, showing yellow teeth. "Malik suspects you have been working with the Americans."

"Malik is a liar!" the boy shrieked, trying to disappear by sinking deeper into the threadbare cushions.

"Malik is dead." Zafir put a finger to his lips to shush the boy's rising whimper. "Now—" He clapped his hands in front of him. "In your university studies do they teach you of the ancient Bedouin custom of *Bisha'a?*"

"No . . . I don't think so. . . ." Sadiq leaned his head back, trying to staunch the flow of blood from his nose. He sounded like he had a bad cold. "I . . . I don't remember. . . ."

"Very well, then." Zafir nodded. "I will instruct you." He rummaged through the small basin of dirty dishes until he found a metal spoon, still encrusted with the hardened remains of some past breakfast. He lit the burner on a gas hot plate and placed the bowl of the spoon in flame. Bits of food flared and popped as it burned off in a smoky yellow blaze. "Here's how it works. I ask you a question . . . then you will give me an answer."

The metal spoon glowed cherry red. The rag in Zafir's hand began to smoke as the heat traveled up the handle and scorched the cloth. "After you have answered, you may prove your honesty by placing your tongue against the hot metal. If you are indeed telling me the truth, it will not burn you."

Sadiq gulped.

Zafir leaned in with the glowing spoon, only inches from the boy's face. "Of course, *Bisha'a* is voluntary. It would prove your innocence, but the choice is up to you."

"I can't . . . I don't . . ."

"Very well," Zafir said, half smiling. "I will take that to mean no." He tapped the super-heated spoon to the tip of the boy's nose, bringing a piercing shriek and a puff of acrid smoke as skin seared in a perfect circle.

Turning his back on the sobbing boy, Zafir began to rummage around the cluttered room. He found it better to let people he questioned stew for a time, wondering what was about to become of them. Their fevered brains did much of his work for him. Amid piles of crumpled food wrappers, paper coffee cups, and old newspaper on the yellowed Formica table, Zafir found what he was after, a cell phone. He snatched it up with a sly grin and began to scroll through the numbers.

"This one is interesting," he muttered, peering up under his wild black eyebrows. He held the phone in front of the boy's eyes. "It is the country code for America, is it not?"

Sadiq's eyes twitched, searching the room like a cornered animal. His chest heaved with fear. "A friend who helps me with my English studies. . . . Please, I do not know what you think I have done. . . . I am a poor student, merely waiting to return to my studies."

Zafir took the vise grips from his pocket and rolled them slowly in his disfigured hand. "So you have said." He knelt beside the trembling boy. "It is very important that I know exactly what you have told the Americans. You will tell me all about your conversations . . . and I will demonstrate the agony your friend Malik suffered before his death this very morning."

Zafir lifted Sadiq's right ankle. Again for reasons of fear or hope or stupidity, the boy put up no struggle. Zafir bound him to the heavy wooden arm of the couch with four quick wraps of the tape. The boy's sandal fell to the floor. Tears streamed from his eyes.

"Yes, yes, yes! I have spoken to an American Air Force agent!" Sadiq blurted. Words began to flow like water from a broken vessel. "He . . . he has killed many of our brothers . . . a very dangerous man. He would have killed me as well if I had not told him something. . . . You must believe me. I did not wish to talk to him, but he forced me."

"This American's name?"

"Jericho." The boy hardly paused at the question. It was far too easy. "His name is Jericho."

Zafir raised an eyebrow. "An Israeli?"

"No," the boy whimpered, chest heaving, eyes darting around the room. "He is American."

"His full name."

"I do not know."

Zafir struck Sadiq across the face with the vise grips. There was a satisfying crunch as his cheekbone cracked. Teeth shattered and gave way.

Sadiq screamed, quivering, trying to make himself smaller. He'd wet his trousers. Pathetic.

"I'm telling you the truth. I . . . I'm not lying anymore."

Zafir struck him again. A piece of tooth flew across the room to land in a dirty soup bowl with a tiny clink. A torrent of fresh blood gushed from his already shattered nose.

"I know you are not," Zafir whispered, leaning in to rest his arm on the back of the couch, looming over the boy.

"S . . . s . . . stop, stop, stop," Sadiq pleaded, shoulders wracked with sobs, spittle covering his chin. "I'm telling you what you want to know. . . ."

"It is much too late to save yourself from *all* pain. . . ." Zafir spoke slowly as he stooped to tape Sadiq's free ankle to the center leg of the couch, leaving him spread eagle on the blood-soaked cushion. "But, if you continue your cooperation, perhaps you may enjoy a quicker death. Let me explain how these events will unfold." He patted the boy gently on the knee. Anticipation of pain brought greater fruit than the pain itself.

"First, I will pull the nails from your toes with my pliers . . . one by one. They come out more quickly than you might imagine so that part of it will not take overly long. . . ."

"Please—"

Zafir raised a hand to shush him. The boy cowered back in silence. "Do not disgrace yourself with begging at this point. We are far beyond begging. Where was I? Ah, yes, after I am finished with your toes . . ." He used the nose of the vise grips to trace a line up the inside of the boy's thigh. ". . . I will move a little higher for a more lengthy procedure. If you were to survive, you would never be able to sire children. But do not worry; your survival is out of the question."

Sadiq bowed his head, sobbing. "I beg of you . . ." His head suddenly snapped up, eyes wide, hoping. "Listen. Here is something—Jericho, he is in the United States, but I believe he is coming back to the Middle East."

Zafir cocked his head to one side. This was news. "When?"

"Very soon," Sadiq said, batting his eyes foolishly, believing he'd bought some time. "He did not say, but I know this man. He is deadly, a cold-blooded killer. If Jericho finds the sheikh he will surely murder him."

"What do you know of the sheikh?"

Sadiq cringed again, preparing himself for another blow. When it didn't come he spoke haltingly. "Everyone knows of the sheikh. . . ."

"What does he look like . . . this Jericho?" Zafir cradled the ball of the boy's right foot, caressing it gently between the rough, clawlike fingers of his disfigured hand. He ran the tip of the vise grips up the tendon on top of the tremulous foot, trailing a white line against olive flesh.

"He is tall . . . very dark hair . . . and a beard. His Arabic is flawless. . . ." The words gushed from his mouth like spilling grain. Sadiq looked on in horror as Zafir examined his toes, pulling them gently apart, one at a time, as one might pluck a grape from the bunch. "He could easily pass for one of us. . . . Ohhhhh . . . I beg of you. . . ."

Zafir showed his teeth again. "All right, then. Beg if you must. I suppose I do enjoy it after all. Please continue. While you beg, I will begin with the nail of your big toe. . . ." He covered the boy's mouth with a strip of tape. "I will not linger on the first one—as a favor to you for this new information. We will speak again in a moment. . . ."

Sadiq broke into a frenzied gyration of vain struggles and muffled screams, but it did him no good. Taped as he was he could move nothing but his shoulders and neck. No one could hear his cries.

Zafir adjusted the screw on the end of the vise grips and snapped the metal teeth shut on the cracked tip of the flailing boy's toenail. This would indeed be enjoyable, but what he really wanted was a face-to-face meeting with this American named Jericho.

CHAPTER 22

USAMRIID
Fort Detrick

"Justin . . . sweetie . . ." Mahoney whispered. She'd unhooked her breathing hose and a puff of condensation formed with each breath on the bubble of her clammy rubber hood. Beads of sweat inched down the small of her back. "I need you to get the Dist." The Dist-Inject was a long-barreled pistol capable of firing plumed syringes or preloaded metal darts of medication. "And draw me some ketamine. Hurry."

"Okay . . . all right," Justin stammered. Cake's "Stickshifts and Safetybelts" blared away on the intercom, the runaway beat only adding to the tension in the air. "How much?"

C-45 squatted on the gleaming tile floor ten feet away, baring yellow teeth. Mahoney's breath caught like a jagged stone in her chest. The big macaque twitched in agitation. She didn't want to do anything to add to it. A small dose of ketamine would have little effect on him at all. Not quite enough might throw him into wild hallucinations and make him even more difficult to control.

"I'd be happy with two hundred milligrams," Mahoney whispered, hoping that would be enough to mean a permanent lights-out. She kept the heaving animal in her peripheral vision, fearing direct eye contact would be perceived as a threat.

Justin came across the intercom, interrupting a wild guitar riff. He was flustered and stuttering. "B . . . biggest one . . . I mean, the only darts we have hold forty cc's."

"Then fill up three, but be quick about it." Mahoney edged toward a plastic broom leaning near the cages.

C-06, the other macaque, bounced and screeched in his enclosure, using his gnawing stick like a club to pound the metal door. He was egging his friend into fight.

"Okay," Justine said after what felt like an eternity. "Got 'em."

Mahoney turned slowly, grabbed the broom, and stepped backward toward the wall. She was surprised to hear the sound of the heavy airlock whoosh open behind her. Justin had defied her order and come in the room.

Now, she had to worry about an enraged monkey and a dumb-ass with a runaway libido.

C-45 went berserk at the new arrival. He'd never responded well to men and the sight of Justin threw him into a fit of shrieking leaps around the room. Needle-sharp claws, capable of shredding the rubber suits, clicked as the thirty-pound bundle of muscle and teeth slid across the bright tile.

"I told you to stay out!" Mahoney snapped.

"This . . . this is all my fault," Justin stammered. "You have to let me help."

"It *is* your fault," Mahoney said, fear keeping her anger at bay for the moment. "Now that you're here, how do you feel about shooting the Dist?"

C-45 had climbed up on top of the cage stacks and now paced back and forth, two feet above their heads—in the perfect position for a flying attack.

"I'm a deadeye," Justin said.

He was showing off again. That was good. It might help to calm his nerves. Megan didn't think it was wise to explain the dire consequences if he missed. This was not the time to mention the fact that no matter how this little adventure turned out, Justin's tenure as her assistant was finished.

So far, he'd been smart enough keep the air pistol hidden. Macaques had remarkable brain capacity to go along with their sharp teeth and angry dispositions. C-45 had been tranqed before. He was sure to attack at first sight of the Dist.

"Okay, Deadeye . . ." Mahoney kept her breath low to keep her face shield from fogging now that she was re-breathing the moist air already in her suit. She could taste the bitterness of her own fear. "As soon as you take the shot, he's gonna go crazy. I'll fend him off with the broom while you reload and hit him again. . . ."

"I'm locked and loaded, Doc," Justin said with far too much swagger to suit Mahoney. "Say when."

"Now!"

Megan was vaguely aware of a soft *whooft* when the dart left the barrel. A nanosecond later, the macaque erupted into a screaming ball of rage. Though Justin had fired the pistol, C-45 locked in on her. The monkey launched from the top of the cage, lips pulled back in a screeching "Kraaaaa!"—intent on ripping away Mahoney's throat.

She sidestepped, feeling the bump as the monkey brushed her left shoulder to crash into the stainless steel table behind her. A thousand-dollar centrifuge, full of test tubes, crashed to the floor, adding another danger with the broken shards of glass. She prayed her suit hadn't been shredded as she spun to face the irate macaque. No time to check now. She could not allow this living buzz saw to get behind her.

Claws clicked as C-45 scrambled on the smooth steel to gain its footing. Thankfully, the bright yellow plume of Justin's first dart hung from the pink skin of its thigh.

Mahoney didn't wait for the animal to turn before she drew back the broomstick like a baseball bat and swung with all her might. The unwieldy suit made it difficult for her to get much power, but the swat sent C-45 reeling against the far wall.

"Aren't you ready yet?" she panted, holding the broom in front of her in both hands, pointed toward the ceiling like a broadsword. "This little bastard wants to kill me."

"Locked and loaded, Doc," Justin said.

The macaque spun on its heels, sliding sideways

across the floor in midturn. Fangs bared, it sprang straight for Mahoney.

"Shoot!"

Justin was as good a shot as he said he was. The second dart hit C-45 center chest catching him in midjump with a pink plume. The macaque went limp and fell just inches from Mahoney's face.

The double dose of ketamine wasn't quite enough to put the agitated beast to sleep, but it slowed him enough that Megan was able pin him to the floor with the broom.

"Hit him with another one," Mahoney panted. Lightheaded, she was breathing more CO_2 than oxygen.

"Another one will kill him."

"Damn you, Justin." Mahoney clenched her teeth. "Quit arguing with me and put another dart in this little son of a bitch. I don't know what kind of bug we gave him, but I'm not gonna go to the Slammer because you let him bite me."

Justin fired another dart. C-45 slowed, and then lay still.

Mahoney held the broom in place another thirty seconds, then staggered back to reattach her suit to a coiled hose from the ceiling. Across the lab C-06 screamed and yipped, driven mad from watching the death of his friend. Mahoney drew three deep breaths of sweet air and then double-checked the door to the other macaque's enclosure.

"Dr. Mahoney . . ." Justin's voice was feeble in her earpiece—wobbly, like he was about to cry. "I think I have a little problem. . . ."

Mahoney turned expecting to find C-45 alive, on the verge of attack. What she saw chilled her even worse.

Justin stood dazed with the Dist-Inject pistol dangling loosely in his right hand. Sticking from the bicep of his blue protective suit was a yellow-plumed dart. It was the first dart he'd fired into the macaque—the dart with a large gauge needle that was certain to contain blood and fluid from C-45.

Mahoney must have knocked the dart loose when she used the broom—and it had landed in Justin's arm.

"Did it break the skin?" she asked, immediately forgiving Justin all his stupid mistakes. She shooed him toward the door and the decontamination chamber, where they'd be able to remove his suit and get disinfectant on the wound.

"Oh yeah," Justin whispered. "Hurts like it went to the bone. What's next, Meg . . . amputation?"

Justin was still half joking. She had to let him know how serious this was so he'd listen to her and follow her instructions to the letter. When she didn't answer immediately, he looked up with terrified, childlike eyes.

Mahoney yanked the dart out of his arm, keeping the sharp end pointed carefully away.

"Seriously, Megan . . ." His voice shook as the gravity of his situation—and his own mortality—slowly dawned on him. Boyish brown eyes, the same eyes that had so often ogled Mahoney, shot around the lab, as if looking for an escape route. He was now absent any emotion but terror. "What about VSV? I read about a woman in Hamburg who got a needle stick and she was okay."

"Well . . ." Mahoney didn't want the boy to give up

hope, but she couldn't lie to him either. Treatments with vesicular stomatis virus were experimental at best. A female scientist in Germany had indeed lived after a contaminated needle stick, but there was no way to be sure if she ever actually contracted the Ebola virus in the first place. "Let's just follow this through with the best protocols we have," Megan said.

"Okay." Justin hung his head, sniffing, tears dripping of the end of his nose. "Tell me the truth though. I mean it. Is this going to kill me?"

"Probably," she said.

CHAPTER 23

12 September
Al-Hofuf

Win Palmer was fond of hammers and, as it turned out, prone to pull one out of his toolbox whenever he was given the opportunity. Quinn didn't mind being a blunt instrument—*pipe-hitters* they called them in Iraq. Professional men who didn't mind doing the dirty work. Deep down, no matter what sort of civilized mold his ex-wife tried to cram him into, Jericho knew he was born for the rough stuff. His heart never truly beat until it was going full bore. And he never felt so alive as when he was hunting evil men—or being hunted himself.

More than fifteen years earlier, shortly before Quinn's first trip to the Middle East, his poli-sci professor at the Air Force Academy had read the class a quote from King Abdul Aziz bin Saud in 1930:

My Kingdom will survive only insofar as it remains a country difficult to access, where the for-

eigner will have no other aim, with his task ful-
filled, but to get out.

Quinn's task was to find out what Farooq had
planned and then kill him—getting out was a secondary consideration.

Access to the Saudi Kingdom hadn't grown any easier since the passing of King Abdul Aziz. It was no
small miracle that roughly twenty-five hours after the
call from his informant, Quinn found himself walking
the stone pathways of King Faisal School of Veterinary
and Equine Medicine in the oasis city of Al-Hofuf.

A tourist visa to Saudi Arabia on short notice was
out of the question—with one exception. Arab member
states belonging to the Gulf Cooperation Council, or
GCC, were immune from the strict travel require-
ments. The country of Kuwait was a member of the
GCC. Posing as Katib Al Dashti, a wealthy Arabian
horse buyer from Kuwait, Quinn was able to forgo the
red tape. A Kuwaiti official friendly to the U.S. let it be
known that Mr. Al Dashti had money to burn and was
in the market for a high-quality Saudi stud horse to
take back to his farm near Kuwait City. The details
were drummed out during Quinn's flight to King
Khaled International Airport in Riyadh and subsequent
three-hour train ride east to Al-Hofuf.

A note was waiting when he checked in to the Intercontinental Hotel. Mr. Othman with the university stud
farm had left his business card and an invitation to stop
by the stables after *Asr*—the afternoon call to prayer.

Quinn had checked the times for the five daily calls

to prayer before leaving the U.S. Everything in the world of Islam revolved around these times. *Asr* fell shortly after 2:30 P.M.

Quinn had grabbed a quick shower and changed into a fresh white *dishdasha* and simple white *ghutra* head-dress. In the lobby, he'd heard the call to prayer from a nearby minaret and followed the lead of other men as they knelt toward Mecca. Even in the five-star hotel, the *Mutawwa'in*—Saudi religious police, more formally known as the Commission for the Promotion of Virtue and the Prevention of Vice—kept a keen watch to see that no one shirked their duty when it came to prayer. Two bearded men with wooden canes had patrolled the opulent foyer, eyeing Quinn with the distrust they showed all under their domain. Both carried themselves with the haughty air of men given nearly unbridled government authority to prey on others—particularly those weaker than themselves. The will of Allah was to be strictly enforced, and as Quinn's political science professor had pointed out so many years before: "Life in a police state is pretty good—if you are the state police."

Though it would have been sweet indeed to spend a few quality moments alone with the two bullies, Quinn had only smiled, trying to conceal his disdain for the draconian measures the men represented.

The cabbie had negotiated a fair price for the quick trip from the Intercontinental Hotel to the university. He'd wanted to talk, but Quinn thought it best to play Mr. Al Dashti as a taciturn Kuwaiti who kept his thoughts to himself. In a country where impersonating a Muslim was against the law, getting caught spying could cost him his head.

Heat waves rippled up from the stone walkways as Quinn studied the concrete buildings, formulating plans as he went. The air was heavy, like the inside of an oven, but with a hint of humidity from the Persian Gulf less than a hundred kilometers to the east to make things even more uncomfortable. University students and staff were evidently wise enough to stay out of the afternoon heat and the walkways were all but deserted.

Quinn stood in the scant shade of one of the many date palms that lined the main paved road. Squinting against a low sun, he surveyed the empty campus, considering his options. Sparrows huddled and chirped in the shadowed fronds above him, unwilling to venture out in the blazing sun. A trickle of sweat ran down the back of both knees. He had no weapons—travel into the Kingdom was dangerous enough—but planned to use whatever was available when the time came. The odor of horse manure and sweet grass hay told him he was near the stables. Oddly enough, the smell had a calming effect. He knew horses—even Arabians—and had always felt better around them while growing up.

Farooq's operation was somewhere nearby, he could smell that, too. It was the bitter smell of something secret—the copper scent of death. Quinn looked at his watch—eighteen hours until his plane left Riyadh for Kuwait City. It would be his first window of opportunity for exit. All he could do now was explore and hope he stumbled onto something.

The main stable was a sight to behold. Arabs held

horses to be their greatest treasures and it showed in the ornate architecture of their barns.

Quinn passed from the blinding sun between thick pink columns supporting a matching stucco façade that rose three stories above the circular courtyard and made his way into the relative cool interior of the barn. He walked slowly down the wide, tiled breezeway keeping his shoulders relaxed, eyes ever on the lookout for danger.

The barn was empty but for a deaf-mute hired boy who shoveled manure into a wheelbarrow while he mouthed the words of a silent song to himself. Large ceiling fans whumped over head; water misters located up and down the ceiling beams sprayed a constant cloud that evaporated in midair. Detailed wrought-iron work decorated eight-foot-tall wooden gates and stall dividers. The scent of clean wood shavings wafted up from the floor of each spacious enclosure. An abundant supply of fresh hay and cool water filled built-in troughs on the walls. These horses lived more pampered lives than average Saudi citizens.

Quinn heard muffled voices as he passed beside the heavy wooden beams and rough, slip-proof concrete that formed the wash rack and shoeing area. A coiled garden hose hung on a peg in the shadows of the inside wall. The medicinal smell of soap and wet horse lingered in the thick air. He stopped next to a portable acetylene torch used for horseshoeing and strained his ears to listen. Angry voices drifted down from an upper-level hayloft that ran above the stalls almost half the length of the building.

Conflict, Quinn thought, as he heard the harsh sound

of a slap on bare skin and a yelp of someone in anguish. *Just where I belong.* He moved forward, reminding himself to think in Arabic so he would remember to speak in Arabic.

He stopped at the base of a thick timber ladder leading up to the storage loft. Voices tumbled down the wooden steps with bits of dust and trampled hay. Again, he heard the cry of a woman. Closer now, Quinn could make out the words.

"Please, this is far from a Commission matter," a female voice pleaded. "I assure you, we have done nothing wrong."

The naive urgency in her words made Quinn scan the barn for a weapon. This was no lover's spat. The strain in her terrified voice was heartbreaking.

"Child of Satan!" a male voice spat. "You will answer for your sins."

"We have committed no sin but to talk with one another. . . ." It was another male voice now, soft and quivering with fear.

Quinn heard the muffled whoof of air leaving someone's lungs followed by a low moan.

"You will rot in prison for your impudence, boy," a gruff voice said. "But first, you will feel the lash. *Khulwa* is a serious matter."

Khulwa was socializing with an unrelated person of the opposite sex—going for a walk, or even having coffee. A university professor in Mecca had been sentenced to one hundred eighty lashes and eight months in jail for being caught at a coffee shop with an unrelated female. It was not unheard of for women to be raped at the hands of overzealous men—punishing their lack of virtue. Such a thing defied understanding, but somewhere in the dark recesses of certain male brains, rape could teach a woman a lesson in chastity.

Up in the loft, cloth ripped. There was a muffled scream followed by a hateful chuckle.

"On your knees," a rough voice spat.

"Tawfiq," the girl sobbed. "Please, help me. . . ."

More laughter. "Tawfiq knows his place."

"I beg of you, sir . . ."

Quinn sprang up the ladder in three quick bounds. Months of working outside the wire in Iraq made moving in the loose, dresslike *dishdasha* second nature. He hiked it up with one hand as he climbed, like a woman wearing a skirt, chuckling in spite of the situation—if Thibodaux could only see him now.

At the top of the ladder, Quinn almost ran headlong into a dutiful member of the Commission for the Promotion of Virtue and the Prevention of Vice. The brooding Mutawwa towered over a young Saudi woman—barely in her twenties—who knelt, quaking before him on a pile of loose hay. Her black *abaya* was torn away revealing a white T-shirt and jeans. Without the heavy black robe, she could have passed for one of thousands of American college students. The man's fist wrapped her long, ebony hair in a thick twist. A delicate chin quivered above her slender olive neck.

The beefy Commission man shot a surprised look over his shoulder, wrenching back the frightened woman's head to bring home the point that he was still firmly in charge. He sneered at the new intruder, his teeth a white gash in a black beard. This Mutawwa was much taller than the two Quinn has seen at the hotel with flecks of gray in heavy whiskers.

"Peace be unto you," Quinn said in Arabic as he hit the startled man in the face with the flat of his hand. The Arab released his grip on the girl's hair and teetered in place like a great bearded tree before a strong wind. Without another word, Quinn heaved him headfirst over the short wooden railing to the tile floor sixteen feet below. The task was easy enough since the Mutawwa's underwear was down around his ankles, providing the perfect hobble when Quinn rushed him. His pious skull cracked like a ripe melon when he hit the concrete.

One down, Jericho's attention snapped to his second opponent. This one was shorter than the first, but with the broad shape of a fireplug. It was impossible to tell his true build under the full white robe, but a thick neck gave the man the look of a wrestler. He was younger than his dead partner, his black beard more sparse and wispy.

The squat Mutawwa pulled himself into a crouch, invoking a whispered prayer to Allah. "Who are you to interfere with Commission business?"

Quinn gave a humble shrug. "*InshAllah*—Allah willing—I am the man who will end your struggles in this world today."

The Mutawwa snatched up a pitchfork, fending Quinn off with the glistening points. In the stalls below, Arabian horses—a nervous lot in the first place—pranced and snorted at the commotion above them.

A block and tackle used to lift the heavy bales of

hay swung on a thick rope from a pulley at the edge of
the loft. In a fluid movement, Quinn sidestepped a fu-
tile jab with the pitchfork and rolled inside the other
man's reach, making it impossible for him to bring the
deadly points to bear. He struck the Mutawwa hard,
bringing the heel of his hand upward with all the force
of his hips. Bone crunched and cartilage tore as the
man's nose all but disintegrated. Clutching the collar of
his cotton robe like it was a judo *gi*, Quinn shouldered
the handle of the pitchfork out of the way and gave him
two brutally effective knees to the groin.

The Mutawwa sank toward the ground with a low
moan. A smear of fresh blood covered his slack face.

Quinn grabbed the block and tackle, yanking it
down to twist the hemp rope around the dazed man's
neck. "Murder . . . is a . . . capitol crime," the Mutawwa gurgled, eyes bulging red.

Quinn kicked him over the edge.

"So is rape," he said.

From the corner of his eye, Quinn caught the fluttering movement of a young student in a white Saudi
thobe and red checked ghutra. Blood oozed from a
split lip. The boy gathered himself up to flee.

Quinn put up a hand. "You will remain here." His
voice, still in clipped Arabic, was little more than a
coarse whisper. The force of it pushed the boy back to
the floor in a slouching, defeated pile.

Quinn knelt to help the embarrassed girl fix her torn
abaya. "What is your name, child?"

"Huwaidah," the girl whimpered. "He is Tawfiq."

She glared at her companion, who'd done so little to try and stop the men from the brutality they'd been about to commit.

Tawfiq, a skinny Saudi youth with a pronounced goiter, stared dumbfounded at the dangling body of the dead Mutawwa. He repositioned his mussed head scarf with shaky hands. "You . . . killed them," he stammered. "You killed them both. . . ."

Huwaidah clicked her teeth, her eyes flicking from terror to rage in the bat of a lash. Her name meant *gentle*, but there was no gentleness in her at the moment. Quinn remembered why soldiers from every army that had tried to conquer the Arab world were so frightened of being captured by the women.

"I am glad he killed them," she spat. "They deserved to die."

"But they were government officials. . . ." Tawfiq swallowed hard, his goiter sliding up and down like a trapped Ping-Pong ball. His voice was a flaccid whisper, devoid of breath. "What will happen to us now?"

Quinn grabbed the wall and leaned over the edge, scanning up and down the shadowed alley. Horses snorted below, sniffing at the blossoming pool of blood from the dead Mutawwa splayed across the tile floor, then gazing up with white eyes at the one dangling over their heads. There was no one in sight. He knew that could change at any moment.

"Tawfiq is right," he said. "We should leave at once. As long as we're not discovered here—and you both remain quiet about what has occurred—things will be fine. There will be an investigation. . . ." Quinn paused to let the youngsters realize the gravity of his words. "But no one need lose their head."

Quinn followed the pair down the ladder. On the ground, he paused long enough to grab a canister of iodine crystals out of a horseshoeing supply box and stuff it into the pocket of his *dishdasha*. Horseshoers used the caustic stuff to treat infections of the hoof. Quinn was familiar with a few other, more explosive, uses that were bound to come in handy.

Once inside the shade of the neighboring barn, Quinn stepped closer to the young couple. "Now," he said. "You must go your separate ways." He gave a stern look to the girl. He was, after all, playing the part of an Arab male. "And cease to find yourself alone with men who are not related to you. It is an abomination."

The pair nodded, heads bowed toward their feet.

"How may we repay your kindness?" Huwaidah muttered, her dark lashes fluttering like a wounded bird as the magnitude of what she'd just escaped crashed down around her.

Quinn smiled softly. It was a question he'd hoped she would ask.

"I am looking for a certain place . . . a place that I believe is also an abomination before Allah." He paused to let her look him in the eyes. "A laboratory where very bad things take place."

Tawfiq's gaze shifted toward the girl. He shook his head, teeth grinding loud enough that Jericho could hear the crunch.

Huwaidah sighed deeply, blinking, coming to a decision. "Yes," she whispered. "I have heard of such a place. The other girls tell awful stories. I thought they were to scare us and keep us from sneaking out at night."

"Huwaidah," Tawfiq snapped. "Mind your tongue. You will be killed."

She ignored him, looking at Quinn with wide, green eyes—honest, resolute eyes that said she could amount to anything if she was not so beaten down. She covered her face with the torn abaya but squared her shoulders, looking toward the far end of the open barn, toward the bright patch of sunlight and blazing pink stone.

"I want to show you the place you are looking for," she said. "You have saved my life, so it is now yours. I do not care if they kill me."

Quinn fought the urge to put his hand on the poor girl's shoulder. Instead, he sighed gravely. "I will not let that happen today."

CHAPTER 24

Fallujah

"The fat man, Malik gave me very little before he . . . left." Zafir pressed the cell phone to his ear with his good hand. "I fear our meeting upset him more than he was able to bear. The boy, on the other hand, proved to be a treasure of knowledge,"

The Bedouin sat on a sun-bleached wooden chair in the scant shade of a café awning. He sipped chai from a chipped ceramic mug as he spoke. Dressed in dark aviator shades, loose cotton shirt, and black slacks, he looked like any one of the hundred other Iraqi men milling around the streets in the war-torn country. All of these men had seen violence—but few relished it as much as Zafir.

"I knew you would be . . . how shall we put it? . . . persuasive. . . . ." Zafir could hear the sheikh's smile in his words.

"I am humbled by your confidence."

"The board is set and the pieces are ready to move into place," Farooq said. "I am anxious to open our game . . . unless, of course, you have information that dictates I should do otherwise."

Zafir fell silent as a platoon of American soldiers—they called themselves Peacekeepers—walked in formation down the dusty street, less than two meters in front of him. They eyed him warily because of his cell phone. Insurgents used cell phones to set off IEDs and holding one in front of an American was a good way to get shot. His throat tightened and he lay the phone down on the bench beside him without a word to Farooq. He took a long, slow breath and forced a smile, waving happily to the passing squad. On the outside he was a picture of calm, a docile lamb wanting nothing more than to comply with the American liberators. Inside, his stomach roiled, aching to cut the throat of the fair-haired boy who brought up the rear. The sheikh's plan calmed him. The boy and thousands of his kind would die soon enough. In time, even the women of the west—the ones who survived—would find themselves behind the burqa. It was the unquestionable will of Allah.

Only when the American patrol had disappeared around the corner a half a block away did he retrieve the phone. The sheikh was accustomed to such delays and the two resumed where they'd left off.

"Allah willing," Zafir said, "I am prepared to begin my part." He knew better than to speak openly on a cell phone. The Americans even listened to each other. Though the chance of them picking up his conversations was slim, it was not impossible.

"You've thought it through?" The sheikh was calm, his voice deadpan.

"I have."

"Then of course you have my blessing," Farooq said, with an air of finality that surprised even Zafir. There was no going back. Zafir caught a hint of newfound respect in his master's words—and it caused his chest to swell with pride.

"There is a small problem," Zafir said. "The boy I spoke with today has been in contact with those who wish to stop your game."

"From the West?"

Zafir gave an affirmative grunt. "There is one player in particular who bears watching. He may try and visit you. Perhaps I should return—"

"You know that would not be wise." Farooq chuckled. "We are on a strict timetable now. You have already made your testament. You have everything you need to begin your journey—including more of my trust than I reserve for any other living soul. My friend, I fear the next time we meet will be in the bosom of Allah."

"Allah willing," the Bedouin said. "But for now, let me tell you all I know of a man named Jericho. . . ."

After he finished the phone call, Zafir sighed. His master now acted as a friend. It was more than he had dreamed could ever take place. But even as he spoke of fulfilling his destiny in the United States, his satisfaction wilted, dragged down by nagging thoughts of the American whore. She would pay for what she had done. Zafir consoled himself with the fact that he would be the one to exact that payment very, very soon.

CHAPTER 25

Fort Worth

"So," Carrie Navarro said, popping her hands against the thighs of faded jeans and leaning back in the soft cushions of the leather sofa. "Here we are again. Think it's worth another go?"

"If you're ready," Dr. Soto said, smiling serenely.

"I'll never be ready," Navarro scoffed, pushing a lock of dark hair out of her eyes. "But I trust you, Doc. If you say I need to watch myself go through this again, then I'll do it. Some hajji bastard's not gonna get the better of me."

"Very well," Soto said. "Close your eyes and relax. Let your mind wander freely. I'm going to count to ten. . . ."

"Where are you now?" Soto asked a minute later.

"Some shithole outside Baquba." Navarro's eyelids twitched.

"Carrie, I'm still detecting a lot of anger from you," Soto said. "I need you to detach—"

Eyelids closed but fluttering heavily, Navarro laughed at that. "I love you, Doc, but that's not gonna happen. Let someone yank out a toenail and come around every few hours and rape you . . . then see how much you can detach. . . ."

"Okay, Carrie," Soto said. "Calm down, sweetheart. If this is too difficult for you, we should wait until a better time—"

"There's never gonna be a good time to go through that kind of hell, Dr. Soto," Navarro whispered. Tears pressed between dark, clenched lashes. "I said I trust you and I do. Besides, I've got more to worry about that just myself here." She clutched her knees until her knuckles turned white. "So, let's do this thing. . . ."

Chibernat Village, Iraq

The duct tape used to cover Carrie Navarro's eyes was crooked, revealing the tiniest swath of light along the frayed bottom edge. She awoke to find herself face-down, hands drawn together and bound cruelly behind her back. Shoulder blades pinned together like a trussed bird, her entire body was one raw bruise. Her head was on fire and her feet felt as if they'd been beaten with a pipe. She tried to move her aching jaw but found it impossible because of a thick cloth gag that held her mouth in an agonizing half-open position. A swollen tongue did little to salve her cracked lips.

Wincing from the shooting pain in her head, she rolled up on one side enough to peer around the concrete cell through the narrow slit in the tape. The rough tile floor was awash in blood and urine. The sudden realization that the odor around her was the smell of her own filth sent her stomach reeling. She had no idea how long she'd been unconscious, but judging from her cramped muscles, she assumed it had been a while.

The squealing metal creak of a heavy door caused her to catch her breath. She pressed her cheek back to the cool stickiness of the floor, watching heavy black boots approach across the tile. A bucket of icy water drove a scream from her lungs.

"Good," someone chuckled in accented English. It was a man's voice, full of contempt. "You are awake." Another bucket of frigid water followed.

Carrie cringed in shock, wriggling away until her back hit a wall. She tried to scream, but with the cruel gag could muster only a pitiful gurgle. She peered through the gap in the tape as the black boots approached her again. A bronze hand, little more than a claw, missing all but a thumb and forefinger, reached toward her face.

"I will now untie you," the voice said. "Clean yourself at once." He might as well have been giving commands to a dog.

He removed the gag first, then without warning he ripped the tape from Carrie's eyes, yanking out her eyebrows and most of her lashes in the process.

"Son of a bitch!" she screamed, moving her jaw back and forth now that it was free.

"You have a fire," the man said. He was tall, with a mussed beard and a wild mane of long, black hair that matched his sullen eyes. "I have yet to decide if that pleases me."

She recognized him as the man who'd pulled out at least two of her toenails with a pair of pliers upon her arrival, tormenting her until she'd passed out.

As Carrie's eyes became accustomed to the stark white light of her cell, she saw two more buckets of water, along with a towel and a coarse bar of gray soap. Three other bearded men stood leering in the open doorway.

As usual, Carrie let her temper get the better of her.

"Afraid you can't handle me all by yourself?" She rolled to a sitting position and dipped her head toward the door. "Is that why you brought your creepy little friends?"

"Oh, rest assured, little dog. I can handle you fine all alone." The man punctuated his words with a swift kick that caught her square in the joint of her hip.

Carrie gasped as waves of pain and nausea engulfed her. "Bastard!" she spat, coughing until she gagged.

The man scratched at his beard, smoothed it, thinking for a moment, then kicked her again. "I know the meaning of these words you use," he said. "You will soon learn better than to call Zafir such names. You may call me a great many things—your master or your tormentor . . ." He smiled. ". . . even your lover. But you must keep a civil tongue in your mouth or I would be most happy to tear it out by the root. And I assure you, in my country, this is no empty threat."

Carrie swallowed hard, trying to regain her composure. It was amazing how pain cleared the cobwebs from her muddled mind. It was as if she could see the pure evil that made up the man standing in front of her.

"How about some privacy while I wash?" she said, rubbing her wrists. "I thought you Arab men were all about covering your women."

Zafir sneered. "That particular nicety is reserved for pious Muslim women. The way you dress in your tight pants and transparent shirt, you may as well be naked at all times. Surely a man can not be blamed when his passions are inflamed around a woman of such wanton behaviors." He threw her a tattered cotton rag. "Now, I will not tell you again so nicely. Clean yourself at once."

Though every muscle screamed at the slightest movement, Carrie resolved then and there that this man would not witness her pain, no matter what he did to her. She rose up on both feet. Wobbly at first, she used the wall to steady herself. It took all her strength just to put her weight on one foot and peel off her soaked khakis. Defiantly, she dropped her filthy underwear to her ankles and kicked them toward the door where the three wide-eyed guards ogled her. She pulled her shirt over her head to find that her bra was already missing. Deep purple lines covered her left breast. Raw bruises blotched her hips and legs.

Concentrating to control her breathing, she strode past Zafir to the two waiting buckets, where she scrubbed herself with the rough soap before pouring the contents of each over her head. This water was warm so she assumed he actually wanted her clean. It sickened her to think why.

Scrubbed pink, she stood naked in front of Zafir letting her arms dangle, unwilling even to fold them lest he think she felt the need to cover herself. She had nothing to be ashamed of. This was his doing, not hers.

"There now." He licked his lips as he took a step closer to her. "Things are much different after one has bathed. Don't you think?"

Carrie shrugged. "I'm not covered in blood and piss, if that's what you mean. But you are still a bastard."

Zafir doubled his fist and hit her hard in the mouth, knocking her against the wall and loosening her front teeth.

He knelt beside her, clawing at her injured breast with his gnarled hand. "You sing like a whipsaw for now," he said. "Let us see how you sound after I have spent some time teaching you. . . ."

Left with nothing to cover herself but a thin cotton shift, Carrie found herself hounded and pestered by the man at least twice a day. She was bound hand and foot almost constantly, freed only when allowed to relieve herself and wolf down a few hasty mouthfuls of bland rice to give her energy before he came to visit.

Early on, a younger guard, barely in his twenties, had thought to spend some time with her. He'd snuck in and promised her he would bring her some extra food if she was nice to him. Zafir caught them before the naïve boy had even begun. Carrie passed out from the beating, but she never saw the boy again.

Days turned into weeks, which melted into months, until she lost all track of time and space. Her only world was a bit of rice and the constant raw anguish of knowing that any echo in the hallway outside her door meant a visit from Zafir. And those visits never failed to bring pain.

She learned his triggers, gauging his moods by the way he approached her, the way he held his crooked mouth. He alternated between the brutality he considered intimate and bouts of unbridled rage, dragging her naked from one end of his bedroom to the other by her rapidly thinning hair.

At first, she'd thought to placate him, to stop the kicking and ease the pain, but she soon found that no matter how hard she tried, her conscience wouldn't allow it. In the end, she merely defied him no matter his mood and let him choose if he wanted to rape her or beat her. More often than not, he did both.

Each and every time, when he was finished and still panting, she looked into his black eyes and called him a bastard.

Carrie had no way of judging how much time had passed. She'd lost a tremendous amount of weight. Her bones jutted out like an inmate in a concentration camp. Her hair was beginning to fall out in clumps, and though she had no mirror, she couldn't imagine he'd want to keep her around much longer. Every day she asked herself if fighting back was worth it. Every day she struggled to make peace with the fact that she'd never see her mother again, that her last sight on earth was the snarling face of Zafir Jawad.

Just when she'd decided to stop fighting and resigned herself to death at the hands of this sadistic madman, something inside her changed. One night, alone in the dark on the cold tile floor, with no sound but the constant echoing drip of her latrine drain in the corner, she lay on her coarse mat of quilts and decided she wanted desperately to go on living. She couldn't put a finger on why, after so many weeks of hopelessness, and couldn't help but wonder if the feeling was fate's way of telling her death was just around the corner.

Zafir didn't visit that morning or anytime that day. One of her guards slid an extra helping of stale rice and a fatty bit of lamb under her cell door. For the first time she could remember, she squatted on the floor and ate in a sort of relative, flinchy peace. Every evening for the next week she ate the extra food her unseen guards provided, then curled up on her rags and spent a shivering night, waiting. She dreamed alternately that Zafir had come to her again or that he had died a brutal death. Each time she awoke, her stomach knotted in fear and she had to crawl to her latrine hole in the corner to vomit away the tension of anticipation.

At dawn of the sixth day of what she began to call her awakening, the staccato sound of gunfire popped outside her room. Loud booms echoed from the cavernous hallway, sending showers of dust skittering down concrete walls. Carrie drew herself into a tight ball on her mat, thinking that at any moment, she would become the victim of a stray bomb. She'd heard American planes overhead many times before. Sometimes they dropped their ordnance nearby, but none had ever ventured this close.

Mortars whumped and whistled in from nearby positions. Grenades exploded for what seemed like an eternity, bending the walls and showering the room in dust. Then she heard voices, American voices rich with New York accents and twangy Southern drawls. Her eyes filled with tears when the door flew off its hinges and five American soldiers in full battle gear filed in to the room.

The men looked like camouflaged giants in their helmets and flak vests. The entire line froze in their tracks when they saw her.

Carrie looked up weakly from her quilts. She blinked her battle-worn eyes at these beautiful men in disbelief. "I hope you kicked some Iraqi ass," she croaked through chapped, swollen lips.

"You bet we did, ma'am." A slender soldier whose name tag read CARTER winked. He handed his rifle to the man beside him and shrugged out of his flak jacket long enough to remove his uniform tunic and drape it tenderly around Carrie's trembling shoulders. She'd forgotten how little her flimsy cotton sheet actually covered.

Specialist Carter knelt beside her, taking her gently by the hand. "Ma'am, are you able to walk?" he said in a rough-hewn Southern voice.

"Are you from Texas?" she asked.

"Wichita Falls," Carter nodded.

"Wichita Falls . . ." She began to sob.

"If you'll come with us"—Carter helped her gently to her feet—"we'll get you out of this place."

The shooting had stopped by the time the soldiers escorted Carrie outside. Two Army medics tried to put her on a stretcher, but she refused, opting instead to leave her horrible prison as she thought she never would—alive and on her own swollen feet. As she stepped from the shadows of her prison into the long rays of early morning sunshine, to draw her first breath of fresh air in over three months, she noticed an open CutVee truck with a bed full of handcuffed Iraqi men. To her surprise, one of the prisoners was Zafir. He slouched in the back, pitiful and beaten, surrounded by his comrades and trussed just as he had trussed her with his hands behind his back.

As she walked to her waiting armored Humvee, Carrie veered away, making straight for the truck. Specialist Carter reached to stop her, but she pulled away, stepping out of the camouflage tunic to stand boldly and nearly naked beside the prisoner transport. The morning breeze pressed the thin sheet against her breasts and the jutting bones of her hips. A huge orange sun rested on the desert floor behind her, marking the starkness of her silhouette.

"Hey, bastard!" she shouted in a hoarse croak, loud enough the entire compound could hear. "Yeah, I'm talking to you, Zafir." Tears streamed down hollow cheeks as she strode closer to spit in the Bedouin's face. "You think you can conquer me with that teeny little thing you call your manhood? You think you can beat me down with a few weak kicks, you piece of camel shit!"

Zafir stared at his feet, red-faced, fuming. The other men in the truck snickered under their breath; one even went so far as to elbow him in the shoulder.

"Well, I got news for you, mister," Carrie continued her rant. "You couldn't conquer a roach. It's no wonder you had to keep a slave. No good Arab woman would take you to her bed without a few kicks to the head." Carrie leaned in, but kept her voice elevated so no one would miss a word. "You only did one thing like a real man this whole time I've been here." She stepped back and pulled the tattered sheet up to reveal her swollen naked belly. "I'm gonna have a baby, you son of a bitch—your baby. And guess what, if you haven't killed him from kicking the hell out of me every day, he'll never know what Islam is! I'll raise him to fight your kind. In fact . . ." She leaned closer to spit again, her voice rising to a screeching crescendo. "I'm gonna name him Christian!"

Dr. Soto dabbed a tear from her eye and sniffed. She set her notepad on the coffee table in front of her. Carrie's chest heaved as if she'd just finished a grueling foot race. Her hands lay motionless in her lap. The corners of her lips glistened, perked into the hint of a smile.

"What ever happened to Zafir Jawad?" Soto asked.

"I'm not sure," Carrie said. "I heard he escaped before they could transfer him to a prison in Baghdad. But I also heard he was killed in another firefight with U.S. forces. Who knows? He's dead to me."

"That's my girl." Soto smiled. "We'll not ever let that man control you again."

"Damn straight," Carrie said. "Never again . . ."

CHAPTER 26

Huwaidah came to an abrupt stop on the concrete walk under the thatch of a date palm, taking advantage of the sparse shade. Without speaking she dipped her head slightly toward a white, concrete building across a wheat field roughly three hundred meters behind the veterinary hospital of King Faisal University. The building was surrounded by pastures, kept verdant by the oasis of Al-Hofuf. Beyond it lay miles of date orchards and pasture lands full of grazing horses, goats, and camels. A complex of barns, not nearly as large as those of the university, jutted off one end of the building. Arabian horses nibbled hay under wooden awnings in the middle of their paddocks, built to provide them shelter from the desert sun.

Huwaidah had been able to repair her abaya so only the most inquisitive observer would notice it had been torn. Since none of the male students would dare let their eyes linger on her, she was relatively safe for the moment. She made the motions of looking for some-

thing in her handbag, averting her eyes from Quinn.
Since they were unrelated members of the opposite
sex—as well as accomplices in the killing of the Mutawwa'in—it was best they not be seen conversing in
public.

"That is the building you seek," she whispered. "I
believe it to be a place of great evil. As you say . . . an
abomination in the sight of Allah."

Jericho let his eyes play around the campus. Students were beginning to move now between classes.
Though King Faisal University prided itself on offering an education to women, the lack of female students
walking the red tile paths was sobering. The crowds of
men wore the red checked *ghutra* headdress and the
ubiquitous white Saudi gown known as a *thobe* in the
Kingdom. Only a handful of women moved between
the somber buildings, always separate from the men,
all covered from head to toe in formless black abayas.

Too much salt, not enough pepper, Quinn thought.

Jericho shooed Huwaidah away with the flick of his
hand. It was too dangerous for her to loiter nearby. He
had no way of knowing if the skinny-minded Tawfiq
hadn't marched straight to the authorities. He would
have to hope the threat of a lash or even the boy's own
beheading for his part in the killings might dissuade
Tawfiq from talking. It couldn't be helped.

Alone now, Quinn stood in the shade of the date
palm for a long while, making notes in a small Moleskine notebook while he studied the building in front
of him, considering his options. Everyone took notes
on a college campus, so passersby didn't give him a
second look.

The northernmost set of stables was connected to the main building by a covered walkway of arched stucco, to provide shade between the barn and Farooq's lab. The horses would, at the very least, give Quinn some plausible excuse for being in the area.

Ten minutes later, he found himself alone as he loafed outside the paddocks. He leaned against the pipe fencing and rested the sole of his dusty shoe on the bottom rail. He didn't have to pretend to admire a dapple gray mare with an almost feline arch to her graceful neck while he scanned the area for surveillance equipment. He spotted two cameras immediately, one tucked under the eaves of the main barn, the other on a post beside the covered walkway leading to the main building that he was sure held Farooq's lab. He saw no cameras around the building itself, but felt sure they were there. A place that manufactured biotoxins capable of killing jumbo jets full of people would be bristling with security, even in a country as insulated as the Saudi Kingdom.

In fact, Quinn was counting on it.

When no guards approached him by the paddocks, he decided to explore the barns. In the shade and relative comfort of the alleyway, Quinn found a red Farmall tractor. It was old, flaking with rust, and had been repainted with several cans of spray paint. A quick check behind the tractor revealed a storage closet with another small acetylene cutting torch and several sacks of grass seed. Bags of fertilizer—their main ingredient ammonium nitrate—were stacked head high against the back wall. Quinn grinned at that, thinking of the iodine crystals in the pocket of his *dishdasha*. Al-Hofuf was situated on the Al-Ahsa oasis, the largest in the world. Though the King Faisal campus itself was dry and dusty, lush fields sprawled for acres to the north and east. The sweet scent of timothy hay and ripening wheat hung heavy on the superheated air.

Jericho had his head in the doorway of the storage room when the first guard approached him from behind.

"I do not know you," the man challenged, ordering Quinn to back out of the room. He was young, no older than thirty, and wore a wrinkled white shirt and khaki pants instead of the traditional *thobe*. "What is your business here?"

"I have come to purchase a horse for my farm near Kuwait City," Quinn said, the Arabic rolling off his tongue like a native. He reached into the pocket of his *dishdasha*. "I have a letter of introduction from Mr. Othman."

"Stop!" The guard raised a stubby revolver that looked as if it hadn't been fired or cleaned for some years. Still, Quinn saw no reason to test it—for the moment.

"Please forgive me if I have done something wrong." He let his eyes play up and down the shadowed barn, acting frightened to put the young guard at ease. He was certain the man wasn't alone. *See one; think two*—the mantra had kept him alive more than once over the years.

Moments later another guard stepped from the shadows of a nearby stall, proving Quinn's suspicions correct. This was the senior of the two, pushing fifty with salt-and-pepper hair, a bulbous, sneering nose and deep-set eyes that challenged and accused everything before them. He wore the same uniform of his partner but appeared to have little of his patience.

"Your name?" he shouted in a tight-throated squawk. Flecks of spit popped from chapped lips at each word. This man had a pistol of his own, a black semiauto Jericho recognized as a Beretta nine millimeter. It looked to be in much more functional condition than the revolver. "Tell me your name!"

If he was to be shot, this would be the one to shoot him. Quinn had no doubt about that. But his demeanor was jumpy, weak. An overly loud voice said he was unsure of himself. That made him at once dangerous and vulnerable. In any battle situation, Quinn subconsciously sorted adversaries in order of possible lethality and weakness—a kind of target progression. The yelling spitter had just earned the number-one spot.

"I am from Kuwait City," Quinn stammered in halting Arabic, hoping it made him sound more frightened than foreign. "My name is Al Dashti. I have a letter from Mr. Othman to look at your horses—"

"I know of no Othman," the spitter said.

The younger guard looked at his partner. "Ramzi Othman," he said. "He sees to the stables for the university."

Quinn nodded. "As I said." He pointed to his pocket. "I have a letter."

"Shut up. You are not in the university stables. You are on private property. We have nothing to do with any Othman or the school. We have no horses to sell to anyone from Kuwait and have no need of any letter."

"Very well." Quinn began to lower his hands. "I apologize for my stupidity and will be on my way."

The older guard motioned with his shiny Beretta, shoving it forward to make a point. "Keep your hands raised." A radio at his side broke squelch. He looked at his partner. "Answer that," he said, apparently not trusting the younger man or his rusty revolver to cover the intruder.

The young guard took the radio from his own belt and checked in. "*Shako mako?*" It was the Arabic equivalent of *What's up?*

"Apologize and bring him inside," a disembodied voice said. "I would like to see his letter."

The guards looked at each other and shrugged. They started to put away their weapons, but the radios squawked again. "Apologize, but do not trust him!"

The older guard frowned at the chiding. He pointed his pistol toward the sunlit opening at the end of the barn's alley. Quinn smiled faintly to himself. Guns or no guns, these men had solved his number-one problem. They were taking him past any security systems and inside the building—right where he wanted to be.

CHAPTER 27

Past the double steel doors, a lone security guard kept watch at a simple wooden desk. He was middle-aged with a neatly trimmed goatee and dressed in the same khaki pants and open-collared white shirt as the two others. Quinn could see no weapon, but assumed he had one tucked away somewhere.

The desk guard glanced up from a crumpled copy of an Al Jazeera newspaper and acknowledged the other men with a grunt. Dark eyes played over Quinn with unconcealed disgust. As Saudis, it was a good bet these men all harbored decades-old tribal grudges against Kuwaitis. Fortunately, they didn't know who Quinn really was. Their grudges against Irish American Apaches were sure to run even deeper.

Fluorescent lights threw a strident glare on the waxed white tile of the hallway. Twenty feet beyond the guard was another set of heavy doors, ornately carved from fine, polished wood. They had no handles and appeared to swing freely.

Other than these and the way he'd come in, the only other exit off the wide hallway was a gray metal door to the left, just past the desk guard. To find out what was on the other side of the blank wall to the right, Quinn would have to make it through the double wooden doors.

"In there." The older, jumpy guard prodded Quinn over the kidney with the muzzle of his pistol, shoving him toward the left.

Quinn took a deep breath to keep from smiling. This one was truly an amateur. No real operator would get close enough to touch him with a weapon.

The professional arrived a moment later as Quinn's captors prodded him into the vacant concrete-block room. Quinn recognized him for what he was immediately—not the top boss, but someone with the authority to make decisions on the spot. He was mature, but not old—maybe in his late thirties—with the confident air that made him keep his chin tilted slightly toward the ceiling and hung a constant half grin on his angular face. His dazzling white cotton robe blended with the whitewashed walls. A red checked *ghutra* only half hid a thick head of curly black hair. A gold Rolex Explorer hung from his bronze wrist.

The man looked down his nose at Quinn with the kind of bored indifference he might reserve for a stray dog.

"Hello, Mr. Al Dashti—"

"Al Dashti," Quinn corrected.

"Yes," the man said. "Of course, Mr. Al Dashti. I am Dr. Suleiman, the chief veterinarian here." He held out a manicured right hand, all but snapping his fingers. "Please, the letter of which you spoke."

Quinn reached in the fold of his *dishdasha*, wishing

he had the Masamune blade Mrs. Miyagi had given him. Whatever was going on in this lab, the chief veterinarian had to be up to his neck in it. He handed over the letter.

Suleiman read it, then paused a moment, letting his eyes slide up and down Quinn. He handed back the letter, then turned without asking a single question. At the door, he paused to speak for a moment in hushed tones to the two guards. The expressions of both men tensed. The jumpy one's shoulders bobbed noticeably at Dr. Suleiman's words. His hand slid almost imperceptibly toward the butt of his pistol.

Quinn's eyes shot around the room, taking quick stock of his situation. The heavy door, whitewashed walls, sealed concrete floor with a drain set in a depressed center—a length of hose coiled on a wall hook like a black snake.

He was in a killing cell.

Quinn was already in motion as Dr. Suleiman stepped from the room into the hallway, timing his first strike with the snick of the door snapping shut. He'd crumpled the introduction letter into a tight ball and tossed it at the older guard's face. The paper was worthless as a weapon, but the man didn't know that. He flinched instinctively jerking his gun hand up to ward off the incoming missile.

Quinn used this split-second diversion to drive the flat of his hand into the younger guard's face, shattering his nose and slamming the back of his head against the concrete wall with a sickening thwack. He slid to the ground leaving a pink smear of blood behind him.

Swelling at the back of his brain would soon stop his heart for good.

As the jumpy guard regained his composure and brought the pistol back to bear, Quinn ran at him with the weight of his entire body. He wrenched the man's wrist and the gun along with it inward toward the startled Saudi's soft belly. Tendons stretched past the breaking point; fragile wrist bones snapped with a sickening pop. His finger convulsed on the trigger. The guard's eyes flew wide as the cold reality of what had happened washed across his face.

"Killed . . ." He coughed, a tinge of blood coating his cracked lips. "Killed by . . . a stinking . . . Kuwaiti . . ."

The man died before Quinn could set him straight.

His two immediate threats neutralized, Quinn stuffed the old revolver in the folds of his *dishdasha* with his cell phone. The other pocket contained the glass jar of iodine crystals. He had to keep from breaking the glass jar at all costs. He checked the Beretta for ammunition. The magazine still held ten rounds. Years of habit and mistrust of machines made him press-check the slide to be certain there was a cartridge in the chamber. Neither guard carried any reloads. That left him with seventeen rounds including the six iffy shots in the rusty wheel gun.

Quinn stood at the door for a moment, hand on the knob, concentrating to slow his breathing. He would have to make every shot count. The two men now dead on the floor had been the easy ones. Now he had to deal with the guard at the table, unknown other personnel, and Suleiman, the real professional of the group—and he'd have to do it all on camera.

CHAPTER 28

Langley Air Force Base
Virgina

Megan Mahoney had never considered herself a worrywart. Working nose to nose with deadly diseases took ice-cold nerves not to mention a certain amount of stoic detachment—but, lately, it seemed that worrying was all she ever did. Gory images of four hundred Ebola-infected airline passengers haunted her dreams. Nagging thoughts of a virus capable of wiping out half the continent kept her stomach in knots, and she found herself eating nothing but junk food. Justin, for all his idiotic flirtation, didn't deserve to be stuck in the Slammer. But he was, and now the poor kid sat with nothing to do but wait and wonder if the tiny needle stick had been enough to infect him with an unknown strain of hemorrhagic fever—enough to kill him.

The Ebola blood variant had jumped almost immediately from one macaque to another breathing the same air. Both had crashed in a matter of hours. It had been two days since she'd had to put down C-45 and injected C-06 with the virus strain contained in the optic jelly. Though the monkey's blood teamed with spaghettilike filovirus it had yet to show a single symptom. Tests on C-12, the macaque she'd put in the adjoining cage, breathing the same air as C-06, remained virus free.

Science was, more often that not, a waiting game, but when she considered what would happen if an Ebola variant escaped into the U.S. population, she wanted to pull her hair out for lack of something positive to do.

Then a man named Winfield Palmer had called. He said he was the Director of National Intelligence and asked if he could please pile a little more on her worry plate.

Now, deep in the lush forests of Northern Virginia, behind layers of electronic and physical security, Mahoney leaned forward in a soft leather office chair, her face bathed in a yellow-green glow from a series of flat-screen monitors.

Beside her, dwarfing a similar chair, a giant of a man with a Louisiana accent had welcomed her to the team like a big brother. He wore faded jeans and a tight black T-shirt that bunched above enormous biceps. His high-and-tight haircut and stern demeanor said he would have been more comfortable in uniform. His name was Jacques Thibodaux and he fidgeted as if he was ready to bounce off the walls.

A pimple-faced Air Force staff sergeant named Guttman sat, big ears pinched between a set of cheap headphones, looking outward from the blinking panel.

His fingers worked a game controller connected to a separate laptop computer on his knees.

"Nothing yet?" Thibodaux asked

Staff Sergeant Guttmann was a prodigy, one of four Air Force enlisted personnel handpicked for their extraordinary hand-eye coordination and almost super-human computer gaming skills to pioneer the advance-ment of a very specific unmanned aerial vehicle, or UAV. Above his head, in ornate golden script was a three-foot blue banner with the motto of his secret unit, Detachment Seven of the Fifty-third Test and Evalua-tion Group: HIC SUNT DRACONES

Here there be dragons. It was the inscription on me-dieval maps for sections of uncharted sea.

"No contact from your friend, sir," Guttmann said. His voice cracked as he spoke, making Mahoney won-der just how old he really was. "I did, however, just take out a Nazi field marshal and two of his zombie underlings using a World War II–era grease gun with extreme skill."

Mahoney wrinkled her nose. These military types were so hard to understand. She shot a look at the Cajun. "Zombies?"

Thibodaux shook his head, muttering under his breath. "This damned multitaskin' generation. While he should be tending to the business of looking out for Jericho, he's playin' Call of Duty—a computer game with Nazis of the living dead or some such thing. My boys love it."

"What's not to love?" Guttman smiled. "Who wouldn't get a kick out of killing Nazi zombies? A bunch of guys in my squadron play all the—"

"You know, Guttman," Thibodaux said, rubbing his jaw with a hand the size of a pie pan. "I got a friend out there, all by his lonesome self in parts unknown, facing some real-life shit that would make your zombie games look like a *Scooby-Doo* cartoon. You might consider showing some attention to your duties at hand."

Guttman, flustered, snapped his personal laptop shut without another word. He glanced at Mahoney, blushing like a schoolboy taken to task in front of a pretty girl.

Thibodaux rose quickly from his chair and strode to the large wall map of the Middle East. He tapped the tiny red dot with a forefinger the size of a sausage between Riyadh and the Persian Gulf. Al-Hofuf, Saudi Arabia.

"Can your bird use its cameras to zoom in or something so we can see how he is? I don't know . . . infrared maybe, like on those Tom Clancy movies."

Guttman sighed, seemingly relieved Thibodaux had decided not to chop his head off. "Sorry, sir. No can do. If Damo was a conventional drone buzzing over a third world country with little in the way of defense we'd be able to get some images. Saudi Arabia would shoot one of those down in a heartbeat. But she doesn't work that way. She floats around up there in stealth mode, out of the picture and out of radar contact— until we need her."

Damo was a new and highly classified UAV. Far beyond the Predator and Reaper drones being used to run recon missions blasting away at insurgent compounds from Kirkuk to the wild and wooly Frontier Provinces of Pakistan, Damo was not supposed to be anything but a few sketches on a Northrop Grumman engineer's drawing board. Three generations past the officially still experimental X47B Pegasus, the U.S. Navy's aircraft carrier launch-capable Unmanned Combat Air System, Guttman's UCAS, was more properly known as the AX7 Damocles. Particularly useful for its ability to loiter unnoticed above an enemy for long periods of time, Damocles could be suspended overhead, ready to strike like the mythic sword hanging by a horse hair. In reality, it had been in operation for well over a year, based out of Eglin Air Force Base in Florida.

Though most UAVs were piloted by officers, the AX7 was launched from the back of a Boeing 747—out of sight of snooping eyes and video cameras—and then controlled by a new generation of gamers from the enlisted ranks whose proficiency test scores had been off the charts. In the hands of a skilled computer dweeb with the right equipment, Damocles could be controlled from anywhere in the world.

Staff Sergeant Guttman was the king of computer dweebs. He checked the systems monitor, touching the screen with a plastic stylus, then made a note on his clipboard.

"I don't know what your friend is out there looking for. That's way above my pay grade, but I can only bring Damo down and into the open if I get the order from that phone." He nodded toward a black handset on the stainless counter beside his joystick and stylus. "If I get the order, Damo is armed with four Tomahawks. But until that phone rings, I can't . . ."

Thibodaux raised his big hand. "We get it, kid. Why don't you just chill and kill some more Nazi zombies. . . ."

Megan stood to go look at the map, to do something, anything but sit and wait.

Then the black phone on Guttman's desk began to ring.

CHAPTER 29

If given the choice, Quinn preferred quick, decisive movement over a lengthy deliberation. It allowed him the freedom to respond to gut feelings. More times than not, such action gave him the clear advantage. There was no doubt Dr. Suleiman had heard the pistol shot from outside the killing room. It was, after all, the fitting conclusion of his execution order. Jericho knew Suleiman was the professional, the one he would have to kill first, but when he sprang into the hall the chief veterinarian was gone.

The desk guard was on his feet, looking toward the double doors. Quinn put a quick double tap between his running lights. The startled man hardly had time to look up. His body spun to the ground in the particular corkscrew fashion of one who is brain dead before they fall.

Without a pause, Jericho rushed for the doors.

Dr. Suleiman met him in a head-on attack, crashing into him with the full weight of his body. The veterinarian was well groomed, but he knew how to fight. He smashed down with both fists in a well-delivered haymaker that sent the pistol skittering across the dimly lit room and out of reach.

Jericho crouched, springing forward like a lineman, using the strength of his legs to drive the Arab backward with the point of his shoulder toward a white marble support column. Flailing out with both hands, Suleiman dragged a tapestry off the wall, bringing the heavy woolen rug down on top of both men. Quinn rolled away, struggling to push free from the tangle of thick cloth. When he got to his feet, he saw a smiling Suleiman holding the thick dowel that had been used to support the tapestry. Five feet long and an inch in diameter, the wooden staff made a formidable weapon in the hands of someone who knew how to use it.

"I do not know who you are," Suleiman panted, a fleck of spittle forming at the corners of his twisted mouth. "But I think you are no Kuwaiti horse buyer. . . ."

Quinn stood facing him, slightly bent at the waist, arms loose at his sides, body quartered away. "I am a messenger," he said in Arabic.

Suleiman raised an eyebrow, dropping his shoulder slightly. "What sort of messenger?"

Feinting with his left hand, Quinn drew Suleiman into a rushed attack. Rolling past the first blow, he caught the doctor on the point of his chin with a brutal upward strike from his elbow. Stunned, Suleiman let go of the staff with one hand but kept a death grip with the other, letting the end hit the ground. Quinn grabbed the man's fist, and stomped hard on the angled wood, snapping the staff in the middle. The jarring shock caused

Suleiman to release his hold on what was left of the weapon.

Quinn grabbed the wooden shard before it could hit the ground. It was two feet long and incredibly sharp on the broken end. Spinning, he drove the splintered point through the startled man's neck so it came out each side like the handlebars on a motorcycle.

"That sort of messenger," Quinn said.

Suleiman no longer a threat, Quinn was met by an empty marble room. Somewhere to his left, he could just make out the soft, eerie whirring of exhaust fans.

Where the building entrance had been sparse and utilitarian, the inner portion was palatial, complete with marble floors and stone pillars. More heavy Arab tapestries of rich maroon and gold draped stucco walls. A long, low table of rich mahogany surrounded by ornate brocade throw pillows occupied the middle of the vacant chamber. Quinn's footsteps echoed off the arched ceiling, twenty feet above his head. A chessboard sat at the end of the low table. Squat pieces, testaments to Islam's prohibition against statues of living creatures, sat lined up on the board and ready for play.

Quinn retrieved the Beretta from the floor and held it in tight against his waist. He scanned the room, searching for any sign of Farooq or his operation. It was a lonely but familiar feeling to be in such a hostile environment thousands of miles from home . . . wherever that was.

The whirring of the fans suddenly grew louder, as if a compressor had kicked on. One of the heavy, floor-to-ceiling plum-colored drapes directly across from the low table rustled slightly, jostled by an unseen wind as if a door had opened on the other side. Quinn prepared himself for an attack, but the movement turned out to be caused by an air intake located in the marble tile behind it.

Closer inspection revealed a glass window on the other side of the curtain. When he drew the heavy cloth to one side, his breath froze in his chest. His free hand slid into the pocket of his *dishdasha*.

CHAPTER 30

Mahoney pursed her lips. She'd never met this Jericho Quinn but could tell from Thibodaux's demeanor he was a good man in serious danger.

The baby-faced staff sergeant spoke into the phone for a quick moment, then pressed the hands-free button on the device.

"Damo's got you on a shadow relay, sir—running your voice in encrypted laser bursts," Guttman explained over the line. "The Saudis won't even know we're talking unless they happen to walk in on you."

There was silence on the speaker. Guttman turned back to the phone. "You still there, sir?"

"I'm here." The voice was surprisingly clear considering the fact that it had to travel from a cell phone no bigger than a pack of playing cards to a drone twenty-seven miles above the earth before being rebroadcast back to Langley. "How do you read me?"

"You're comin' in slurred and stupid, as usual, beb," Thibodaux laughed, breathing an audible sigh of relief to hear his friend's voice.

"Glad to hear it," Quinn came back. "Listen, has the boss gotten hold of that plague doctor yet?"

"She's sittin' right beside me," Thibodaux said.

Megan leaned toward the phone out of habit, as if closing the gap another few inches might make it a little easier for her voice to travel thousands of miles. "Megan Mahoney with the CDC."

"I'm looking at some pretty bad stuff here, Doctor."

"Can you describe it?"

"Roger that," the voice said. "I've got what looks like two airtight rooms behind glass observation windows. The rooms are divided down the middle.... That wall looks to be airtight as well, but I can't be sure from where I'm at. They're set up like hospital wards but—" Quinn's voice stopped abruptly.

Mahoney opened her mouth to say something, but the big Cajun held up his hand to shush her.

"He could be handling . . . a problem," Thibodaux whispered. "He stops talking, we stop talking.

There was a muffled pop on the line that reminded Megan of a large metal pan being dropped to the ground. Garbled voices followed, and then two more pops in quick succession.

Quinn came back on the line, calm as if he'd just gone to answer the door. "Had a couple of visitors," he said simply. "I could sure use your help, Jacques. They keep popping up every time I try to get the job done."

"I wish I was there, *l'ami*," Thibodaux said. "I hate sittin' on my thumbs stateside while you get to play World of Warcraft with the bad guys."

"Dr. Mahoney." Quinn's voice was somber again. "I'm thinking this is some kind of a test facility where they could watch their experiments with the disease progress. No one has tended to the people in these rooms for quite a while. It looks like a horror movie in there. The sheets are filthy . . . blood everywhere."

"How many?" Mahoney heard herself ask. She had seen Ebola wards firsthand in Africa and could imagine what the rooms looked like.

"Five," Quinn said. "It's hard to say, but I'm pretty sure three are Americans . . . some of our missing soldiers. I think one of them is dead already. . . ." The unmistakable sound of a sniff came across the line. "There's a little girl in there . . . maybe seven years old. She's still moving, but I think the woman next to her is dead. . . . Anything I can do to help her, Doc? Could I put on a mask or something and go in there?"

There was an earnest goodness in the voice that stopped Mahoney's heart in her chest. To be sent on this sort of mission, he had to be a capable and dangerous man. She hadn't expected any semblance of mercy.

She looked helplessly at Thibodaux.

"He's got a little daughter of his own," the Cajun whispered. "He'd never say it, but it kills him to be away from her."

Mahoney nodded, understanding. Her jaw set in a firm line. "Listen to me," she said. "This is going to be hard. . . ." Her voice caught as she imagined this man, this father, standing on one side of a filthy glass window, separating him by mere inches from a child in unimaginable agony. She took a deliberate breath and plowed ahead, staring at the floor, unable to look Thibodaux in the eye. "It's a horrible thing . . . but you've got to leave her in there. From what we know so far, these poor souls are infected with a highly contagious, airborne variant of a hemorrhagic virus. If it were to get out, thousands . . . hundreds of thousands would die. You must not go anywhere near them, mask or no mask."

Mahoney's eyes welled with tears. She hated to cry in front of people, fearing they might see it as a sign of weakness. A look at both Thibodaux and Guttman's glistening eyes showed her she had nothing to worry about in that regard. That didn't make what she had to do any easier. Though a death sentence had been pronounced on the victims in the lab long before her conversation with Jericho Quinn, she was the one pushing for a fast execution. She tried to console herself with the tired rationale that such an end would be more humane, but the grim truth was that such humanity didn't matter. The virus could not be allowed to escape the confines of that lab.

"Your only option is to destroy that place." She shivered as she said the words. "Believe me, it's the kindest thing you could do for the child."

"I hear you, Doctor." Quinn's voice came across the speaker again, full of composure now. "Jacques, get Palmer on the line. Let him know I've got three photographs for him. I'll send them your way as soon as I get to a pickup point."

"Roger that," Thibodaux said, raising a dark eyebrow. "Photographs?"

"Yeah," Quinn said. "Head shots, like these guys make when they prepare their last will and testament . . . right before they strap on a vest full of nails and explosives—martyr portraits. There were five of them, but

I've taken care of two of the problems since I came to the lab. . . ."

"You have names?" Thibodaux asked

"Afraid not," Quinn said. "Just photos. But I also have a small case, about the size of a box of rifle ammo. Looks like it's supposed to hold twenty glass vials about two inches long each. There are only seventeen left in the case and they're all empty. Don't know about the other three. . . ."

Guttmann's mouth fell open. "You think the three people in your martyr photos are bringing that virus to the U.S. in those vials?"

Mahoney ignored the young sergeant. "Can you give me a better description of the vials?" she said.

"Glass . . . maybe a hard plastic . . . clear . . . about the size of a tube of lipstick. Each vial has an inner glass container, slightly smaller, that fits inside the larger. Both have screw-on tops with rubber seals."

"You could get a hell of a lot of virus in a vial that size," Thibodaux mused. "Couldn't you, Doc?"

Mahoney nodded slowly, making some notes as she spoke. "Depending on the culture medium you'd need to keep it viable, enough to infect thousands—maybe more."

"That settles it," Thibodaux said, smacking his huge hand on the table. "Jericho, get the hell out of there and let us blow that place to kingdom come."

Guttmann stepped in front of his control panel, guarding it. "I can't . . . I mean . . . I couldn't fire the Tomahawks without permission," he stammered. "I'd need authorization for that from way higher up than you. This is only supposed to be a surveillance op. . . ."

"He's right," Quinn said. "A missile would destroy the place but start a war with the Saudis at the same time. If we destroy the evidence they'll have a hard time buying off on our claims of a deadly virus. Besides, I still haven't found Farooq. Give me an hour. That'll give you time to get your permission. In the meantime, I have an idea that might solve our problem. If you don't hear from me in an hour and five minutes, bring your little buddy out of orbit and zap us to Hell."

"Okay, *l'ami*," Thibodaux sighed. "An hour and five it is, but be sure to give yourself plenty of time to scoot out of there. I'm afraid Mrs. Miyagi will take away my new toys if you get yourself killed. I'm getting' sorta attached to that Beemer." His words were frivolous, but his face was creased in worry. He leaned forward against the counter, resting his face in his big hands. "No shit, Jericho. Be careful."

"I'll talk to you again in an hour."

"Roger that," Thibodaux said, straightening up with a groan. "I'll call Palmer."

Mahoney paced to the map as the line went dead. She put her finger on the small dot over the oasis city of Al-Hofuf.

"Here there be dragons," she whispered to herself.

Quinn stuffed the photographs inside his *dishdasha*, outside his T-shirt and facing away from his skin so he wouldn't ruin the images with sweat. He'd need them preserved as well as possible if they hoped to get any sort of ID on the terrorists that remained alive.

As he walked past the second observation window,

he noticed a black intercom box on the wall between him and the three soldiers. He almost passed it by, but one of the men stirred on a filthy cot. In his early twenties, the boy was soaked in sweat, blinded by the ravages of his disease. His name tag read MEEKS—the missing Air Force TACP from Fallujah.

Jericho pushed the button, swallowed hard before he could speak. "Sergeant Trey Meeks . . . we're here to take you home."

Meeks tried to rise, but, too weak, made do with tipping his head toward the noise. "Who's there?" His pitiful croak ripped at Quinn's heart.

"Another American . . . OSI," Quinn said, resting his head against the wall. "Hang on for a few minutes more and I'll take care of everything.

"Air Force?"

"You bet," Quinn said.

"An American," the boy sighed. Exhausted from the effort of just a few words, he fell back against his sodden cot, wracked with spasmodic coughs. When he finally calmed, he turned back toward the window and blinked serenely. Though blind and covered with unimaginable gore, the corners of his cracked lips turned up in the slightest hint of a smile. "I knew you'd come."

CHAPTER 31

Thirty-five minutes later, Jericho stacked the last fifty-pound bag of ammonium nitrate fertilizer on top of a pile as high as his chest. The barn's cramped storage room was thirty feet from the lab's outer wall, but he didn't want to risk moving explosives back and forth across the open ground. He couldn't help but chuckle at the irony of it all—an American, smack in the hotbed of Middle Eastern terrorism, manufacturing an IED—an improvised explosive device—much like the sort insurgents in Iraq and Afghanistan used to kill U.S. troops almost every day. Like the bombs they used to kill thousands in a Colorado shopping mall.

Jericho's device was far more crude. He only hoped it would be as effective.

Given time, enough foolish bravado, and the right materials, virtually anyone with access to the Internet could build a bomb. For Jericho, time was at a premium and he had to make do with the materials he had on hand.

Like Timothy McVeigh's Ryder truck that had demolished the Murrah Federal Building in Oklahoma, the main component in Quinn's explosive was ammonium nitrate. It was powerful stuff, capable of inflicting incredible damage. It was also relatively stable, needing an initial concussive blast and a fairly sizable booster to provide detonation. For that, Quinn had to bet on a little old fashioned ingenuity and a whole lot of luck.

He had roughly a ton of fertilizer—less than half of that used by McVeigh—but he hoped the dusty grain and hay loft would add to the explosion. Rummaging behind the old Farmall tractor, he was able to scrounge up three ten-gallon cans of diesel fuel. These he poured into holes he cut in three bags of fertilizer. Into the top bag, he nestled the two pony bottles from the portable oxygen-acetylene cutting torch. Detonating a bomb was a little more problematic if you wanted to live through it. For that, Jericho needed a trigger he could activate remotely.

The first thing he'd done on his arrival to the Saudi Kingdom was purchase a cell phone with a local number. Wiping the sweat from his forehead, he switched this phone to vibrate before lashing it to the neck of the oxygen tank with a short length of hay twine he found on the floor.

A search of the barn's cleaning cabinet provided the necessary ingredients to mix with the precious iodine crystals he'd swiped from the horseshoeing box. This mixture would provide his blasting cap.

Preparations for his crude bomb complete, Jericho took a deep breath and opened the bottle of purple crystals. They began to evaporate as soon as he removed the lid. Pouring the entire bottle of metallic flakes into a plastic cup, he carefully mixed in the liquids from the cleaning closet to form a slurry of purple mud the consistency of thick pancake batter. He said a little prayer of thanks that he'd had a high school chemistry teacher with enough foresight to use *The Anarchist's Cookbook* as a text. The finished product brought a smile to his face.

While it was wet, Quinn's purple mud was relatively stable. When it dried, the slightest tremor could set it off like a blasting cap. He'd watched his chemistry teacher blow a hole in a phone book by barely touching a marble-sized dab of the dried stuff with a yardstick.

Up to this point, he'd worried more about getting caught than blowing himself to pieces. Now that was about to change. In the confined, fertilizer-filled air of the storage room the tiniest spark at the wrong time would spell disaster.

Jericho began to smear the wet purple mixture over the face of the cell phone. The heat was sweltering and the edges of the mud began to lighten and dry before his eyes. He consoled himself with the fact that if someone dialed a wrong number and called his phone right then, Farooq's twisted experiments would be destroyed along with him.

Giving everything one last look, he gingerly touched the handles on the oxygen and then the acetylene bottle, giving them a twist until he heard an audible hiss from each.

Peeking out the storage room, he looked up and down the alleyway and, seeing no one in the failing light, shut the door behind him. He'd give the purple mud ten minutes to dry in the stifling heat.

Then he'd need to make a phone call.

* * *

"What do you mean he is *here*?"

Sheikh Husseini al Farooq slouched in air-conditioned comfort in the back seat of a black Lincoln Town Car limousine. Slender fingers clutched a car phone so tightly his manicured nails turned an opaque blue. His normally purring voice rose a half an octave. "I am *here*. How could such a man gain access to the Kingdom?"

"This I do not know," Zafir said on the other end of the line. "But I am sure he is there. I tried to call Dr. Suleiman, but there was no answer. Security does not pick up either. I have already sent men to check, but I beg of you, my sheikh, leave the area at once. I fear it is not safe—"

"Nonsense," Farooq cut him off. He pushed the button on his door console and the tinted window hissed down a few inches. A warm breeze hit him in the face, rich with the sweet odor of horses and new-mown hay. Farooq loved horses, the smell of them calmed him as much as a drug. "Stop worrying, my friend. I am surprised he made it this far. That is all. This is a beautiful evening. The sun sets on our beloved oasis, and, Allah willing, we are as safe as—"

The air suddenly grew thick, heavy, as if stacking up against itself. A terrific roar filled the dusky night. The limousine shook as if in the jaws of an earthquake. Alarms screeched all across the university parking lot. Grains of sand began to rain down as a black column of smoke enveloped his precious laboratory. The squeal of horses filled the void of the explosion.

Terrified Arabian horses bolted in every direction, snorting, tails flagging in blind panic. White-robed students poured from shattered glass doors and concrete buildings, surprised from their evening classes. Some stared in awe at the smoldering crater where Farooq's laboratory had once stood. Some ran after the loose horses, spurred on by anxious professors and stable hands anxious to get the expensive animals back under control before they killed themselves.

None of the horses wore halters. This, along with their crazed attitudes from the explosion, made them almost impossible to capture. Each horse had a gaggle of at least five students chasing vainly after it, ropes or feed buckets in their hands, like a pack of inefficient dogs. But, as Farooq peered over the rim of his tinted limousine window, he saw one man trotting easily beside a muscular blood bay. Both hands holding the horse's flowing mane in a firm grip, the man moved in a loping cadence alongside the prancing animal. In four quick strides, the bay surged from a trot to a canter, stretching out its neck as it changed gait and effectively yanked the man up and onto its back in one beautiful, fluid movement. In a fleeting instant, horse and rider disappeared into a swirling cloud of dust and blowing debris.

If ever there existed a man who could come as a thief into the Kingdom and produce such an explosion right under their very noses . . . the man on the blood bay horse would be him.

"My sheikh?" Zafir's frantic voice snapped Farooq back to his cell phone. "Are you there? I hear screaming. What has happened?"

"We have copies of the video records from the laboratory on our remote server?" Farooq's voice grew quiet as he struggled to control his breathing.

"Of course," Zafir said.

"Very well. I will review them."

"I will come at once."

"You have another mission." Farooq sighed. "Our timeline is already set in motion. I will have Raheem retrieve them. I fear our medical project is no more. . . ."

There was silence on the other end of the line.

"No more?"

Farooq ground his teeth. His nostrils flared. "I must know who did this to me," he spat. "I will deal with him in my own way." He rolled up the window and rested his head against the cool leather seat, suddenly exhausted. "In any case, your duty is before you, my friend. Your time is far spent. The others should have already moved. In the end, our saboteur has done nothing but take a few pawns. The American devils do not realize it, but with our opening moves, the game is already won."

Jericho guided the big bay with his knees, pointing it toward a throng of white-robed students who milled under rows of palm trees and the buzzing glow of streetlights. Stars peeked intermittently from a brilliant indigo sky through clouds of smoke and falling ash. The horse, a strong-willed gelding, was a flighty one. Jericho had passed on the chance to make his escape on a Palomino mare that had looked much gentler. His ex-wife was a blonde so he'd decided to take his chances on the brunette.

He glanced at the TAG Aquaracer on his wrist as he slid from the prancing animal. He took a loose lead rope from a waiting student and slid it over the sweating horse's arched neck, looping it around the animal's nose to form a makeshift figure-eight halter. He handed the end to the astonished student with a smile and slight bow. The train to Riyadh left in two hours.

He still had time for a shower.

CHAPTER 32

14 September
DNI Alternate Offices
Army Navy Drive
Arlington, Virginia

Mahoney rolled an empty glass vial back and forth in her open hand, holding it up to study in the soft glow of Win Palmer's green desk lamp. They knew so much about these terrorists . . . and still, they knew so little.

The Director sat behind his desk, thinking deeply. Beyond him, slouched on an overstuffed couch along the far wall, Quinn nursed a can of Diet Coke. Thibodaux sat across from him, looking at a loose stack of photographs from Farooq's lab.

"We need to tell Sergeant Meeks's family something," the big Cajun said, "even if it's a lie. Let them know their boy's not lost out there . . . missing forever."

"In time," Win Palmer agreed. "When this is over. Right now, what we have to worry about more than anything is panic—and I'm not speaking only of the population. You'd be surprised at how often I hear the term 'absolute containment' used from the Gang of Five in our little briefings."

Megan scoffed. "That's what they called the solution to their problem with Northwest 2—'absolute containment.'"

Palmer gave a somber nod. "What happened there is not something anyone is proud of, Ms. Mahoney. But most believe it was a necessary evil."

"How much about this does your Gang of Senators know?" Thibodaux asked.

"They don't know everything," Palmer said. "But they do know about the virus. Two very influential generals have spent a considerable amount of time bending their ears with an endless list of the deadly possibilities. Carpet bombing the hell out of any area that the virus shows up in has been discussed as a more than viable option— even here in the U.S. I don't mind telling you, these people are scared out of their wits."

Quinn leaned back, swallowed up in the burgundy cushions of Win Palmer's couch. "Then we have to stop these guys first." Tendons in his arms bunched as he sipped on his can of Diet Coke. He was still rumpled from traveling through a dozen different time zones in three days and though he'd recently shaved, already sported a healthy five o'clock shadow. He looked up at Mahoney from the glossy color copies of the martyr photographs he'd brought back with him from Al-Hofuf.

"What do you think, doctor? Could they transport enough virus in that vial to hurt us?"

"More than enough," she said. A shiver crawled up her back and left both arms tingling. She held the vial-within-a-vial up to her eye, between her thumb and forefinger. "This holds about ten cc's—a scant two tea-spoons. Considering the fact that the sprayed droplets of a single sneeze appear to be enough to pass the virus, I'd say they could put enough liquid in here to kill half the Eastern seaboard before we could contain it . . . *if* we could contain it. . . ." Her voice trailed off.

Thibodaux chimed in.

"Stuff this deadly," he mused, rubbing his thick jaw-bone. "They'd want to be careful not to let it out of the bag in their own sandbox. It's one thing to infect your enemy, but if it's as deadly as you say it is, this could wipe out the entire Middle East without too much of a problem. Those guys always looked a little on the sickly side to me anyhow." He pointed to the pho-tographs. "The ones transporting the virus might end up as martyrs, but I'd lay odds the higher-ups in their chain of command have other plans besides killing off half of Islam."

Jericho tossed his empty Coke can in a wastebasket beside the sofa. He looked up at Palmer, who sat be-hind a mahogany desk, freckled fingers steepled in front of his ruddy face, elbows on a leather desk blot-ter, listening.

The Director of National Intelligence leaned back in his chair, as if to study the nine-foot ceiling as he spoke. "Exceptional work, Jericho—bringing these photographs back. We've uploaded them into Immi-gration and Customs Enforcement, TSA, the Bureau, and every other facial-recognition database we have. Hopefully, ICE or State will nail these bastards as they're coming in. Biometric programs aren't foolproof, but if one of them uses an ATM or smiles at the right camera, we should be able to get a preliminary location."

"Still just the two names?" Thibodaux asked, dwarfing an office chair across from Jericho. He hadn't been traveling, but it was clear from the dark circles under his eyes that he hadn't slept much either.

"Just the two younger ones," Palmer said. "Both are under thirty and appear to come from poor Bedouin families. Hamid is the jowly one. The one with the mole beside his nose is Kalil." The DNI shrugged. "We're running the unsub through Interpol and State. Defense found a picture that's a possible match, but they can't seem to locate the damned file with a name."

"The old fella looks like a mean son of a bitch," Thibodaux sneered, scooping up the martyr photos. "This mole ought to make it easier for your biometrics to key on ol' Kalil. Damn thing looks like a dog tick. . . ."

"Maybe," Palmer said. His voice was calm, but worry lines stitched a high forehead. "I hate to say it, but until we get some kind of nibble, there's not much we can do. You all may as well go home and get some rest. I have a feeling you're all going to need it."

Mahoney moved closer to Quinn, sitting on the couch beside him. He'd taken several digital images of the lab and they were spread out on the coffee table in front of him. She was close enough to smell the soap from his recent shower. His dark hair hung in loose ringlets, still damp. He had the look of a freshly bathed wolf, clean from all the blood but with the deadly look of a recent kill still smoldering in his eyes.

Mahoney had never been around someone who ex-
uded such charisma. Her scientific brain told her it was
chemical, but her emotions didn't care where the feelings sprang from. They were just as strong. She let go
of a stupid, fleeting wish that she'd worn something
less severe than khakis and a white button-down.

Jericho Quinn was a handsome man, there was no
denying that. He was shorter than the big Marine by a
good four inches, but tall enough. A little on the gaunt
side with hungry brown eyes to match the hollows in
his cheeks. Athletic arms strained against the tight
sleeves of a black polo. A curl of dark hair visible
above the third button said he was no chest-waxing
metrosexual. Quinn was a square jawed, five-o'clock-
shadow-by-noon man's man. He oozed danger, but
something in her primordial self woke up and screamed
that this was the kind of man who would protect her
and their cubs. . . .

Mahoney shivered in spite of herself. Afraid it was
visible to the others, she feigned a sneeze.

She thumbed through the lab photos from the coffee
table, eager to take her mind off thoughts of Jericho
Quinn. Though taken through thick glass, the images
were of surprisingly good quality and the torment on
the victims' faces was all too evident.

Mahoney studied the drawn face of the poor child,
horrified by what she saw. She glanced up at Jericho,
showing him the photograph. "Didn't you say their
eyes looked . . . flat, I think you said?"

"Ummhmm." He nodded. "The way you described
Ebola, I'd assumed it was part of the disease."

Megan looked at the photo of the girl again. She took a small magnifying glass from the table and ran it over the other faces.

"Oh, my . . ." she gasped. The muscles in her jaw tensed and bunched as she fought the urge to vomit. "One of the virus samples I have back at Fort Detrick is made up almost entirely of aqueous humor—the fluid from inside the human eye. It looks as though they were trying experiments with a portable medium for the virus other than blood."

Thibodaux's brow furrowed. "Oh ye yi! You mean to say those bastards sucked the juice out of that little one's eyes?"

Mahoney dropped the photos back on the table. "Her and all the rest."

The big Cajun doubled both fists and stared hard at Jericho. "I hope you took care of the ones that done this, Chair Force. . . ."

"Working on it," Quinn said.

"Well." Thibodaux rose slowly to his feet. "This is gonna be a pleasure."

Kim called before they made it out of the lobby. Mahoney had remained behind to make a few phone calls of her own on Palmer's STU phone. Jericho waved Thibodaux on. "I'll meet you back at Miyagi's," he said as he took the call. Instead of going on without him, the big Marine went outside and sat on the steps, unwilling to leave a man behind for any reason.

The call was short, a simple session where Kim filled him in on Mattie's newest achievements. This time, she'd been accepted to play in the prestigious Anchorage Youth Orchestra. His ex-wife never actually chastised him directly. Instead, she let the implications of his absence do the work for her, praising the great achievements and success of their daughter, in spite of the absences brought on by his "important job" and "save-the-world" overseas missions. She was extremely skillful at slowly beating him to death with backhanded compliments. "She's doing amazingly well, considering she misses her dad so much. . . ." It was Kim's way of saying Mattie would be playing in Carnegie Hall if only Jericho were there to cheer her on. Still, he beamed at the news. At five years old his little girl was a musical prodigy on the violin. Kim was an excellent violinist in her own right; years of dedicated practice had seen her play in Seattle, Los Angeles, and New York. She had a permanent seat with the Anchorage Symphony and had over twenty students of her own. But privately, Jericho felt Mattie's superhuman ability had more to do with inheriting his talent at languages. Music was, after all, just another language. He said nothing of this to Kim, more than happy to let her take the credit. Instead he listened quietly and told her he loved her. There was no way to tell her what he was actually doing. She'd never know he'd gone to Saudi Arabia—he wondered if she'd care if she did.

"You doin' okay, Chair Force?" Thibodaux asked as he and Quinn walked across the parking lot toward their bikes, a stone's throw from the Pentagon.

"I'm all right," Quinn said. "A little worried about

my daughter, that's all." The whir of a thousand cicadas droned from the surrounding greenery, in harmony with the memory of Kim's parenting sermon that still buzzed in his head. A dazzling afternoon sun reflected off hundreds of parked cars. The evening rush hour had already begun, clogging the arteries that fed D.C. proper. The Jefferson Davis Highway and 395 had slowed to a lethargic trickle.

"I don't like to get in another man's business," the Cajun said, "but you appear to be a mite conflicted—and in my experience conflicted men are apt get themselves killed."

Jericho felt his stomach tighten. It was difficult enough to gain the trust of an operator like Thibodaux. The last thing he wanted to do was jeopardize it with screwed-up thoughts of ex-wives and dying home fires. They had a job to do and a high level of trust between them was vital. The best way to engender that trust was to be honest.

Quinn stopped and looked up at the big Cajun. "Before Palmer recruited us, I told my wife I'd quit." Saying the words was like throwing up on the dinner table, then waiting for a reaction.

Surprisingly, a huge grin spread across Thibodaux's face. "Hell, we all promise 'em we're gonna quit every once in a while. Just like they promise us they're gonna lay off the brownies while we're deployed." He shrugged and began to walk toward the bikes again. "I make all kinds of promises to get in her panties."

Quinn laughed. "I wish I'd thought of that last time I was in Alaska."

"It ain't even a lie if you mean it at the time." Thibodaux winked.

"You're away from home as much as I am," Quinn said, relaxing by degrees as they walked. It felt good to be able to talk to someone. "And you still decided to have a big family?"

The Cajun looked out over the Potomac. "I dunno. My child bride wanted to have a mess of kids. It was all part of the deal from the get-go with her. Who was I to say no when the process is so damn enjoyable?"

Quinn sighed. "Yeah, Kim was always on my back trying to have more kids."

Thibodaux stopped in his tracks. "Well"—he chuckled—"if she was on *your* back, it's a wonder you even had the one."

"I'm serious, Jacques," Jericho said. "You seem to have the family warrior thing all figured out."

Thibodaux resumed his long strides, thinking a moment before he spoke. "My granddaddy once told me there was only two things in the middle of the road: a yellow stripe and a dead possum. I don't want my boys to stand anywhere near the middle of the road and I figure the best way to guard against that is for them to see me fight for what I believe in. Besides," he said, "I don't know if you are aware, but there's a war on."

"I hear you."

"Anyhow," Thibodaux went on, "my wife and I get along much better when I'm not there underfoot all the time. I honestly believe if I was a mailman or something that kept me home every night she'd wind up shootin' my ass."

At their bikes now, Jericho nodded. "Thanks for the words of wisdom."

"Hell." Thibodaux smiled. "Even stone-cold killers need to talk now and again. The point is, you shouldn't hold this kind of shit in. It's like being mentally constipated. That's what conflicts us, and that which conflicts us doth get us killed. You may quote me."

"Thank you, Dr. Daux Boy."

The men both turned to watch Mahoney step from the double glass doors and into the parking lot.

"Doc Daux Boy says that woman there done gone and got all Matthew 4:19 on you."

Quinn raised an eyebrow. "Since when did you start to quote the Good Book?"

"My granny was a sure 'nough Bible scholar. Whenever I had some little gal after me, Granny'd say she was Matthew 4:19—fishin' for menfolk."

Standing at the rear of his BMW, Quinn opened the aluminum side case to retrieve his padded black gloves and leathers. He took his helmet and fiddled with the GPS display inside the visor as he spoke. "Seriously? You think the good doctor was flirting with you?"

"Not me, dumb-ass," Thibodaux laughed. "She's been oo-awing you with her baby blues from the get-go. I saw her fall when she first heard that honey-sweet voice of yours over the com-line from Al-Hofuf."

Quinn shrugged on his armored jacket and waved off the idea. It was warm so he flipped the switch that flushed the jacket with coolant. Mahoney was still twenty feet away, a wide smile across her face. Her broad, swimmer's shoulders were thrown back as she walked. Low rays of sun turned her hair into a golden halo—not blond but not red.

"You could do a hell of a lot worse," Thibodaux whispered.

"She hasn't said more than ten words to me," Quinn said, his voice hushed.

"Just because she ain't thrown her hook in the water don't mean a thing." The big Cajun winked. "You mark my words, brother, she's fishin'."

Mahoney stopped, shaking her head slowly back and forth when she saw the two men dressed in their sleek Transit Leather jackets beside the tall BMWs. Her eyes were wide with wonder. "Whew," she gasped. "You run around the world blowing up terrorists and ride big honkin' motorcycles when you come home. What do guys like you do when you have a midlife crisis?"

Thibodaux gave Quinn an I-told-you-so smirk. "Well, beb, in this kind of work, we'd be damn lucky if we didn't pass midlife somewhere back in our teens. But, if I do happen to live a little longer, I plan to sire myself a couple more sons." He hooked a thumb over his shoulder toward Jericho. "I reckon he'll settle down and marry his ex-wife. . . ."

Thankfully, Quinn's cell phone saved him from the conversation with a pestering buzz.

It was Palmer.

He listened a moment, then snapped the phone shut, eyes hard on Thibodaux.

"Surveillance cameras on the Postal Museum picked up a match to our number-two martyr, Kalil."

"The one with the dog-tick mole on his cheek," Thibodaux said. "Got it." Helmet in hand, he climbed aboard his GS and let it run through the electronic diagnostics before he started the motor.

Jericho turned to Mahoney. "Palmer has Metro Police watching the guy. Sharpshooters are moving up on the scene now, but he wants us there yesterday."

"They can't approach him," Mahoney warned. "If he deploys the virus everyone around the Museum could be infected."

Quinn bit his bottom lip. "It's worse than that," he said. "The Postal Museum is directly across the street from Union Station. It's rush hour. I don't know how many thousands of commuters go through there every day."

Mahoney ran a hand through her hair, looking across the Potomac into downtown D.C. "Like Palmer said, we have to think containment here. If the virus goes airborne anyone exposed to it will have to be stopped where they are and kept there. That means shutting down the Metro trains coming in and out of Union Station. . . ."

"Being done even as we speak," Quinn said. "D.C. SWAT and FBI HRT are en route to set up a perimeter to keep folks quarantined until we can mobilize National Guard troops . . . if it comes to that. No one is being told exactly what they're dealing with, but they know it's serious—some sort of flu."

"Good thinking," Thibodaux threw over his shoulder. "Any kind of flu sounds better than bleeding-outta-your-eyes Ebola."

Quinn looked at his watch. "Listen, Doc, I hate to

drag you into harm's way, but you're our resident expert. I'm gonna need you to meet us over there."

Mahoney turned toward her Toyota, then back again. She nodded toward the 395 bridge that would take them across the Potomac River and into D.C. proper. An endless procession of cars inched along, brake lights flashing. Construction on the lanes going north into the city squeezed inbound traffic into a single chute, making it crawl as slowly as the clogged outbound lanes.

"It'll take me an hour to get there in the 4Runner," she said. "You'll be able to cut lanes on the motorcycles, but I'm dead in the water."

Jericho popped open an aluminum case and handed her a helmet. "This is my ex-wife's. She's sort of big headed so it might be a little loose."

Mahoney put up both hands. "Oh, no, I . . . are you sure?"

"Come on, Dr. Mahoney, I'm a safe driver." He grinned. "According to the CDC, we're only about six times more likely to die in an accident on a bike than a car."

"Your really know how to convince a girl," she said. "I guess we're all dead anyway if that virus gets out. I may as well come along for the ride." She blushed, holding the helmet in front of her like a shield. "If I'm going to be clinging to your waist, I wish you'd call me Megan."

"Okay, Megan, I'm Jericho." He patted the bike's rear seat with his black glove. "This is easier if you get on first."

He couldn't help but wonder if maybe he didn't

hope—just a little—that what Thibodaux said about her fishing was true. He took her hand, helping her swing a leg over the tall bike, catching the scent of her perfume as she moved. White Shoulders—Kim wore White Shoulders . . . He swallowed, pushing away the thought.

"There's a cord coming out of the left side of your helmet," he said, once she was situated. "I need to plug it in to this socket. . . ." He pushed the small jack into the connection a half inch below her left thigh. "You and I will be able to talk to each other. I can talk to Thibodaux by radio, but your commo is only hardwired to me."

"Got it," Mahoney said, sounding much more capable than he thought she would.

"Hey, Boudreaux," Jacques's voice crackled across the intercom in Jericho's helmet. "I'm thinking we might not even make it across on the bikes in time. That traffic's murder, beb."

"The GS is just an oversized dirt bike," Quinn said, settling himself aboard, hands on throttle and clutch. "You feel comfortable doing a little off-road?"

"Not really," Mahoney said from behind him. She sounded a little queasy at the thought.

"You know me, brother!" Thibodaux flipped his visor shut and gunned the BMW's boxer engine. "*Laissez les bon temps rouler*!"

CHAPTER 33

Quinn eased his GS out of the parking lot and into traffic along the Old Jeff Davis Highway, giving Mahoney a quick moment to get her riding legs under her.

"Rule number one," he said, thankful they had the intercom. "When I'm going less than fifteen miles an hour, you sit still. No shifting around or you could interfere with what I'm doing. Faster than that and feel free to stand on the seat if you want."

"Okay," she stammered. "Just don't forget I'm back here when you go ripping off the pavement."

She clung to his waist as if she might fly away. Her right arm rested just above the butt of the pistol under his Transit Leather jacket.

"You with me, Jacques?"

"With you, beb."

"Okay, the Mount Vernon bike path runs along the river. We'll jump the curb here and take that to the Arlington Memorial Bridge, then across toward the Lincoln Memorial about a mile up. The sidewalk's pretty wide." Mahoney tensed, tugging him closer. Even through the armored jacket, he could feel the weight of her against his spine. He shook his head to chase away a fleeting memory of riding with Kim. It was too easy to get nostalgic with the feeling of a good woman behind him on the bike. . . .

Loose gravel and red dirt spun from his rear tire as Quinn jumped the curb and crossed an open patch of ground before cutting north on the smooth pavement of the Mount Vernon Trail. He punched a button on his right handle bar. While he waited for the dial tone, he explained what he was doing to Mahoney. "I'm going to give Palmer a quick call."

He could feel the doctor nod her head behind him, but she said nothing.

The phone rang once before the DNI answered.

"Palmer."

"Sir," Quinn said. "We're doing a bit of creative navigation to reach our target. I'd appreciate it if you'd let D.C. Metro and the U.S. Park Police know not to get in our way."

"Consider it done," Palmer said. "Last report has Kalil walking along Massachusetts Avenue in front of Union Station. He's wearing a gray T-shirt, khaki slacks, and brand-new white tennis shoes. There's a Metro cop on horseback across from the taxi stand by the flagpoles. He's got eyes-on but has orders not to approach."

"Roger that—"

Quinn leaned hard to the left, narrowly evading a pack of angry in-line skaters who scattered like quail before the roaring motorcycles. "Gotta go, sir."

Both Quinn and Thibodaux made liberal use of their horns. That, along with the sound-muffling qualities of their helmets, protected them from the steady torrent of cursing that followed them down the path from each bicyclist and jogger who had to leap out of their way and into the thick foliage. Three spandex-clad cyclists on graphite racing bikes rode straight into the river in front of the Navy-Marine Memorial.

Ducking and dodging, Quinn flew up the path, paralleling the stalled traffic on the George Washington Parkway. He felt Mahoney tense, heard her catch her breath as he darted across the access road, weaving in and out of the creeping traffic below the gray stone breastwork of Arlington Memorial Bridge. He accelerated to climb the grass embankment to the sidewalk that would carry under the Eagle arches and across the bridge. The inbound traffic to D.C. was indeed lighter, but Quinn kept to the wide walk. He leaned over the handlebars, throwing his weight forward to keep the front wheel down as the powerful motorcycle cleared the bridge in a matter of seconds. He cut left at the Lincoln roundabout, then took to the dirt beside the Reflecting Pool. Thibodaux stayed tight on his tail, hollering like a joyful schoolboy at each twist and turn.

Quinn was sure he'd have to have to peel Mahoney off his back when they stopped.

At least a hundred middle school students in crimson T-shirts parted like the Red Sea when they looked up from loitering at the base of the Washington Monument. Girls and a couple of the boys screamed at the top of their lungs.

"Damned little mouth breathers," Thibodaux grumbled as his bike threw up a cloud of red dust, narrowly avoiding a pack of kids who walked toward him with their heads down listening to music. "That'll teach 'em to take out the earbuds."

Two minutes later saw the riders shoot past the Smithsonian Museums, then up Louisiana Avenue toward Union Station. Two blocks away they took to the street, falling in with evening traffic to keep from arousing suspicion on their approach.

"Got him," Thibodaux's voice came across the speaker in Quinn's helmet. "He's leaning up against a construction barricade along First Avenue. Gray T-shirt and khakis. I can see his big ol' mole face from here . . . dammit! I thought Palmer said the locals were going to stay out of this. . . ."

Quinn found himself stuck behind a produce truck without a clear visual on the target. "What do you mean?"

"Looks like the D.C. mountie has decided to ride on over and chat up Mole Face."

Quinn downshifted into third and cut between the curb and the delivery truck, gunning the throttle to zip quickly out of the driver's blind spot. He wasn't so worried about making the trucker mad, but he wanted to be seen.

He made it around just in time to see the mounted officer tumble from his horse. A gunshot cracked above the din of traffic as a second uniformed D.C. officer approached Kalil on foot. The other officer went down as well, grabbing an injured thigh with one hand while he clawed for his weapon with the other.

"Where the hell are those shots coming from?" Thibodaux screamed into his mike.

"Kalil has backup," Quinn snapped. He scanned the

flowing melee of commuters and tourists among the road construction barriers. Most of them hadn't heard the shots or even noticed the downed officers. Mahoney, to the credit of her scientific brain, looked high. She was the first to see the shooter.

"There," she said. "Behind some scaffolding to the right, above the construction at two o'clock. There's a man with a rifle."

Quinn maneuvered his BMW around a parked taxi to stop behind the relative cover of the engine block. "I see him," he said. "Jacques, we got a gunman on a cherry picker about a half a block in front of the Securities and Exchange Commission. . . ."

Kalil's head snapped up. He spun on his new tennis shoes and sprinted toward the row of shadowed pillars at the entrance of Union Station. If he made it inside, he could disappear—or worse, deploy the virus in the crowded terminal.

Thibodaux roared past, heading for the rifleman. "I got the shooter," he said. "You bag Kalil."

"Careful," Quinn warned. "See one, think two."

"Always, beb." Thibodaux hopped the curb to ride a wheelie across the open pavilion under the row of American flags. Bullets thwacked off a full-size replica of the Liberty Bell as he tore by, picking up speed to make for a poorer target.

"Go!" Mahoney yelled, smacking Quinn on the thigh to get his attention. She'd vaulted off the back of the bike and now stood beside him, helmet in her hands. "Get him. I'll be right behind you."

Quinn gave her a quick thumbs-up and goosed the engine to speed across the pavilion toward the open doors, standing on the pegs as he hopped the opposite curb.

Evening commuters in D.C. were used to a certain amount of chaos and were only just beginning to understand they were in danger. Some, having lived through the 2002 sniper attacks, zigzagged across the open ground, seeking shelter behind whatever they could find. Others stared up blankly with open mouths, like sheep.

Kalil pumped his arms, running like he was on fire as the big BMW closed the gap behind him. Quinn was able to squeeze his bike through the south doors seconds before they shut, just feet behind his target.

Once inside the cavernous station, Kalil ducked to the left, sprinting with all his might past a long set of low tablelike benches under the vaulted archways and toward the Main Hall. With his speed up to get through the doors, Jericho overshot the turn.

The BMW's back tire spun on the slick marble, throwing up a thick plume of white smoke. Quinn slammed his foot on the ground, pivoting the bike, making him thankful for his heavy boots.

Kalil tore through the arched portal at the end of the marble corridor, running as if pursued by the devil himself. Sliding on the slick floor, he darted right, entering the Main Hall, shoving startled tourists and commuters as he vanished around the corner.

Jericho gassed the throttle, shifting into third gear by the time he reached the opening and leaned into his turn. His heart sank as he rounded the huge ionic columns to find a man in blue overalls mopping the glistening wet marble. Kalil had slipped as he ran past and knocked over the mop bucket. He was up again and moving fast.

Already leaning well into his turn, Jericho felt the bike begin to slide. He straightened her as best he could, and cranked the handlebars hard right, laying on the power to drift the rear tire sideways at high speed and stay in his turn without spilling. He needed the tire spinning fast when he cleared the water. The roar of the BMW's boxer twin echoed in the vaulted chamber as Jericho slid around the corner like a flat-track racer. The bike squealed and smoke poured from the rear tire when they hit dry marble, leaving a line of black rubber twenty feet long. Jericho straightened the front wheel, eased off the gas a hair, and took his first breath in five seconds.

Out of nowhere, a burly D.C. Metro cop with a snarling German shepherd trotted directly for him. Weapon drawn, the officer shouted unintelligible orders. The dog barked like it hadn't been fed in days. Evidently these two hadn't gotten the order to disregard marauding BMW riders inside the Capitol Beltway.

Ahead, Kalil cut left, sprinting, dwarfed by the towering architecture of Union Station's Main Hall. He leapt up the wooden stairs of the cozy Center Café, an ornate island some twenty feet high in the middle of the teaming station.

Quinn ignored the shouting cop and shot past him, popping the clutch. He gained speed as he approached the staircase, close enough he could almost reach out and touch Kalil. Gassing the bike, he yanked up on the handlebars enough to bring the front tire into a high wheelie as he hit the stairs. It was a rough ride, but he let the BMW have her way and she rumbled up the steps like a willing horse up a rocky slope.

At the top, Kalil shoved aside startled diners, tripping to splay across the first table. He crashed to the floor in pile of minestrone soup and halibut fettuccini. Momentarily stunned, the Arab clamored to his feet, intent on going down the staircase on the opposite side to shake his tail. Jericho shoved a vacant table aside with his knee as he brought the motorcycle to a skidding halt in the middle of the dining area. Crystal glasses and china plates shattered against the plush carpet. Silverware clattered to the floor. Kalil had to weave in and out of a dozen such tables, giving Quinn time to do his job.

Still straddling the GS, Quinn planted both feet, drew the Kimber from the holster under his jacket, and shot Kalil twice in the back of the head.

Startled diners looked up, some with forks suspended before gaping mouths. The terrorist sprawled headlong over a table, splashing a bright swath of blood across the white linen cloth. What was left of his face was planted squarely in a plate of linguini and clam sauce.

Jericho watched in horror as the tiny glass vial left the dead man's fist intact, but rolled toward the edge of the restaurant floor to fall over the edge.

"Don't move!" Mahoney screamed.

The Metro cop stood on the floor of the Main Hall, his barking shepherd straining at the leash in one hand while the other held a glass tube of liquid. He'd seen the vial fall and reached instinctively to catch it.

Megan stood like a statue at the bottom of the stairs. Both hands were raised, palms open and unthreatening toward the big policeman. Her smile was ashen, her voice halting.

"Officer . . ." She willed a calm tone into her shaky words. "Listen to me very carefully. If you drop that vial, we all die. . . ."

The deafening roar of fighter jets overhead rattled the building, drowning out all conversation.

CHAPTER 34

Quinn dialed the phone to Palmer before he'd even holstered his pistol. The DNI put him on hold and made a quick call. Outside, the fighter jets pulled away, thundering back toward Langley.

Once Mahoney told everyone within earshot that the vial held sarin gas, it was a fairly simple matter to keep people away. The Metro cop handed the clear vial over without a fuss. Megan slipped it inside a padded, hard-shell plastic tube she'd brought just for that purpose. She slumped, relieved, but shaking with the knowledge of how close they'd come.

Thibodaux's voice brought her out of her stupor.

"You okay, Doc?"

She looked up to see a wide rip in the leather of the Cajun's motorcycle jacket, running parallel with his elbow. Another creased his thigh.

"What happened to you?"

"Turns out Kalil's backup boys were pretty handy with their shooters."

Jericho was already off his bike, examining the torn leather. "Are you hit?"

Thibodaux laughed. "They the ones that's hit, beb." He poked two fingers through the bullet holes in the jacket. "Lucky for me, I'm ATGATT."

Mahoney raised an eyebrow.

Jericho smiled, turning to take off his helmet. He motioned a group of Japanese tourists away from the Center Café and Kalil's bleeding corpse. "All the gear all the time." He chuckled. "The armored riding gear Palmer had made for us saved him."

Over the strenuous objections of the mayor of D.C., the feds—who were, after all, really the ones in charge of the capitol—had Union Station locked down for five hours while the area around Kalil was searched for other vials of virus. The body and the glass vial were placed in an airtight "coffin" and transported via armored CDC van back to the BSL-4 at Fort Detrick with a full security detail.

"Y'all hear those flyboys come by?" Thibodaux said, wiping his brow with the back of a big hand. "Talk about a close one."

Quinn released a deep breath. "Too close."

Megan shivered as she began to understand what they were saying. Not only had they come within the brink of exposure to a deadly hemorrhagic virus, they'd very nearly been bombed to oblivion by their own government.

"The Gang of Five?" she whispered.

"Yep," both men said in unison.

"I think we just about got dropped in the grease," Thibodaux said, his forehead furrowed in thought.

"When this is over"—Jericho looked at Thibodaux—"you and I need to pay a little visit to the halls of the Senate Hood and have a chat with our Gang of Five."

CHAPTER 35

FBI Special Agent Bob Chaffee leaned back against the edge of the metal table and exhaled through his prominent nose like an angry bull. His thinning blond hair was combed straight back, plastered to his scalp with gel. A dark suit jacket was folded neatly on the table to his right.

The Arab man handcuffed to the wooden chair in front of him wasn't talking and Chaffee was beginning to look foolish in front of his new partner.

"I think we're supposed to call someone with the CDC," a portly customs inspector with gray hair offered from the other side of a metal government-issue desk. His name was Ernie and he was a likeable enough sort for a grandpa. Chaffee thought the man a little too sweet faced to be a gun-toting U.S. customs officer.

"The hit was flagged for national security," Chaffee

tossed the words over his shoulder to Ernie, but his steel blue eyes still locked on the suspect. "Last I heard the Bureau retains jurisdiction on national security matters no matter what some CDC doctor puts in a computer field." He opened his fist to reveal a clear glass vial about two inches long.

The prisoner's eyes focused intently on the vial, following it as a cobra might follow the bobbing of a flute. Beads of sweat glistened on his forehead, though the room was cool enough that Ernie had to wear his dark blue grandpa sweater.

"What's in this thing, Hamid?" Chaffee asked. "Drugs?"

Liz Miller, Chaffee's Betty-Bureau-Blue-Suit partner, chimed in. "There is a flag that pops up to say specifically we're supposed to notify CDC. Maybe this is some sort of swine flu. I've read theories that Al Qaeda is trying to weaponize it. . . ."

Special Agent Miller was an attractive enough woman, tall and triathlete fit with a pile of flaming red hair and a splash of freckles across her cheeks. Fresh out of Quantico, she thought she actually had something to offer to an investigation—some unique insight from her twenty-six weeks of study that trumped Chaffee's twenty-three years on the street. What she had yet to learn was when to shut her yap and observe.

Chaffee shook his head. He was not about to call the CDC. The CDC was supposed to call the FBI. That's the way things worked. He'd show this nubile newbie just how terrorism investigations were done.

Loosening his tie, he rolled up the sleeves of his custom-made white shirt and folded his arms across his chest. It was important he let the suspect know he was prepared for the long haul.

"So, Hammy," he said, hoping the Arab was smart enough to get the pork innuendo. "Let me tell you what we do know. You came in this morning on the 9:06 flight from Dubai. Your passport is in good order, but . . . and this is a big but, my friend . . . your visa has some problems. The thing is, it's not even a very good forgery. Visa fraud is a felony, you understand me?" Chaffee craned in close, inches from Hamid's twitching cheek. "You understand prison, shit for brains?"

"Allahu akbar," Hamid whispered.

"What did you say?"

Hamid hawked up a throat full of phlegm and spat. Yellow mucus dripped from Chaffee's nose and chin.

He wiped it of with a handkerchief, pausing a moment to gaze at the office door before he doubled his fist and hit the prisoner hard in the jaw. Handcuffed, the Arab was unable to catch himself. Both he and the chair pitched onto the rough carpet, face first.

"Bob!" Agent Miller grabbed Chaffee by the shoulder, but he shrugged her off, towering over the prisoner.

Hamid lay on his side, panting, but still tight-lipped. A trickle of blood ran from his nose, spotting the scabby carpet.

"I'm calling the CDC," Ernie whispered from behind the desk. "This is getting out of hand."

Chaffee wheeled, a shock of gelled hair hanging down across a pink face. "Don't you even think about it, old man. I told you, this is a national security issue. I'll have your ass for hindering my investigation if you so much as touch the phone." His starched shirt was askew, half untucked. One sleeve hung unrolled and unbuttoned, loose around his wristwatch.

A beige desk phone began to chirp. Ernie snapped it up. He, listened for a moment, nodded curtly, and then extended the handset toward Chaffee.

"Plain fact is I already called them, Bob. This is Dr. Mahoney with the CDC. She wants to talk to the agent in charge." The inspector's jowly face tightened. "And you've made it pretty clear to all of us that that's you."

Chaffee snatched up the phone, and then promptly slammed it back on the receiver. He threw up his hands in disgust. "You're an idiot, you know that, Ernie." He hooked a thumb over his shoulder. "Three thousand people died in Colorado. This guy could be connected to that and you call in the disease police. Unbelievable!"

"The computer hit said to call them." Ernie stood his ground. "When you go back up to Mount Olympus with all your other Bureau gods, I have to answer to my boss. I followed protocol."

"Shut up." Chaffee turned away. "You're a disgrace to the badge."

Agent Miller touched his arm. "Bob—"

"Don't you Bob me," he snapped. "Sit back and shut your yap. You might learn something useful." He hitched up his suit pants, making certain his sidearm was snapped securely into the holster on his belt. Handing her the glass vial, he rolled up his dangling sleeve and turned his attention back to Hamid.

"Hold on to that for me. It's evidence and I'm gonna need both of my hands."

* * *

"They hung up on me."

Megan Mahoney sat in the back seat of her Toyota 4Runner, dwarfed by three black parachute bags containing biohazard suits and portable air units. She lowered a cell phone from her ear in dismay.

Thibodaux sat behind the wheel, whipping expertly in and out of traffic. He took the spur road off highway 267, following the signs to the International terminal. It was midmorning and the commuter gridlock had let up enough that an aggressive driver could make good time, particularly going away from the Beltway. He glanced in the rearview mirror at Mahoney.

"Sure you had the right number?" he said, slamming on the brakes to avoid rear-ending a Boar's Head meat van.

"I spoke to the customs inspector." Mahoney nodded, redialing and getting nothing but a busy signal. "He said he was putting on someone from the FBI."

"What's the Bureau doing there?" Quinn sat in the front passenger seat, his eyes shut, head back.

"Beats me," Mahoney said. She couldn't blame Quinn for resting. Since Win Palmer had put Hamid's name and photograph on every lookout in the Western world, they'd been to Reagan National airport twice and Baltimore once, checking possible hits. Until now, they'd been false alarms, look-alikes. She'd assumed this one would be the same until they'd hung up on her. She'd dealt with the Bureau before, and though most of the individual agents were highly capable and pleasant enough, the agency had a certain inertia to it that could be difficult to overcome. "From my experience these guys can be mighty parochial."

"That's an understatement, *cher*," Thibodaux said. "I'm fixin' to get us right up by the door. We'll crash their party no matter if they invite us or not."

Quinn had his door open before Thibodaux put the Toyota in park. Mahoney handed a black bag marked XXL to Thibodaux just as a security guard in a gray uniform and yellow vest strode up. He was bald in the back, but his remaining hair was cut in a long flattop, pointing skyward like a smokestack, badly in need of a trim.

"You can't park that here," the guard said, nodding toward a sign along the curb. "Tour buses only."

"FBI," Thibodaux barked.

"Oh, uh . . ." the guard stammered. "Okay."

"Damn." Thibodaux grinned as the three walked away from the Toyota toward the terminal door. "No wonder the Bureau's so parochial. Their name's like a damn magic word."

"We had to be telling the truth." Quinn grinned. "Who would lie about being FBI?"

When Hamid hit the ground, the arm of his chair had snapped, leaving him cuffed not to the entire piece of furniture, but a stout club of heavy wood.

"What do you think, Hammy?" Chaffee said, stooping to lift the panting Arab back upright. He could get inside this guy and he knew it. "You feel like talking or should I ask my partner and her chubby friend to step out for a moment so I can shove that little vial of yours down your throat?"

Hamid said something, barely audible, under his breath, more of a squeak. Agent Chaffee grinned. This was too easy. . . .

Hamid struck like a snake, grunting with exertion as he brought the heavy wood across Chaffee's forearm. Bones cracked. Chaffee screamed, plowing into the Arab. The pain in his arm sent waves of nausea through his gut. His head reeled, but he knew he had to close the distance between himself and the club or risk being brained—especially now that his gun hand was useless.

Bellowing like a bull, Chaffee charged the far end of the room, taking the Arab along with him. Hamid slammed into the wall first, woofing as the air left his lungs. Unfazed, he continued to use the club, striking wildly but landing blow after blow on the agent's back and shoulders. Chaffee rained left hooks into the Arab's ribs, keeping him pressed against the wall with the point of his shoulder. He kept his broken wrist wedged against his own sidearm, fending off Hamid's snaking hand as best he could. It was only a matter of seconds before the Arab would have his gun.

"Somebody shoot this son of a bitch!" Chaffee yelled as he felt the Glock slip from his holster.

He heard two quick pops and Hamid went limp. The gun slid away with a muffled thump against the carpet.

Chaffee was vaguely aware of the smell of gunpowder as he let the Arab's body slump to the floor. Nausea brought on by the excruciating pain in his arm and a cold gush of adrenaline flowed back with full force. He staggered once, lowering himself to the floor with his good hand, cradling the broken arm across his lap.

Betty Bureau Blue Suit towered over him, her issue Glock still trained on a gurgling Hamid. Ernie too had found a pistol somewhere under his sweater and stood, aimed in at the threat.

A cool tickling caused Chaffee to touch his face. His hand came back bathed in red. Miller's second round had caught Hamid high in the shoulder, shattering his collarbone and spraying Chaffee with blood.

"Bob," Agent Miller said, her voice a half an octave higher than it had been. "You good?" She kicked the pistol away from Hamid's twitching hand.

"I'm fine," Chaffee winced, cradling his wounded arm. When he twisted around to thank her, his eyes locked on the shattered glass vial at Agent Miller's feet.

CHAPTER 36

Palmer's fury had shown in his twitching face after Quinn told him of the near miss with the fighter jets at Union Station. He'd vowed to keep any further communications about the virus out of the hands of the Gang of Five until he'd checked back with the Hammer Team. Until that time, he advised them to fly low and handle things as discreetly as possible.

Jericho's OSI badge and a few moments of explanation to TSA and a harried airport police sergeant had gotten all three of them past the screening point with the bags of biohazard gear. Their real roadblock turned out to be a pudgy airline gate agent wearing blue uniform shorts and a wrinkled white shirt. Apparently, Mr. Brandon Milford felt as if it was his solemn duty to safeguard the magnetic lock on the door leading to the back corridor of the International Terminal. Had it been left up to Jericho, he would have been happy to choke out the hairy-legged little butterball with the lanyard from his name tag.

Instead, he was content to let Mahoney explain their way in. Jericho would save his energy for the moments when his particular skills were needed and let the good doctor handle the diplomatic niceties.

Thibodaux leaned against a concrete pillar beside him, looking on smugly with a raised eyebrow. "She's losin' her temper," he said, taking a flat toothpick out of his mouth and dipping his head toward a red-faced Mahoney. "See how her butt cheeks are startin' to clench inside her khakis?"

"Sounds like you've made a study of this," Quinn mused.

"Oh, yeah." Thibodaux grinned. "When I see my wife's tail end clench like that, it's time to hunt a different piece of real estate. Means she's fixin' to throw a frying pan or somethin' heavy at my head." The big Marine tossed the frayed toothpick on the floor. "If I was this guy, I'd be gettin' ready to duck. . . ."

"I need authorization," the gate agent said, folding his arms and setting his egg-shaped face as if it were granite. "You're not going back there until someone answers the phone and I get authorization. It won't do you a bit of good to get testy with me. I'll punch the code and let you in." His nasal voice had the annoying whine of a mosquito. "*After* I get authorization."

"Excellent," Mahoney said. "Call and get it."

"I have," Milford said. "They don't answer."

"Call someone else, then." Mahoney threw her hands in the air, shaking her head in dismay. "Call the airport police. We just talked to one back at security. He said you'd let us in."

The gate agent shook his head emphatically. "The

airport police are not on my list of people to call. You say you're federal. You know they wouldn't have any jurisdiction over customs anyway. Look, I'm really busy right now. You have a seat over there and I'll give them another call in a few minutes. I'm sure someone will answer then.

Mahoney stood, dumbstruck. She turned to look over her shoulder at Quinn. Her butt was indeed clenching. He tapped the pistol under his jacket. *Want me to shoot him?* he mouthed.

She looked back to the gate agent, who sat as immovable as a stone.

Quinn looked at his watch. They'd all expected someone from customs would be waiting out front for them. He pulled out his cell phone to give Palmer a call. Before he could hit the send key, Mahoney's honey-sweet voice filled the air, menacing as a swarm of vengeful bees.

"Okay, Brandon Milford." Mahoney jabbed her finger at the ID badge around the pudgy man's neck. "You want to see officious, I'll show you officious—how about I get the President of the United States to give you a little ring?"

"You better use smaller words, Doc." Thibodaux chuckled. "*Officious* seems awfully big for this guy."

Mahoney's gaze burned into Milford's sodden eyes. Even from fifteen feet away in the waiting area, Jericho could see the man's chins begin to quiver.

"How about this, then?" she said. "How about you continue to use your unfettered power to keep me on this side of that door and all the while, the virus that's lurking on the other side will work its way through the air and into the heating and ventilation system. You're such a great physical specimen it won't have any trouble worming into your pasty little system in no time flat. In about four hours' time you'll be bleeding outa your eyes. Projectile diarrhea won't begin to describe your condition. All the cells in your body will begin to liquefy. . . ." She leaned across the high counter, gently stroking the back of Milford's dimpled hand. "The pain will be so bad you won't even be able to scream . . . and somewhere along the way your tiny little balls will turn black and fall off—"

Milford punched in the code and waddled away.

Seconds after entering the sterile hallway, Jericho heard two distinct pops. He drew his Kimber, recognizing the noises for what they were. Thibodaux had his pistol in hand as well.

A disembodied voice stopped them outside the white door emblazoned with the blue and white eagle logo of ICE: IMMIGRATION AND CUSTOMS ENFORCEMENT.

"You from CDC?"

Megan held her credentials up to the Plexiglas box mounted beside the speaker. "Dr. Megan Mahoney . . ." She shot a glance at Quinn and Thibodaux. ". . . and associates."

Quinn stepped to the speaker, his gun discreetly behind his thigh. "We heard shooting. Everything all right?"

"We're secure," the voice said. "But we have one FBI agent with a broken arm and a badly wounded suspect. . . ."

"Buzz us in," Mahoney said. "I can help until para-medics get here."

There was a long pause before a female voice came over the speaker. It was strained, teetering on the verge of full-blown panic.

"The Arab had a small vial with him," the voice quavered. "It's been compromised."

Mahoney swallowed. "How compromised?" She motioned both Quinn and Thibodaux over and had them take off their jackets, pointing toward the half-inch gap at the bottom of the door. Quinn realized what she wanted and used the thick leather to plug the void, backing it up with Thibodaux's.

"Shattered," the voice said. "Broken, shot to hell, spilled everywhere . . ."

"Give us a minute to suit up," Megan said, already pulling her orange biohazard suit and attached breathing unit from the bag. "We're coming in." She turned to Quinn. "It may be too late, but we need someone in maintenance to turn off the HVAC as quick as possible."

"On it, *chérie*." Thibodaux was already punching numbers into his cell phone.

Mahoney hung a Bluetooth earpiece in her ear and called her office while she pulled the thick, rubber-coated zippers on the suit. She gave her location and requested a level-four hazard team and security detail.

Quinn called Palmer, who used his connections to throw up an immediate quarantine around Dulles under the guise of a chemical spill, grounding all departing flights and diverting inbound traffic to Reagan or Baltimore.

"Listen, Doctor." The voice on the intercom had a catch in it, as if she was trying to control a sob. "I . . . I think I got some of the liquid on my foot. . . ."

Mahoney shot a worried glance at Quinn. "We'll be in in just a moment."

Checking each other for correct fit and seal in the bulky hazard suits was labor intensive, and though Quinn and Thibodaux had been through the same procedure twice before in the last six hours, they were all exhausted. Mahoney took extra time inspecting their gear. Unsure of what to expect on the other side of the door, both men kept their sidearms in small nylon pouches next to the portable breathing units attached to their waists.

After an agonizingly slow five minutes Mahoney pronounced them "sealed" and the magnetic lock clicked open. Thibodaux resecured the heavy leather jackets at the base of the door inside.

The customs office was in a shambles. Papers from loose file folders were strewn across the industrial blue carpet as if the area had been hit by a tornado. The remnants of a wooden office chair lay broken on the floor. A man in a sweat-stained white shirt huddled against the far wall holding his arm in his lap, his red power tie hanging loose and askew. A tall woman with flaming red hair and a gun on her hip stooped beside him, her jacket behind his head and a slender arm snaked around his shoulders. Worry lines creased her freckled nose. It was impossible to tell if she was trying to give comfort or get it. Likely a little bit of both, Quinn thought.

A graying customs inspector, the tail of his uniform

shirt hanging out over a paunchy belly, hunched above a wounded Arab. The inspector's arms were bathed in crimson up to his elbows as he worked frantically to staunch the flow of blood. Red flecks dotted his face and stained the front of his uniform shirt. The Arab groaned, his mouth opening and closing like a fish drowning in the open air.

Quinn let Mahoney take care of the FBI agents while he knelt beside the customs inspector. Thibodaux stood next to him.

"Jamal Hamid?" Quinn bent in closer so the wounded man could hear the muffled buzz of his voice through the clear plastic face shield. "We know what you have done. We know what you have brought into our country."

Hamid's eyes fluttered, startled to hear someone speak to him in Arabic. "You know nothing," he gasped. Pink blood foamed at the corners of his mouth. One of the shots had torn through a lung.

"We've already captured the others," Quinn lied. "You are the last. It is over."

Hamid closed his eyes, pained more from the news than from his wounds. "Impossible. Zafir was not . . . Zafir has . . ." He broke into a ragged coughing fit. As the coughing subsided, his olive face turned to ash, the muscles relaxed. He was bleeding internally, no matter how much pressure the customs inspector put on the wounds. "Not possib . . ." He gasped, shaking his head in disbelief. "Zafir . . . not possible . . ." His head lolled to one side. The customs inspector checked for a pulse, then shook his head.

"He's gone."

Thibodaux sighed. "Maybe we should consider bloodletting as a form of enhanced interrogation. Hamid just gave us the name of the third man."

"It's a start." Jericho rose to his feet with a groan. "Zafir isn't an uncommon name in the Middle East." The clammy suit seemed more confining that his motorcycle leathers—or maybe it was just the thought of the surrounding virus and the memory of the horrors he'd seen in the Al-Hofuf lab.

Mahoney had turned a garbage can upside down on top of the broken vial and moved the two FBI agents to the other side of the room, as far from the damp spot as possible. She tried to get them to sit down, but the man refused, violently jerking away.

"Should we get them out of here?" Quinn asked, nodding toward the two agents.

"Not yet," Mahoney said through clenched teeth. "Can't take a chance on letting anything spread beyond this room. Our mantra has got to be 'contain, contain, contain.'"

Quinn noticed how strong the doctor's Georgia accent had become under stress. He found it oddly attractive considering the circumstances.

"What was in the glass tube?" Agent Chaffee asked. "Bird flu?" He had a nasty bruise on his right forearm. The way he babied the thing it was likely broken.

Agent Miller's green eyes were dilated and wide, as if she stood awestruck at some passing celebrity. Flecks of dried saliva crusted white at the corners of her mouth. Quinn felt sorry for her. She looked young and this was probably the first time she'd even drawn her weapon other than at the firing range. Now she'd killed a man and had enough sense to know she was in grave danger. She was in shock, but less so than her more experienced partner.

Looking at Chaffee's beet-red face, Quinn noticed tiny hairline cracks in the man's teeth, probably brought on by years of jaw clenching. This was the kind of agent who lived his entire life in a state of near apoplectic stroke. There was no talking to people like that so Quinn made it a point to direct his words toward Agent Miller.

"Okay, Liz," Quinn said. "These guys don't travel alone. Did you notice any associates hanging back when you took this one into custody?"

"It was a plane from Dubai, jackass," Chaffee scoffed. "There were two hundred Arab guys who got off with him. They could have all been his associates. . . ." He winced, clenching his eyes shut until a new wave of pain subsided. When they opened he glared at Mahoney "I asked you a question. What was in that vial?"

"Have a seat, Agent Chaffee," Mahoney said. "We have a team on the way. There'll be medical personnel to take a look at your arm."

"She's right, Bob," Miller said, trying to paste a smile over the strain on her face. "Just sit down and rest."

Mahoney's Bluetooth flashed on her ear, casting a pulsing blue halo around her hair inside the hood. "Hold on," she said. "I have an incoming call. It's probably my team."

Agent Chaffee jerked away from his partner. He grabbed a fistful of Mahoney's rubber suit with his good hand, spinning her around. His eyes were wild with a mixture of rage and hysteria. Spittle flew from his twisted mouth as he screamed, "You listen to me. The FBI has national security juris—"

Jericho reacted in a flash, slapping Chaffee hard across the ear with a cupped hand that sent him staggering backward. He followed up with a swift knee to the groin and snatched the agent's Glock from his holster before he hit the floor.

"*You* are not in charge, Agent Chaffee," Quinn said, his even voice belying the fury and speed he'd used to pacify the man. "Now sit still and let us handle this as best we can." He nodded to a stupefied Mahoney. "Go ahead and take your call."

CHAPTER 37

"Megan?"

"Yes . . ."

"It's Justin. Where are you?" His voice was frantic as if he was bursting with information. At first, she was afraid he was calling with bad news about his symptoms from the needle stick. Then she remembered he should have been in the Slammer, incommunicado.

"Justin?" she said. "Where did you get a phone?"

"I was going crazy in there, Meg," he said. "I convinced Dr. Kraus to let me out."

"Roberta let you out of the Slammer?" Mahoney gasped, throwing a puff of condensation on her face shield. Justin must have been putting some serious moves on the tall German scientist for her to cave in against such strict protocols. Kraus had always joked that she had a thing for his dimples.

"I'm not even feeling sick. Anyway, I promised her I'd stay in the BSL-Four containment and do some work."

"I'll bet you did."

"Anyway," Justin said, "that's not the important part. I'm pretty sure I'm going to be fine."

"Justin, I'm kind of busy here," Mahoney sighed.

"I know, but I think you'll want to hear what I've got. Check this out, Megan. We injected C-06 with the optic jelly on the eleventh and paired him with C-12 as a breathing buddy, right?"

Mahoney looked at her watch, doing the math. She felt her legs go a little wobbly, wondering where such a conversation was heading. "Right. That would have been about ninety-six hours ago—roughly four days . . ."

"A little over that," Justin said. "But here's the deal. I couldn't sleep so I checked C-12 last night around midnight and he was clean. Then, I ran another test about three hours ago. He's got it, Megan. His blood is swimming with filovirus. The virus is contagious, but not right away. My blood is still okay so it looks like I'm home free."

"Symptomatic?" Megan found herself chewing the inside of her cheek, an awful thought working its way to the fore in her exhausted brain.

"C-12?" Justin said. "No, he's fine. But I when I went to check on C-06 half an hour ago, he had blood literally gushing out of his nose. He's crashing, Megan, and he's crashing fast. The virus in his blood has changed. The protein sheaths are dissolving. I think that's what makes it turn contagious."

"It's been a long time since my head's seen a pillow," Mahoney said. "Run down the timeline with me so I can make sure I have it straight."

Justin plowed ahead, unaware that he was talking about anything but captive crab-eating macaques.

"Okay, Meg, here's what we've got. The macaque we injected after we had to put C-45 down—C-06—didn't become symptomatic after we injected him until the fifth day, but his breathing buddy in the next cage, sharing nothing but air, caught the virus sometime during the fourth night. . . ."

Mahoney's eyes fell to the overturned wastebasket. She was struck by a sudden, sickening thought. Justin had no idea about the real ramifications of what he was saying.

"Do me a favor," she said weakly. "Check the contents of the glass vial we brought in yesterday." Going from call to call on suspected terrorists she'd not had time to look at it herself.

"Already done," Justin said. "It's not a virus at all. It's some kind of shellfish toxin. There's enough in the vial to kill one man almost instantly, but that's all."

"A suicide drug . . ." Mahoney's voice trailed off. Her eyes shot around the room. The carpet around Hamid was soaked in a dark, rapidly spreading stain. Droplets of the Arab's blood had splattered like rain both during the fight and subsequent shooting. Chaffee's face and hair were flecked in red. The customs inspector looked like a Civil War surgeon after a brutal amputation. "You're saying C-06 passed the virus before he showed any symptoms whatsoever?"

"Yes. Do you know what this means?" From the jubilant tone in Justin's voice, it was obvious all he was thinking about was that it meant he was clear of any infection from his needle stick.

Megan teetered on her feet, clutching at the edge of the table with her glove to remain standing.

"Everything all right, Doc?" Quinn took her arm to steady her.

The bulky hood moved back and forth slowly, swishing as Mahoney shook her head. She whispered, feeling as if she might vomit.

"Pandora . . ."

CHAPTER 38

"If I'm not mistaken the Soviets already have something like this," Win Palmer said, leaning back in the customary thinking spot behind his heavy desk to stare at the ceiling. Quinn was beginning to think the man had answers to all his problems etched somewhere up there. "Didn't they get some kind of airborne hemorrhagic virus?"

"Supposedly," Mahoney said. "I think they had better luck with Marburg. . . ." She sat hunched over on the couch, elbows on her knees. She was still stunned from the discovery that Arab terrorists had found a way not only to make a variant of the Ebola virus airborne, but contagious before—if only just barely, according to Justin—the carrier showed any symptoms of the disease.

Her head snapped up. "Don't y'all see? A person with this . . . this Pandora form of Ebola would be the mother of all Typhoid Marys. We . . . I mean the CDC . . . the government has all kinds plans in place for quarantine in case of plague, tularemia, smallpox—all sorts of biological pandemic. But we'll never even see this coming. People won't even know they're sick while they're passing it to their families . . . the checkout lady at the grocery store, the guy who holds the door open for them at the bank. . . . Imagine the underground Metro stations with their moist crowded air. . . ." She took a deep breath, nodding her head as if to bring her thoughts into focus. "Over the last two decades HIV/AIDS has crept like a slow burn over the entire world. It's infected tens of thousands of people—most generally transmitted through unprotected sex. Even the most flagrant individual is more discreet about having sex than he is with his breathing. We're such a mobile society, in a matter of hours after Zafir becomes contagious, hundreds of people he has infected will get on airplanes and buses, taxis and subways. . . ." Megan slumped as if she had already lost.

"How long?" Thibodaux asked, pacing beside the door. He was a doer and all this talking made him visibly twitchy. "How long do we have until Zafir is hot?"

"These guys aren't stupid," Quinn offered. "Megan, you think it's safe to say they'd wait until they were out of their own country before they infect themselves with Pandora?"

"I'd think so," she said. "This virus is so deadly I'm sure the guys who don't want to be martyrs will insist on it."

Palmer, who generally seemed content to sit back and listen, tapped a pencil on his leather desk blotter. "You called that one correctly. The Saudi deputy foreign minister sent word six hours ago that he was closing the borders to all incoming traffic. They've stationed Saudi military personnel at all border crossings. Trains, buses, and aircraft coming into the country have been halted until further notice. They're blaming it on swine flu. It's stirring up quite a scare over there. Jordan, Syria, Lebanon, and Iran have all followed suit. Egypt is bound to be next.

"We need to play this extremely close-hold." Palmer continued. "We could end up with ten dozen more FBI Agent Chaffees staring down our necks if we let other agencies get involved in the reality of this thing." Palmer leaned back and stared up at the ceiling some more. At length, he let the chair tip forward and rested his forearms on his desk. "I'll work up a story for all the networks. Zafir is the biggest terrorist since Carlos the Jackal; that ought to get their juices flowing. I'll release his photograph to all the wire services and get everyone in the country looking for him. We'll leak it that he has nuclear material. There's no such thing as a kill order on NCIC, but we'll let everyone know he should be considered armed and much too dangerous to approach. Scary enough to keep local law enforcement at a respectable standoff distance."

"That'll work if we find him before he goes contagious on us," Mahoney mused. "You say the Saudis shut their borders six hours ago? Someone with influence in the Kingdom must have expected people to start getting hot at about that time. If we go with that pattern, Kalil came in first, followed about twenty-four hours later by Hamid. That would put Zafir arriving sometime today."

"Makes sense," Quinn said. "I got a call from one of

my OSI buddies in Iraq a couple of hours ago. My informant, Sadiq, has gone missing. He says there was quite a bit of blood on the floor of the kid's apartment so no one's holding out too much hope of finding him alive."

"I suppose they were all in the john," Thibodaux snorted. "And didn't see a thing."

"A neighbor remembers a guy with a deformed hand walking up the stairs sometime on the eleventh. That would have been shortly after Sadiq called me." Quinn scribbled in his black Moleskine notebook as he spoke. "DOD finally came up with a name to go with the third martyr photograph we gave them. Zafir Mamoud al Jawad. He was arrested with a bunch of other insurgents outside Baquba sometime in oh-seven. The report said they had American hostages. Should have gone to trial, but he escaped his Iraqi police detail along with some other prisoners and got away in the desert. He's a Bedouin, real tough guy, missing three fingers and part of his left hand, apparently from some sword fight."

"Now we're gettin' somewhere, beb." Thibodaux bobbed his big head. "So we figure Zafir was still in Iraq on the eleventh. Let's say he left on the twelfth, how long would we have from right now until he was contagious?"

"If the virus in him reacts like it does in the macaques," Mahoney said, "and supposing he infected himself as soon as he left the Middle East, maybe a day." She walked to a poster-size calendar Palmer had on his wall above a mahogany credenza that matched his desk. The September scene was a photograph of two sailboats racing in cobalt water of Cabo San Lucas.

Taking a red marker from a mug on the credenza, she drew a big circle around September 16. In the center of the circle, she wrote *10 a.m EDT*.

She looked at her watch. "I don't know how we're going to do it, but before ten tomorrow morning, we need to find Zafir Jawad and kill him."

"Eighteen hours," Thibodaux moaned, leaning back in a huge, yawning stretch. "I guess I can sleep after I'm dead."

CHAPTER 39

Zafir removed his shirt to kill the leader of the three cocaine smugglers. He used a short knife with a silver eagle head on the hilt he'd bought from a street vendor in Nuevo Progresso—across the Rio Grande in Mexico. The night was inky dark, but he couldn't risk getting caught. Not now, not when he was so close. U.S. Border Patrol agents were everywhere and the dying drug smugglers provided them with a job to take their minds off chasing illegal aliens—especially those from the Middle East.

The knife was an inexpensive weapon, nothing like the fine steel Zafir was used to in his homeland, where such a blade was often used to take a life. The eagle-head blade was easily sharpened, as cheap knives often were, but easily dulled—much like most of the people Zafir knew. By the time he'd removed the head of the first cocaine smuggler, he had to stop and use a flat piece of sandstone from the river to bring back the edge. The other two smugglers looked on, trussed like goats as he tended to his gruesome work. Their eyes sparkled with that strange sort of glowing shock Zafir had come to appreciate. Lying on the their bellies, hands and feet behind their backs, neither moved, paralyzed by the sheer terror of watching their companion lose his head to a person who was an obvious expert at such things. Their mouths were taped, but Zafir guessed they wouldn't have made a sound if he'd done nothing but tie them.

These were young, cocky men from the nearby city of Reynosa, who had made the mistake of many in the lower echelons of criminal organizations, believing that since their boss commanded respect, such respect automatically trickled down to their level. Zafir had never heard of the Ochoa cartel, and when they'd thrown the name out as something that should certainly strike fear in his heart, he'd only laughed and stabbed the apparent leader in the belly. He'd knocked the other two senseless with a rock.

His grizzly task completed, Zafir leaned the dead smuggler's body against the base of a thorny acacia tree. The head, eyes locked wide as if still wondering how such an awful thing had happened, he placed in the lap of its previous owner along with the backpack of cocaine. When Zafir reached for the second smuggler, the young man's eyes rolled back in his head and he began to writhe against his bonds, wracked with sobs. The high-pitched buzz of his screams purred against the duct tape stretched across his mouth. Zafir paid no attention and dragged the boy to the tree beside his headless friend, where he dropped him like a sack of garbage. The last smuggler was quieter, whimpering softly as Zafir dragged him to the tree by his belt and dropped him on the opposite side of his dead compatriot.

This done, he retrieved his shirt from where he'd left it on a willow shrub by the Rio Grande and knelt beside the quivering men. Up to this point, he hadn't said a word.

Turning the knife slowly in his good hand, he let the blade glitter in the scant light from a sky of endless stars. He held the freshly honed point to the eyeball of the writhing one, causing him to freeze in the middle of his gyrations.

"When I remove the tape from your mouth, I need you to scream as if you'd just lost an eye," Zafir whispered in fluent Spanish. "Here," he said pressing the point home with a satisfying pop. "Let me help raise the volume. . . ."

Frenzied howls from the terrified drug smugglers drew nearby Border Patrol agents to the riverbank. The responding agents' radio reports quickly brought every agent in the sector, hungry to witness the brutality of such a bloody scene. Zafir was able to slip past what were normally heavily manned observation posts completely unmolested.

He estimated he'd walked almost seven miles before he saw the yellow flicker of a tiny campfire in the woods. He moved in slowly, picking his way through the clumps of prickly pear cactus and thick thorn brush. The night was hot and choked with dust. But for the tangle of so many bushes, it reminded Zafir of his home. Through the darkness, he heard lilting laughter.

As he inched closer, he saw two Mexicans, a man and a woman, sitting on a white limestone boulder beside the dying embers of a fire. The woman's belly was stretched tight under a black shirt as if she carried a huge ball. She was pregnant and very near to giving birth.

Zafir was about to move by, fearing contact with anyone that would slow him down. Then he heard the young husband mention in a soothing voice that his cousin would be arriving soon with a truck to take them to the hospital in McAllen.

He listened to the giggling couple while he knelt in the shadows of dry grass. They dreamed together about the birth of their son, how he would be born in America and experience all the fruits of such citizenship. Zafir smiled at the thought. Very soon America would experience some very bitter fruit indeed, but this young couple would never see it. Their cousin's car would get him to the Harlingen Airport, where he could fly to Fort Worth. Farooq's contacts in Los Angeles had provided him with a California driver's license under the name of Jorge Ramirez. The sheikh's influence was everywhere.

Quietly drawing the pistol he'd taken from one of the drug smugglers, the Bedouin looked at his watch. It was a U.S. Navy Seals dive model, given to him as an ironic gift from the sheikh. Tritium numbers glowed an eerie green in darkness. It was almost midnight. He began to move toward the sound of laughter.

Time was short and he had business with an old friend from Baquba.

CHAPTER 40

Fort Worth

Carrie Navarro hardly had enough energy to hit the button on the blender for Christian's banana milkshake. Lately, work had been such a battle. Her new editor at the *Star Telegram* was nearly ten years younger than her with no real-world experience beyond being a livestock reporter for the farm and ranch section, but still he felt it necessary to change every story she wrote to the point that she didn't even recognize it by the time it came out in print. Not only was he an ass, he was an incompetent ass, and that was unforgivable. Still, there was little she could do about it but scream, since he happened to be the publisher's nephew. She'd dealt with her share of idiots over the course of her career, but the fact that this one was her boss made it more of a challenge. If her life's experience had taught her anything, it was to prioritize the things that stressed her, and the pimple-faced editor of the political section, mired up to his little pierced eyebrow in nepotism, was not going to be one of her stressors, not today anyway. She had plenty of things to give her ulcers without worrying over that little weasel.

It was late, almost time for the news. Christian's bedtime had come and gone, and Carrie felt a twinge of guilt for being such a rotten mom. Of course he was more than happy to stay up and now sat cross-legged on the floor looking at his favorite Dr. Seuss book. She compensated for her lack of mothering skills by making them a couple of grilled cheese sandwiches and banana milkshakes—a late-night snack that would have caused her own mother to throw a bona fide fit. Again, it wasn't something she was going to let get to her. Dr. Soto had helped her with that.

Paper plate of sandwiches in hand, Carrie flopped down on the couch and patted her lap.

"Climb up here and keep Mama company, little man," she said.

Nights were not as scary as they had been before she started seeing Dr. Soto, but they were still dark and still lonely. Unspeakable memories popped into her thoughts when she least expected them, particularly if she didn't keep her mind occupied. Despite his cruel beginnings, Christian proved more than a pleasant distraction. He was her life.

No matter the violent way he came into being, this amazing child had saved her. He was smarter than any other three-year-old she'd ever heard of, already reading hundreds of words. He spoke Spanish as well as he spoke English—and he spoke English like a child three times his age. But more importantly to Carrie her son was a gentle soul. He doted on his mother as if he somehow sensed her inner fears, crying when she cried, often reaching up to touch her cheek with his tiny fingers for no apparent reason. It was as if he was as much in awe of her as she was of him.

Christian cuddled up in her lap, Dr. Seuss book in one dimpled hand, a quarter of grilled cheese sandwich clutched in the other. Who would have thought she could get so much joy out of watching the little guy chew?

"You read," Carrie said, picking up the remote. "Mama will see what the talking heads have to say before we go to bed."

"Talking heads." Christian giggled. "You're funny, Mom. . . ."

Carrie took a bite of sandwich as she flipped through the channels. She preferred her local news to the cable networks. The reporters and anchors still wore too much makeup, but most of them had enough meat on their bones to look a little more human than the big-haired stick-figure beauties on CNN.

. . . USE EXTREME CAUTION. DO NOT APPROACH, scrolled along the bottom of the screen, followed by a toll-free number. Carrie sat up with renewed interest. She'd missed the lead-in and the blond, female member of the anchor team of Kip and Jane was running down the top story of the evening. Jane Baily wore big glasses and kept her hair straight, hanging past her shoulders, looking more like a sixties-era flower child than a news anchor. That's why Carrie trusted her.

". . . authorities tell us they're looking for this man

in connection with the theft of highly dangerous radio-active material. They're warning people who may see him—and this includes law enforcement—not to attempt contact. Don't even approach him, they're telling us. Anyone who sees the man in the photograph we're about to show should call the number at the bottom of the screen immediately. Let's go ahead and bring up the photograph. . . ."

"This is like something out of the movies, Jane," Kip said, looking somber without his trademark sparkling grin.

"Here we are," Jane said as the photograph came up on the screen. "Authorities aren't saying where he's supposed to be or where he's going, but the man is identified as . . ."

A bite of cheese sandwich fell from Carrie's gaping mouth. Her bare toes clenched at the carpet.

"Zafir!" she cried. "NO . . . I can't . . ."

". . . of Middle Eastern descent," Kip continued. "Zafir Jawad is missing three fingers . . ." Kip and Jane kept up their banter. Carrie heard nothing but the whoosh of blood pulsing in her ears.

"You're hurting my leg." Christian wriggled to escape Carrie's fingernails on his thigh. Squirming around to face her, he looked up with an olive complexion and deep-set eyes identical to the man staring at her from the television.

A thousand bees buzzed inside her. Her skin crawled as if writhing in a bed of poisonous snakes. Trembling so hard she worried she might crack a tooth, Carrie reached for the phone beside the couch. It rang as her finger brushed the receiver.

She screamed, memories of months of torment and pain flooding her system like an illness. If Zafir was in the United States, she knew exactly what he was after.

In her lap, Christian began to cry.

CHAPTER 41

16 September, 0130 hours

Jericho opened his eyes when Winfield Palmer's Bombardier Challenger touched down in Texas with a puff of smoke and a muted squawk of tires on tarmac. Designed by Bill Lear, the CL 601 had roughly the same cruise speed and only slightly less range than a Gulfstream IV—the more famous sister jet on which every spy in the world of fictional espionage seemed to fly. This particular CL 601 was registered to the Federal Aviation Administration. Just as Quinn and Thibodaux served as Other Governmental Agents, the Challenger was an Other Governmental Aircraft—one thing on paper, but quite another in point of fact. The pilots were paid through the FAA payroll system, but took their orders from the Director of National Intelligence. Without a very close inspection, both pilots and aircraft would blend in with the thousands of other boring cogs of the civil service gears that made up the unwieldy bureaucracy of the United States government.

The sleek plane bounced once, then settled into a smooth ground roll. The seats were plush—comfortable leather that leaned all the way back for long overseas trips. Teetering on the razor's edge of complete exhaustion and delirium, he'd collapsed into a dreamless sleep as soon as the jet had jumped off the ground at Langley. A two-hour nap had done little but add to the kinks in his spine and the unshakeable feeling that he was walking around with his head inside a barrel of crude oil. He tried to swallow but felt as if he had a mouth full of talcum powder. Accustomed to the freedom of the wind on his motorcycle, airplane air was among Jericho's most hated substances.

Blue taxiway lights shot by the windows as the jet rolled into Fort Worth and past Alliance Airport's iconic snow-cone-shaped control tower.

After the photo of Zafir went public, there had been no shortage of leads. Thousands of people phoned the number to say they'd seen the fugitive. Some even claimed to be him. Agents from virtually every organization in the government took part in trying to locate the fugitive (though none of them knew the real story beyond that he should be considered a highly "toxic" target). There was no way to check all the tips, but they couldn't stand by and do nothing.

Then, call screeners sent forward a report from a Border Patrol agent in South Texas who said one of his prisoners had seen the photograph on the television while in the hospital after having his eye cut out by a "devil bandit" on the banks of the Rio Grande. According to the agent, the prisoner had nearly broken his handcuffs trying to get out of his bed when he saw the picture on the news. He swore this was the man who had cut out his eye and sawed the head off his friend.

Moments later, the call had come in from Carrie Navarro and they finally had something to go with.

"One-thirty in the morning." Thibodaux yawned. "That's two-thirty in my brain. I know we're tryin' to save the world and everything, but I feel like I've been stomped to death."

Mahoney gathered up the sheaves of notes she'd worked on during the flight and stuffed them in a black ballistic nylon briefcase. There was no attendant to lord over their safety, and she stood to take a bag out of the overhead while the plane was still moving. "Can I ask you something, Jacques?" she said, holding a pen in her mouth as she worked the compartment's latch.

"Fire away, *l'ami*." The Cajun yawned again, holding both arms above his head like huge goalposts as he gave a shivering stretch.

"You don't cuss very much for a Marine," she said.

Thibodaux grinned as he unfolded himself out of the plush leather seat. "My child bride only allows me five non-Bible curse words a month."

"Yeah, but she's back at Cherry Point," Quinn said. He straightened his pistol and situated the Masamune blade at the small of his back. "How's she gonna know?"

"Let me tell you somethin'." Thibodaux raised an eyebrow, as if he alone held the knowledge of a dark and dangerous secret. "I can't count the times I've looked death square in the yap, but none of that scared me near so much as that little Italian woman between my sheets. Believe me, beb, she'd know."

Quinn leaned in so Mahoney couldn't hear him. "You do realize that *shit* isn't a Bible word?"

"Really?" Thibodaux said, wide eyed. "Dammit!"

Through the windows, Quinn could see a Bell Jet Ranger helicopter as the Challenger slowed. Strobe lights flashed in the night. The rotor turned, spooled up and ready to go. Men in blue jumpsuits moved toward the belly of the 605 before it had even stopped, ready to unload the duffel bags of gear at the first opportunity.

"The chopper will take us to the helipad at Texas Christian University," Quinn said, leaning on the back of his seat to watch the chopper out the side windows. Even in the shadows he could make out dark semicircles of sweat on the men's coveralls. He braced himself for the Texas humidity, knowing it would hit him in the chest like a wet towel. "Palmer has a car waiting for us at TCU," he said. "Navarro's house is just a few miles from there. He's set up a place for us to do our surveillance in a vacant house across the street."

Bouncing in her Nikes with a contagious buzz, Mahoney seemed to have a limitless reservoir of perkiness. Quinn was relieved she showed some level of human mortality when she actually rubbed her eyes and yawned like a lioness, wide and long enough he could count the fillings in her teeth.

"Sorry about that," she said, putting the back of her hand to her mouth as the yawn turned into a full-body stretch. "We've got less than eight hours left . . . if we're lucky." She looked down the aisle at both men. "I could be dead wrong about the timeline, you know. Even as we speak, Zafir could be spreading this thing like some kind of Johnny Ebola Appleseed."

"What else can we do?" Quinn arched his back, trying in vain to pop his spine.

"I'll tell you what." Thibodaux fished a protein bar out of his camouflage backpack and ripped it open with his teeth. "Once we locate Zafir, the most sensible thing to do would be to drop some napalm on his ass—toast him and the germs that rode in on him." He swallowed the bar in three bites and washed it down with a gulp of water from the SIGG Aluminum bottle he carried everywhere.

"And kill everyone around him. . . ." Mahoney said through clenched teeth. "Maybe we should declare martial law and force everyone to stay in their homes for the next three months." She ran a hand through her hair, mussed from the long flight. She sighed like an exhausted runner, still miles from the finish.

"No one would have the stomach to enforce a nationwide quarantine until people start dying," Jericho said. "Most of our National Guard troops are just kids—even the ones who've done a tour in the Middle East. I'm not sure they're up to shooting the local barber just because he leaves his house for food." He studied Mahoney in the stark light of the cabin. Her eyes were wide and round, like a frightened little girl. "Palmer trusts your timetable and so do I. He's convinced we can do this without losing too many innocents. We hold off as long as we can before we tell locals what's really going on. As soon as it leaks out what this manhunt is really all about, there's a very real possibility cool heads will not prevail."

"I don't like it." Mahoney groaned. "It's no good. If we're all there is . . ."

"Oh." Jericho gave her a wink. "We're not *all* there is." He punched a number in his cell phone as they walked down the boarding ladder.

"Brother Bo," he said. "We're on the ground. You and your boys ready for a little excitement?"

CHAPTER 42

Gail Taylor, the sturdy girl behind the Avis counter at the Dallas Fort Worth International Airport, had at least three tattoos. A delicate hummingbird sipped nectar from a yellow cactus flower on her left wrist. The alluring red petals of a briar rose blossomed in the swell of pale flesh above the loose V in the front of her peach-colored cotton blouse. When she turned to retrieve the keys to his rental car, Zafir caught the glimpse of a third. It was some kind of tribal design, reminiscent of something he had seen on natives of the South Pacific islands, visible along the narrow strip of exposed flesh above the waist of her jeans and below the hem of her shirt, just where her buttocks came together.

The pious side of Zafir found such an open display of sexuality revolting. The rest of him couldn't pull his eyes away. He was not unaccustomed to seeing women with tattoos. It was common for Bedouin women to draw intricate designs on their hands with henna dur-

ing weddings and other celebrations, but none were so
wanton as this.

Gail Taylor was pleasant enough. She was in her late
thirties, with an oval face, and carried her extra weight
around her hips. She had a graveled, whiskeyed tone to
her voice that made Zafir's heart beat faster every time
she spoke. He was happy when she turned her attention
away from him and to the business of her job.

Bubbling over with giddy energy, she worked through
all the papers he needed to sign with an eagerness that
surprised even Zafir. In all his travels, he'd never rented
a car and he fretted over this one moment more than
any other part of his plan—even his death. Above all
else, Zafir hated to look foolish

The jiggling briar rose tattoo peeked out when Gail
filled in the paperwork, leaning over the chest-high
counter to show him where to initial when he declined
unneeded insurance. He'd trimmed his coarse beard
into a neat goatee and cut his windblown hair in the
style of an American movie actor. She touched his
scarred hand gently, as if it made no difference that he
had a claw there instead of fingers.

Feeling heady, he pulled away, struggling to gain
control of his emotions. He was not used to a woman
who paid attention to him of her own accord.

"And this . . ." He coughed, swallowing hard. "This
is the GPS?"

"Yep," Gail said. "You just punch in the address of
where you want to go." She pressed her breast against
his shoulder as she demonstrated. "It'll even talk to
you in Spanish if you want."

"English will do." Zafir smiled, straining to look pleasant. "I need the practice."

"What's the address?" Gail's red fingernail poised over the little colored screen.

Zafir paused. In his lust to find Carrie Navarro, he'd only thought to get to the city where she lived. He'd assumed finding her in a place as open as America would be simple enough.

"West Fort Worth," he said at length.

"That's an area." Gail Taylor giggled. "Not an address. I have to put in a street and numbers." She tapped the back of his hand with a red fingernail.

"I understood everything was mapped here in the U.S.," he said, feigning his best Mexican accent. "Can you not type in a name and have the GPS give me an address?"

Gail gazed up at him, batting big, cowlike eyes. There wasn't an ounce of guile in them.

"Well, no . . . that wouldn't get us anywhere, not with this little guy. You'd need a computer for that."

"I have no computer." Under the lip of the counter, out of the girl's line of sight, Zafir clenched his good fist. He had no time for this.

"My jackass manager shut down our Internet or I'd help you look it up on our computers. I guess you could go to the library, but my guess is you don't have a library card. . . ." Gail suddenly brightened. "An iPhone would do. They're just little computers anyhow. I have one in back with my stuff."

"You would show me how to use it, this little computer iPhone of yours?" Zafir smiled, willing himself to relax, though his instinct was to strike this woman as hard as he could.

Gail mistook his seething anger for passion and lowered thick, black lashes accented by peach eye shadow to match her blouse. Her full cheeks flushed pink. "I could do that."

Charm was not Zafir's strong suit. He did not have to play games with women. They did as he told them to do and he did to them as he pleased. The importance of his mission pushed him forward. He knew he was a wanted man and needed to get out of the public eye as soon as possible.

"Perhaps we could go somewhere . . . more private," he said, clenching his jaw.

The fleshy woman stepped back, letting her hand trail along his arm. "Mr. Ramirez . . ."

He hung his head, to hide the fire in his eyes. "I hope I have not been too . . . how do you say it . . . aggressive."

"Why, Mr. Ramirez . . . I . . . I think I'd like that very much," she said. "We meet some real weirdos here, but I can tell you're not one of them." She glanced at the digital clock on the wall behind her. "It's a quarter to six. I get off in fifteen minutes. Tell you what, you buy me breakfast and I'll help you find what you're looking for." She touched him on the arm again. "*Everything* you're looking for."

"I would be most happy to buy you breakfast in return for your kindness," Zafir said. In his mind's eye, he saw the plump thing in a burqa. She was much too forward with him, a complete stranger. In the Kingdom, breakfast alone with an unrelated male would have earned her a hundred lashes.

"Meet me back here in fifteen minutes," she said. "I'm so hungry I could eat a cow." She lowered her gaze. "I can promise you one thing. I'm a lot more fun to be around when I'm not hungry. . . ."

CHAPTER 43

Zafir wiped a smeared droplet of Gail Taylor's blood from the iPhone with the tail of his shirt. The infidel woman had been overly helpful, falling all over herself as she showed him how to use a free people-finder website to find Carrie Navarro's address in her small, handheld computer. She'd played the part of bold lover almost to the end, giggling and winking until he'd taken the eagle-head knife out of his duffel bag and passed it slowly in front of her flushed face.

Remembering, Zafir lifted his collar to his nose and smelled the scent of the American woman that lingered on his clothing. He rolled down the window of his car and breathed a deep breath of the humid morning air.

Imminent death, he thought, was a liberating thing indeed. The notion of its certainty endowed him with a sort of heady focus he'd never before experienced, even in the heat of deadly conflict. His perspective changed. No longer would it be important to fret over fingerprints he might leave behind. Stains of the American woman's blood on his clothing would never cause him a problem. The sloppy manner in which she'd died didn't matter. And the fact that he'd left his DNA on her body was something from which he could walk away and never give another moment's consideration. The filthy woman had obviously been of loose morals to flaunt her body the way she had—with him, a complete stranger. She was a common whore and deserved what she got. Was he not a man? Did he not have natural tendencies and desires that such a wanton woman would inflame with her behavior?

At the end, when he'd already begun his work with the eagle-head knife, she'd been so pitiful, so utterly without spirit, absent even a hint of the strong will possessed by his old friend Carrie Navarro. Gail had whimpered and begged. Her eyes covered in garish makeup, eyes that had once flirted with him, had snapped wide in abject terror. She had pleaded for mercy as long as her tremulous chest held a breath—when the only merciful thing to do would have been to kill her more quickly. The woman's weakness made Zafir despise her, but it had made him hate Navarro even more.

He drove on into morning traffic on the littered streets of East Fort Worth near Gail Taylor's scabby apartment off a frontage road that ran parallel to Loop 820. He passed a western store with a giant red cowboy boot out front and a McDonald's restaurant with its golden arches rising heavenward like a heathen idol. A line of coffee worshipers queued in the drive-through waiting to show their devotions to their morning fix. Used-car dealerships sprawled along the access road.

Stores selling every kind of goods imaginable from mobile homes to baby clothes lined the littered streets. Zafir shook his head at such decadence. America the wealthy, America the fat, America the arrogant. Soon, in a matter of weeks, stores and restaurants as far as the eye could see would stand vacant. Those few infidels who were left alive by the hand of Allah would be too frightened to venture into public places among the rotting corpses of their neighbors.

The heady memories of Gail Taylor ebbed away like a receding tide with each new breath. A single burning desire drew Zafir forward like a flaming string through his heart. Though his death was a certainty, he had to survive the moment. He had to make it to Carrie Navarro's home, to take care of the unfinished business with her. What happened beyond that was irrelevant. At first he'd thought to try and save his son, send him away somehow, back to the sheikh. But such a thing was impossible. No, he would take the boy from the pitiful shadow of his harlot mother—take him and allow him the great honor of dying as a glorious martyr alongside his father, where he belonged.

Zafir glanced up in the rearview mirror of his rental sedan, scanning as he merged into the heavy traffic of Loop 820. He headed south, toward the highway that would bisect Fort Worth and take him to Carrie Navarro. His instincts told him there was someone behind him, someone who followed him like a jackal follows the lion—plodding just far enough behind to be out of danger. Such instincts had never failed him before. But this time, he had to be mistaken. If the Americans knew where he was, they would surely kill him before he drove another mile. He'd heard the reports. They had shot Kalil in the back of the head without ever trying to arrest him. He had no idea what had happened to Hamid, but assumed he also was out of the game. The Americans could not know everything, but they surely had some idea of the risk these men had posed. They had no reason to follow him and every reason in the world to want him dead.

He moved to the fast lane, and then slowed to fifty miles an hour. Angry drivers honked and shouted obscenities out their windows as traffic stacked up behind him, and then merged into other lanes to pass. If there was anyone following him, he was extremely good at his job.

Zafir shrugged off the feeling and checked the GPS mounted on his windshield. The numbers showed he would arrive at Navarro's in thirty-one minutes. He smiled, leaning back against the headrest to savor the thought.

What he'd done to Gail Taylor was nothing but an enjoyable diversion. A frolic. He'd been easy on her, made her death come relatively quick. Carrie Navarro had to atone for the things she'd said to him—for the humiliation she'd put him through in the eyes of his subordinates.

And Zafir would make certain that her atonement would be slow and painful.

CHAPTER 44

Mahoney sat on the carpet of the empty house, knees drawn up to her chin, her back against the peeling robin's-egg blue paint on the living-room wall. The house smelled vaguely of cinnamon, mildew, and motor oil. Four dead roaches and a twitching cricket formed a pile of sweepings on the linoleum floor beneath Quinn's chair in the vacant dining room fifteen feet away.

Bo Quinn and four other bikers from his "club" had roared up on their Harleys at the TCU helipad and followed the team in the early-morning darkness to Carrie Navarro's quiet tree-lined street west of Trinity Park. All the men looked like the sort Mahoney's father had warned her about, the kind you didn't want to meet in an alley on a dark night. She had smiled inside when Bo had dismounted his bike, and yanked his brother toward him in a back-slapping embrace. Jericho appeared to know the other members of the club as well, shaking their hands and hugging each of them in turn.

Bo's sandy hair was cut short, though it was still long enough to cover his ears. While his companions all sported full beards or goatees, the younger Quinn had only a healthy growth of stubble, which, if he was anything like his brother, he could have sprouted in less than a day. Like the others, he wore faded jeans and a denim vest over a dark T-shirt. An indigo rocker under the angry-looking black octopus on the back of the vest was emblazoned with the word DENIZENS in embroidered red letters four inches high.

Bo was the only member of his group not completely sleeved in tattoos. While the other men's muscular arms were covered in multicolored images of big-breasted women, eyeless skulls, and blazing guns, Bo Quinn had only one visible piece of ink. Occupying the entire inside of his veined right forearm was a jet-black octopus, identical to the one on his vest, eight arms trailing around a single angry eye.

Bo's second in command appeared to be a tall Viking of a man with a scar that ran from his right eyebrow across his nose and to the bottom of his opposite jaw. Called Ugly by the others, he was bald but for the shoulder-length patch of hair on the back of his scalp, which he pulled back into a blond ponytail. A green jailhouse tattoo of a spiderweb covered the left side of his face, drawing attention to the jagged scar. The man had hugged Jericho, grinning as if they were long lost cousins. Caught up in the reunion, he'd embraced Megan as well. She'd been surprised that he'd smelled faintly of cookie dough along with the lingering odor of pipe tobacco. When she closed her eyes, she could picture a kindly old uncle. When she opened them, she saw a bloodthirsty pirate. At first, Megan had found it disconcerting the way the men, who were the type her mother would mention in the same sentence as the phrase "gang rape," exchanged pleasantries as if meeting at a family reunion over a plate of slaw and barbecued ribs.

"Pleased to meet you, ma'am," Ugly had said, his face a picture of earnestness behind the green web of prison ink. A diamond stud adorned the scarified cauliflower nub of what was once his left ear. "I'll lead the way," he'd said, climbing back aboard his bike. "Y'all follow me. . . ."

Carrie Navarro had gone to her mother's home nearly sixty miles away. Palmer pulled some strings and got the Bureau to stand up a protective detail out of an abundance of caution, though none of her protectors knew exactly who she was or why they were guarding her.

The vacant house Jericho and his friends were using for surveillance was directly across the street from Navarro's now-empty nest. Hidden in the trees at the far corner behind Navarro's modest white frame home, Thibodaux was able to maintain a visual along the south and east sides of the house. From their position across the street, Mahoney and the Quinn brothers could watch the front as well as the west side. Both Jericho and Bo had agreed that it provided an excellent location that would give them a "tactically superior advantage" when Zafir arrived. Megan listened to the men and wondered what it must have been like growing up in the Quinn home.

Bo Quinn had insisted on pulling his new Harley-

Davidson Night Rod inside the vacant house, unwilling to leave it outside to be caught in the cross fire if things "went rodeo" on them. The low-slung motorcycle now sat like a flat black locomotive in the middle of the living room.

Despite the urgency of capturing Zafir Jawad, the Quinn brothers chatted calmly about Bo's new bike, how fast it was for a Harley—Jericho had plenty to say concerning this—and how much horsepower Bo had been able to milk out with a few modifications.

"She's American and she scoots, Jer," Bo had said, nodding smugly. "A hundred and fifty miles an hour, right out of the box. I'd like to see your German bike do that. . . ."

Over time, Mahoney noticed a smoldering intensity about the two men that began to make her feel a little light-headed. At first she blamed it on fatigue, but realized it was much more basic than that. Though they shared the same strong jaw and propensity to grow a quick beard, the brothers were like night and day. Where Jericho was dark, Bo was blond, with the sun-bleached look of a surfer. Four years Jericho's junior, Bo was much more flamboyant in his manner, strutting his muscles as he moved like a body builder in the middle of a contest. Jericho was more subtle. He looked every bit as strong, and, for all Megan knew, might have a couple of tattoos of his own hidden somewhere under his polo shirt or 5.11 Tactical khakis. Whatever he had, he didn't flash it.

By the time they'd been waiting five hours, boredom and the men's easy banter had worn away any semblance of inhibitions in Megan.

"You two are so different," she heard herself say. "You grew up together, and you seem to like the same things, and yet you appear to have ended up on polar opposite sides of the law."

Bo laughed out loud, slapping his knees with both hands. He slumped beside her on the ratty tan shag carpet, letting his back slide down against the wall.

"I'm a lost cause, Doc," he said. "Our folks were so proud of Jericho, especially when he got the appointment to the Academy. That was like a three-hundred-thousand-dollar scholarship, wasn't it, Jer?"

"I don't know. Something like that," Jericho grunted without looking up from his rifle scope pointed across the street.

"Well—" Bo let his head fall to one side so he looked directly at Megan. "Everything our parents saved not having to pay for Jericho's college, they got to use on my bail money." He shrugged, maybe, Megan thought, a little sadly. "Like I said, a lost cause. Tough to live up to a brother like that one, I'll tell you. I can barely string five coherent words together in English. He was rattling off three different languages before he got out of high school. We had a really cold winter his sophomore year so he stayed inside and learned to speak fluent Japanese. Funny thing though, he never could figure why the girls liked me more. . . ."

"How about we stay focused?" Jericho said. He leaned back from the Remington 700 sniper rifle mounted on a short, tripod-like table and stretched his back. A box of cartridges that read .300 WINCHESTER MAGNUM sat on the table beside his left arm. Each looked the size of Megan's finger. The room was dark and the curtains drawn but for a thin gash a foot in front of the rifle barrel. He sat far enough from the threshold so as not to be seen by anyone across the street.

"He's been like this for as long as I've known him," Bo went on, the edge of mischief sharp in his voice. A pistol bulged at the waist of his black T-shirt. The cuffs of his faded jeans rode up over heavy riding boots to reveal white socks as he rested his arms across bent knees.

"Don't pay any attention to my wayward brother, doctor," Jericho grumbled. "He doesn't have the opportunity to talk to that many honest women."

"As a matter of fact," Bo said, "I'm not entirely certain such an animal exists."

Megan smiled at that. "What did you mean when you said your brother's been like *this*?" She dipped her head toward Jericho.

"You know." Bo shrugged. "The responsible one. Taking care of things." The muscles along his neck tightened as he spoke. Where Jericho's strength was wiry and deceiving, Bo Quinn had thick, visible power like the knotted roots of a short but sturdy tree.

"Chair Force, you there?" Thibodaux's disembodied voice crackled across the radio clipped to Quinn's vest.

"Go ahead," Jericho said.

"Just checkin' in," Thibodaux said. "I still got no movement out here."

Bo took a BlackBerry phone from his belt. Using it like a walkie-talkie, he pressed a button and checked on all his men. Each reported no movement. Moon and Cujo covered the alley behind Navarro's house. Ugly and Mean Jim waited up on Lafayette Avenue, toward Trinity Park about a quarter mile away, acting as a back-up team in the event reinforcements were needed. They had the house surrounded.

"Bo's guys report no contact," Jericho said into his mike. "Nothing on this end either." He didn't say it, but Megan could tell from the tension in his voice that he was as worried as she was that Zafir might wait until he was contagious and spread the disease for a while before paying a visit to Navarro, if he showed up at all.

The sun had come up hours before. Heat waves were beginning to shimmer off the cars parked along the live oaks lining the curb. Modest homes, most built in the early seventies, were strung up and down the block, each with a familiar look of its cookie-cutter neighbor. The siding or brick color changed on every other house and some had scabbier lawns than others, but other-wise, they were the same. Two houses to the west, a bass boat loitered on a gravel pad alongside the empty driveway. It was faded by years under the hot Texas sun. The healthy crop of weeds and low tires on the trailer said few of those hours had actually been on the water. Several homes up and down the block had motorcycles in the driveway or parked along the curb. The Denizens' Harleys wouldn't cause a second look.

Returning the BlackBerry to his belt, Bo leaned back against the wall again and took a long pull on his bottled water.

"What's all this about these guys gettin' seventy vir-gins if they die for the cause?" He spit a bit of wood from his toothpick on the floor. "Pardon me, but that just don't seem like Heaven in my opinion. Now . . ."

He winked at Mahoney. "Promise me seventy experienced women and I might be willing to strike some kind of a deal. . . ."

Jericho glanced up from his rifle scope long enough to shake his head. "My brother, the religious philosopher . . ."

Bo ignored him. "So," he said, grinning at Megan with a face that looked eerily like a more lighthearted version of his brother. Judging from the other members of the Denizens motorcycle club, he had to be leading a hard life, but he appeared to be absent the worry and stress Jericho carried around on his shoulders like a backpack full of moral responsibility. "You dating anyone?"

Mahoney shook her head, blushing in spite of herself. She wondered what she'd say if the other Quinn asked the same question. "No. My job . . . my life doesn't lend itself to dating. . . ." Mahoney wondered why that was true. Other doctors in her office dated all the time. Some of them partied like little rabbits. Maybe she'd never extended herself. It was depressing to think she was now in her thirties and had never really had a serious relationship. She would never admit it to this man, but though she was no virgin, she was far from experienced.

"Outstanding." Bo put his hands on his knees.

"What?" Megan winced, suddenly afraid Bo Quinn could read her mind.

"I mean the part about you not dating anybody. After we're done here, and we whack your little terrorist friend, how about you and me get some breakfast? What do you say?"

"Knock it off, Bo," Jericho said. "She's not your type. And by that, I mean she's got a brain between her ears."

"Ha, ha, ha." Bo wagged his head back and forth. He winked at Mahoney as he got to his feet with the slow groan of someone who'd been in a recent fight. She caught the glimpse of a white scar, almost an inch wide, running above his right hip at the waist of his jeans and disappearing over his kidney. Hand on the butt of his pistol, he readjusted the tail of his T-shirt and leaned a shoulder against the wall to peer out a gap in the living-room curtains. He took care not to touch them and cause any movement that could be seen from the outside. "I always wanted to be like him, you know—when we were growing up. . . . Except when it came to girls. He moved way too slow for my taste in that regard."

"At least I *had* taste." Jericho chuckled. "That was the difference."

Mahoney closed her eyes. She enjoyed listening to the two men banter. Though they were fiercely competitive, there wasn't an ounce of animosity passing between them.

"I guess it would be difficult"—Mahoney smiled, unable to resist the urge to pick on Jericho—"having a brother who goes around bent on saving the world all the time."

Bo gave a little shrug. "Like I said, he's been like that my whole life. It's all I've ever known. Always watching out for the one weaker than he is." A mischievous sparkle gleamed in Bo's eyes. "He doesn't like to talk about it, but there was this Eskimo girl back when we were younger—"

"I'm not kidding," Jericho said, still glued to his rifle scope. "Knock it off."

"Hey, Jericho." Bo raised a brow. "You invited me here, remember? Besides, it's not like I wasn't there, too. This is my story as much as it is yours." He turned back to Mahoney, chuckling and waving off the implied threat. "Anyhow, we were riding our bicycles along the Coastal Trail in Anchorage. I think he was in the ninth grade at the time . . . fourteen or fifteen, and I was maybe eleven. I was lucky he would even hang with me. Well, not far from Westchester Lagoon, we rode up on a bunch of college boys harassing this homeless native gal. She'd had a little too much to drink, and the boys were probably high. It was sort of a perfect storm. They were . . . you know, shoving her around and calling her a muk. . . ."

"Muk?" Mahoney asked.

"Short for *mukluk*," Bo said. "It's like the N word of the North—pretty rude thing to say, really. Anyhow, just as we peddled by, one of the guys took a swipe at the old gal's shirt and ripped it half off. Things went from bad to worse in a hurry. They started to grope her and she cut loose with a terrible howl. I remember, it about the scared the pee outta me. Everything was way the hell out of hand—and then my brother flew in from his home planet of Krypton. . . ."

Jericho scoffed.

"I was just a kid, you understand," Bo went on. "Didn't know what to do. But my big brother jumped off his bike in a heartbeat, wading into among those college boys like they were nothing more than three mosquitoes—"

"As I recall, you waded right in there with me."

" 'Course I did," Bo scoffed, more serious than before. "But I had your example."

"I just enjoyed a good fight back then." Jericho shook his head. "That Eskimo woman provided me with an excuse."

"You still like to fight." Bo's eyes gleamed at the memory. "You know what I remember most, Jer? When you'd finished with the first two and had that biggest son of a bitch on the ground, pounding his face bloody with your fist . . . that boy was sobbing and slingin' snot something awful by then. I expect he was afraid you were gonna kill him. He said something like, 'Why are you doing this? Who cares about a drunk Eskimo?' You remember what you told him?"

"What?" Mahoney leaned forward in anticipation. "What did you say?"

Bo snorted. " 'Who cares about a drunk Eskimo?' the kid says, and my big brother just keeps hittin' him and says, 'It's my job!' Can you imagine such a thing? A fourteen-year-old kid telling someone that saving a woman was his job . . . like he had some sort of God-given calling to look after other people. . . ."

"That's about enough storytelling," Jericho said. "I was in it for the fight and you know it."

"Whatever you say, big brother." Bo smiled, looking at Megan with a long sigh. "I gotta tell you though; I think I started to worship him from that moment on."

Cujo's nasal voice squawked across Bo's Black-Berry, rescuing Quinn from any further roasting.

"Boss"—the biker was breathing hard—"You're not gonna believe this . . . but it's rainin' rag heads out here."

Mahoney sprang to her feet. Jericho sat up, away from his scope.

"Say that again, Cuj," Bo said.

"Aye-rabs!" Cujo said. His voice was jubilant as if was shouting *BINGO!* "We got us two in custody."

CHAPTER 45

Bo offered up the phone. "I think we're into your bailiwick, Jer."

"Hey, Cujo, this is Jericho," he said. "What do you mean 'in custody'?"

It was clear from the muffled grunts in the biker's voice that he was on the move as he spoke.

"Moon spotted two guys sneakin' up the back alley a couple houses down from you. We was able to work our way up a deep creek bed to get in behind 'em. Then we waited under a magnolia tree and conked 'em on the head as they tried to sneak by. Jacques checked 'em out. He says it's not the guy you're after, but they're definitely the bad guys."

Thibodaux's drawl broke squelch on Jericho's radio. "Neither one is Zafir, beb," he said. "Both got all their fingers and toes . . . so far at least."

"And you're sure they're Arabs and not from Mexico or Central America?"

"Chair Force," Thibodaux grumbled into his radio. "You're killin' me, pal. I have spent a day or two in the

Sandbox my own self. Neither one of 'em has an ID, but they were 'Allah Akbar-in' me to death 'til I gagged their sorry faces. . . . And, lest you get too worried we smacked some poor member of the local mosque, one of 'em has a copy of Zafir's martyr photo folded up in his back pocket. They're either the SOB's backup or they belong to his fan club. Either way . . ."

Jericho peered through the rifle scope across the street at Navarro's front door while he thought. "Get them out of sight as fast as you can. Zafir's out there somewhere and I don't want to tip him off."

"Where's Moon?" Bo said two minutes later as Thibodaux and Cujo huffed in from the backyard, each carrying a bound and gagged Arab over his shoulder. A wave of heat and humidity rolled in with them when they opened the door.

Thibodaux dropped his prisoner unceremoniously in the middle of the living-room floor, well away from Bo's Harley. "Moon stayed behind to keep his good eye peeled in case Zafir shows up. Sorry we couldn't call earlier, Jericho. We sort of had our hands full."

"Moon's okay then?" Bo asked, checking out the front window.

"He's fine, boss." Cujo looked around the room, still holding his Arab over a broad shoulder. "I left the sawed-off with him."

A prodigious beer belly rolled over the top of the biker's jeans, completely hiding his belt buckle. He wasn't as tall as Thibodaux, but he was every bit as muscular and the extra weight around his middle didn't seem to hold him back at all. Completely bald, each side of his polished scalp was tattooed with matching black lighting bolts. He sneered, showing a gold front tooth.

"Where you want this one?"

Jericho pointed to the wall opposite the man Thibodaux had brought in. He took a deep breath, considering his options. The real problem was not how to interrogate the captives; the problem was doing what needed to be done in front of Mahoney.

"I need someone on the rifle scope," he said, looking at the doctor. "If Zafir shows up, we don't want to miss him."

Mahoney nodded, taking a seat in front of the gun. Her mouth was set in a sort of nervous half grin.

"You shouldn't have to shoot anyone," Jericho consoled her. "Just keep an eye on the front of the house. Sing out if you see Zafir. Remember, we still have Ugly and Mean Jim up the street."

"I'm fine with watching out for Zafir," Mahoney said. She stared hard at the two Arab men, studying them with the eyes of a scientist. "What are we going to do with them?"

Awake now, both men peered over the top of their duct-tape gags with dark, sullen eyes. One of the men was considerably older than the other, well into his forties. The younger of the two was barely twenty. Both were clean shaven and wore simple cotton T-shirts and blue jeans. At first glance, most Texans might believe the men were Mexican.

"Shouldn't we ask them if they know where Zafir is?" Megan said.

"That is exactly what we have to do." Jericho shot a quick glance at Thibodaux, then turned back to Mahoney. "There is a near hundred-percent chance he's only a block or two away. Right now, I need you to do me a favor and keep your eyes on that scope."

"I understand," she said, though he knew she didn't . . . not yet.

He stepped closer, directly beside her, and put a hand on her shoulder. She flinched at the suddenness of his touch.

"Listen to me," he whispered. His body was directly between her and the younger Arab. "You've told us over and over how deadly this virus is. We have to do whatever it takes to find Zafir and stop him. I can't have you making eye contact with that kid against the wall."

"Why?"

Jericho bit at his bottom lip, choosing his words carefully. "Because you're not like the rest of us here in this room. You're a nice person. You have a kind heart. This guy will study you like you study germs. Once he sees that kindness in your face, he'll cling to it with everything he's got." Jericho leaned in, close enough that a lock of her hair brushed against his cheek. His lips were only inches from her ear, whispering. "He'll begin to think he has a chance."

"Doesn't he?" Her voice was barely audible.

"No."

Mahoney pressed her eye to the rifle scope and didn't look up. Jericho had no idea what she thought of him now, but he was pretty sure she wouldn't think much of him in the next few minutes.

Without the luxury of time, Jericho snapped into action. Stooping over his black Eagle Industries duffel, he gathered the things he'd need. "Cujo," he said, screwing a Gemtech silencer on the threaded barrel of the custom .22-caliber Glock Miyagi had issued him. "I need you to carry the big guy into that back bedroom. Be sure and draw the blinds." He turned and spoke several quick phrases of Arabic to the younger, more slightly built man leaning against the wall, explaining his plans. It was important the boy ponder what lay in store for his companion—and eventually himself. Both men's eyes narrowed, brimming with pure, unabashed hatred.

Jericho checked to make sure the magazine was full, then tucked the pistol in his waistband. He bent to rummage through the duffel bag again, coming up with a small pair of pruning shears and a roll of white first-aid tape.

"Bo." Jericho looked up at his brother, who towered like a sullen statue over the slumped younger Arab. "You mind waiting out here with him?" Jericho needed someone strong enough to keep the guy in line if he decided to make a fuss. But more than that, he didn't want his kid brother to be a witness to what he was about to do. Killing the enemy in the heat of battle was one thing. Enhanced interrogation methods required an awfully cold heart. He wasn't entirely sure how Thibodaux was going to handle it.

"Jacques," he said, using the pruning shears to point

at a standing lamp to the left of the front door. "Rip the power cord out of that." He flipped the hall light switch on and off to make sure he had electricity. "Bring it with you to the back room. We're going to need it."

Behind the rifle, Mahoney shuddered.

CHAPTER 46

Megan ached to plug her ears, but she could feel the young Arab watching her.

The interrogations had started off quickly, with a muffled scream drifting down the dark hallway almost as soon as Jericho had shut the door behind him. She could hear Jericho's voice speaking in gentle, clipped Arabic phrases, but she had no idea what he was saying. The seconds seemed to ooze by and Mahoney found herself pressing her eye against the rim of the rifle scope so hard she was sure she'd formed a pink ring in her skin.

The bare lightbulb in the dining room dimmed slightly, followed by another long, agonizing moan from the back room. Jericho's voice popped down the hall again throwing out more rapid-fire questions in Arabic. Twice more the light over her head flickered, then went out altogether. A moment later Thibodaux opened the door and stepped into the hall. His face was drawn tight as a stone. He motioned Bo toward him. "Go out to the garage and flip the breaker back on."

The sour smell of urine and fear wafted up the hall-way.

"Will do," Bo said. He looked down at the stricken younger prisoner, who was now slumped forward, staring between his own splayed feet. "Watch him for a minute."

Thibodaux stayed at the door. "I got him. Go get the breaker."

Bo ran for the garage.

Mahoney leaned into the rifle until her fingers turned white, struggling inside to come to terms with the situation. Her emotional brain told her the things going on down the hall were immoral. Civilized beings didn't lower themselves just because the people they fought were uncivilized. Civilized people didn't harm others but for the most dire of circumstances. She was a doctor and the physician's prime directive was: First, do no harm.

But her forebrain, the part of her that let her look at things rationally, reminded her she harmed living things virtually every day. She'd always consoled herself that her particular brand of pain was absolutely necessary. She wasn't experimenting on defenseless bunnies to invent some new brand of women's eyeliner. She was trying to rid the world of the most deadly plagues known to man. The things transpiring in the back room were just as necessary, no matter how distasteful. They'd moved far beyond research. If an enemy had to be tortured in order to save thousands, wasn't that okay? It was all for the greater good. It was exactly what she told herself each time she injected an innocent monkey with some horrific virus, then cut out its brain to study the effects. Cause untold suffering in a few, all for that greater good—to save humankind. No matter how awful Jericho Quinn's actions, Mahoney couldn't bring herself to blame him. The lab animals she tortured were completely without guile. The men Quinn worked on wanted every American dead. She slumped against the rifle as her eyes filled with tears—not for the man sobbing in the back room, but for Jericho Quinn.

"You sneaky son of a bitch!" Bo's voice yanked Mahoney out of her moral wrestling match and back into the real world.

Somehow, the young Arab had freed his hands and came up with a thin box cutter Cujo must have missed in his sock. He'd lashed out at Bo, catching him with the razor blade just below the knee.

Bo kicked out, connecting with the Arab's ribs. His legs still taped, the man rolled away, but came up again with the blade. Blood pouring from a long gash in his jeans, Bo whipped the pistol from his waistband at the same instant Megan realized she had a rifle in her hands. She spun in her chair, bringing the weapon around in a flash. Her finger tightened on the trigger.

"Holy hell," Thibodaux's voice boomed down the hall. "Y'all don't shoot him!"

Mahoney froze. At this distance, she had to look over the top of the scope to make out her target. Seeing the growing swatch of fresh blood on Bo's pant leg filled her with the overwhelming urge to blow the

Arab's head off. If he happened to look at her face now, she was pretty sure he wouldn't be seeing any mercy.

The Cajun was large enough he took up most of the hallway, but he moved with incredible speed. Snapping out with a left foot, he kicked the box cutter from the startled Arab's hand. He grabbed the man by the back of his belt and the scruff of the neck and hoisted him to chest level before slamming him facedown against the carpet. Any remaining fight the young Arab had left him along with the blood that gushed from his nose.

Mahoney felt her hands begin to shake and eased her finger away from the trigger.

Thibodaux squatted to wind fresh tape around the groaning prisoner's hands. "We can't talk to him if you blow him to pieces, you know." His jaw muscles tensed as he worked.

Jericho suddenly appeared from the bedroom door, making his way solemnly down the hallway toward the stunned prisoner. His eyes shifted to Thibodaux and he shook his head. Over his forehead, running in a dripping arc from his hairline to his right eyebrow was a line of fresh blood. At first Mahoney thought he must have cut himself; then she realized it wasn't his blood.

Jericho nodded toward the prisoner, asked him something in Arabic. He slouched against the wall without moving. He ignored the question completely and muttered a sullen prayer to himself. Jericho shrugged, and then breathed the sigh of a truly exhausted man. He squatted beside the prisoner, thumping him in the forehead to make certain he had his attention. The Arab's face stayed pointed toward the floor, but his eyes rolled slowly upward, staring in an unspoken challenge. Jericho stayed where he was, less than a foot from the man who had just tried to kill his brother. He fired off another line in Arabic, softer this time and more deliberate. The younger man's eyes fell again. His entire body began to shake as if suddenly stricken with a fever.

"That's the first reaction we've had from this yahoo," Thibodaux said. "What did you say to him?"

Jericho groaned, pushing off the wall to get to his feet. "I told him his friend had talked but we needed to confirm his story. That he bravely endured unmentionable pain, but in the end it had done him no good. Then I told him it was his turn."

Mahoney stood, holding the rifle to her chest like some sort of security blanket. She didn't know what to do with herself. She wanted to scream. She wanted to tell Jericho that she'd thought it through, that she understood why he had to do what he'd done . . . what he was about to do. She was sure he'd be able to see it in her eyes, if he'd just look, but he refused to meet her gaze.

"Jacques," he said softly. "Let's get this one moved to the back room. . . ."

CHAPTER 47

Bo's BlackBerry squawked from the holster on his belt, freezing everyone in place and buying the young Arab a moment of reprieve. A gravel voice with a thick Texas accent suddenly broke squelch.

"Bo, this is Ugly," the voice said. "We got a towel-head in a light blue Pontiac rental car coming up the road. He's eyeballin' that gal's house pretty hard. Looks like he's your guy. He's missing a couple of fingers. . . . Wait, I think he's stopping. . . ."

"Watch yourselves," Bo warned, clenching the grip of the pistol in his fist.

"Hang on, Bo," Ugly said. "Watch him, Jim! Shit, he sees us—"

Ugly's voice stopped abruptly, covered by the staccato sound of gunfire both over the phone as well as outside and up the street.

"Talk to me, Ugly." Bo rushed toward the door, gun in hand.

Jericho went after him, grabbing him by the shoulder. "Wait!" he said. "Don't just rush out headlong. We don't know how many there are out there. Our lives aren't the important thing here. We have to do this the smart way."

Bo shrugged away, using the barrel of his gun to push aside the window blinds. "Shit! I can't see anybody. They must be just over that rise."

Jericho stood to his left, scanning up and down the road. "Nothing," he said through clenched teeth as more gunfire erupted outside.

"Ugly! Jim!" Bo snapped. "What the hell's going on?"

He was met by nothing but silence. "Dammit!" Bo hissed through clenched teeth. "I'm gonna go check on them."

"I'll come with you." Jericho stepped to the door. "Remember, no matter what else happens, we can't let Zafir get away."

A deadly look clouded Bo's face. "I hadn't planned on it, brother."

Ugly's gritty voice popped across the radio again, broken this time and higher in pitch. "Jim's down! He took a bullet in the guts. . . . The son of a bitch shot me, too, but I think I got him. . . ."

Jericho's heart raced. "Bo," he snapped. "You tell him to watch out! This guy's not dead until he's DRT."

"Okay, boss . . ." Ugly's voice came back across the radio before Bo could issue the warning. It was still high-pitched, but slower, calming down. "Yeah, I got the bastard. Looks like he's dead—"

The pop of small-arms fire peppered the air again, followed almost instantly by the roaring *slap, slap, slap* of an American motorcycle engine.

"Hey!" It was Ugly's voice again, screaming, panting as if he was running down the road. He kept the mike keyed as he moved. "Boss! You better get out here! He's getting away. . . . Hey, get off my bike!"

CHAPTER 48

"I need to borrow your Harley," Jericho said as he threw his leg across the Night Rod parked in the middle of the living room. "You go check on your guys, I'll go after Zafir."

"Take her!" Bo said. "But remember, she's not a two-story building like your Beemer. You gotta watch the corners." He kicked open the front door, a pistol in his hand. "Now go! We'll take care of this end."

The Night Rod came to life with a deafening roar, straight-shot dual mufflers shaking the walls of the little house. Jericho shot a glance at Mahoney as he kicked the bike into first. She smiled. "Bo's men are hurt," he yelled. "See if you can help them. I'll take care of Zafir." Quinn tapped the Bluetooth device in his ear. "Jacques, sorry to leave you with the baggage. Give Palmer a call and he'll send someone to pick them up. I'll call out my locations on the radio. Get to the car and follow me as soon as you can."

"We got this, beb," the big Cajun yelled over the thumping motorcycle engine. "I'll be right behind you."

Jericho goosed the throttle, burning the Harley's fat rear tire through the carpet as he hopped the threshold out the door. He shot off the front porch and landed with a thud in the front yard, planting a boot on the concrete sidewalk to keep from spilling. Bo was right. The bike had very little ground clearance and she was a beast at low speeds. Up the hill, nearly a hundred yards up the street he could see the Pontiac. It was dead and steaming in the middle of the road where Ugly had put several rounds through the radiator. Both bikers were on the ground but looked to be alive and sitting up. A man on a red motorcycle disappeared over the crest going east on Lafayette.

Jericho took the hill four seconds later and caught sight of the fleeing bike, which now had almost a full block of lead. He leaned forward, rolling on the throttle. Slow speed handling could be forgiven in a bike as fast at the Night Rod. It handled remarkably well on the straightaway and Quinn was easily able to able to spur a respectable hundred and ten miles an hour out of the Porsche-designed engine by the time he bounced through the second intersection. On a flat-out race, he wondered how the Night Rod would stack up against his GS. On the twisties of a real-life street pursuit, it wouldn't have even been a contest. Thankfully, Ugly rode an American bike as well. Even though Zafir had a head start, Quinn began to close the distance.

Less than fifty yards ahead now, the red bike slowed to take the sweeping left turn using all four lanes of Montgomery Street at the bottom of a long hill. A Fort Worth city bus ripped through the intersection, missing the speeding bike by inches. Quinn made the decision to slow down enough that he didn't make the same mistake. He couldn't do anyone any good if he was smeared across the front of a bus.

The Arab cut left again, turning off Montgomery to roar east along the wide parking lots of the Fort Worth Stock Show grounds. Quinn had studied a map of the area immediately surrounding Navarro's house, but at a hundred and twenty miles an hour it didn't take him long to move into unfamiliar territory. He flew past huge, arena-like livestock barns on his left, each arched building giving way to the next in a long series. Light poles were nothing but a blur. Street signs were unreadable as they zipped by. Seconds later he passed a covered gate on his left, leading into the stockyards. There was a sign large enough he could read it without wrecking Bo's motorcycle. The irony made him chuckle despite the danger. HARLEY AVENUE GATE.

Cars were spread out along the two-lane road, moving slowly, spaced just enough that Zafir was able to weave in and out of them without too much trouble. Still, he had to reduce speed in order to maneuver. He wasn't quite the rider Jericho was. Few people were.

Even on the low hog, such weaving twisties were child's play for Quinn and he leaned from side to side, darting back and forth among the traffic in a sort of zigzagging dance. He added power, accelerating to feel the pavement whir just inches beneath his knees as he leaned the bike into each shallow turn. If not for the fact that he was chasing a man whose blood carried a virus that could wipe out the entire western hemisphere, it would have been fun.

"Jacques, are you with me yet?" Quinn yelled into the Bluetooth, wind whipping his face.

"Five by five, beb."

"Outstanding," Quinn yelled, keeping his voice up to be heard over the rush of oncoming wind. On the back of the speeding bike it was like trying to talk during a hurricane. "I'm still behind him . . . going east on Harley Avenue around the back side of Trinity Park. We're heading toward University Drive."

"Half a mile back," Thibodaux said. "We're comin' up on Montgomery and Harley now. I got the doc with me."

Jericho started to ask about the prisoners but decided he didn't care. He had his hands full with the Night Rod and miles of flesh-eating pavement.

Focused as he was on the fleeing Zafir, Quinn didn't see the black pickup screaming up from behind until it was almost on top of him.

Ride like everyone is on crack and trying to kill you. It was a mantra he and his brother had repeated to each other hundreds of times growing up in a motorcycle family. His father had drilled it into both of them as boys. As it turned out, the approaching pickup had exactly that in mind.

Quinn leaned hard to his right, scraping a metal foot peg on asphalt as he took the sharp turn into the tree-lined park. Moving too fast to react, the oncoming truck shot past the intersection. It slammed on the brakes, tires squealing and smoke pouring from the rear of the vehicle as the driver threw it into reverse and tore backward toward the turnoff.

In the vibrating side mirror Quinn saw the pickup pass the intersection, then slide to a stop on the gravel shoulder, only to peel out and turn to fall in behind him again, pouring on the gas.

Quinn gritted his teeth. On the bike, he'd have the advantage of maneuverability and speed, but the truck could make mistakes. If Quinn made one, he'd go down and at these speeds that would spell disaster.

He cursed himself for not expecting something like this. Kalil had had more than one person backing him up. Zafir would surely have more than the two losers stupid enough to get caught in front of Navarro's house.

"We have company," Quinn shouted into his headset as the gleaming silver truck grill loomed larger and larger in his side mirror. "Black Chevy pickup. Newer model."

"We're coming up on the park now," Thibodaux said, worry stitching his voice.

"Don't fret about me," Quinn shot back, as the pickup bore down on him. "I lost sight of Zafir about ten seconds ago." His heart sank as he spoke the words. "He was heading east toward University. You stick with him. I'll handle this guy."

Forty feet behind him, the black Chevy closed the gap. In the thick of Trinity Park now, Quinn cut between two trees, leaving the pavement to take a red gravel jogging path to his right. He heard the roar of the big block engine behind him and ducked between a picnic table and a public toilet to avoid getting flattened. Unable to negotiate the narrow pass, the pickup had to go wide, overcorrecting and bouncing across the manicured lawns. Gunfire clattered through the perfect rows of oak trees as the passenger stuck the pug barrel of a submachine gun out the window.

"Don't worry, Chair Force," Thibodaux's voice came across the Bluetooth. "We got Zafir in our sights. He's going south on University."

Quinn didn't have a chance to register the good news. The truck bounced around the stone toilet buildings, coming in at an angle now from the opposite direction. He could see the gun barrel bobbing out the open window as the passenger continued to fire in short, deadly bursts.

Quinn let off the throttle long enough to draw his Kimber and transfer it to his left hand. As the pickup came around the second bank of toilets, he leaned in, riding toward it, keeping a line of picnic tables in between them to avoid getting run down. The Kimber held eight rounds and Quinn used all of them to spray the open window as the two vehicles passed each other like jousting knights.

He didn't have time for this. Zafir was getting away.

The passenger side of the windshield turned white from the impact of the 10-millimeter rounds. The machine gun tumbled out the window and the shooter collapsed, both arms flailing loosely in the wind.

For a moment Quinn thought he'd hit the driver, but the pickup continued to move, throwing up a cloud of dust. It spun around, coming back for another try.

Quinn downshifted, realizing his gun was dry. The speed and agility of the Night Rod were his only allies. He'd have to stop the bike to change magazines, and in the time it took to do that the Chevy would run him down. Worse, Zafir would be as good as gone.

The chest-thumping roar of an oncoming Harley suddenly shook the trees. Quinn's head snapped to the left, astounded to see his brother materialize like an apparition from a thicket of cottonwoods, ripping in from the far edge of an open field.

Bo's lips were drawn back in a youthful grin. His denim vest flapped in the wind. He pointed toward the black pickup as he bore down, making quick eye contact with Jericho. Sizing up the situation, Bo used a technique he called *kissing*. It was akin to what professional drivers called *pitting*—using one vehicle to strike another in just the right spot to cause the driver to lose control. On a motorcycle, the move required more finesse—and the result was a little different.

Instead of striking the Chevy, Bo maneuvered alongside it, keeping his bike about three feet away and in the driver's blind spot. About the same time the driver realized there was another motorcycle in the picture, he yanked the wheel hard over, trying to run down his new adversary. Instead of trying to evade, Bo accelerated, angling toward the pickup and rolling effortlessly over the side and into the bed. He came up on his knees as the Harley tumbled out of control and slammed into an oak tree with a sickening crash.

Before the driver could react, Bo shot him three times through the back glass. He looked up at Jericho, who now rode alongside the bouncing pickup, nodding toward the twisted remains of the motorcycle with a grimace.

"Don't try that with my bike!" Bo yelled above the wind. The truck was already beginning to slow. "Now go! I'll take care of this."

"Tell me you have eyes-on, Jacques." Jericho took to the pavement again, racing through the Botanical Gardens and turning east again to try and cut the gap between himself and the others. He caught the green light at University and flew into the intersection heading toward the spaghettilike maze of highways a block to the south. Quinn knew that if he was on the run, that's the direction he'd go. He gambled that Zafir would do the same, scanning the trees and side streets. Cars moved lazily up and down the four-lane under the glare of a morning sun. They showed no evidence that a motorcycle had just sped past.

"Jacques!" Quinn called out again as the maze of buttressed overpasses and sweeping concrete ramps loomed in front of him. "Coming up on the freeway now. You've gotta tell me which way to go!"

"West! West!" Thibodaux's gumbo-thick voice flooded across the Bluetooth in Quinn's ear. "Take a left on the West Freeway, then keep left onto I-30. We're still on the freeway running alongside. Doc's runnin' the GPS. She says we got another ramp a mile or so ahead where we can join you."

"You still have eyes-on, right?"

"Roger that," Thibodaux said. "We're on the road above him. Can't get to him from where we are, but I can see the son of a bitch plain as day, rippin' down the interstate like he don't have a care in the world."

"Stay with him," Quinn said, leaning the bike hard right to follow the signs toward Interstate 30. "Get Megan to call 911 and report him as a DUI—"

Quinn had to swerve to avoid a tow truck that drifted into his lane, narrowly missing a TEXANS DRIVE FRIENDLY sign post. Directly ahead, a gray-haired man in a black BMW sedan slammed on his brakes for no apparent reason. Quinn cut the bike back to his right again, finally finding a clear lane. If Zafir and his men didn't kill him, one of these city drivers seemed bound to.

Desperate for information, Quinn called out to Thibodaux again. "I'm taking the access ramp now. Tell me if he gets off the highway."

"You got it, beb," Thibodaux said. "He's still below us. Another half a mile and we'll be right on top of him. We're gonna lose sight of him for a sec, but he's got nowhere to go. . . ."

"I'm on the interstate now." Quinn called out the exit numbers as he shot by them.

"You're a mile behind us," Thibodaux said.

Quinn poured on the throttle, thankful for the Night Rod's powerful Porsche engine. Merging onto the four-lane interstate, he sped past a Texas Highway Patrol unit working radar on a pullout. He glanced down at his speedometer and grinned when he saw the needle bounce over a hundred and twenty. The state black-and-white fishtailed on the pavement, throwing up a curtain of gray smoke as it fell in behind. This was one way to make sure he had some backup.

The siren wailed mournfully as Quinn took the inside lane to fly around a swaying tandem tractor trailer. Wind from the big rig shoved him around like a rag doll and he sped up to one-thirty-five to move around quickly. The highway trooper was in a regular Chevrolet Impala instead of one of their interdiction Camaros so he had a little trouble keeping up.

Thibodaux's frantic voice suddenly crackled in Jericho's ear. "We got two marked cop cars gettin' in behind Zafir. . . . Looks like they've spooked him. . . . He's doubling back! Repeat. He's coming back at you!"

"On the other side?"

"Smack dab at you, beb!" Thibodaux said. "Into oncoming traffic. Maybe he'll wreck and solve all our problems for us."

"We can't be that lucky," Quinn spat, more to himself than the Cajun. He let off the gas, allowing the Highway Patrol car time to catch up as he scanned the road ahead. Traffic had slowed to seventy-five with the trooper's siren screaming in the background. Jericho had to weave the bike in and out between the rapidly congesting packs that had only moments before been well spaced along four lanes of interstate. Without a helmet or even a pair of sunglasses, he was well aware that a piece of flying gravel could blind him—or even knock him off his speeding bike. Remnants of a blownout tire or any other road debris that happened to be in his path would have deadly consequences. He leaned into the wind and rolled on more throttle, pushing the dangers out of his mind.

They were nothing compared with what he had to do next.

Zafir's motorcycle suddenly appeared in the distance, growing quickly from small speck on the horizon. Horns blared. Cars and trucks parted like the Red Sea before Moses, swerving in both directions to avoid the oncoming missile.

With both Harleys traveling over eighty miles an hour it wouldn't take long to close the distance between them. Instinctively, Quinn tightened his thighs, squeezing them against the tank of Bo's bike. He'd made the mistake of firing his pistol dry and was left with few options.

Traffic opened up on the wide highway as the two men bore down toward each other. Zafir was hunched forward, leaning over the handlebars as far as he could, as if riding on a sport bike instead of the big cruiser he'd stolen after his gunfight with the Denizens. His head snapped up when he saw Quinn, recognizing him instantly as an enemy.

Quinn let off the throttle, slowing to seventy but aiming the Night Rod directly at the oncoming motorcycle.

Distorted by buffeting wind, the Arab's face pulled back into a tight smile, as if he knew what was about to happen. As it turned out he had no idea.

With each bike traveling over seventy miles an hour, it took them less than two seconds to close the hundred yards between them. Quinn released the left handgrip to snatch the Masamune blade from the scabbard in the small of his back. A fraction of a second later, he pressed on the right grip, leaning away as he passed the other bike. The men's knees missed each other by mere inches. Quinn kept his left arm extended, holding

Yawaraka Te's gleaming blade at head height, parallel to the blur of passing pavement.

He felt a shudder as the sword connected with Zafir, but at such speed was unable to turn and check his accuracy without dumping the bike. He heard a grinding crash and the squeal of a dozen car brakes as highway traffic screeched to a halt. It took him another hundred yards to bring the Night Rod skidding to a stop on the inside shoulder.

The Highway Patrol car slid to a halt on the loose gravel behind him. Sidearm drawn and dead-steady, the aggressive trooper bailed out like an enraged guard dog and screamed for Quinn to drop his blade.

Quinn let the sword fall, gritting his teeth when he heard the seven-hundred-year-old steel ring against the pavement. Still straddling the bike, he raised both hands high over his head. He could feel the trooper's pistol trained directly at his back.

"You freeze right where you are, ninja boy!" the lawman boomed. The "or I'll kill you" was implied.

"I'm a federal agent," Quinn yelled over his shoulder, keeping his hands in the air.

"Is that a fact?" the trooper said, his voice icy with professional calm. "So, the feds are hiring ninjas now to go on sword patrol? Frankly, mister, I don't care who you are. You better have a damn good reason for choppin' that sombitch's head off."

Thibodaux and Mahoney came up on the eastbound lanes and screeched to a stop on the far shoulder. "He's one of the good guys," Thibodaux called out, his hands in the air so as not to alarm the trooper any more than he already was. Quinn turned his head just enough to see Mahoney running toward the tangled wreckage of the red Harley where it was piled up along the guard rail. She'd taken the time to throw on a protective hood and gloves but wore no other safety gear.

Two more black-and-whites skidded to a halt on the gravel shoulder. Now that he had more guns on the scene, the original trooper finally allowed Quinn to lower his hands and show identification.

"What the hell is OSI doing hacking people to death on my highway?"

"We need to get a perimeter set up around the body," Quinn said, nodding toward the center of the interstate. He watched from a distance as Mahoney stooped to examine the wreckage. "I know this seems odd, but we need to locate the head and make sure no one gets near that either. This guy has some seriously contagious diseases." Quinn looked at the three troopers, capable lawmen all, but none over thirty. He thought they might not even know what hemorrhagic fever was. "The stuff he has makes swine flu look like diaper rash."

"Well, why didn't you say he was sick?" the first trooper on the scene scoffed, looking at Quinn through narrowed eyes. "That's a damn good reason for choppin' someone's head off with a sword. . . ."

Quinn ignored him. He put the Night Rod on its center stand and started to walk toward the wreckage where Zafir's body was plainly visible. Surprised to see Megan stand and remove her protective hood, he broke into a run, adrenaline still pumping from his wild ride.

Twenty feet away he noticed all the blood had

drained from Mahoney's face. "What?" he said, slowing to a trot. "What is it?"

Megan closed her eyes, raising her face toward the sky. Her shoulders were shaking. "Zafir Jawad lost his fingers during the first Gulf War," she said. "This guy still has the stitches from where his were amputated no more that two weeks ago. He's a decoy. We let the real Zafir get away."

CHAPTER 49

Zafir smiled to himself as he drove. Surely Allah the merciful smiled upon his mission. One of the sheikh's servants, a man named Isam, had called to warn him.

The Americans knew. There were people waiting at Carrie Navarro's house. It made sense that Farooq would send someone to watch over him, someone to protect him from such things and ensure he was able to complete his assigned move in the Game. Zafir gripped the wheel of his rental car until his fingers turned white and pondered the bravery of such men. Their death was now a certainty—if not from the duties of protection, at the very least from the ensuing plague. Such was the purest of devotion to Jihad.

Navarro had now gone into hiding. He cursed the infidel Jericho for finding the photographs. It had been stupid to leave them in the lab . . . but who would have imagined someone making his way into the Kingdom undetected? Zafir consoled himself with the fact that in the end, none of that would matter. Photographs or not, millions of infidels would ultimately die a horrific death from the virus he carried within his body. A smile spread over his face at the thought, but turned into a shiver as considered what the illness would do to him first. He reached in his pocket to touch the small vial of poison that would rescue him when the pain was too great to bear. In the mirror he saw beads of sweat on his brow and wondered if he might not be contagious earlier than Suleiman had believed.

Zafir pulled over at a highway rest area on the edge of Fort Worth to look at Gail Taylor's iPhone. He'd spent months learning everything there was to know about Carrie Navarro while she'd been his prisoner. There was no place for her to hide. He used the remaining fingers of his disfigured hand to punch a name into the search engine just as Gail Taylor had showed him. He caught a whiff of her heady scent again on his collar, but pushed it from his mind. In no time he found the address he wanted and entered that into the GPS on his dash. In Iraq or the Saudi Kingdom finding the specific address of a person might take days and require the torture of many relatives. The Americans made it so easy. Sophisticated technology cut away privacy like an well-sharpened axe.

Zafir put the car back into gear and pulled out of the rest area to join the flow of interstate traffic heading west, into the sun. Finally so near his goal, he felt a familiar stirring, a warm rush, low in his belly. Very soon, Navarro would experience indescribable agony. She would die—but it would not be the virus that killed her.

CHAPTER 50

Carrie couldn't stop her hands from shaking. The walls of her mother's three-story farmhouse were beginning to close in around her. She found it difficult to breathe, let alone think. For the first time in five years, she lit a cigarette. The terrifying notion that Zafir Jawad was in the United States was more than she could wrap her brain around. With the help of Dr. Soto, she'd only just come to grips with the nightmares of her past life. Now this man who'd committed unspeakable acts of cruelty for so many months had reared his head again. The mere thought of his face made her retch.

She took a long drag on the cigarette, willing it unsuccessfully to calm her twitching nerves. Christian lay on his belly in front of the television holding his nose at the smoke and watching a Transformers cartoon. Her mother had stepped into the bedroom to take a phone call from a neighbor.

Two federal agents—neither looked old enough to

shave—occupied the living room by force, trying to seem inconspicuous. She could tell from their barely concealed sneers that neither considered this a top-shelf assignment. One sat on the recliner in the corner reading a paperback spy thriller. The other stood by the window talking to his wife on the cell phone about her shopping habits and their mountain of credit card debt. Both had their jackets off and their pistols were exposed. At the foot of the one reading the book was a discreet black case Carrie knew contained some sort of machine gun. It would not be enough. Pistols, rifles, swords, or atom bombs—it didn't matter. She knew Zafir. He was too smart. If he wanted her, she was a sitting duck. No matter where she hid or what anyone did, he'd find her. There was no getting around it. He was too close, too strong. She alternately clenched her fists and relaxed them as Dr. Soto had taught her, struggling in vain to calm her erratic breathing.

She stubbed out her cigarette on one of her mother's china saucers, fighting off the feeling that the room was getting smaller. Her eyes shot from her little boy to the back door and she suddenly realized what she had to do. She couldn't just sit still and wait for him to come kill her.

Smiling at the two agents as she passed the adjoining room, Carrie walked into the kitchen. Pretending to rummage through the refrigerator, she scanned for possible weapons, finally settling on an eight-inch chef's knife from her mother's wooden block. Wrapping the blade in a rolled dishtowel, she stuffed it down the waist of her jeans, over the small of her back. She tugged the tail of her loose cotton T-shirt over the top of her pants to cover it, then stood at the kitchen door. She motioned to Christian, touching a finger to her lips to keep him quiet.

"Hey, little man," she whispered, fighting to keep up her tremulous smile. "Go put on your shoes."

CHAPTER 51

Jericho stood at the edge of the highway watching the growing crowd of stranded commuters as they got out of their cars to look at the grizzly scene. A fist of worry gripped his chest. Fort Worth PD had set up barricades, keeping dozens of well-tanned onlookers in cowboy hats, big hairdos, and ball caps at bay. A Channel 4 news helicopter touched down less than fifty yards from the crash scene.

"You think the Navarro girl is okay?" Mahoney asked.

"Her mother's house is an hour away from here by car," Jericho sighed. He'd never felt so beaten. "She's got protection."

"I just called and talked to the agent in charge out there," Thibodaux said. "Sounds like he's about thirteen, but he swears everything's hunky-dory. No sign of any bad guys out his way. That leaves us with zip for leads when it comes to finding Zafir."

Mahoney took out her iPhone. "What did you say Navarro's mother's name is?"

"Juanita," Quinn said. "Juanita Calderon."

Mahoney worked the iPhone for a moment. Lights flashed in her eyes as she scrolled through a series of screens. Suddenly she groaned and turned the device around so both Quinn and Thibodaux could look at the color display. "When I type in Carrie Navarro I get a link to a photo of her accepting an award from her newspaper. Look who's standing beside her."

"Her mother, Juanita Calderon," Thibodaux read the screen.

"And when I do a people-finder search for Juanita Calderon in Weatherford, Texas . . ."

She touched the face of her iPhone. Both men moved in beside her now, watching the new page load. They watched a satellite image with a pulsating blue dot over a white farm house. Thick green woods crowded the neighborhood, each home with at least five acres of land.

"I'm guessing that's Juanita Calderon's house," Thibodaux said.

"She's listed in the phone book," Mahoney said, biting her lip. "And if we can find her this easily, so can Zafir."

The Channel 4 news chopper was just spooling down in a vacant pasture when the Hammer Team crawled through the barbed-wire fence beside it. The burly Jacques Thibodaux took the lead as they made their approach. Though Quinn was more than capable when it came to physical confrontation, in the short time he'd been working with Thibodaux, he'd found it was a time-saver to let the giant Cajun's physique press the issue if an issue needed to be pushed.

The chopper pilot, a sensible-looking man with mussed gray hair wore a green David Clark headset with a tiny mike situated over his mouth. He busied himself on the radio while a lone reporter, who appeared to be the only other occupant of the helicopter, sat in the back seat rummaging through a giant blue duffel of camera gear and microphones.

"Hey there," Thibodaux said, grinning. "*Comment ça va, beb?*"

The reporter, a thirty-something Ken doll look-alike didn't even look up. "Tell this hick we've got a deadline to meet, Steve," he mumbled to the pilot, as if he couldn't be bothered to converse with mere mortals. "I don't have time to talk. Tell them to run along and get away from the chopper." His sockless penny loafers and pink oxford button-down suggested his name might be something like Biff.

Thibodaux threw a tired glance over his shoulder at the others.

"OSI." He held up his shiny new black credential case and gold badge. "Pains me to say so, but we're with the Air Force. I'm gonna need to borrow your helicopter."

"Beat feet, dude." Biff smirked, still fiddling with a foot-long camera lens. "I'm gonna have to call bullshit on that one. Our Air Force doesn't have any jurisdiction over civilians on American soil. Posse comitatus and all."

"You're right. . . ." Thibodaux turned and looked at Quinn again. There was a twinkle in his blue eyes. "I tried to be nice," he sighed. "Really I did." His back suddenly seemed to flare wider as he loomed over the simpering reporter. The friendly twang fled and his voice grew deadly quiet. "Tell you what then. How 'bout this for logic? I'm bigger'n you and we're taking your chopper."

Biff looked up from the camera, his eyes flung wide at Thibodaux's menacing tone.

Quinn nudged Mahoney out of the way as Thibodaux grabbed the reporter by the scruff of his starched oxford collar and heaved him out the door and into the field stubble.

The Cajun cocked his head toward the smirking pilot. "You got any problems with Air Force OSI workin' on American soil, my friend?"

"Steve Akers," the man said, grinning. "USMC retired. Hell, welcome aboard. That kid's been a pain in my ass since he started. Can't say I'm sad to see him go."

Quinn and Mahoney scrambled in the back as Thibodaux climbed in front where he'd have more leg room. "Good to meet you, Marine," he said, nodding in greeting as he adjusted a second headset.

"Welcome, Air Force," the pilot said.

Thibodaux shook his big head emphatically, nearly dislodging the headset. "I'm zero-three-six-nine, pal." He gave the numerical code for a Marine Corps MOS of Infantry Unit Leader.

Akers raised a seasoned eyebrow, then pulled up on

the collective to lift the helicopter off the grass. The bird shuddered slightly, flying out of the chopper's own rudder wash and into clean air, picking up speed.

"Thought your fancy creds said you worked for the Air Force?"

"Long story," Thibodaux said. "I'll tell you on the way to save the world."

CHAPTER 52

A single policeman slouched in the unmarked Ford Crown Victoria out front of Juanita Calderon's white frame house. This was all Zafir had to see to confirm what he needed to know. Carrie Navarro was in the house.

It was a fluke that he was even aware Juanita Calderon existed. Early after Carrie had become his guest, he'd seen to it she was given paper and a pen to write her family a letter. She'd been smart enough not to trust him, even then, so he'd sent in an underling, a young fighter from Samarra, to give her the materials. Navarro had written the letter, but the stupid boy had fallen in love with her. Zafir had caught them alone together and been forced to kill him.

Carrie's letter had been addressed to a post office box, but it had provided him with a name and a city. With Gail Taylor's iPhone and the instructions she had provided before he killed her, it had been easy enough to perform a search on that name. The P.O. box was in a place called Weatherford so when he found a Juanita Calderon in that city, he knew he had the correct place. Night after night he'd sat outside Carrie Navarro's cell door and listened to her whimper for her mother. It made sense that the stupid cow would go there when she felt threatened.

Zafir's heart raced. At long last he was on the brink of his long-sought objective. He licked his lips, tasting the memory of her.

He sat behind the wheel of his rental car on the adjacent block, looking through a grove of cedar trees between two houses. Juanita Calderon's home sat in the middle of a lavish subdivision at the outskirts of town. Each house was at least two stories with a well-manicured lawn and corral. A few even had roping arenas. There was at least one boat or motorcycle parked in almost every driveway. Some had horses in small paddocks; behind their houses. Calderon's was among the oldest, presumably it had been the ranch house before the land was parceled off for development, but it was still impressive with a sprawling, wraparound cedar deck and two huge oaks in the spacious front yard.

Zafir looked around, planning his approach. Beside him was a wrought-iron gate with a cutout of a man on horseback chasing a longhorn cow. Beyond the gate, three horses grazed with their heads down in the pasture hemmed in by the trees. He'd bought a pair of binoculars at a Wal-Mart on the edge of Fort Worth and used them to scan the neighborhood. At the fence paralleling the street, two llamas looked on stupidly as only llamas can look. Calderon had neighbors, but each house was situated on a large wooded lot, giving them plenty of space in between. Such space would give Zafir cover as he approached.

He put the rental car in gear and drove down the pitted asphalt road adjacent to Calderon's street. He struggled to keep his heart from racing as he made the turn, now less than half a block from Carrie Navarro. Breathing deeply, he kept up his speed so as not to draw the attention of the policeman in the Crown Victoria and turned into the long limestone driveway of a gray brick two-story, three lots away from his target. There were no vehicles out front, and Zafir took the gamble that the occupants were not at home. If they happened to be home, he was prepared to kill them quickly. Americans weren't accustomed to sudden violence in their own backyards. They would surely try to negotiate when they should be fighting.

Zafir glanced up the street, making certain his arrival hadn't raised the attention of any inquisitive onlookers. The policeman out front was a heavy man with a glowing red face. Rounded shoulders pressed against the window and looked as if they might pop open the car door at the slightest movement. He was obviously lost in a daydream, complacent in his peaceful town, certain that nothing violent would ever happen to him. Zafir marveled that a country capable of producing some of the finest warriors in the world could be so lax at home. It looked all too easy. But no matter how overweight, policemen had radios and Zafir needed time to mingle with the population after he indulged himself with the American whore.

Gravel crunched beneath tires as he brought the

rental car to a stop on the far side of the gray house. He eased the door shut without slamming it and walked across the sun-parched side yard toward the rear patio, breathing a sigh of relief when no one came out to challenge him. Tiny brown grasshoppers clicked and buzzed away from his feet. A sturdy palomino horse trotted up to the back fence and snorted, staring at him with huge brown eyes. A line of thick oak trees beyond the barn made a perfect green backdrop for the animal. Zafir suddenly found himself caught up in the moment, captivated by the beauty of the scene. To the ancient Bedouin, the horse was everything, a prized posses-sion. The feeling was bred into Zafir to the deepest marrow of his bones. For the first time, he grew tearful at the thought of dying. He raised the flat of his good hand to his heart. Surely there would be horses in heaven.

His eyes still moist, his heart jumped in his chest when he turned. Little more than a hundred yards away, a young woman with dark hair slid open a glass door and stepped into the bright sunshine of Juanita Calderon's redwood deck. She wore tight blue jeans and a simple white T-shirt. Even from a distance Zafir was warmed by the familiar curves and swells of Car-rie Navarro's body. She was healthier now, more full figured after having their child, but still beautiful to look on, and, he could tell from the way she threw her head, still just as brazen.

Zafir's jaw dropped when a small child stepped through the same glass doorway and clutched Na-varro's outstretched hand. His head spun at the sight of his son. Even from a distance it was easy to see the boy carried himself with a confident air, just like his father. For a split second he thought again about trying to spare the child. His head throbbed and he wondered if it might not be too late. It did not matter now.

The Bedouin began to run, ducking quickly around the horse barn and into the dark tangle of wild grapevines, briars, and oak trees. He would kill Navarro and take the child with him. In the few short hours they had left alive, Zafir would teach him the true way of Islam. In the end, his son too would become a glorious martyr and find his reward in Paradise.

CHAPTER 53

Four minutes from Juanita Calderon's house, Quinn began to take long, slow breaths, willing his heart rate to slow. Mahoney had shown enough forethought to bring his M4 when they'd jumped in the rental car and it now hung loaded and ready, suspended on a single-point sling around his neck. He reached behind his back to touch Yawaraka-Te's hilt, assuring himself the ancient blade was still there. He'd reloaded the 10 millimeter tucked in an inside-the-pants holster over his right kidney. If it was possible, they'd take Zafir out with long guns—giving them the safety of distance—but something told Quinn the Bedouin would be too smart for that.

Steve Akers, the chopper pilot and former Marine, dropped the bird low, skimming the tops of the trees. He followed the rise and fall of the natural terrain in what was known as NOE—nap-of-the-earth flying. It was a technique used in Vietnam to protect chopper pilots from heat-seeking missiles—go low and go fast. The technique had the added benefit of keeping the thump of the helicopter's approach dampened by the foliage and terrain. Akers flew more like an artist than a technician and coaxed every ounce of speed out of his machine.

The side doors were slid open and a warm, humid wind roared through the cabin. In the front seat Thibodaux checked the magazine in his M4.

Mahoney stared out the open door, eyes locked on the trees as they whipped by in a green blur, less than ten feet below the skids. The wind fluttered the leg of her khakis, pressing the cloth against the smooth curve of her calf. Thick reddish blond hair whipped across her face, but she made no attempt to push it away.

Quinn tensed when she suddenly spun toward him, looking him full in the face. If she'd noticed him looking at her, she didn't mention it.

"It's after ten," she yelled above the roar, tapping her watch. "We're well inside the safety zone. If he is here, there's a good chance he's gone hot. . . ." Her face was drawn, her normally rosy lips pinched and pale.

Quinn put a hand on her shoulder, trying to calm her. "Palmer has the Texas Highway Patrol and the National Guard moving now to cordon off the area. We *will* stop this. And we'll stop it here, one way or another."

"If he didn't get a cup of coffee along the way . . . or ask for directions . . ." Her chin quivered as if she might break down at any moment. "He only has to get Pandora to one other person we don't know about and their plan has worked. . . ."

Quinn opened his mouth to stay something else, but Akers cut him off.

"Tallyho at two o'clock!" The pilot held his hand up, knifelike and pointed right of the helicopter's nose. "According to my GPS, that white two-story up there should be your target." He twisted in his seat to throw a tense look over his shoulder. "And you're not gonna like what you see."

CHAPTER 54

Carrie moved quietly, making up her plans as she went along. She had no idea where she was going, but she knew she had to move. Sitting still would drive her crazy if it didn't get her killed. She carried Christian as she went, telling him they were playing a hiding game so he wouldn't make a fuss. Her mother might hang up the phone and come looking for her at any moment, the guards could discover she was missing and haul her back inside. Engrossed in worry at the thought of getting caught, she kept careful watch over her shoulder as she made her way down the long flight of wooden stairs leading from the red cedar deck.

As she came off the last step, she ran headlong into Zafir.

A liquid scream curdled in her throat. The Bedouin folded his arms and looked hard into her face, sneering. She'd forgotten how tall he was. With his back to the sun, his body was a dark silhouette, larger than life. The monster's eyes fell on Christian and his cruel mouth relaxed, hanging open in awe.

Carrie put the boy gently on the grass, without looking down. She wanted to scream, to warn the others inside that he was here. But her lungs felt heavy, her tongue refused to follow her brain's commands. With the air-conditioning running full bore, she doubted if anyone inside would hear her anyway. Her brain screamed for a way out. She stood rooted in place, unable to lift a finger while before her eyes, this vile, evil man stooped and gently mussed her little boy's hair like a long lost uncle. He whispered in hushed tones, speaking in Arabic, smiling softly as if he were actually capable of kindness. Carrie knew from long experience that was impossible.

The muscles in her arms twitched as she struggled to free herself from the paralysis. Half breaths escaped her nose in tormented sobs. Her mind raced, thinking of her poor child who was about to witness his own mother's murder.

Zafir released her with a vicious slap.

"Christian, run!" Carrie hissed, the words gushing from her lungs like air from a ruptured tire. Tears gushed down her face as if from a broken dam.

But the boy stood fast, clinging to her leg. He stared up wide-eyed at the dark man who looked so much like him.

"No need to run, my child." Zafir smiled, transitioning smoothly to English like the wily devil that Carrie knew him to be. "I am your baba. . . ."

The thought of her little boy calling this horrible man father was more than Carrie could bear. Without another thought, she jerked the knife from her waistband, slashing wildly at Zafir. Her rage helped free her muscles—but he was faster. He'd faced blades before and a few unaimed gashes on his forearm did not faze him.

He swatted the blade from her hand as if it was nothing more than a troublesome fly. It clanged to the ground, wedged at an angle against the wood of the bottom step. Zafir stomped hard with the sole his heavy boot, snapping the sharp steel just inches above the hilt.

"You are a fool," he jeered, grabbing her by the wrist. "You thought you could kill me with a ridiculous kitchen tool?" Rivulets of dark blood ran along his arm, dripping from the remaining fingers of his disfigured hand. He spat on the ground in disgust. "My son would have been a woman if I had allowed you to raise him."

"You can't have him!" Carrie moaned. Her lungs began to lock again as memories of this man's power flooded her body and mind. "You . . . can't . . . I . . . I won't let you take him!"

"You?" He laughed. "And what could you possibly do to stop me?" He grabbed the neck of her T-shirt, tearing it away. "Have you got a spoon in there to go with your knife?"

The sneering smile faded from Zafir's darkening face. His voice grew ice cold. "I will do as I please." He drew her to him, squeezing her trembling cheeks between his fingers. "Shall we find a quiet spot in the woods for . . . how do you Americans say it? Old times' sake." His lips hovered inches from hers. The familiar metallic odor of his breath stabbed at her memory.

Carrie spat through pursed lips, catching him full in the face.

Zafir slammed his forehead brutally against the bridge of her nose. Blood gushed from her nostrils. A fountain of colored lights shot through her brain. She staggered backward, tripping over the wooden steps to sprawl backward onto a flagstone walkway.

'Mama!" Christian cried out. Screaming in rage, the boy kicked Zafir in the leg.

"Ah." Zafir smiled, scooping up the squirming child. "My son has fire. He is just like me, don't you think? How long has it been, Carrie? I know you must have missed our times together, my love." Suddenly calm again, Zafir touched Christian on the tip of the nose. Blood dripped from his wounded arm onto the boy's shorts and bare leg. Carrie felt her stomach heave. She turned to throw up on the grass.

Zafir went on, lost in his twisted fantasy. "The awful things you said to me that day when you were released—they do not matter anymore. I am quite certain that after Zafir Jawad has held you in his arms, no other man has been good enough." He raised an eyebrow. "Am I wrong when I assume that few nights have passed that your thoughts have not turned to me?

"I must admit, Carrie, my bird—" He set the boy on the ground, patting him on the head with a blood-soaked hand. "I have spent many nights with a picture of you in my mind's eye . . . and in that picture I see the time in which I will end your life."

Towering above her, Zafir drew a long knife of his own. Sunlight glinted off the blade as he turned it in his bloody fist. His lips drew back in a yellow snarl.

"Allah be praised for delivering you to my hand—"

A thundering roar shook the air as a helicopter rose

like an apparition from the live oak trees beyond the yard, appearing out of nowhere. Two men with rifles stood, one on each skid, as the aircraft bore toward them like a falcon coming in for the kill.

Zafir's head snapped around, forgetting Carrie to focus on this new approaching threat. Christian pressed his hands to both ears against the deafening noise.

Carrie sprang to her feet, still reeling from the vicious head butt. In her right hand, she clutched the broken shard of the chef's knife.

"Zafir!" she screamed above the thumping din of the chopper. "There's something you need to know!"

The Bedouin turned back to face her, startled to see her standing.

Lunging forward, she plunged the broken blade into his eye, pushing it home until she felt the shuddering scrape of steel against bone and she could push it no farther. Zafir clawed at his face with his gnarled hand, trying to fend her off with the other. He wailed in agony. His legs peddled backward as if creating distance from his tormentor might help him escape the pain.

Carrie flailed with both hands, slapping at Zafir's arms, clawing blindly at his face and neck until he fell writhing and screaming on the ground.

"Stay away from me!" she screamed. "I'll kill you! I swear I'll kill you if you touch my son!" Her voice cracked in a hysterical rage. Backing away but never letting her eyes leave Zafir, she reached to find Christian and dragged him to the far side of the deck.

Vaguely aware that the helicopter had set down in

the backyard, she watched through blurry eyes as people in large rubber hoods ran toward Zafir with guns in their hands. She swayed for a long moment on wobbly legs before finally sinking onto the grass beside her son.

CHAPTER 55

17 September

Jericho peered through the six-by-six-inch observation window at the newest patient at the BSL-4 containment. Mahoney and Thibodaux stood on either side of him. Bo stood back a few feet, along the startlingly white tile of the far wall. Though he was a tough and grizzled outlaw biker, he had no stomach for what was on the other side of the air seal and heavy metal door.

Inside the innermost room of the Slammer, Zafir Jawad lay shackled to a metal hospital bed by one ankle. Blood seeped through white surgical bandages wrapping the left side of his face, covering his sightless eye socket. His dry, hacking cough was audible through a black intercom box on the wall. But for the dignity afforded the dying patient, the scene was eerily reminiscent of the lab Quinn had visited in Al-Hofuf.

Palmer worked with the military and had the entire BSL-4 containment unit at USAMRIID turned into a modified version of the Slammer. No one on the Hammer Team had been within breathing distance of Zafir without protection, but out of an abundance of caution, everyone who'd had any sort of contact with any of the three would-be martyrs or their backup agents was put under quarantine. Zafir occupied the actual Slammer. A test of his blood had shown that the virus was still fully encased in the protein sheath at the time of his capture, so all but Carrie and her son, who'd been in physical contact with his blood, were allowed to commingle inside the BSL.

Quinn pushed a silver button flush with the white tile wall. "Zafir," he said, "we'd like to give you the opportunity to tell your side of the story."

"Imbecile!" Zafir scoffed. He turned gingerly, wincing in pain to face the wall away from the observation window. "Do you not see that I am at peace with Allah? I have prepared myself to die long ago."

"I know you believe you are prepared." Quinn kept his voice low, belying the hot torrent that churned in his gut. He firmly believed anger had little place in his chosen profession. Dispassionate action was always better—but he was human. "Things have changed in a great way since you began your plans." He paused. "Many, many things."

"Tell me . . ." The Bedouin turned again, despite his pain, tilting his head toward the door, narrowing bloodshot eyes. The flesh around his lips hung loose around his mouth, giving him a grotesque, clownlike effect. Pandora was beginning to take her toll on his body. "Are you the one called Jericho?"

"I am indeed."

Zafir swallowed, nodding almost imperceptibly. "Then I will tell you this about the sheikh. He is a very wise man. Make no mistake, he will find out who you are and he will come for you."

"Tell me where he is and I will go to him."

"He will flay the skin from those you love." Zafir's voice rose from a hoarse whisper into a menacing growl. "He will send your women—"

"As I said—" Quinn pressed the intercom again, interrupting the tirade. His patience was at an end. "Circumstances have changed. Do not forget, we are in possession of your suicide drug. You will have the opportunity to die, as you wished, but, as you are fully aware, your death will not come as quickly. Perhaps you remember the faces of the American soldiers and the innocent young girl you infected with this same virus back in Al-Hofuf. . . ."

Chains clanked against the metal bed as Zafir jerked against his shackles. A hollow scream—the wailing roar of a damned soul—poured from the intercom box until Quinn pushed the button to silence it.

Three doors down from Zafir, in another soundproof room, Carrie Navarro and her son sat on the edge of a hospital bed behind a glass partition. A careful examination of Zafir's blood showed a ninety-nine-percent chance that his virus had not yet matured to the contagious phase when they'd had contact. Because of this—not to mention all the poor woman had been through—Megan had allowed mother and son to be housed together. But there was still a great deal to learn about the Pandora virus, so they were not allowed to roam around with the others.

Mahoney pressed the intercom button as they walked past their isolation room. "Hey, Carrie. Hey, Christian. How's it going in there?"

Everyone in the hall waved. Christian waved from the safety of his mother's lap. Carrie smiled. "Hey," she said wanly. Her physical recovery was going to be much easier than her mental one. Luckily she had her little boy and, Megan thought, as she looked at Thibodaux and both of the Quinn brothers beaming through the glass, that lucky little boy now had three extremely protective godfathers.

"You know, my brother's still stuck on his ex-wife, right?" Bo sidled up next to Mahoney after they said good night to Navarro and walked down the long hall toward the outer lab and the room that would serve as their chow hall and common area for the next two weeks of quarantine.

Under the pitiful gaze of a love-struck Justin, Megan grinned, tossing her head in the best flirt she could muster. "I'd heard that."

"Well," Bo said, "the big dude from Louisiana tells me Jericho took you for a spin on his Beemer. If you're not sick of Quinn boys after all this, I could take you for a ride on a sure-enough American bike when we get out of this place."

Mahoney looked at Jericho, who shrugged.

"I can only vouch for him as a good kid brother," he said. "Beyond that, I'm pretty certain he belongs in prison."

"Hey dude, *malum prohibitum* not *malum in se*." Bo

hooked a thumb toward his chest, showing off his Latin. "The things I choose to do are wrong, only because *The Man* says they are. Nothing I do is inherently bad." He raised a brow, looking directly at Megan with a sly grin. "Well, almost nothing."

Megan bit her bottom lip. The notion of taking some time away from work with the rough-and-tumble Bo Quinn was an interesting proposition. After spending the past few days getting to know men like Jericho and Jacques, she just couldn't come to grips with going back to the plain-vanilla types she'd dated in her previous life.

Though the idea of being alone with Bo the biker terrified her as much as the thought of getting a tattoo, it beckoned to the same sense of exploration that had pulled her into field research in the first place. She'd heard of women who married soldiers, police officers, or firefighters and when they divorced or found themselves alone for whatever reason, always went back to someone from the same adventurous ilk. Such men were what they knew—and in the end, she supposed, the very thing they craved.

Justin steadfastly refused to leave the BSL, making up reason after reason he should stay. Once they'd all come in and shared his air, he was committed and had to stay for the duration. Now he plodded along a few steps behind Megan wherever she went, his shoulders stooped, his face hangdog. Completely intimidated by the muscular biker with a tattoo of a black octopus on his forearm, the poor kid's chin quivered when he spoke. His eyes fluttered as if he might break into tears at any moment. Megan knew it was cruel, but she had to stifle a giggle every time she saw him.

Thibodaux walked a few yards ahead talking on his cell phone, waving his free arm as he spoke in animated Italian to his Delta-Whiskey. He suddenly spun to face the others, blocking any further progress down the hall. Moving his head slowly from side to side like a disbelieving buffalo, a huge grin smeared across his face. "It must have happened before my last deployment to Iraq. . . ."

"What?" Mahoney asked, though the answer was written all over the big Marine's face.

Thibodaux grabbed Jericho by both shoulders with his huge paws, dancing him around in a tight circle. "Yet once again, *l'ami*. Yours truly is gonna be a papa. . . ."

"Good grief, Jacques." Mahoney's mouth fell open. "How many will this make?"

"Seven," Thibodaux said, lost in the idea of having another child.

"As a trained epidemiologist, I think I need to have a talk with your wife," Mahoney said. "There must be something in the air at your house."

"Oh there was, beb." The big Cajun winked a glistening eye. "Her feet."

"You think we got it all?" Mahoney asked Jericho, after everyone else was asleep and the two of them sat in the chow hall. A carton of butter pecan ice cream sat on the table between them.

Quinn sighed. He was exhausted down to the marrow of his bones, but his mind raced with thoughts of a dozen scenarios, none of them good.

"I don't know," he said. "But we can account for the martyrs because of the photographs. I only found three vials missing from the case in Al-Hofuf. If we assume that each martyr brought a vial of toxin to commit suicide, we got them all. There could be another lab, but my guess is Zafir would have been a little more on the smug side had there been others with the virus walking around somewhere out there."

Mahoney stuck her spoon in the ice cream and leaned forward on the table, resting her chin on folded arms. "It's almost too overwhelming. . . ."

"I guess most things are," Quinn said, "if you think about them too long. You're the one who decided to name this particular virus Pandora."

"It fit," Mahoney said.

"In the Pandora myth," Jericho said, resting his hand on top of hers, "do you remember what was left in the box after our girl opened it and let all the evil stuff out to torment the world?"

"Ah." Mahoney smiled. "*Hope*."

"That's right. Hope," Quinn said. "I have to hope for the best, or I'd go crazy doing this kind of work."

"Yeah, about that." Mahoney sat up again. She took another bite of ice cream before pointing at him with her spoon. "I wanted to talk to you about this job of yours."

"What do you mean?"

"Well." Mahoney shook her head, leaning back in her chair to look him up and down. "I've been following you for less than a week and I feel as though I've been beaten half to death. I can't imagine doing this sort of work all the time. I think my head would explode."

Jericho chuckled. "You don't give yourself enough credit, Doc. You stayed icy calm out there, through all of this. It's not so hard, what I do. Win Palmer is right. I'm a hammer. Someone gives me a nail to hit and I hit it. Simple really, especially when the world is full of so many nails."

"But it's so taxing," Mahoney said. "On you and your family."

"That it is."

"Then why?" she asked. "Why *do* you keep doing it?"

Jericho thought for a long moment, tapping his ice-cream spoon on the edge of the carton. His mind drifted back to when he was fourteen and happened on the college bullies on the Coastal Trail in Anchorage. He scooped another bite of ice cream and grinned.

"It's my job."

EPILOGUE

Northeastern Afghanistan

Sheikh Husseini al Farooq used an olive wood walking stick to negotiate the rock-strewn trail in the mountainous region near the Khyber Pass, southwest of Jalalabad. The evening was cool, the shadows barren of the air he so desperately needed. The wizened old coffee bean of a village headman moved down the path with the dexterity of a mountain ibex. His barrel chest swayed back and forth as he waddled swiftly on short, crooked legs toward the dark entrance of a stone hut built into the side of the cliff.

The sheikh stopped, resting on the stick to catch his breath. He knew where they were going now so it didn't matter that the headman outpaced him. Another man might have been embarrassed that the old man was faster considering the fact that he carried the sheikh's two heavy bags. But Farooq was used to others doing the work for him. He was accustomed to opulence, fine silks—and getting exactly what he wanted.

All that had changed because of an infidel named Jericho.

Two days after the unthinkable capture of his servant Zafir Jawad, a source from Baghdad sent word to Farooq's safe site in the mountains of Northern Pakistan. He was now the most wanted fugitive in the Global War on Terror. The messenger had flaunted the news, as if it was something of which to be proud. But Farooq knew better. His friends in the Saudi government had turned against him at once. With a bounty of five million U.S. dollars on his head, he didn't know whom to trust. Government spies in Pakistan could be purchased for a cup of strong coffee. Iraq was out of the question, and the Saudis had made it clear they would be happy to have him beheaded and collect the easy reward. He had embarrassed them, and for that, there would be no forgiveness. From the time he'd heard the news, he'd been constantly on the run.

At length, he hiked up the hem of his long woolen coat and started after the headman, panting at each treacherous step until he collapsed inside the filthy little hut.

Farooq spoke only rudimentary Pashto, but like many of these unlearned border people, the headman spoke smatterings of at least four languages—his native Pashto, Persian Dari, Pakistani Urdu, and thankfully, Arabic. They all came in handy in his opium-smuggling trade. If pressed, he probably spoke enough Russian and English to ingratiate himself with military patrols.

Once they were seated on threadbare, lice-ridden cushions, the headman's stooped wife brought in a wooden tray of butter tea and flat bread. Small dots of indigo dye tattooed her forehead, cheeks, and chin. The more dangerous of the two, the old woman made no effort to conceal the scowl in the jade of her flint hard eyes. Farooq accepted the strong tea with both hands and offered a smile to the woman. Afghan females in general were vessels of a fiery temper—extremely volatile if left unchecked. In Farooq's experience, green-eyed Pashtun women were the worst.

"I am in need of a place to set up the computer," Farooq said at length, taking the time to finish his foul-smelling tea before getting down to business.

The headman smiled, tipping his cup to lips covered by a sparse mustache. It was the color of the chalky rocks outside his rough home. The air in the confined room was full of smoke and the sour odor of human confinement.

"Ah," he sighed in a nasal, high-pitched voice. "You have a computer, but you would need a satellite phone to connect to the Internet."

"I was told you could help with that," Farooq said, impatiently pursing his thin lips.

"You know the Americans often monitor signals sent up on satellite phones?" For an illiterate drug smuggler, the headman had an excellent knowledge of the ways of the world. Though he lived in a stone hut, decades of fighting Russians and Americans alike had taught him to keep up with technology.

"I am aware of this," Farooq said. "I plan to send no messages that will bring American Predators to bomb your homes. I will be looking at nothing of interest to them."

The headman sat motionless, like one of the stones that made up his house.

"You can help me, then?" Farooq finally said, breaking the silence.

"Indeed," the headman said. In the corner, his green-eyed wife muttered something under her breath. He ignored her. "Our valley is perfectly suited to speak with the night sky."

He waved a weathered hand at his wife, motioning her out of the corner where she lurked in the shadows. "Here, pour our friend another cup of tea and then fetch me the phone."

Farooq accepted the second cup, peering into the greasy sheen under the glow of the smoking oil lamp. Taking a sip out of polite necessity, he set the cup to one side and unzipped his computer case. He'd been trying for a week to connect to the Internet, one of the many things he'd taken for granted back in the Kingdom. It was important he find out about this man Jericho.

The old woman produced a black phone, roughly the size of a brick, rolled in a greasy woolen rag. The headman took it and the two men went outside, into the gathering dusk. Pinpricks of light began to appear as stars filled the darkening sky. Farooq opened his case and booted up his computer while the old man cranked a rusted Chinese generator next to the front door of his hut. Next, he turned on the satellite phone and waited for a signal. Surprisingly, he got five bars almost instantly.

The old man took a dented square tin from his pocket and held it toward Farooq. It was *naswar*, Afghan snuff—a potent mixture of pulverized tobacco, lime, and indigo. Farooq raised his hand, feeling a little sick at the thought of putting such a mixture in his mouth. He bowed his head to politely decline. Grunting, the old man opened the tin and tucked a pinch of the dark powder inside his bottom lip behind rotten teeth.

The computer finally connected with a familiar ping. Farooq settled in as comfortably as he could on a flat boulder with the computer in his lap and began to type. Reflections from the screen flashed across his face as he searched every database he could think of. He only needed to find out who this Jericho was. After that, he could go to him and exact a proper revenge for Zafir's death—for ruining everything. Farooq still had money. Not as much as he would have liked, but there would be enough for his purposes, stashed in a safe deposit box in Pakistan along with an Uzbek passport no one knew about but him.

Farooq knew little about the man he hunted. Iraqi insurgents had placed a price on his head early in the conflict. According to his informants, they dubbed him the *Ifrit*—what the Americans would call a genie—because of his ability to appear out of nowhere and inflict so much harm on them. His given name was Jericho and he was thought to be a member of the U.S. Air Force.

Farooq searched every military website he found but none of them were useful—until he happened on a link to an Air Force Academy alumni page. He clicked through dozens of years of graduation lists, checking seven different cadets named Jericho before he found one who had graduated with high athletic honors with a degree in foreign languages—Chinese and Arabic.

His name was Jericho Quinn.

Farooq's fingers trembled with bottled rage as he continued to type. He followed link after link and came up with nothing. He had a name, he even had the state where the infidel grew up—Alaska—but he could find nothing more than a few swimming scores from secondary school. There seemed to be nothing about the man once he'd left the university.

Clicking through the pages, Farooq suddenly stopped. A smile spread slowly across the bones of his narrow face as he read an article from an Alaska newspaper dated just weeks before.

Madeline Quinn, daughter of Kimberly and Jericho Quinn, won a prestigious seat in the Anchorage Junior Youth Symphony . . .

Jericho Quinn had a little girl and now Farooq knew where to find her.

AUTHOR'S NOTE

A long time ago, a wise partner warned that I would find two kinds of people in our line of work—those who would run toward the sound of gunfire and those who would instinctively hunker down to save their own skin. Lucky for me, most of the folks I've worked with fall into the former category.

In researching this book, I relied on the expertise and experience of many brave men and women—countless soldiers, sailors, airmen, and marines who've spent more than their fair share of duty in the Sandbox, separated from home and family. Most of them cherish their anonymity.

Brad Abravanel's intimate knowledge of the CDC proved invaluable. He walked me through dozens of pandemic scenarios during our many hours at the pistol range. When it comes to deadly viruses, Laurie Garret's *The Coming Plague* was the ultimate resource, though I believe it was the most frightening book I've ever read.

Sonny C. got me started riding BMWs the moment I first saw his 1150 GS Adventure. Many thanks to the people at advrider.com for all the wonderful information about adventure riding, and the folks at Aerostich for producing such a cool catalog to dream over during our long northern winters—and from which to outfit Jericho Quinn and the Hammer Team with riding gear.

My wife, an insightful and talented writer herself, provided much needed cutting criticism and support. I appreciate her more than she can know. Molly Mayock, a gifted screenwriter, was a huge help with her thoughtful cinematic comments.

Though he wouldn't want it, Drew A. needs a hearty thank-you for many colorful insights into his experience in the United States Marine Corps.

I owe a debt of gratitude to my agent, Robin Rue, and her assistant, Beth Miller, for their years of patience in my behalf, as well as to Gary Goldstein, an editor, mentor, and friend.

There are bound to be errors here—I take responsibility for all of them. Some are unintentional, others are by design. After all, I'd hate for any of my comrades at arms to feel like I've written a textbook for the bad guys.